Devotion

BOOK III OF THE MARTYR SERIES

By MC Hunton

ISBN: 978-1-955479-09-7

DEDICATION

For found family.

CONTENTS

ACKNOWLEDGMENTS

To the Pendemics, without whose (sometimes brutal) feedback this series wouldn't be where it is today.

To Talia, for early morning breakfast dates and helping work through the challenging topics in this novel.

And to Leslee, whose artistic genius brought my characters to life.

CHAPTER ONE

Darius Jones's world was a swirl of pain and light.

The blow came in beneath his chin. Swift. Unrepentant. It knocked his head backward, and his teeth gnashed together, catching his flesh between them. The sweet, metallic taste of blood flooded over the top of his tongue and trickled between his teeth.

Darius swore as he gingerly wiped his mouth with the back of his hand. A pink slurry smeared across the beige fabric wrapped around his knuckles. He pushed his tongue out, exploring the raw spot inside his lip. Stinging pain shot through his cheek, and he winced.

"Keep your hands up."

The words rang out sharp in the room. They bounced off the mirrored walls before being absorbed by the black, padded floors beneath Darius's bare feet. Thorn Rose stood across from him. Even in training, she was fierce and tightly wound. She widened her stance. The defined musculature lining her calves and thighs showed through her red leggings, and her bare stomach was rigid and ready as she brought her forearms in to cover her face. Her intense, half-empty, black eyes watched him from the gap between her wrists. She wasn't wearing guards or gloves, and raised

1

tendrils of scarred skin wrapped around her left thumb to the back of her hand.

"You live *here*," she said. "Protect your head. Don't leave any openings."

"Got it," Darius said.

"When you strike, strike quick." She demonstrated, and her left fist popped out. As it flashed by, Darius caught sight of the *Peccostium*. The mark of the Sins sat, black and evil, just below her wrist joint. A tangled mess of furious white scars surrounded it, dripping down to her elbow. Her arm snapped back into its proper spot, standing guard by her jaw. "And return here. *Always* return here."

Darius nodded and held his hands up, too.

"Okay," Thorn said. She took a deep breath and slowly exhaled it from her nose. Her thin brows came in heavy over her eyes. "Try again."

Darius flew at her.

He threw his right fist toward Thorn's chin. She swiftly deflected—ducked down and to the left. He turned to keep her in front of him where he could more easily defend himself. They circled for a moment. Slowly. Meticulously. The soles of their bare feet made soft, sliding sounds against the padded floors. Thorn's dark eyes focused intently on Darius's as they sized each other up.

Darius feinted to the left then came in for another strike on Thorn's opposite side. She anticipated it, redirecting the blow with her arm and spinning out of the way. When she twisted around, her elbow came in at Darius's ribcage. The hit was light, but it knocked him off balance, and he stumbled.

"God damn it!"

"You're too tense," Thorn said. Her arms dropped from their offensive position, and she reached up to tighten the elastic holding her long, black hair to the base of her skull. From looking at her, no one would have guessed they'd been at this for almost twenty minutes now. Where Darius was sweaty and tired, Thorn looked as fresh as she had the minute she'd walked into the room. She propped her hands on her hips. "You're getting worked up and making stupid mistakes. Maybe we should be done for the day."

"No," Darius said, almost too quickly. Thorn's expression furrowed, skeptical and observant. He ignored her and pressed on. "I'm fine. I've got it. I just have to focus."

And he needed the outlet—to expend as much energy as he could *now* so that he could fall asleep tonight.

"You're *exhausted*," Thorn argued. "Take a couple of days to recover."

"I don't need to recover," Darius said. "All the other trainees do this daily. I can, too."

Thorn raised one eyebrow high on her head. "The other trainees are working with Chris's Tactical team, and you're healing most of them up at the end of the day. You are working with me, and no one here can fix *you*."

Darius shook his head. He didn't want to acknowledge how right Thorn was—how much more rigorous his work with her was compared to what Chris and TAC did with the others—because it would mean adjusting his schedule and training *less*. Their sessions were intense and thorough, and they left Darius so tired he could hardly keep his eyes open at night.

Which was exactly what he wanted.

"I'm fine," Darius said again. He rolled his shoulders and held his hands in front of his face. The muscles in his legs groaned, but he ignored them. "Let's go."

Thorn glared at him for a moment longer before she took another deep breath, planted her feet, and raised her guard. "Relax," she told him, and her eyes focused hard on his, peering so intently into them that Darius was half convinced she knew what he was doing—and why he was doing it. "Don't get stuck in your head."

Her mouth tightened. Now he was confident she wasn't talking about the fight anymore. He felt a red heat rise upon his cheeks.

"I'm fine," Darius said for the third time. Repeating it

would make it true, he told himself. He hoped Thorn would believe it—maybe then he would, too.

"You've got to be *better* than fine."

He lunged for her again.

The last six months were a whirlwind of elation and depression—of victory and bitter defeat. Another Sin had been destroyed for good, leaving only four intact and one floating around looking for a host. If that wasn't enough of a reason for the Martyrs to celebrate, Nicholas Wolfe certainly was.

When Teresa Solomon, Humility, had eliminated Pride and died in the process, everyone assumed it meant all Virtues had to sacrifice their lives to take down the Sins.

Nicholas had proven them wrong. Sloth was dead, but Nicholas wasn't.

Not *technically*.

Thorn dodged Darius's attack. As he blew past her, she spun and struck him between the shoulder blades. He flew forward, sprawling to the ground.

"Had enough?" Thorn asked.

Darius growled and hopped back to his feet. Thorn was already in position again, expression static and unreadable, her form so perfect that Darius couldn't even guess at any next move. He rolled his shoulders and braced himself. Facing her was different than facing any other Martyr here, and it wasn't just because she was the best person on the team at hand-to-hand combat.

It was because Thorn Rose didn't have a soul.

The energy that had once made her human had been cleaved into pieces—torn from her, bit by bit, when Wrath had possessed her over one hundred years ago—and even after she'd managed to escape, it had never come back together. Darius had come to rely on his Virtue senses when he sparred with the others. He could feel their energy, which gave him an unfair advantage in fights. He could "see" them without seeing them—know how close they were, anticipate their moves based on the warm aura that emanated from their very beings. Thorn didn't have one.

The circling continued. Darius felt tension rising in his shoulders. The anticipation, wondering when Thorn would come at him, grew with each passing second. Her deep, void-like irises zeroed in on his. He took a slow breath, and Thorn's words swam in his mind.

"Don't get stuck in your head."

He rolled his shoulders, felt the muscles loosen—

Thorn moved quickly. Her left hand came at him again. Gently open, fingers curled, as the heel of her palm moved toward his stomach. Darius glanced out of the way. Barely. When Thorn flew past him and her back was turned, he tried to counter-attack, but she was too fast. She spun expertly, and his fist missed her face—striking, instead, against her arms, which she'd raised to defend herself.

"Better," she said, and he caught a glimpse of her through the gap between her wrists. There was a small smile on her thin lips.

"But not good enough." He wiped the sweat from his brow, and at that moment, Thorn rushed in. He wasn't ready. Her jab flew toward his face. He managed to turn, but as he did, Thorn ducked down and swiped her foot out in a wide, arcing kick. She knocked Darius's legs from underneath him, and suddenly, he was airborne.

Darius landed so hard on the padded floor it forced the air from his lungs. For a few agonizing seconds that felt like hours, he couldn't breathe. His diaphragm froze, shocked into silence, and his lungs tightened in his chest. A deep, aching pain, an emptiness, and the fear that this feeling would last forever overwhelmed Darius's senses. He felt his heart beating hard in his throat, and his mouth gaped open, gasping for air he couldn't bring in.

Thorn knelt by his side and immediately propped him up. Her right hand wrapped around his bicep, her grip almost painful, as her left palm flattened against his back and moved in firm, tight circles.

"Yeah," she said. Her voice came out hard and angry—

more self-reproachful than targeted at Darius. "We're done for the day."

Darius shook his head. Still gasping, still aching, he shook his head fervently and tried to wave Thorn off, but she was stronger than him, and he still couldn't breathe. At last, his body seemed to remember what it was built to do, and his chest opened up. He took a deep breath, coughed, and waved his hand again.

"I'm *fine*—"

"This isn't up for debate, Jones," Thorn snapped. Her grip hadn't loosened around his arm, and the hand pressed to his back now held him steady. Darius could feel her slender fingers stretched out between his shoulder blades, rising and falling with his harsh, uneven breathing. "You need more rest."

"I *don't* need rest," Darius said. He pulled himself out of her hands and clumsily stood up. His chest still ached—still felt hollowed out the same way it had last September, when Saul, Juniper, and Lindsay had burned to death, caught in the crossfire between the Martyrs and the Sins, and a week later, when he and Eva had gone to spread Saul's ashes…

Suddenly, Darius's mind was full of rattling gunfire, the stink of burned rubber, and spilled blood. He shook his head. "I need to train."

Thorn slowly got to her feet. Her arms crossed as her dark eyes took in his expression then moved quietly down to the hand he had pressed against the empty spot between his lungs. Darius hadn't realized he'd raised it, and he quickly dropped it back to his side. Thorn's focus came to his face again.

"We're *done*," she said. "Go wash up. We'll get back at it in a couple of days."

She didn't let him argue. He opened his mouth to do so, but she threw him a dangerous look and turned away, striding to the women's locker room. Darius watched after her, breathing hard, until she disappeared. Movement on top of the weight rack to his right made him turn, and he spotted a small, blue-scaled lizard with massive, leathery, red wings folded at its sides.

Sparkie, Thorn's Familiar, the corporeal part of the energy Wrath had ripped from her, tilted his head as he stared at Darius. Darius wasn't sure, but he thought even the animal looked reproachful—like it was reminding him to do as Thorn asked and take a shower, too.

And she'd know if he didn't. She and Sparkie were one and the same. If Darius tried to keep working, he couldn't hide it from her. Not with half of her soul in the room.

So, he took a deep breath, exhaled it in a sigh, and walked into the men's locker room.

Then he was alone.

The long, narrow room ran along the back of the gym, a tight strip between it and the pool. The smell of chlorine filtered in through the door across from Darius. White tile, white walls, and bright white lights made the locker area blindingly sterile and boring. Almost too boring. Without the chatter of people bouncing off the hard walls or the background noise from showers running and hand dryers blasting hot air, Darius had almost nothing to distract him from his thoughts.

Nothing but sore muscles.

He groaned and walked to the far end, past alcoves of lockers and changing areas, to the showers. He grabbed his gym bag, hung it on a hook, and stripped down. His white shirt clung to the sweat caked across his chest and down the divot of his spine. Pulling it over his shoulders highlighted the acute soreness in his arms. He threw it and the rest of his clothes into a pile on the ground. Then he opened the shower door and turned on the water.

While he waited for the water to get hot, Darius leaned against the frame and caught a glimpse of himself in the mirror hanging across the room.

God, he couldn't blame Thorn for wanting to call it quits.

Dark, sleepless circles made his green eyes look tired.

He'd been too lazy to shave the last couple of days, so a fine layer of stubble lined his sharp jaw. Even his *body* looked worn thin. Since joining the Martyrs over a year and a half ago, Darius had gone from sickly skinny to slim and toned, but now his olive skin was speckled with the shadows of bruises he hadn't let heal before jumping back into the ring. He gently touched his hand to a deep, green and purple mark at his side. The memory of a bullet ripping through him at that exact spot, leveling him before he could heal Eva's wounds, made him wince and close his eyes.

Then Eva was all he saw.

He couldn't wait anymore. He stepped into the shower before it got hot and shivered in the lukewarm spray. When the water finally warmed up, Darius tilted his head back and let it berate the top of his skull. It poured through his short, dark brown hair, over his face, and down the back of his neck. His body reacted to it. Muscles—tense from training, from tossing and turning every night, from gripping anxiety and guilt—allowed themselves a few moments to relax. His legs felt weak beneath him, and Darius leaned his shoulder against the wall. He took a deep breath of the hot, humid air and let it out in a sigh.

"Fuck."

Darius paused inside the locker room door and gazed out the window. Thorn waited for him, sitting on the same exercise mat she'd slammed him into less than a half-hour before. Like him, she had showered and dressed. Her damp, black hair fell against her shoulders, and she'd changed into fresh clothes, though Darius didn't see why. She never broke a sweat when they trained.

If Darius hadn't known better, he would have thought she was meditating. Her eyes were closed, legs drawn up beneath her, and hands folded peacefully in her lap. Her sleeves extended to her palms, where her thumbs stuck through holes in the wrist cuffs, covering her *Peccostium* and the scars around it.

The two of them had made a routine of meditating together twice a week, and he knew when she was focused and when she wasn't. Right now, Sparkie betrayed her agitation. He walked in little circles by her knee, his wings and tail twitching occasionally. Darius heaved a sigh. He couldn't hang out here forever; Thorn was not above coming in if she thought he was taking too long. So he opened the door. Thorn's Familiar froze as he walked back into the gym, and her eyes shot open.

"You didn't have to wait for me," Darius said. He adjusted his bag on his shoulder as Thorn got to her feet.

She didn't respond, instead taking a quick moment to look him over. Darius wished he'd thought to wear long sleeves, too, to hide the bruises starting to color on his forearms.

"Let's go grab some food," Thorn said at last. Darius got the feeling it wasn't what she *wanted* to say by the way her intense focus looked him over—as though she expected him to unravel like a poorly sewn sweater.

"I'm not hungry," Darius said. It wasn't technically a lie. He hadn't had much of an appetite in the last few months. A single eyebrow raised high on Thorn's head, and Darius let out a rough chuckle. "What?"

"Jones—"

"Don't 'Jones' me," Darius said, and he made his way toward the door.

Thorn followed, reaching her hand down at the exact moment Sparkie leapt up to grab it. His tiny claws latched onto the fabric on her arm as he scurried up to her shoulder.

"I won't *Jones'* you when you start taking care of yourself," Thorn said. Darius walked into the courtyard, and she was fast on his heels. "You need to take a break—"

"Jesus, Thorn, how many times do I have to tell you that I'm fine for you to believe me?" Darius snapped. Now that they were out in the courtyard, Darius's voice carried through the massive, concrete cavern. This space was large enough to house several hundred people comfortably, but it had been a long time since that many had lived in the Underground. Now, the room was vacant. Huge, empty planters lay in a grid-like pattern through the center of the room. Alcoves around its edge boasted of more prosperous times when the Martyrs had entertained hobbies, classes, and other extracurriculars that had since faded away. At the far end of the room, near the elevator, a handful of people were sitting down to a late dinner—mostly researchers done for the day. They all simultaneously glanced up from their meals, and Kenia, the Martyrs cook, craned her neck over the counter toward them.

Darius cleared his throat and spoke a little more quietly this time. "I'm sorry, it's just—I've been seeing Abraham once a week, and honestly, I could do with a little *less* people worrying about me." Thorn's frown only deepened. Darius put on a strained smile. "I've been taking care of myself since I was *ten*. I know what I'm doing."

"Then *do it*," Thorn said, but the sharpness in her voice dulled a bit. A glint of concern passed between her dark eyes, sending an awkward yet grateful jolt through Darius's chest. She took a deep breath and opened her mouth to say something else, but before she had the chance, both of their phones sounded a sharp, familiar alarm.

Code Black.

The tension between them shattered. Thorn and Darius shared a look—his eyes wide and haunted, hers narrowed into furious slits—and they took off. Their shoes slammed hard against the concrete tiles as they sprinted across the courtyard. Thorn reached the far side first. Her Forgotten Sin strength gave her speed and endurance Darius couldn't compete with, even when he wasn't exhausted from nonstop training. She didn't waste time waiting for the elevator; she instead rushed to the door beside it and threw it open. Sparkie leapt from her shoulder and disappeared into the stairwell.

But Thorn paused and waited for Darius to reach her. Then, they climbed the stairs two at a time. She pulled ahead again, opening the door to the first floor before he reached the landing so they could fly through it together. The uppermost level of the Underground was a flurry of activity. Darius felt dozens of souls moving. The hallway from the elevator was narrow, flanked by the garage and the tactical room. People moved about in there, buzzing like hornets.

As the hall opened into the entrance and waiting room to the hospital ward, Darius spotted a tall, slender man speaking quietly with one of the nurses. His black hair fell to his shoulders, and his mouth set into a hard frown behind his goatee. Dark, half-empty eyes landed on Thorn and Darius as they entered the room. He dismissed the nurse with a nod and turned toward them.

"Alan," Thorn said. "What's the situation?"

Alan Blaine, the founder of the Martyrs and Thorn's uncle, took a long, slow breath. "One of our TAC units was ambushed at a police checkpoint leaving the city. Two others came to the scene to relieve them. They were outnumbered. Outgunned."

Thorn's mouth tightened into a fine line. "Gluttony."

"We must assume," Alan said, "though he was not on the scene, for which we are *very* lucky. All six of our people were injured, but none have died… not yet."

He passed Darius a dark look.

"Which units were involved?" Darius asked. His throat tightened against the words.

"The Fourth, Fifth." Then Alan paused, and he gave Thorn a troubled look. "And the First Response Units."

Thorn's porcelain skin paled. A flash of fear so cold, so palpable, that it sent a shiver down Darius's spine flooded her expression.

"Elijah and his team are preparing triage for severe trauma," Alan went on, and he turned away from Thorn and took in Darius again. "You will want to be in there."

Darius brushed past Alan and sprinted across the length

of the waiting room. He couldn't *feel* Thorn, nor could he hear her, but he knew she'd be right behind him.

"She'll be fine," Darius said. He glanced over his shoulder to see Thorn following close on his heels. "I'm sure she's fine."

Thorn's forehead knitted into a tight furrow, but her eyes glistened with a carnal, wild panic. "She fucking better be," she whispered.

Darius swallowed hard as they rushed through the double doors.

The hospital ward was empty. It usually was. Despite the Sins' increased activity and the influx of injured Martyrs returning from patrol, patients rarely stayed hurt for long now that Darius was around. Hospital cots and privacy curtains dotted down the long room. Over two dozen individual beds sat, clean, crisp, and untouched.

Darius strode past them and through another door on the far end of the ward. Where the hospital was empty, the triage room moved with warm, positive energy. Darius could feel Dr. Harris and a team of nurses darting around, preparing the unit for an influx of people. The thought made Darius's aching stomach twist. He pushed through the swinging door.

"Darius," a tense voice said. Elijah Harris stood by the back wall, scrubbing his hands and arms with soapy water as his wife and head nurse, Colette, tied a medical mask around his face. "I hope you never tire of hearing me say, thank *god* we have you."

"Glad to be here," Darius said, though he was anything but glad right now. He walked past Elijah, Colette, and the other four nurses standing ready in the room. Raquel Hernandez, the one nearest the door, watched Darius intently until he met her eye. They shared a brief, anxious nod.

"Thorn," Elijah said, his tone weary, "you know the rules."

Dr. Harris turned his steely gray eyes onto Thorn as she came through the doorway. Even with his nose and mouth covered by a mask, Darius could see the frown in his expression. His brown hair, graying at the temples, poked out from the bottom of his green medical cap as Colette pulled it over his head. Thorn looked up at a large screen on the far wall where the six incoming TAC members' vitals were laid out. Darius wasn't an expert, but he'd picked up enough to know it wasn't looking good.

Thorn pointed at the top chart. "Chris is—"

"Getting worked up won't help her," Elijah snapped, "or anyone else here. Get in position."

Darius's stomach twisted, and he glanced at Raquel to see tears glistening around her brown irises. An alert sounded from a speaker in the corner of the room, and every eye turned toward the entrance. Thorn, for once seeming to listen to someone other than herself, stood at the back of the nursing staff with a forced calm. Her mouth set into a fine line as she stared through the windows and into the garage beyond them.

A tense hush fell.

Then the sensation of warm energy came into Darius's awareness from above and spiraled downward. Light shone through the glass. Tires screeched to a halt.

"Let's move!" Dr. Harris called.

Darius forced the door open as Raquel, Colette, and Elijah ushered their team out with stretchers and rushed upon a battered, black SUV. The metal sides were dented and pierced—bullet holes ripped through the outer shell and left the reinforced doors scraped and misshapen. Almost every window was shattered. A big, burly man opened the driver's side door, blood pouring from a wound on his scalp like a crimson waterfall down his face. Pebbles of glass shards sprinkled onto the concrete floor as he stepped down. Darius moved toward him, but he shook his head.

"I'm fine," he said, waving his hands. His fingers shook, and his palms were covered in blood. "Help the others."

"Conrad, come here," Colette said, and she grabbed the bleeding man by the arm. Together she and Darius lowered him back onto a stretcher. As soon as his backside hit the cot, he collapsed onto it.

"Darius!"

Raquel's voice echoed through the dark parking garage like a howl. The sound pierced deep into Darius's chest, into his soul, and he rushed around the side of the vehicle to where she and Elijah had opened the rear hatch. He felt the blood drain from his face, from his hands, from his feet as the room around him went cold and numb.

The back was full of bodies.

Moving, groaning, *bleeding* bodies. Five Martyrs lay crumbled together, clutching onto one another in a desperate and harrowing attempt to hold themselves together.

And they *needed* to be held together. The gray interior of the vehicle was the color of rust and reeked of the sweet, metallic scent of blood. Raquel and Dr. Harris were pulling people from the back. Jason Nichols. Seth Graves. Amelia Chan. They were all dazed, barely clinging to consciousness. Darius moved toward Liz Wright, Conrad's partner in the Fifth Response Unit, as Raquel and another nurse transferred her from the SUV to a stretcher. Power surged to his hands, eager for a release, and he drew them closer to her…

But Liz shook her head and gestured a pale, shaking hand back to the vehicle.

"Chris," she said. Her voice was harsh and gravelly. She coughed, and blood speckled her purpling lips. "Get Chris."

Darius's heart sank as he spun around to see Elijah crawling backward from the SUV. His green scrubs were painted in heavy, scarlet swatches. As he drew back and came to full height, Darius heard the sickening sound of liquid dripping onto the floor—

"Chris!"

Thorn. Her voice filled with an aching desperation. She came tearing from the triage room, her black eyes wide and terrified as she swiftly moved between the other nurses and injured Martyrs until she'd forced her way to where Dr. Harris was laying Chris onto a stretcher.

Thorn grabbed it, and she pushed it toward the triage doors, Darius guiding it from the other side. He could feel Dr. Harris behind them, moving to handle other casualties while they waited for Darius's healing touch—

His touch.

As Thorn forced them through the doors and pulled the stretcher out of the way, Darius cupped one hand to the side of Chris's face. His thumb gently stroked her cool cheek while his other pressed tight against a wound he could see through the shredded fabric at the crook of her neck. Her black turtleneck was saturated in blood.

"Shh," Darius said, opening up the boundary between them. He felt energy pour out of him, flowing from his healthy body into Chris's broken one like a river emptying into a dry lakebed. Her eyes rolled backward, and she gasped. Darius urged more power forward. "It's okay. We've got you."

He glanced at Thorn. She didn't look back. Her eyes were focused on Chris and Chris alone.

More wounded were carried through, and the triage room exploded with noise and chaos. Darius's ears filled with the sounds of Elijah yelling orders, groaning and crying Martyrs, and the harsh beeping of machines. He tuned it all out and zoned in on the patient between his fingers. Chris's skin was still cold and sallow, her lips a shade of blue that made Darius too nervous to let go. Her eyelids had stopped fluttering, but instead of becoming more alert, they'd shut hard and hadn't opened again. Darius pushed more energy into Chris while Thorn ran her fingers through her yellow hair. Brown streaks of tacky blood held it together in clumps.

"Don't you do this to me," Thorn murmured so quietly only Darius could hear her over the raucous noise filling the tiny room. Emotion crackled the last word. Thorn cleared her throat. "How many times do I have to tell you, *you're not allowed to die.*"

She wouldn't die. Darius wouldn't let her.

He closed his eyes and focused, searching with his Virtuous senses to find where Chris needed healing the most. He felt it in his stomach—mirrored as a deep, heavy aching in his abdominal wall and the organs behind it. He moved his hand to her waist, lifted her shirt, and pressed his fingers against the seeping wounds on her gut.

Then he drove his healing energy forward again. It focused on and centered in her core, draining Darius. He closed his eyes and clenched his teeth as his head began to swim, but he didn't stop.

Not until he felt two tiny, metal items push out from a hole in Chris's flesh and into his palm.

Darius raised his hand and tilted the bullets into a tray by the side of the cot. They landed in the basin with a soft *clink-clink!*

At last, Chris began to move. It started in her hands. Where Darius was still holding the crook of her neck, Chris reached up and wrapped her fingers around his wrist. Darius's heart skipped a beat, and he paused in his healing. Chris's green eyes opened. She stared at the ceiling, her pupils constricting with the light.

"Oh, thank god," Thorn murmured.

Chris turned toward her, brows furrowed, mouth open. Then she looked to Darius…

The reality of the situation struck her. Her confusion dissolved, and her eyes filled with wide terror. The sounds of the room roared to life around Darius with a thunderous boom. Dr. Harris calling out orders. Raquel and the others responding in turn. Footsteps. Alarms. Swearing—

Chris sat up on the cot, sucked in a sharp, painful breath, and pushed Darius away.

"Heal the others," she growled, grabbing at her stomach where the wounds were still not fully healed. "I'm fine. Go."

"I'm almost—"

"I said *go!*"

Chris pushed him further back, wincing again. Thorn grabbed her and lowered her back onto the cot. Then she turned to Darius and gave him a dark nod, which he returned before moving to his next patient.

Seth Graves was barely better off than Chris. He was laid out on the cot beside her, his face ashen, jaw shaking. Raquel and Colette were prepping him for Darius—cutting clothing away from the bullet holes tearing through his stomach and right thigh. As he approached, the two nurses moved away to help Dr. Harris. Seth turned his head toward Darius as he came up to the side of his cot and let out a frantic laugh.

"Fuck, Darius," he grunted through chattering teeth. Darius pressed his hands against Seth's stomach, and the other man groaned in relief as healing power surged into his body. "I didn't think we were gonna make it this time..."

"What happened?" Darius asked. It was a technique Dr. Harris had recommended Darius try a couple of months ago when the first big influx of injured Martyrs had started to come in. Talk while you work on them. Ask questions. Keep them busy. It helped everyone stay calm.

"Police checkpoint," Seth said. He swore and tilted his head back. "Never had a problem before, but as soon as we stopped, they started firing. Chris was hit before we knew what was happening. Thank god backup was so close, or we'd be laid out in a morgue somewhere..."

Darius nodded, but he wasn't really listening. His brain was struggling to keep up with the words coming out of Seth's mouth—struggling to make sense of them. The power flow from his body was slower than he was used to. Or maybe he just perceived it as slow. He looked over his shoulder at Liz Wright, lying on the next cot over, and it felt like he was looking at her through water. The hairs at the base of his neck began to tingle...

"Jones?"

A hand wrapped around Darius's bicep. The lack of a warm aura told him it had to be Thorn's. He ignored her, focusing on the flesh molding beneath the heel of his hand. A metal slug forced its way through the entrance wound and into his palm.

He dropped the bullet into another little tray. It rolled in a semi-circle before stopping, drawing an arc of deep crimson against the chrome behind it. Darius's bloodstained fingers quivered, and he shook his wrist to steady them.

"You need to sit down," Thorn said, firmer this time. Her grip tightened around his arm, and she tried to guide him away from the chaos—away from where four other TAC members were still bleeding out on the tables. Dr. Harris didn't notice—or he didn't care. Jason Nichols suddenly shook violently. Elijah was at his side in seconds. Colette cut through Jason's shirt and pulled it open to expose his chest. He'd been shot only once—near his heart.

"We're losing him!" Elijah yelled into the room.

Darius pulled out of Thorn's hands and rushed past Liz, past Conrad, past a handful of nurses, and came upon Elijah's side. Thorn followed close behind him. He felt her grab his shoulders as he reached down and placed his palms directly over Jason Nichols' heart. Jason's eyes met his, wild and frantic, as he grabbed Darius's hand with ice-cold fingers.

"Don't let me die," he choked out. Blood bubbled at his lips, and tears poured down his cheeks. "I'm not ready to die!"

"I've got you," Darius said. Power followed the path from his soul, through his arms, into his fingertips, and began weaving into Jason's flesh and bone. Jason shook again, and Darius pushed until his face went cold and his hands started to quake. That tickle at the base of his neck became a blaring warning. The hairs stood up on end, sending goosebumps across his shoulders and down his arms. Something inside of him screamed, "DANGER!"

He ignored it, kept pushing forward—

Darius didn't even notice his vision go gray, nor did he hear Thorn's voice calling his name as she pulled him backward, and he fell into her arms. Jason convulsed again. The monitor beeped faster and faster until—

It stopped entirely and rang out in a single note, as deafening as the silence of a heartbeat.

The next thing Darius knew, he was staring at the ceiling, and Thorn's face obscured his vision.

"Jesus fucking christ," she growled. She ran her fingers through his hair, much like she had with Chris. He was surprised at how gentle they were against his scalp and thought he could feel them shaking. "What the *fuck* is wrong with you?"

He tried to sit up, but his head was still swimming, and the movement made him nauseous. His stomach buckled, and before he could stop himself, Darius turned sideways and dry-heaved onto the triage room floor. Cold, sticky sweat made his shirt cling to him, and his nose, lips, and hands felt clammy. The squeaking of sneakers on the tile floor, the motion of hot energy as the nursing staff moved around them, hardly registered. He tried to sense Jason Nichols in the room, but his aura had disappeared. Darius's stomach dropped, and Thorn's words cut like a scalpel.

"What's wrong with me?" he managed to get out through a gasp. "I'm just one Virtue, Thorn! And I'm trying, but—"

His guts twisted again, sending him hunched over in another bout of heaving stomach acid between his clenched fists on the tile. Hot water stung his eyes as he laid his forehead against his wrists. Thorn's hands found him again, this time wrapping around his shoulders to steady him as she pulled him up. When he looked at her, her expression was tight with painful sympathy.

"You've done enough," she said. "More than enough."

"But Jason—"

"We can mourn him later," Thorn cut in. "Right now, focus on the people we helped. Wright is going into surgery, Carter and Chan don't have any life-threatening injuries, and Graves and Chris are healed enough to get through the night—because of *you*."

Her sharp brows furrowed over those deep, black, and

fervent eyes. The attention was so focused, so *uneasy*, that it filled Darius with a heavy block of guilt. He shook his head and looked away, and his eyes landed on a cot just six feet from where he sat. Someone had draped a sheet over Jason Nichols. All Darius saw was the outline of a body—empty, without a soul.

It had been a long time since he hadn't been able to save someone. Almost six months exactly.

When Eva Torres had been shot and Darius hadn't been there for her.

CHAPTER TWO

Liz Wright lay on the hospital bed, her gown backward and opened enough to show the wounds on her stomach. She closed her tired, brown eyes and let out a soft sigh. Like Chris and most members of the Tactical Unit, Liz's body was marked by rough scars from old battles Darius hadn't been around to heal. A bullet injury at her side. A slash near her hip. They stood out, pale on her brown skin.

And they struck a stark contrast with the long, red surgical cut extending from the bottom of her bra to just above her belly button. In the two days since the attack, Darius slowly and systematically healed the survivors. Liz was the last. This was their third appointment. Dr. Harris had felt that her injuries had been too severe to fix all at once.

"Are you sure you're up to this?" he asked.

Elijah stood on the other side of Liz's bed, arms crossed around a medical tablet as he watched Darius with cold, steely eyes. Liz looked up at him as she nervously pulled a strand of dark, wavy hair behind her ear. Darius sighed and nodded.

"I was up to it yesterday," he said, trying to keep the biting tone to a low murmur. He hadn't hidden his displeasure with Alan and Elijah's decision to put him on restricted duty—no training with Thorn, no overtime, and no extensive healing sessions. "I told you—I'm feeling great."

The doctor glanced at his pad and typed a few notes. "Well, that *does* ease my concerns about you collapsing on my triage room floor. I don't care that all the tests we ran on you came back normal. Until *I'm* sure you really are 'feeling great,' we're going to take things slow." Darius opened his mouth to argue, but Elijah raised a finger. "Ah—this is non-negotiable. This evening, I expect you to go down to the kitchen, grab some dinner, and go to bed early. Doctor's orders."

"*And* the Tactical director's orders."

Chris Silver walked through the double doors to the hospital just in time to hear the tail end of Elijah's speech. She strode in with a sense of authority she still didn't seem to have a full grasp of. Her head was held high, her shoulders square, and she gave Darius a friendly but firm look as she gently elbowed him in the side. Then, she turned to Liz. An almost guilty glint shone behind her eyes as she touched Liz's fingers. "How are you feeling?"

"Good," Liz said, awkwardly glancing between Elijah, Chris, and Darius. "Would be even better if we could just get this over with…"

Chris smiled, and Darius felt himself smile, too. He glanced at Elijah and raised his eyebrows in a good-natured jab. "Am I good to go *now?*"

Elijah shrugged. "By all means." He opened a palm and gestured at the woman lying on the bed between them.

With Elijah's watchful eyes trained on him, Darius laid his hand against the soft skin on Liz's stomach and opened the gates. Power flowed freely from his fingertips and palm, pouring deep into Liz's wounded abdomen. Though he couldn't see the internal damage recover, he was getting better at feeling the sensation of it through the energy exchange. Soon, the stream slowed to a trickle and then nothing at all. When Darius pulled back, Liz's stomach was a canvas of healthy brown skin and old scars.

"There," Darius said. He held his hand out to Liz and helped her sit up. "Good as new."

She thanked him, and Elijah ordered her to see Colette for a final check on her vitals before she was free to go. As she got to her feet and walked away, the doctor turned back to Darius, drew out a juice box out of his pocket, and tossed it over.

"I told you," Darius said, laughing at the ridiculousness of it all as he pulled the straw out. "I'm feeling *great.*"

Elijah's lips pursed together, and he shook his head. "I need you to be at your best when you're in here," he said. Darius's smile faded. He saw Chris shift out of the corner of his eye—felt her watching the side of his face. Dr. Harris went on as though she wasn't there. "When I have a crisis situation, I can't stop to worry about *you*, too. Take care of yourself."

Then he walked away, leaving Darius and Chris standing awkwardly by an empty hospital cot. Darius stared after him, unfocused, and a guilty surge made his stomach uneasy.

"Sounds like he's been talking to Alan," Chris said. She passed Darius a smile that didn't reach her eyes. "He had almost that exact same conversation with me two nights ago."

"Because you wanted to wait for your healing?" Darius asked as the two of them started on their way out of the hospital ward. He drained the juice box in three big swallows and tossed it in a bin by the doors as Chris opened them.

She nodded. "Yep." Then she frowned and mimicked Alan's dark, formal tone with startling accuracy. " *'Christine, you cannot expect to take care of your team if you are not taking care of yourself first.* '"

Darius cracked a smile. The day after the attack, Chris had tried to instruct him to heal the rest of her people before he addressed her wounds, but Alan had stepped in. He made it clear Chris was a higher priority than anyone else. She had been furious, but Darius was relieved.

"He's not wrong," he said with a shrug.

Chris cast him a humored look. "Neither is Elijah," she shot back with a smile, but concern crept in at the edges of her eyes. "Speaking of Alan and Elijah, did they approve you for shooting classes?"

They reached the foyer beside the elevator, and Darius didn't respond as he opened the door to the stairwell. Chris paused, crossing her arms and fixing him with a stern, compassionate look. At last, Darius sighed.

"Shooting classes, meditation, and my work with you are the only things I *am* approved for," he said shortly. When Chris's frown didn't soften, Darius raised his shoulders and smiled sheepishly. "Unless *you're* going to kick me out. Tactical director's orders."

He pushed his grin wider, and Chris relented. Her mouth eased up into a smirk, and she rolled her eyes as she stepped past him.

"As long as you tell me you're good," she said with a shrug, "that's enough for me."

They spiraled down the dimly lit stairwell, their footsteps echoing through the concrete chamber as they moved six levels down. A solid, locked door sat at the bottom landing.

"So," Darius said as Chris typed her access code into the handle, "how are the new guys doing in the recruit class?"

Chris grimaced. The light on the door glowed green, and she pulled it open. "They're… new guys," she said, like that answered anything.

It did.

Six months ago, in the same incident that had claimed Eva's life, the Martyrs' old TAC director was killed in action. Jeremiah Montgomery had been manning their getaway vehicle in a car chase through midtown when a Programmed cop landed a lucky shot in the back of his skull. He'd died instantly, his energy blinking into nonexistence as their car veered through oncoming traffic and crashed into a streetlight.

Darius didn't remember much after that. He'd been thrown through the windshield and knocked unconscious. By the time he'd woken up, almost twenty-four hours later, Chris had already been promoted to Jeremiah's position.

Since then, whatever spare time Chris had that wasn't taken up by her patrol shifts in the city was now spent preparing schedules, planning team training routines, and organizing a new recruitment initiative she'd been trying to instill for years. She had enlisted Darius's help, which suited him just fine. He needed the distraction, and Chris needed the support.

"That bad, huh?" Darius asked. They stepped into the basement, and his senses filled with familiar tastes, smells, and sounds. Damp, dirty floors. Hot, moist air. Moaning water pipes, roaring and rumbling in a way that made it feel like the whole place was alive. The door closed behind them, and the handle locked with a mechanical *"whir."*

"They're untrained," Chris said. "None of them had any experience with weapons or combat. It'll take time. I wish it were taking a little *less* time… I'm worried about our presentation tomorrow. If it doesn't go well, Alan might cut the program."

Darius's stomach tightened. Since starting this project four months ago, they'd only pulled in three people, and not one was approved for work outside the Underground yet.

The two of them fell silent as they made their way through the basement. The long, wide corridor passed branches of narrower, darker passages. A white pathway marked the floor in glow-in-the-dark paint, arrows and labels etched into the floor making this labyrinthine mess more sensical. Darius had thought he'd get lost down here, but now that he attended shooting classes once a week, he found it surprisingly easy to navigate.

As they followed the primary walkway, motion-activated lights blinked to life and flickered from the mouths of the intersecting halls. All but one. As he and Chris neared the shooting range, one of the passages remained fully lit. Stevie and part of her maintenance team were working on a vent in the ceiling. Her black hair was pulled back in a clip, and she wiped her dirt-streaked brow as she stabilized the ladder. When they passed, she glanced up and smiled. They waved, and Chris turned toward the shooting range.

When she opened the door, the class looked up to see them.

"About damn time," a woman called across the concrete room. Her voice had a light Irish accent and a heavy dose of good-natured teasing. "We've been waiting here a whole three minutes!"

Mackenzie McKay, the director of the Discovery half of the Research and Discovery Unit, was standing with a handful of established Martyrs from all walks of the Underground's non-Tactical operations. Elena Cortez and Caleb Claytor from the Gray Unit. John Waters from R&D. Nicholas Wolfe, tucked into the back.

The former Virtue stood apart from the rest, one arm around his chest while the other was raised, pressing his fingertips against his mouth. He'd lost weight since he'd sacrificed Diligence and half of his soul to destroy Sloth; it showed in the hollow spots beneath his cheekbones and in how his tailored shirt no longer fit so perfectly. His face had acquired a couple of new creases in the last few months, and his temples were starting to show white hairs among the blonde. Darius met Nicholas's gaze as he entered the room, and those powder-blue eyes focused on him. They looked duller. Something in their flatness reminded Darius of Thorn's black stare.

Cold. Half-empty.

A chill rushed down his spine, but he smiled all the same as he walked across the room.

The class gathered around a table in a rectangular control booth. To the left, Conrad sat by the gun locker, one thick arm hoisted behind his head while he stared at a phone in his lap. A large, soundproof window on the far wall looked down at six firing lanes. The limited space meant Chris ran several shooting classes throughout the week as they trained every Martyr in the Underground on essential Tactical Unit skills.

Just in case, she had told Darius months ago, they had an emergency and needed more personnel.

"We just finished healing Liz," Darius said. Mackenzie pushed a pair of virtual reality goggles off her bright blue eyes and up her forehead. Her pixie cut stuck up in all sorts of strange angles. Darius gestured to her hair. "Dyed it again?"

Mackenzie's face broke into a grin, and she raised her eyebrows. The piercing through the left one disappeared behind loud, orange bangs.

"You like it?" she asked, but she didn't wait for an answer as she ruffled the fiery mop with her fingertips. Her nails, painted a vibrant purple, contrasted with the new color. "I was itching for a change."

Chris cleared her throat and gestured to the table in front of them. "Since we're *three minutes* behind schedule," she said, giving Mackenzie an obliging look, which the Irishwoman returned with fervor, "let's get started. First, safety."

As the class focused on her, Chris squared her shoulders and clasped her hands behind her back, holding herself with easy authority. Her green eyes moved across the room, and she ran through their gun safety protocols with the practiced repetition of someone who had said this hundreds of times before. Darius knew the speech by heart: firearms were to remain unloaded, pointed at the ground, with fingers off the trigger until every student reached their designated firing lane. Breaking the rules didn't just mean leaving the range—you could lose your spot in the class entirely.

When she wrapped up the rules, Chris moved on to today's agenda.

"We are going to do five sets at fifteen yards. When each one is done, you will hear a tone in your headset, at which point you will remove your clip, put the gun on the stand in front of you, and step back. I'll come to your station, talk about your performance, and then we'll start the next set. Is everyone clear?"

She looked around, and six heads nodded. "For those of you with real weapons, Conrad will assign you an unloaded firearm and five full clips. Caleb and Mackenzie, you're still on the VR."

Mackenzie groaned as she pulled her goggles back over her face. "I can't *believe* I'm not allowed to use an actual gun yet."

"You can't even hit a virtual target," John said, giving her a charming smile as he walked around the table and gently touched the small of Chris's back. Chris stiffened a bit—the same way she always did when John tried to engage her in affectionate displays while she was working. He didn't notice, or he pretended not to, as Mackenzie tilted her head in his direction.

"It's all fun and games down here," she said. Darius couldn't see her eyes behind the tinted lenses, but he imagined she was winking. "But don't worry—get me in front of a Sin, and I'll shoot 'em right between the eyes."

Mackenzie raised her hands, clasped them together with her pointer fingers extended, and mimed taking aim and firing a handgun.

"You two, stop messing around," Chris said. She stepped away from John, and his expression fell as Mackenzie smiled sheepishly.

"Sorry, boss," she said.

Chris raised her brows, grabbed the second pair of virtual reality goggles off the table, and tossed them to Caleb. He fumbled the catch, nearly dropping them to the ground, and Chris's mouth tightened patiently as he pulled them over his platinum blonde hair. When he was done, she gestured to him and Mackenzie. "Go take lanes one and two."

With a quick salute and dramatic flair, Mackenzie spun on her heels and grabbed Caleb by the elbow. His face went pink. "C'mon, spy boy," she said. "Time for us dunces to get to work."

They grabbed VR weapons from a rack by the door and headed out. Darius felt them descend the short stairway before turning left and making their way to the two furthest-left firing lanes. Chris turned to the rest of them. "Everyone else, get a weapon. Conrad?"

Chris glanced over her shoulder to find Conrad frowning down at the phone in his hands, completely unaware of the rest of them. A pair of tiny, wireless headphones stuck like little black bugs from his ears. When Chris repeated his name, louder this time, he finally looked up. With a distracted air, he pulled one of his earbuds out. A man's voice poured through it, loudly enough for Darius to hear it from the other side of the room.

"Y'all ready?" he asked.

"Yes," Chris said coolly. "Turn that off when you're on duty."

Conrad rolled his eyes as he shut off his device and slipped it into his front pocket. The class filed toward him, and Chris glared at him while he opened the weapon locker before she turned to Darius and forced a smile onto her face.

"Don't miss," she said.

"That's the goal."

Darius got in line for a weapon with the rest of the class. All but John. He'd stayed behind to talk quietly to Chris, and though Darius couldn't make out what was said, Chris's firm "I told you, I'm *fine*" gave him an idea. When John came and stood behind him, Darius threw him an awkward smile.

Minutes later, the class stood at the end of their firing lanes, their unloaded firearms laid flat on the metal stands in front of them. Darius was situated between Elena and Nicholas. He felt out of balance with Elena's comforting warmth on his left while Nicholas, to his right, was cold and empty. On Elena's other side, Mackenzie was firing wildly at targets only she could see, swearing the whole time. Darius looked down the line at the target set up fifteen yards away when Chris's voice rang out through his headphones.

"The range is hot," she said, repeating the same instructions she gave at the beginning of every class. The routine had to be dull by now, but Chris's tone was professional and inscrutable. "Load your weapons." Those of them using real firearms snapped their first clip into place. It clicked in Darius's hands. Chris continued. "When you hear the tone, you may begin firing."

A low, steady beep sounded in Darius's ears, followed by the hammering of three firearms going off at once. The noise was muted through his ear protection. He took a deep breath, raised his weapon, and pointed it at the paper target. It was strange how foreign the gun still felt in his hands. Heavy, cold, and deadly. It seemed mismatched, a healer wielding a tool with only one purpose: to end another life.

But it was an important skill—a *crucial* skill. Knowing how to fight and defend himself was something he couldn't afford *not* to know. He had faced the direct consequences of this problem more than once, and every time, people died.

People he may have been able to protect.

He fired his weapon, pulling the trigger until he'd counted fifteen bangs, at which point he removed the clip, put down the gun, and stepped back from his stand. He peered down the lane to see… nothing. Every shot missed. As the rest of the firing petered out, a tone in Darius's ear told him the first set was over. He removed his headset and shook his head.

He had to be better than this.

"Darius? Are you okay?"

Elena's voice snapped him out of his thoughts, and he turned toward her. She pulled her headset off, too, and a wisp of rich, brown hair fell into her face. Swiping it back behind her ear, she looked him over, and her eyes filled with concern. Like many of Eva's old friends, she had taken to asking Darius how he was doing any time he so much as scratched his nose.

"Oh, yeah," he said dismissively. He glanced at her target

and saw all her shots clustered together in the silhouette's chest before he looked further up the room. Chris was at the far end, speaking to Caleb and Mackenzie, slowly heading down the line to the rest of them. Darius shook his head. "This just feels weird. I'm here to save people, not kill them, but if I want to be approved to join TAC as a field medic, I've gotta pass my assessments…"

He took a deep breath, let it out in a slow stream, and turned back toward his lane.

"Well, you won't get approved with aim like *that*," Elena teased, her full lips turned up in a smile. "Have you passed any of the others?"

Darius sighed and shook his head. "Just the one for resilience to Direct Influence, but that's hardly an accomplishment. As a Virtue, the Sins can't get in, even if they *wanted* to."

"What about your combat skill test?"

"Thorn won't let me take it," Darius said. His tone darkened, and he cleared his throat. "She says I'm not ready."

"Yeah…" Nicholas scoffed on Darius's other side, and Darius jumped as he turned around. He hadn't realized Nicholas was listening in. "She's never gonna let you go out on TAC assignments."

Heat rose to Darius's cheeks, but Chris's warm aura approached before he could say anything. He turned around just in time to see her frowning at his target. "Didn't I tell you not to miss?"

She smiled, and he gave a half-hearted chuckle. Like the rest of the room, she had a pair of sound-buffering headphones around her neck, and she pulled them on again. "I want to see what you're doing. Everyone, PPE on!" The room was a flutter of movement as the rest of them put their eye and ear protection back in place. Chris stepped up to Darius's side and gestured to the firearm on the stand in front of him.

"Show me," Chris said, this time her voice both loud in his ear and muffled beside him. The others around the room turned toward him, and the attention felt as hot as human energy on that first morning as Kindness. Darius cleared his throat, snapped a fresh clip into his weapon, and held it up. The paper silhouette stared back at him, shamefully perfect despite the fifteen rounds Darius had already fired toward it. He took a deep breath, let it out in a stream, and pulled the trigger.

The bullet clattered into the trap behind his target. He swore under his breath.

"It's your wrist," Chris said. She approached his right side and extended her arm along his to grip his hand and guide the weapon.

"You tend to curl this way when you're about to shoot," she said, her hold firm, as she gently tilted the pistol to the left. "Try to keep a straight line from shoulder to fingertip."

She demonstrated this by extending her pointer finger. Darius lifted his from the trigger and put it against the side of the gun.

"Right," Darius said. He had a strange sense of déjà vu, like they'd talked about this before. They probably had. Darius was doing so much shit that sometimes it all blurred together. "Sorry."

Chris grabbed his shoulder reassuringly. "Don't sweat it. This is why we're running classes. Try again."

She took a step back. Darius felt her energy behind him, her eyes on the back of his head, as he set his shoulders, aimed down his sight, and pulled the trigger.

A hole ripped into his silhouette's shoulder. Barely. If the target had been a real man, Darius would've clipped him.

But he'd landed a shot, and he allowed himself a moment to punch the air in victory.

"Good," Chris said with a smirk. "Now, just do that six inches down and to the left, and do it every single time."

Then she walked back toward where Mackenzie and Caleb were still struggling with their fake guns, fake targets, and very real complications. Elena threw Darius a smile while Nicholas just shrugged and got back to work. On

Nicholas's other side, John watched after Chris. Darius noticed a tight grouping of holes in his target's chest.

When the tone beeped to start their second round of shooting, Darius did better. More than half hit the target, scattered about like he'd thrown marbles and hoped for the best, but it was better than nothing. As he removed the clip and set his gun back down, smiling to himself, he looked down the lanes. Elena was perfect again. Nicholas, just better than Darius, but John—

John had missed every single shot.

<hr>

"I think Lina *cheated*."

Mackenzie stomped up the stairs, leading Darius and the others as they made their way up from the lower level. Caleb frowned as they rounded the first set of steps.

"What do you mean?" he asked.

"She passed her marksman assessments after less than three weeks of practice!" Mackenzie said, throwing her hands in the air. "And I know for a *fact* all she did to prepare was read the damn gun manual and take a few test shots."

"Have *you* tried reading the manual?" Elena asked. Caleb chuckled, and Mackenzie glared at them over her shoulder.

"Har-dee-har," she said as she opened the door to the courtyard. "I made a bet with her that all of my Discovery team would get cleared for emergency TAC duty *way* before her Research team did, and we're falling behind! I figured we were a shoo-in."

"You're worried you'll be why our team loses, huh?" John asked as he and Chris walked through the door last, hand-in-hand.

Mackenzie groaned. "At this point, I'm just crossing my fingers that she can't read a damn book to become a karate expert overnight, or I am *boned*."

They all laughed, and Darius basked in it. The last six months had been hard. The first time a Sin had been destroyed, the ones left standing had gone quiet. This time, they were roaring. Incidents with the remaining four and their Puppets were on the rise. The Martyrs had lost a lot of good men and women in the last year and a half, and those losses still stung like open wounds, so the rare moments like this, filled with laughter and joy, felt brighter.

A soft *ding!* called out behind them, and Darius turned around as Alexis Claytor stepped off the elevator. Her bright, icy blue eyes moved over the group before she looked down at her watch. "How was class?"

"Great," Mackenzie said. She elbowed Caleb in the ribs and tilted her head against his shoulder playfully. "Your baby brother here gets to move on to real weapons next week!"

Caleb's cheeks went pink as Alexis looked between them, her thin brows raised slightly into her platinum blonde hair. "Do *you* get to move on to real weapons?"

Mackenzie provided a dramatic frown and flung her hand dismissively. "Of course. Soon. Eventually."

Darius and the others laughed, and Elena gazed over the courtyard. "Looks like Kenia's making barbecue tonight," she said, gesturing to where the older woman was setting up trays of savory chicken and blackened corn on the cob. "Who's up for dinner? I head back into town tomorrow for my next shift, so you won't see me for another two weeks…"

Then she raised her eyebrows, tilting her head toward the courtyard.

"Is that *guilt?*" Mackenzie asked. "You're trying to *guilt* us into eating with you before you go on assignment?"

"Not guilt," Elena said. "*Persuade.*"

"Well." Mackenzie raised her hands in the air. "Consider me persuaded. Who's in?"

"Not us," Chris said as she let go of John's hand and came to Darius's side. John hastily wrapped his arms around his chest. "We've got a presentation to prepare for."

Mackenzie's nose wrinkled up in a grimace. "Oh, right.

That's tomorrow morning, yeah?"

"Yep," Chris said.

"Good on you," Mackenzie said, and she grabbed Chris's shoulder. "You'll do great. The plan is golden." A flattered flush rose to Chris's cheeks. Mackenzie didn't wait for her to respond as she turned to John, Nicholas, and the Claytor siblings.

"Do *you* guys have presentations to prepare for?"

"No—" Caleb began. Mackenzie didn't let him finish. She just linked her left arm into the crook of his elbow, grabbed Elena with her right, and started stalking off toward the kitchens.

"You heard the man! Let's get going!"

Alexis hurried to Caleb's side. John laughed, hugging Chris awkwardly before he darted after Mackenzie, too. Nicholas followed at the back, like a quiet shadow in their wake.

"It's crazy," Chris said, and Darius turned toward her. "A year ago, I *never* could have imagined seeing Alexis and Caleb Claytor eating dinner with *Mackenzie*."

Darius laughed. "And it's all thanks to you."

Chris frowned. "What do you mean?"

"It's your training procedures," Darius said as they approached the elevator. "Your combat and marksmanship classes, and my Influence classes—they force units to work together who wouldn't normally." As they waited for the elevator, he looked back at the Martyrs gathered for dinner. TAC teams sat with researchers, nursing staff with Intelligence officers. The blending was beautiful. "You should be really proud of yourself."

"It's not just me," Chris said shortly, but the shadow of a smile betrayed her gratitude at the compliment. "It's everything that's happened to us in the last couple of years."

"What's that?"

"Death. Loss. Pain." Chris shrugged, and Darius's mood fell. "*You* and proving that the Sins can be stopped. I've lived here my whole life, but it hasn't felt like a home before.

Now, it does."

She smiled at him, but instead of making him feel better, Darius felt empty. A home, where the ones they loved were sent out to die. Where children grew up without mothers, or never grew up at all, or grew up so fast they never had the chance to be children in the first place. Darius's jaw tightened as he looked at his feet, and he caught Chris watching him out of the corner of his eye. When the elevator doors opened, they got onto the platform and made their way up without a word.

It was late by the time Darius and Chris finished going over their presentation. The lights had been dimmed for the evening, casting the hallway in darkness, and Darius stifled a yawn as Chris locked her office door behind them. Based on his senses, they were the only two still up working this late. The topmost floor of the Underground was quiet and cold. At the same time, a warm haze of human life murmured beneath Darius's feet, lazily shifting as the Martyrs walked through their respective evening routines and went to bed.

Bed. Darius's stomach twisted up as he thought about going to bed. It was his least favorite part of every day.

"That took longer than I thought," Chris said through a yawn. Darius glanced down at her as she rubbed her eyes with her fingertips. "At the end, the slides were all blurring together, and I'm a little worried about the numbers."

She forced a laugh, but Darius heard a nervous tightness under her warm tone. His own anxiety melted a little, and he gently nudged her with his shoulder. "Chris, it's great."

"Yeah," she said, but she shook her head. "You're right."

"Convincing," Darius said. She laughed.

"I just need this to go well."

There it was. Tension shuddered over Chris's shoulders,

drawing them up. She'd changed from her Tactical uniform turtleneck into a v-neck shirt, which highlighted the hard lines in her throat even more. Ever since Chris's promotion, Darius had watched as pressure molded her body into a tangled knot.

"You've got to stop stressing so much," Darius pressed. "You're going to snap in half."

He attempted a smile, but Chris didn't return it. For a few seconds, the two of them walked in silence until they reached the waiting room. Finally, Darius cleared his throat, and they paused.

"Alan wouldn't have made you the TAC director if you weren't the best person for the job," Darius said. Chris glanced to the side, her gaze drifting to the dark glass doors to the garage. He frowned and leaned in a little closer. "You get that, right?"

"Tell that to *Conrad*," Chris said with a scoff. "He's made it pretty clear he thinks Alan made a mistake."

"Forget Conrad," Darius said, waving his hand, and Chris finally looked at him. "Don't let him get into your head. No one's better for the job than you."

Chris didn't say anything, and she didn't have the chance to. A familiar warmth entered the Underground from above, and Darius turned toward the garage doors. Chris followed his gaze as yellow light blared through the glass. A green hatchback parked by the entrance, and a man stepped out. Bright headlights outlined his skinny body as he made his way toward the Underground. He moved in a perfectly straight line with a rigidity Darius knew came from a hyper-vigilance that bordered on superhuman.

"What's Jacob doing here so late?" Chris wondered out loud. Darius was about to shrug when a voice behind him made him jump.

"We've got a meeting."

Darius and Chris turned back toward the offices to see Thorn's strong, lean silhouette walking down the hallway. He'd been wrong—they *weren't* the only ones working late.

He glanced at his watch.

"Now?" he asked. "It's almost eleven."

"You know how Jacob is," Thorn said. Then she turned to take Darius in, a cool, unreadable expression on her face. Darius's stomach flipped again. The way she watched him with her dark, keen eyes made him worry.

Chris quietly looked between the two of them before settling on Thorn. "What for?" she asked, breaking the tension. Darius and Thorn turned to her.

"I assigned him to scope out the city and look for more police checkpoints," Thorn said. "I don't want a repeat of last Friday." She glanced over Chris quickly, and Chris's mouth tightened. Then Thorn took a deep breath and looked back to the door as Jacob reached it, grabbed the handle, and pulled it open. His car had been left running. The sound of the engine hummed into the room and disappeared as the door swung closed, like a mouth had shut and swallowed the noise behind it.

Jacob paused just inside. His brown eyes darted between Darius, Thorn, and Chris, and his tongue slipped out from behind his teeth to wet his lips. "Didn't think anyone else would be up," he said.

Thorn didn't respond to that. "What have you got for me, Locke?"

Jacob reached into his pocket and flashed a small, silver data chip. His eyes didn't leave Thorn's face, and he shoved the item back into the safety of his pocket. "What you asked for. It's all here."

Thorn nodded. "Great. Let's go see what kind of fucking mess we're in."

She began to walk back down the hallway. Jacob moved to follow her, but as he reached Chris and Darius, he stopped and held out his hand. Darius was taken aback, but he gave it a firm shake.

"Good work," Jacob said quietly. He looked between Darius and Chris, nodding in both directions as he did it. His curly, graying hair stuck out at the edges of a faded, orange ball cap. "Great work. The Martyrs need guys like you keeping them safe. Keep them safe, yeah?"

Darius nodded. "Of course."

"Good," Jacob said. He nodded, quick and sporadic. "Good."

"Locke?" Thorn said. She had paused at the turn in the hallway, and her expression was hard to read. "You okay?"

Jacob nodded, muttered a quick goodbye to Darius, and sped off. When Darius heard the door to Thorn and Alan's waiting room click shut, he turned to Chris. She shook her head.

"It's still so weird when Jacob's around," she murmured as she and Darius walked toward the elevator.

"What do you mean?" Darius asked with a frown.

"I remember when he first came into the Underground," Chris said, taking a short, shallow breath. "My mom and Jeremiah were on the TAC team that responded to the incident."

"When he killed his family?"

Chris's eyes widened. "You know about that? *Jacob* doesn't even know about that…"

"Thorn told me," Darius said. "On the flight to Spokane last year. She said Pride's old host used him as an assassin and that he was Programmed to… well, you know."

A lump formed in Darius's chest as he hit the elevator button.

"Yeah." Chris nodded solemnly. "When we found him, Isla Diamandis—she was Pride at the time—Programmed him to kill his family and then himself. When Mom got there, the wife and girls were gone already, but Abraham had somehow restrained Jacob. You know the rest. Alan had to Deprogram him, and all that time in Jacob's head messed with it."

Darius knew, all right. Thorn had explained it as permanent brain damage. Jacob was constantly flooded with stress hormones, which made him jumpy and paranoid.

"Anyway," Chris went on. "We were told not to talk

about what he'd done under Pride's Programming because, even though Alan tried to hide the memories, he and Thorn were concerned he'd find out and have another episode."

The elevator dinged, and the doors slowly slid open. "Do you worry he'll be violent again?" Darius asked as they stepped onto it.

"No," Chris said. "Not really. He's more protective of the Martyrs than anyone I know. More than Thorn, even." Darius raised his brows in disbelief, and Chris laughed. "I'm serious! When he was really bad, Jacob asked Alan to add additional Programming to make sure he couldn't hurt a Martyr. He didn't want his paranoia to get our people killed."

Darius nodded slowly, and his mouth pulled into a subtle frown.

"So," he pressed, "why is it weird to see him now?"

Chris let out a slow, dark chuckle. "Jacob's younger daughter was eleven," she said. "The same age I was at the time. Listening to Mom and Jeremiah talk about how the Sins had made a parent murder his own kids… little girls like *me*… It stuck with me, and it was really hard to see past that Programming."

The elevator arrived at the main level, opening to the courtyard. As they stepped off, Darius sighed. "Pride used him," he said as they walked through the dim, concrete room. In the emptiness, their footsteps echoed like quiet voices whispering in the distance.

"Like a tool," Chris agreed, nodding. "And he got her back. About ten years later, Jacob's intel helped us kill Diamandis. It didn't feel like enough. It never does."

Chris's voice darkened, and Darius glanced at her. She didn't meet his eye, and they walked to the eastern wing of rooms in silence.

CHAPTER THREE

"I'm not sure I like these numbers," Abraham Locke said, running a hand down his clean-shaven face. He frowned at the digital projector screen at the far end of the table from where Darius was standing. It highlighted rows of figures and statistics: fifty-seven people considered for the Martyrs, with just over three percent joining. That boiled down to two people in the last four months. "They don't seem that impressive."

Chris fumbled with the remote. She'd been in this room dozens of times since her promotion and hundreds before that, but today the smoothness she usually moved with felt jerky and nervous. She had forsaken a casual outfit for her Tactical uniform, Darius assumed as a way to present herself more professionally, and she adjusted the hem of her black turtleneck as she clicked to the next slide. Before she spoke, she glanced up to where Darius was operating the computer. He took a deep breath, raising one hand, palm up, in front of his chest; Chris squared her shoulders and breathed, too.

"They don't seem impressive now," Chris agreed, glancing at Abraham, "but we're working on a small scale to test the concept. As you see here, we could see four to five times as many people when we expand the process."

Abraham gave an unconvincing nod but didn't argue further. Chris's eyes swept across the conference table. It was long enough to seat twenty people comfortably, but today, only the seven directors of the Martyr leadership were gathered here. Lina, her caramel-brown hair woven into a neat plait down the back of her head, sat on Abraham's right while Mackenzie, Alan, and Thorn were across the table. Everyone watched Chris with a quiet respect that the new TAC director didn't seem to know what to do with.

"Miss Silver, would you explain the process in more detail?" Alan asked plainly. He clasped his hands on the table, his back straight, as he considered her. "You and I have spoken about it at length, but I believe the rest of the room has less of an understanding of what is happening here."

A pink flush rose across Chris's face. "Yes, sir, that's coming up next…"

Then she turned back to the screen and clicked another button. A flow chart came to life.

"The ultimate goal of this program is to recruit more people into the Martyrs," Chris said, using the clicker to draw more text and images up as she spoke. "The procedure we've been working with is pretty simple: when civilians are involved directly in an incident with the Sins, we track them down and see if they would make good potential recruits.

"Now." Chris clicked her button, and a list generated down the page. "We don't consider just anyone. We look for certain criteria: aged between twenty and forty-five, good physical health, and no close family ties, social circles, or strong career goals. We also do a background check for mental health issues or violent criminal records. If they don't fit what we need, they're eliminated from consideration."

"What do you do with the ones who *do* fit?" Mackenzie asked. "Just… show up at their front door and ask if they wanna go to war?"

Chris gave a nervous smile. "Yes and no. Most of these

people have experiences they can't explain. If they were Puppetted, they might have blocks of missing memories or injuries they can't account for. Others saw things they didn't understand. So, we send Thorn and a TAC team to their apartment and tell them we can answer their questions. If they agree to come to the Underground, TAC brings them in to talk to Alan. If they don't want anything to do with us, Thorn Programs their memory of the meeting away entirely."

Lina took a short, sharp breath. "They've been coming to the Underground? Isn't that a security risk?"

"We've taken as many security precautions as possible," Chris said. "They must agree to come in blindfolded to ensure they don't have any idea where the Underground is. The ones who decide to join after speaking to Alan are put under the same Programming the rest of us have gone through to protect our location. The ones who don't are brought back to the city, and again, Thorn erases their memory of the whole thing."

Abraham frowned, and he considered Darius. He looked a lot like his older brother, but where Jacob was stretched thin and squeezed out, Abraham had a healthy roundness to his long face. His expression mirrored one he often wore during their therapy sessions: probing and thoughtful.

After a moment, he turned to Alan and Thorn again. "This seems a lot like what we did with Cyrus Murphy."

A heaviness fell into Darius's chest. Cyrus Murphy had been one of the orphans he'd taken in before he found himself with the Martyrs. In fact, Cyrus was the *reason* Darius was with the Martyrs. Thorn had grabbed Cyrus during an incident with Envy almost two years ago. When Jacob had brought him back to New York, Envy had found and killed him.

Tension moved around the room like a cold current. Mackenzie and Lina exchanged an uncomfortable look while Chris focused on Darius. Thorn turned to watch him, too, but her eyes were less concerned. More curious.

Darius cleared his throat.

"Yeah," he said. "It's definitely similar. The whole goal with Cyrus was to avoid as much Programming as possible, right? That's always been one of the biggest concerns with recruitment. Programming is complicated, and since Wrath feels whenever Alan and Thorn use their Influence, we can't do it in the Underground without alerting her to our location. So, if we only talk to people who are already a good fit, it limits how many people we Program. The goal is not to use any Programming at all unless we're dealing with someone we are seriously considering."

Alan nodded quietly, and one corner of Thorn's mouth turned up in a small smile. Darius nodded toward her as Lina leaned forward on the table.

"But Cyrus was killed," she said, her voice hesitant, as she looked between Darius and Chris. "Have any of these other potential recruits been hunted by the Sins? I don't feel comfortable doing something that could make people targets…"

Thorn shook her head. "Cyrus Murphy was a target for the Sins *before* we picked him up. He was able to fight Envy's Influence. She had him Puppetted, and he broke free. That's not something most people can do without training… *unless* they've had long-term exposure to a Virtue. Hell, that's the only reason we picked him up, too."

"And we can be *sure* none of these people are being watched by the Sins?" Lina asked.

"If they are, the protocol is different," Chris said, and all eyes in the room shifted back toward her. "In a situation where we find people for whom it's *dangerous* to return to the city, whether because the Sins used them to commit a crime or their family, friends, or homes have been jeopardized, we use a hybrid of our old system and the new one we're testing now."

One of Abraham's thick brows raised. "Our old system… you mean bringing them straight to the Underground without any other warning?"

Chris's jaw tightened, but she nodded. "Yes. Only now, we sedate them so they don't know how to get here, and Dr. Harris has set up a handful of the old, unused medical offices as private rooms. They stay secured there until Alan and Darius can explain what's happened to them, heal their wounds, whatever they need."

"This feels like kidnapping," Abraham said with a sigh.

"It's either that or let the Sins kill them," Chris said.

"How many people have we considered for recruitment?" Alan asked sharply, getting everyone back on task.

"We've looked at people from just over thirty incidents," Chris said. She took a deep, shaky breath. "About sixty people."

"And of those, how many came to the Underground for more information?"

Chris paused before she answered. "Eight."

"What's the next step?" Lina asked. "When they get here?"

"That's where Darius comes in," Chris said. She seemed a little relieved to be back on track with the presentation they'd put together, and she focused on her slides. "He goes in to get a vibe check on them, just chatting with them to get a feeling using his Virtue instincts. So far, we haven't had anyone send up red flags." She gestured to him, and Darius nodded.

"If he likes the look of them," Chris continued, "we move to the next phase where Alan and Darius explain the whole situation. Everything. Sins. Virtues. Forgotten Sins." Chris glanced around the room, lingering a little on Alan and Thorn before she turned back to the screen. "This includes showing off Sin and Virtue power through healing, because this is a hard pill to swallow without immediate evidence sitting in the chair next to you."

"Damn," Mackenzie said, raising her eyebrows. She clicked her tongue piercing against her teeth. "We're just opening up the *whole* bag, huh? People don't freak the fuck out?"

Alan cracked a rare smile. "Oh, they do."

"New people always do," Thorn defended. "No matter when we tell them. Earlier is better."

She threw Alan a stern expression, and he provided a curt nod in return.

"Plus," Chris said, "they have more evidence than we've had in the past: Darius can heal them. Everyone we've talked to so far has believed us."

"All *eight* people?" Abraham asked.

"Yes. And two of them decided to join. That's a twenty-five percent success rate once we explain the war we're in. Technically, it's higher than that since one of those recruits also brought in her older brother." Chris gave Abraham a half-smile. "Do you like *those* numbers?"

He let out a warm but awkward chuckle. "Okay, that is better," he said. "But what about the people who come here and still don't want to join? How do we stop them from being a security breach?"

Chris gestured an open palm at Thorn. "Thorn brings them back to the city and instills some simple Programming to hide their memories from however long they were with us."

Lina frowned. "That Programming isn't necessarily permanent," she pointed out.

"If the Programming dissolves," Thorn said coldly, her mouth set into a hard line, "that means I'm dead, and you all have much bigger problems than a handful of people in New York who know about the Sins."

An uncomfortable silence fell, and everyone at the table exchanged dark looks. Darius watched the side of Thorn's face. She didn't take her focus away from Lina, and Lina glanced down at her hands.

"Besides," Chris said, clearing her throat and demanding attention again, "we use the same protocols as before. They're blindfolded when they're brought back to the city, so even if Thorn's Programming *does* disappear, they can't tell anyone how to get to the Underground."

"I do like that bit," Mackenzie said, crossing her arms and leaning back in the chair beside Thorn. "Quite frankly, I don't give a damn if people know what war we're fighting, so long as the Sins can't find us and turn this whole place into Martyr soup."

Thorn nodded in agreement as Abraham sighed and rubbed his eyes.

"I agree. This strategy seems pretty sound," he said, but the tone of his voice felt skeptical. He put his hands back down and turned his attention to Alan. "But you've tried to recruit in the past, and it caused a lot of problems. Even if people don't have strong ties to the city, or anywhere else in the world, for that matter, it doesn't mean they don't have *any* connections. How can we guarantee new recruits don't try to keep in contact with those people? Asking them to cut out everyone in their lives is… Well, to be honest with you, I don't know if it's possible."

"We all did it," Darius said. Everyone turned to him again. "I had more than that orphanage the Sins destroyed," he said bluntly. "I had a whole community of people at the street market I could have gone back to. Once I realized what was happening here and that I wouldn't be leaving, I haven't tried to connect with them at all. I'm sure it's the same for you." Darius gestured toward Abraham and Lina. "Jacob isn't your *only* family, right? Have you reached out to anyone you had to cut out? *Any* of you?"

Darius looked around the room. Mackenzie stared at the table, her lower lip pinched between her teeth. Lina's right hand toyed with a silver pendant around her throat. Abraham shook his head. "No," he said.

"Then we wouldn't have any higher risk than we already do," Darius said.

Chris looked at him and gave a grateful smile. Aside from Thorn and Alan, Chris was probably the *only* person Darius knew who didn't have to abandon people outside the Underground. She hadn't had connections to cut.

"We were *all* recruited," Darius went on. "The only

difference is we were recruited after something awful happened to us. As far as I know, everyone here came in after some attack."

"Not Holly," Mackenzie offered with a single-shoulder shrug. "That little genius found *us*."

"To our great benefit," Alan added.

Darius nodded in their direction. "Besides Holly, then."

"If anything," Abraham argued, but his cheeks turned a little red, and he began to roll up the sleeves of his plaid, button-up shirt, "that proves my point even more. Almost every person here is fighting because the Sins destroyed their lives, but you're talking about recruiting new members who aren't connected to this mess at all. What right do we have to ruin theirs, too?"

Thorn raised a brow, crossed her arms, and shot Abraham a dark look. "How the *fuck* do you figure we're ruining lives? We're not blackmailing anyone. We're not *coercing* them to stay. We're just giving them the option, and if they don't want anything to do with it, we make sure they don't remember what's happening and send them back to live their cushy little lives in New York City."

"Cushy little lives?" Abraham said, his mouth dropping open. He let out a scoff, and when he went on, his voice was louder. "That's a callous take. Not everyone here has had a hundred years to get over the tragedies that brought us together, Thorn. I certainly haven't forgotten how hard it was to jump into this life."

Silence fell like a storm cloud, and Darius looked wide-eyed between Thorn and Abraham. Thorn's jaw had tightened, and her gaze was as fierce as ever, but she swallowed hard and didn't argue. After a beat, Lina grabbed Abraham's forearm on the table. It was like a spell was broken, and he let out a chest full of held breath in a sigh.

"Listen," he went on, more evenly now, as he raised his hands. "My job isn't to blindly agree with everything proposed at these meetings. I'm *supposed* to ask questions." He looked around at them all, avoiding Thorn's hot glare.

"We're the good guys, right? And I want to make sure we really think through pulling people into this mess. When people join us after losing everything to the Sins, the fight can be cathartic. It might even help them handle the trauma they've been through. Hell, for some of us, the Underground is our only option. Without this place, Jacob would be dead." His throat constricted around the word, and he cleared it before continuing. "But the fact is, Martyrs don't have an easy life. Mental health is fragile, at best. This is a *hard* path, and it feels… I dunno… irresponsible to drag more people into it."

"As irresponsible as letting the Sins *win?*"

Chris's voice was quiet but heavy. Her discomfort at the spotlight faded, and she looked down at Abraham with an almost offended expression as she crossed her arms.

He shook his head. "I'm not saying that."

Chris raised a hand. "You are, though," she said, indicating for Darius to cut the presentation. He obliged, and the screen retracted back into the ceiling. Behind it, a whiteboard was nailed to the wall. Chris grabbed a marker and turned back to Abraham, pointing at him with the butt of the pen. "You want to talk numbers? Let's talk numbers."

She started scribbling on the board. "In the last eighteen months, how many TAC members do you think we've lost?" Abraham stared and said nothing as Chris wrote the number, extra-large, so no one could miss it. Then she drew a hard, red line beneath it. "Twelve. That's just since Darius joined us. Twelve of my men and women are gone. That number is even higher if we look at non-TAC. Teresa Solomon. Sara Park. Eva Torres."

Darius's stomach lurched at Eva's name. Chris's eyes drifted his way before she cleared her throat and turned back around.

"Now, how many new people have we brought in since then, *not* including the recruits I found using these new protocols?"

She looked right at Abraham, and his face went even

darker before he finally said, "Three."

"Three," Chris repeated, and she wrote that number down, too. "And one of those three is among the dead, so really, just two." She stood back and looked at the board before considering the room again, her bright green eyes filled with determination. This time, they didn't focus on Abraham.

"In eighteen months, our TAC team decreased by *one-fifth*," she said. "And our total loss count for the whole of the Martyrs? More than a *tenth*. How long can we keep *bleeding* people before we aren't strong enough to survive? The Sins don't have to find the Underground to destroy the Martyrs. They just need to wait for us to starve ourselves until we waste away to nothing."

Silence filled the space. Alan glanced around at his team proudly, while Thorn watched Chris with the same level of admiration Darius himself felt for the new TAC director.

"Look," Chris went on. She leaned forward, placing her hands flat on the table. Blonde hair cascaded around her shoulders and framed her face in a bright yellow veil. "I understand how hard this will be for people. Being a Martyr is *not* easy, but the work we do is *so* important. I have fought like hell for this organization, and I'm not about to watch it die. If we don't bring more people in, if we don't *seriously* figure out how to solve this problem, it will."

More quiet air as people absorbed that. Then Mackenzie let out a whistle.

"Talk about ending on a high note." She looked around the room. Abraham glanced down at his hands on the table, and Mackenzie's eyes landed on Darius with a wink.

"I believe it's time we take this to a vote," Alan said, getting to his feet to stand beside Chris. He lifted his right hand. "All in favor of integrating Miss Silver's recruitment procedures into our current systems?"

Darius raised his hand and watched as every Martyr around the table did the same. Thorn's fingers shot into the air immediately, followed by Mackenzie, Lina, and, finally,

Abraham. A smile formed behind Alan's goatee.

"It's settled," he said, placing a palm on Chris's shoulder. "Miss Silver, please start training your teams on a rolling basis to implement these new protocols."

Darius's chest swelled as Chris smiled so widely that it pinched the corners of her eyes and revealed a line of pink gums around white teeth. Thorn got to her feet, her mouth turned into a smirk that came as close to beaming as Darius had ever seen it. Mackenzie jumped up, let out a whoop, and clapped her hands together. Even Lina smiled, but Abraham still looked unconvinced.

After discussing the details of what it would take to start integrating Chris's system, Alan dismissed them. Chris wrapped Darius in a tight embrace before she darted off to her office. While the conference room emptied, Darius watched as her hair whipped around the corner. Her door opened and then clicked shut, and Darius felt her energy hurrying to her desk. Even when she sat down, she buzzed with excited movement. He smiled.

"She needed that win," Thorn said.

Darius turned around as she stepped up beside him. Lina and Abraham moved past, heading toward the waiting room, as Thorn crossed her arms and watched the same spot on the wall where Darius had been focused—the spot beyond which both he and Thorn could feel Chris's aura.

"It's no wonder she got it," Mackenzie said. Her staticky energy moved up to Darius's other side. "That girl's put a *lot* of work into this."

"They both have," Thorn said, and she put a palm on Darius's shoulder. Her fingers felt oddly cool through his clothes. "I hope you're ready. With more recruits, you're going to have your hands full."

Then her grip tightened, just a bit, and her mouth went thin. Darius's stomach did a little flip.

"I think I can handle it," he said, trying to keep his tone confident. He thought Thorn was going to challenge him, but she didn't have to. Mackenzie did it for her.

"How hard can it be?" she said, counting off on her fingers as she went on. "Just tack on a few more sessions of those 'how to not get dicked over by Direct Influence' classes you're teaching, plus healing up all our wounded and dying, plus training to pass your shooting and combat assessments so you can heal those wounded and dying on the scene, and don't forget to eat and sleep, while you're at it… Oh! And how many new Virtues have you found?"

Mackenzie nudged him and raised her brows until her piercing disappeared behind her bangs. Darius let out a laugh, but even he thought it sounded hollow.

"Isn't that last one *your* job, too?" he quipped, and Mackenzie shrugged.

"*I'm* not the one with a built-in Virtue compass." She winked and wrapped an arm around Darius's middle to pull him in for a half-hug. "In all seriousness, though, Jones, you're taking on a lot. If you need help, you know where to find me."

Then she said her goodbyes and wandered off to the Research and Discovery headquarters. Darius watched her go, acutely aware of Thorn's gaze on the side of his face, wondering if she knew how frustrated he was with his search for the Virtues.

Because he hadn't found a promising lead in *months*.

"G'night, Darius."

Darius glanced up from his computer screen. He'd been staring at the bright glow for so long that Parker Boseman's young face was blurred in the dim light of the R&D headquarters. She was nothing more than a fuzzy shape, dark smudges where her eyes and mouth belonged beneath a mop of tight ringlets. He forced a smile and threw up a hand.

"Night, Parker," he said. "Thanks for all your help."

She beamed. He didn't have to see her features in detail

to know it. Her wide mouth cracked open in a smile, shining white against her bronze skin, and she bounced a little on the balls of her feet.

"No problem," she said. "I'll see you tomorrow."

Then she ducked out of the room. Her energy seemed to skip down the hallway as she headed to the lower level, where the rest of the Martyrs were gathered.

Mostly asleep, Darius thought, as he looked at his watch. It was almost ten p.m.

He groaned, rubbed his tired eyes with his fingertips, and turned back to his screen to open the file Parker had sent him. In the last six months, the research half of the R&D department had built a massive backlog of potential Virtue leads, and Darius was painfully behind in analyzing them. He wanted to say it was because of all the other things he was working on right now, but he knew the real reason was a lot more complicated…

The list was massive. Hundreds of articles. Hundreds of incidents.

Hundreds upon hundreds of hours wasted looking in the *wrong* place and coming up empty…

For three nights, while Chris was busy integrating her new systems into the TAC department, Darius had done nothing but read through headlines, scan articles, and glance at pictures, hoping to get some sense of where they should be looking. Parker had done the heavy lifting, sorting the leads into a dozen categories and subcategories, from location to incident type.

But none of that seemed to matter. When Darius had found the article that led them to Nicholas, it felt *different*. Important. Part of that "Virtue compass." Everything landing on his desk now was aimless. Sometimes a glimmer of a good feeling, but nothing that made him feel as confident as that one article had.

A warm sensation flickered to life above him and began to spiral into the Underground. Darius focused on it and frowned. Abraham and Lina were rarely out this late.

Darius turned back to his work as they quietly moved. He expected them to head straight to the lower level, but the energy paused in the foyer before Lina broke away and made her way toward the R&D headquarters. Darius glanced at the door when it opened a few minutes later. Lina didn't seem surprised to see him sitting behind his desk.

"Good evening, Darius," she said warmly.

"Hey," he said as she walked past him to her workstation at the back of the room. "Cain kept you up?"

Lina laughed. "He's all alone out there. I can hardly blame him for wanting company. He *did* manage to get Abraham pretty tipsy tonight."

Darius chuckled. "*Abraham* got tipsy?"

Lina's smile faded. "He doesn't usually drink so much." The last word drifted off, and she shuffled some items on her desk. Seconds later, she lifted a couple of books and glanced up at Darius, finding him watching her. She gave a short sigh. "Today is the fifth anniversary of my sister's death."

A clamp tightened around Darius's chest. "Oh," he said with that awkward cadence of not knowing what *to* say. "He has seemed a little off lately… I'm sorry."

"Thank you," Lina said, her hand moving to the pendant around her throat. Darius looked at it closely for the first time. It was shaped like a teardrop, with four Hebrew letters etched into it in a square pattern. "This year was harder than others. Stella was the same age I am now when she got her diagnosis, you know." Darius hadn't known, but he nodded anyway, his face tight in empathy. A pink flush rose to Lina's cheeks. "I'm sorry. I didn't mean to bring it down—"

"No, no," Darius cut in, raising his palms. "It's totally fine. Do you want to talk about it?"

Lina smiled and shook her head. "I'm all right. We did a lot of talking today."

"How's Abraham?"

"Drunk," Lina said with a wry laugh. "But okay. I'm sure he'll feel otherwise in the morning. You'd think, as our counselor, he would have better tools for this kind of thing, but I suppose it's easier to help others than it is to help ourselves."

She paused, clutching her books to her chest, and the edges of her eyes drew in with concern. As she watched him, his throat went tight.

"C'mon," she said at last, walking to his side and gesturing her head toward the door. "It's late. This can all wait until tomorrow."

Darius forced a smile, shut off his machine, and got to his feet. The two of them headed into the hallway, and Darius lingered for a moment, heaving a sigh before he flicked off the light.

A few minutes later, he walked into his room, turned that light on, and the emptiness looked back.

Darius stood in the doorway and took it in. Drab, impersonal, and *boring*. A queen-sized bed sat in the center, flanked by simple oak tables. One dresser. Darius had moved here just shy of six months ago when the old room he had lived in since coming to the Underground proved too depressing of a reminder of everything he had lost since then. He hadn't done much to make the space feel more his. The only personal item he had was a red, leather-bound book: the Bhagavad Gita Teresa had given him. Instead of keeping it out, he'd tucked it away in a side table drawer, untouched.

With a sigh, Darius closed the door and got ready for bed. As he changed into his sweatpants, he looked at himself in the mirror hanging from the back of his door. All his bruises had finally disappeared, and his tawny skin looked healthier than it had in weeks. He wondered when they'd let him train with Thorn again. Somehow, he was *more* exhausted without it.

Darius lay on his back and stared at the ceiling. The bed felt cold and overlarge. Before the Underground, he'd slept in a pile of wiggling children, their bony elbows and knees poking into his ribs and back. Later, Eva had curled by his side, her warm, human energy draped around him like a blanket.

He was not accustomed to the empty space. It felt confining.

Time crawled by as Darius flipped and turned, opening his eyes moments after forcing them shut time and time again, and sleep dangled just out of reach. His brain was busy with thoughts about Lina, about Abraham, and about Eva.

With a groan, Darius flopped onto his back and forced his concentration onto his breathing, blindly hoping to slow his mind down. He focused on his hands, gently tapping his thumbs against the pads of his fingers. With each tap, he grounded himself in his surroundings. What could he see and feel? Sense and hear? The dark ceiling. His sheets, cool against his bare chest. The Martyrs' warm energy hovering in nearby rooms. A loud, shrill alarm—

He knew the sound. That familiar, heart-wrenching sound.

Casualties.

Darius leapt out of bed, all weary hopes of sleep shattered.

CHAPTER FOUR

Broad hands slipped under the hem of her shirt, lifting it until it tangled around her elbows and pinned her arms above her head. The hands came back down, following the curves of her sides, touching each rib. Fingertips slipped beneath her bra. Cold, human energy made the early spring weather feel cooler, and even the bare flesh of his stomach pressed against hers didn't warm her. None of it did. Not the touches. The caresses. The feeling of his lips against her throat. Her collar. Lingering a little before moving lower.

Jay's deep, husky voice murmured against her chest. "Teagan?"

The movement slowed. Thorn hardly noticed. Her dark eyes were focused on a poster tacked to the wall behind Jay's head, staring into the face of some musician from the 2080s she'd never bothered to learn the name of. It didn't matter. None of this did.

"Tea?"

Those strong hands pulled back.

Chris had two of her TAC units fully trained to start looking for potential new recruits, and while Thorn knew logically how crucial this was for the Martyrs, she was struggling with the *logistics* of it. Between Chris and Darius, Thorn had two people prepared to work themselves into an early grave. An *earlier* grave. How the fuck did they think they were going to manage training green Martyrs on top of their other responsibilities? Thorn needed to—

"Jesus, Teagan, why did you agree to come over if you're not up to this?"

Jay Coons pushed himself off the wall, away from Thorn, and propped his hands on his hips. He was shirtless—god, Thorn didn't even remember him taking it off—and the top button of his jeans was unclasped.

Fuck. Now she remembered what she was here for.

"Sorry," Thorn said, and she half-meant it. It had been a while since she'd seen Jay, and the *idea* of sex sounded great... an hour ago. The minute she showed up, though, she remembered *why* it had been so long.

"*Sorry?*" Jay repeated. "If you don't want to be here, I don't *want* you here."

"I never said I didn't want to be here," Thorn snapped, untangling her arms from the shirt Jay had pulled over her head. It tugged at her gloves, dragging them down, and brushed against the *Peccostium* on her left wrist. A disorienting sensation shivered up her arm, along the thick lines of her scars, and into her bones. A flicker of resentment came to life in her chest as she threw the shirt to the floor. "I just have a lot of other shit going on—"

"Then go," Jay cut in, and Thorn's resentment bubbled. "Do whatever else you've got to do."

"Look," Thorn snarled, adjusting her gloves and pulling them higher. "I don't owe you a fucking *explanation*, and if I say I want to be here, I want to fucking be here."

"Oh yeah," Jay said, raising his eyebrows. "Clearly. By the way you stood there and did *nothing*, I can tell you want to be here. It's a pretty fucking big turn-off if I'm the only one into it."

"You want to talk about turn-offs?" Thorn spat, crossing her arms. "What about your shitty attitude?"

Jay's eyes widened. "*My* attitude?" He let out a laugh and

threw one hand up indignantly. "That's a lot coming from you!"

"Another big turn-off?" Thorn went on. "Waking up Mrs. Steinman again, unless you *like* it when your neighbor pounds on your wall."

"At least she doesn't punch *through* it!"

The resentment roared into fury, and like a goddamned Pavlovian response, Thorn's body came with it. The cold indifference flickered with a false heat of passion in her core. This was all she and Jay did anymore. There was a time when things between them had the illusion of normalcy: dinners, drinks, and sex.

But in the last year, all they did when they got together was fight then fuck. The pattern had been fine at first—better than the nothing she felt outside of it—but Thorn was getting tired of patterns. Tired of fighting. Tired of feeling fucking *angry*.

But she kept coming back anyway. She looked Jay over. His body was tense, the streetlight outside casting it in soft shadows. The muscles in his abdomen stood out in a contrast that made him look more in shape than he was—younger, too, like when Thorn had first met him four years ago.

"What?" Jay said, hands back on his hips. Chest pushed out. The sliver of his boxers showing above jeans that had slipped down, just barely, giving the line of hair stretching from his naval a longer runway. And his anger, his god damned *anger*.

"No smart-ass response?" he went on. "Just gonna hit something?"

Just like that fucking dog and the bell. Thorn strode up to him and shoved him backward. The backs of Jay's knees hit the couch, and he fell onto it. Thorn put a hand on his chest, pushing him deeper into the uneven cushions, and caught his lips in a rough kiss. He opened his mouth, almost like he had planned to argue, but instead, he dove into hers. His hand wrapped around the back of her head, pulling her closer—

An alarm on Thorn's phone blared to life and killed the fire in her stomach as abruptly as if she'd been shot. For a moment, Jay disappeared. His apartment disappeared.

And all she saw was Chris's face, white and bloodied, just like Donovan's had been.

Thorn leapt away from Jay, grabbed her shirt, and snatched her satchel off the floor. Sparkie, pressed tightly inside the bag, looked into her bright, red phone screen. A flash of relief flooded down Thorn's spine, but that relief quickly drowned. Jay groaned and ran his hands down his face.

"What the *fuck*."

"I've gotta go," Thorn snapped. She opened the door and rushed down the steps, pulling on her shirt as she hit the sidewalk and ran north. Sparkie tore from her satchel, his red, leathery wings vaulting him into the sky as he headed straight toward the Upper East Side, where the alarm in Elena Cortez's apartment had just been set off.

Even this late at night, the streets were busy as Thorn sprinted from Jay's apartment to where she parked four blocks away. One man stepped into her path and slurred, "Where you running to, beautiful?" Thorn pushed past him so hard that he tumbled over a garbage bag sitting on the side of the road and vanished behind it.

A black, nondescript motorcycle stood against the curb, and Thorn jumped onto it. She pulled her kevlar bike jacket over her shoulders, put her helmet on, and tore away so quickly that her tires peeled on the asphalt. The scent of burning rubber coated Thorn's tongue and the inside of her nose as she headed to 3rd Avenue. She hit the bridge, punched a few icons on a digital dash, and Chris's name lit up the corner of Thorn's visor as her helmet radio tapped into the TAC director's feed.

A barrage of voices immediately poured into her ears.

"—have blockaded a two-block radius," Conrad Carter was saying. "From East 77th to East 75th—"

"Get through it," Chris ordered into the mic. "Whatever it takes."

"Roger that," Carter replied.

"What's our status?" Thorn said. She tapped a couple more icons, and a city map filled her screen. Red dots moved along it, marking where Carter's vehicle was closing in on Elena's apartment. Sparkie was already above the building, spiraling in furious circles. Thorn caught a flash of movement as two people in black body armor sneaked along the side of the building.

"Carter's looking for a way through the blockade," Chris said. "Graves and I are on our way in."

As Thorn sped down East River Drive, swerving in and out of the cold commuter energies around her, Sparkie pulled in tight and plummeted from the sky. Just as Chris opened the front door to the complex, his wings furled open and caught him like a chute. He clung to her shoulder, and Thorn's heart tightened. Through her helmet speakers, she heard the distant sound of a battering ram slamming into wood.

She was five minutes away. Five minutes was a long time to have her team in the middle of an armed combat situation. A long time for Thorn to listen to them fight, able to do *nothing*.

As TAC voices continued to come through, a muddled mess of orders from Chris as she moved up the stairs and Carter complaining that he still couldn't get past the blockade, Thorn snarled into the mic, "Is Andrews on?"

"Here." Holly Andrews broke through. Just hearing the security lead's steady voice added a tense stability to the chaos.

"Can you cut out the police radios?" Thorn asked.

"Already done," she said. Above the yelling, the stomping, the sudden sound of rapid-fire gunshots going off, Thorn thought she heard the clacking of a keyboard. "The First Response disruptor is live and active, but all it's gonna do is stop any cops inside from communicating with the ones on the street. The blockades won't be affected."

Thorn *had* to get through that line, and she didn't like her options.

But she didn't have any other choice.

"Okay," Thorn growled. "Give me two minutes."

She tore off East River, exited onto 97th, then turned south to 2nd Avenue. The city felt cold around her, energy zipping by, because even at eleven fucking p.m. New York City was still alive and breathing. Thorn reached out with her power, pushing her Influence in a wide arch around her body as far as she could, and issued a simple command to anyone inside that bubble:

Get out.

Cars pulled to the right and the left, parking awkwardly on either edge of the one-way street. Drivers leapt out, not knowing why, not understanding that the sudden need they felt to run, to get away from this place, came not from their own minds but from Thorn's. She cleared a path through vehicles as they left the road. Lurkers, drawn to the police line to gawk at what was happening, darted east and west, disappearing down alleys, between buildings, and into Central Park.

In the distance, somewhere in North Brooklyn, Thorn felt another energy surge to life as Wrath woke up.

"We've got half an hour before Hunt gets here," Thorn said.

She could see the blockade now. A police cruiser was parked across 2nd Avenue, preventing drivers from entering the area at 77th. The officers looked at the motorcycle. Thorn felt for their auras, latched onto them with hers, and pushed in more Influence with the confidence that she belonged here. They watched, unconcerned, as she veered onto the sidewalk and zipped around them.

"Carter, *now!*"

Thorn could feel where Carter and his partner, Liz Wright, were turning—their fuzzy auras at the edge of Thorn's range, coming up 75th to another police stopping point. She pushed her Influence out to the cops there, too, and suddenly the TAC unit was inside.

A blast of gunfire sounded in Thorn's ear.

"They've got SWAT up here," Chris shouted, and Sparkie cried out furiously from her shoulder. "I could use some backup!"

"How many?" Thorn asked.

"Enough to be a problem," Chris said.

Thorn swore as she careened around the corner and slammed her bike to a stop in the middle of the sidewalk outside Elena's apartment building. The area had been vacated. Within a two-block vicinity, Thorn sensed a fraction of the energy she should have felt nestled to sleep at almost midnight on a Monday. A fire lit up in her chest.

This ambush was planned.

Thorn leapt off her bike, leaving the electric engine engaged, and grabbed a pistol from the satchel cinched around her waist. Carter's vehicle whipped around the corner and screeched beside her as Thorn flicked off the safety and chambered a round. Then she ran into the indistinct, brown building, shouting into her mic.

"Fourth floor!"

Darkness flooded the hallway and staircase—the power had been cut?—but it didn't matter. Thorn's visor adjusted to night vision, allowing her to see as she sprinted up the stairs. She heard shouting, shooting, sobbing. Felt the huddled energies of the families who hadn't vacated the premises hiding together in their apartments as gunfire blasted three stories above them. The sounds were muted, dull from her adrenaline and the noise-canceling effects of Thorn's helmet, but she could still hear the voices.

"Entrance secured!" Chris said.

"We're here," Carter growled. "Comin' up!"

"Lay down your weapons!"

Thorn didn't recognize that one. Male. Younger than she expected. He had to be one of the officers. She could feel them. Four energies she didn't know inside unit 403. Two

Martyrs outside: Chris and Seth Graves.

But she couldn't feel Elena.

"Any sign of Cortez?" Thorn asked. She was only one floor away now. The energies were more distinct. Graves shouted something. Another gunshot went off. The cop shouted another order.

"Not yet," Chris said.

Thorn's chest constricted. That didn't mean anything, she told herself. This was New York. Elena could have left after she set the alarm off. She could have gone out the fire escape. Sprinted down the street. Joined the horde of people Thorn had sent away, safely into the anonymity of the city.

Fourth floor. More shouting. Thorn rushed down the hallway.

She had to know for sure.

"Thank god," Chris began, but Thorn ran past her, directly into the apartment.

And she came in shooting.

Pushing out her Influence, Thorn filled the studio with cloudy confusion. The officers faltered, hesitating as they tried to make sense of the conflicting commands inside their heads, just long enough for Thorn to make her way through the doorway without getting shot to fucking pieces. She pulled her trigger in rapid succession, hitting one, two, three of the men, missing the fourth. Two fell backward, struck in the chest plates. One immediately blinked out as Thorn's bullet went under his chin, severing his spinal column.

She kept pushing. Behind her, Graves guarded the door while Chris slipped into the room. Thorn heard the fourth officer shout something, heard more gunfire, and felt another SWAT member blink out of existence. She ignored it all as she rushed to the bathroom. Sparkie landed at the crook of her neck and froze.

The reinforced door was decimated. Rammed from its hinges and hanging from a mangled lock. A shower of bright red sprayed the walls behind it.

Thorn's eyes moved to the floor.

Elena lay shattered by a leaden rainfall of rifle fire. Blood speckled her throat, her chin, her face. Bare, brown arms spread out, exposed by the thin straps of her satin nightgown, which hadn't always been deep crimson, Thorn was sure, but now that color was all she could see. Dark eyes stared up at the ceiling, cold and lifeless.

The constriction around her chest worsened. Suffocating. Her breath caught, and a cold sweat of dread and rage and *hatred* blossomed along her body. She felt her lip curl into a snarl, and she turned around. A sound erupted from her mouth: a raw, hoarse roar exploding into the room. Everything seemed to move in slow motion. Two of the SWAT team were dead, one squared off with Chris near the exit, screaming for backup that wouldn't come, and the fourth yelled at Thorn from the far end of the room. She filled with loathing fire.

How many lives was one Martyr worth?

Time caught up to Thorn as she raised her weapon and pulled the trigger. The officer by the door, his rifle pointed squarely at Chris's chest, spluttered as the shot hit him beneath the armpit, where his armor didn't have the coverage to protect his fucking heart. He fell to his knees in the doorway, gasping for breath. Thorn's finger tightened again to finish the job—

A bullet slammed into her shoulder, cutting through a seam in her jacket.

Thorn's back collided with the splintered doorframe, cracking it more, and the gun flew from her hand. Blood poured from the wound and down her arm. She looked up. Locked eyes with the fourth officer. Something about him felt different. He paused, his pistol pointed right at Thorn's sternum.

"Hands behind your head," he commanded, and he took a step forward, looking between her and the animal by her throat. "Ma'am, put your hands—"

Sparkie screeched as Thorn charged. The officer shot her again, but she muscled through as it thudded painfully against her kevlar. He scrambled to adjust his aim; Thorn attacked.

She rammed into him so forcefully that the two of them flew backward. His heels caught one of his dead companions, sending them both toppling over and crashing into the back of Elena's couch. Chris screamed something to her, and the cold energy of the other officer finally blinked to nothing, but none of it mattered.

The colors in the room seemed to mute. The deep, red blood turned to shadow, and the blacks grew blacker as Thorn threw one punch after another into what little of the man's face she could see beneath his visor. He grabbed at her, tried to pry her off him, but Thorn spread her legs, anchored herself so firmly to the ground that his weak attempts did nothing more than make her angrier. Soon, the smooth skin across his cheeks and chin was slick with blood, and his strength faltered. His grip around her weakened, and Thorn thrust her hand beneath his helmet strap. Closed her fingers around his windpipe…

"Thorn, *stop!*"

Chris's voice cut through, a light in the fog. Color came back to the room. Wrath's energy, a pulsing, intermittent beacon of evil, was close enough now for Thorn to be uncomfortable about it. The man pinned beneath her legs had stopped fighting. Behind his visor, Thorn could just see his eyes, the color of cognac, go wide.

"I've got Cortez!" Carter screamed.

Thorn glanced behind her as he forced his bulk away from the mangled bathroom. Elena draped from his arms, her skin dusky, her lips a shade of purple that made Thorn's stomach sick. She turned back to the officer and tightened her grip. He gasped, grabbed her arm, and tried to pry her off. Thorn hesitated.

That difference she'd noticed in him before… she knew what it was now.

His energy.

Most of the cops in this damned city had been so

thoroughly corrupted by Gluttony's incessant presence that they felt like ice. Painfully cold. Like frigid wind coming off the Atlantic on a January morning. This man, though…

He felt like Chris.

"Wait!"

Her voice again. Chris wrapped her fingers around Thorn's shoulder. "We can use him! He could know how they found out about Elena!"

Those cognac eyes stared deep into Thorn's, full of the animalistic fear all human beings have when they realize they're close to death, but his held something else, too. Determination. Drive.

In some ways, he reminded her of how Darius had looked that first day they'd found him, running back into a bloodied bar, ready to die for what he believed in. She loosened her fingers, and the man took a gasping breath.

"Okay," Thorn said. "Let's go."

As she spun him around, he tried to stand, but she must have given him a mild concussion because he stumbled and fell again. Thorn pulled his arms behind his back and forced him to his feet.

"Where are you taking me?" he asked.

"Graves," she said into her headset, ignoring the officer as Chris led the way. Thorn followed, dragging a cop fifty pounds larger than her down the stairwell as though he was a petulant child throwing a tantrum. "You have the sedative in your kit?"

"Yes, ma'am."

"Good," Thorn growled. "We're going to need it."

CHAPTER FIVE

Darius walked through the hospital ward at eight in the morning, a to-go cup of hot coffee in each hand. His eyes ached, and his body felt clammy the way it always did when he didn't get enough sleep the night before. Even a hot shower hadn't made him feel better. He stifled a yawn and nodded to Raquel at the nurses' station.

"Has Chris been back there all morning?" he asked.

"Yep," Raquel responded without looking up from the medication bin she was sorting. "She got here at 0530." Her voice sounded weary, too. Like Darius, Raquel had been woken up by the alarm and rushed to the hospital ward to find Elena Cortez dead, four TAC officers sporting superficial wounds and deep mental trauma, and an unconscious police officer in the back of Chris's car.

"You okay?" Darius asked. He'd asked it seven hours ago, too, but he was starting to doubt everyone who said "yes." Were they all like him, telling the same lie because it was easier than admitting they weren't?

Raquel shrugged, throwing a look over her shoulder. Her brown hair was pulled up into a messy bun that was more messy than bun right now. Flyaways framed her face and made her look fuzzy. "I'll feel better when we get *him* out of here."

She gestured into a wide alcove behind the nursing sta-tion. A knot formed in Darius's stomach.

"Soon," he said. "Alan's talking to him today."

Raquel nodded, and Darius headed into the alcove. Four newly-renovated, private medical suites, two to each side, faced each other across the tile floor, while a fifth door looked back at the nurses' station from the far wall. Darius paused by the first room on the right.

Unfamiliar, hot energy paced back and forth.

Darius swallowed hard and made his way to the fifth and final room. He fumbled with the to-go cups for a moment, pinning one between his forearm and stomach while he opened the door. A blast of cool, stale air hit him.

Even after pulling out all the paperwork and digitizing it to transform this old office into a monitoring terminal, the place still smelled musty. Bulky, plastic storage shelves lined the walls on either side, packed with boxes of data chips and miscellaneous electronics. Surveillance equipment covered a table in the center of the room, and Chris sat behind it, staring up at a massive, paper-thin screen installed on the opposite wall. Darius looked at it.

A man walked around the hospital suite in an open-backed gown. The bloodied armor and uniform he'd been wearing when he came in had been cut off so the nursing staff could treat his injuries, though Darius couldn't say it had helped. His face was still heavily swollen from the nose down; streaks of dried blood caked to the buzzed sides of his head and matted the longer hair on top. Every so often, he stopped to tap on the concrete walls, and his gaze found the camera lens. He stared right into it, and Darius's throat ran dry.

"Who is he?" Darius asked.

Chris looked up and inhaled a deep breath. Her blonde hair fell loose around her shoulders. "Gabriel DuPont," she said. She typed a few strokes into the keyboard, and a hand-ful of files spread out on a monitor at the corner of the desk.

"He joined the Nineteenth Precinct two months ago," Chris went on. Darius lowered into a chair on her left. He gently touched her shoulder with the bottom of one of the to-go cups, and she glanced down at it. "God, thanks. You're a saint." She took it, raised it to her mouth, and wrinkled her nose the way she always did on that first sip now that she'd switched to taking her coffee black.

"So, he's a rookie?" Darius asked, surprised. He didn't imagine a lot of rookies made the cut for the SWAT team.

Chris shook her head and set her coffee down. "No. He spent eight years on the force in Pittsburg. According to the records Holly dug up, his wife had an affair and still somehow managed to get everything in the divorce. He put in for a transfer afterward."

Darius nodded, but the tightness in his forehead hadn't relaxed. DuPont moved away from the camera, walking toward the door. The back of his gown slipped open, and Darius caught the gnarled edge of thick, healed flesh a couple of inches to the right of his spine.

"That's a nasty scar," he said. "Injured on the job?"

"Yep. Hostage situation. He managed to get everyone out alive and spent a couple of months in the hospital recovering. From what I read, he's lucky he's not paralyzed."

DuPont turned back around, frowning as he fixed his gaze on the camera again. He strode right to it, threw his hands up indignantly, and spoke, though no sound came through the muted speakers. His shrewd, coppery eyes narrowed, and Darius's stomach felt uneasy. The man was hard to read, but Darius didn't like what he *was* reading… It didn't match up with what DuPont had done. He didn't feel like a killer.

A dark shadow obscured the space beneath the door.

"Right on time," Chris said.

DuPont spun around as Alan walked into the room. Chris hit a button on the keyboard, and the speakers mounted to the wall on either side of the screen crackled to life.

"Good morning, Mr. DuPont," Alan said in his standard, professional cadence. Darius remembered the tone. It was the same one he'd had when Darius had first come to the Underground, too. Alan shut the door behind him and stood in front of it. As soon as DuPont saw his face, he patted his thighs like he was looking for something in pants pockets. Alan continued. "How are you feeling?"

"Am I being detained?" Gabriel DuPont's baritone voice was as sharp as his eyes and deeper than Darius expected.

Alan shook his head, his veil of straight, black hair shifting as he did. "No," he said. "You are not."

"So I'm free to go."

"No," Alan repeated. DuPont's jaw tightened, and his broad hands curled into fists at his side, but he maintained his composure. Alan didn't indicate he noticed, but Darius knew better. The Martyr leader gestured to a pair of metal chairs along the wall. "Please, Mr. DuPont, take a seat. We have a lot to discuss."

"I'm not speaking without a lawyer," DuPont said. He seemed unfazed by the fact that Alan was two inches taller than him—and fully clothed. Even in nothing but an open-backed gown, the officer held himself with unyielding confidence.

Alan raised his eyebrows. "There are no lawyers here."

"The law states—"

"The law is irrelevant," Alan cut in. "I have no interest in arresting you, nor do I particularly want to keep you here for any longer than I have to, but before I let you go, I have questions, and you *will* answer them."

The two men stood in silence for a moment. Chris and Darius froze as though they were in the room themselves. Chris leaned forward on the table, her fingers clasped together and pressed against her lips as she watched DuPont with dark curiosity.

"I have questions, too," DuPont said. He wasn't bulky, but his arms were thick and strong. Darius wondered if he was sizing Alan up, trying to decide if he could take him down. "Where am I? What division is this? Are you with the FBI?"

"Mr. DuPont," Alan said, shaking his head, "you are under the mistaken impression that you have a say in what happens here. Let me outline the situation as I see it."

He moved forward, now standing close enough for DuPont to reach out and touch him. The officer squared his shoulders and held up his left palm while his right froze at his hip.

"I'm gonna need you to take a step back."

"Last night, you murdered a woman in my charge," Alan said, ignoring DuPont. For the first time since he entered the room, Darius caught a note of anger. It was so thoroughly buried that he rarely had the chance to see it. It glistened in Alan's black, half-empty eyes and twisted the corners of his lips. "You broke into her apartment and gunned her down while she was in her *nightgown*. She was shot no fewer than thirteen times. To be frank, you are fortunate that all I am asking you for is information. Why was she a target?"

DuPont said nothing. His jaw shut so firmly that the muscles along his neck tightened.

"I have rights," he said.

"You do not," Alan replied. He took another step. "Now tell me—"

DuPont threw a right hook toward Alan's face. Chris and Darius leapt to their feet, but just before DuPont's hit landed, Alan leaned out of the way. He reached up with one hand, caught DuPont's fist, and squeezed it. Even through the camera's tiny mic, Darius heard the crunch. He winced as DuPont screamed.

"Holy shit," Chris breathed.

Alan released DuPont, and the officer staggered away, holding his hand, his eyes wide and horrified. His fingers were twisted into unnatural angles, already pooling deep purple where the bones in his knuckles bulged like boils.

Alan's expression remained impassive as he took another step forward. This time, DuPont moved back.

"Why was she a target?" Alan demanded again.

"What the fuck is *wrong* with you?"

"Mr. DuPont," Alan said evenly. "*You* attacked *me*."

Darius let out a breath, not realizing he'd been holding it, and sat slowly back into his chair. Chris did the same, her green eyes suddenly alert and fully awake. On the monitor, Alan and DuPont continued their posturing. "I guess it's a good thing Thorn didn't want to interrogate him," Chris murmured. "If Alan's angry enough to break his hand…"

"She'd have killed him," Darius said with a groan, rubbing his tired eyes with his fingertips.

Chris nodded, then she shook her head. "But this isn't helping anything. If he wasn't going to cooperate before, there's no way he will now. We can't *force* him to talk."

Darius's head snapped back up to the screen as an idea struck him. "Maybe we can," he muttered.

Chris frowned. "What?"

"I'll be right back." Darius hurried into the hospital ward, walked two rooms down, and opened the door. Alan turned, startled, as Darius came in. Face-to-face, he could see more of Alan's rage. It seemed to hover around him, feeding into the space, poisoning it. His mouth curled downward, and he gave Darius a warning look.

"Mr. Jones, this is not the time," he started, but Darius shook his head and held up his hands.

"I'm not healing him," he said, and Alan's eyebrow twitched curiously. "I'm here to get him to talk."

Realization dawned on Alan's face, and he gave Darius a curt nod as he backed away. Gabriel DuPont stared at him, his eyes narrow, his mouth twisted into a look of contempt. As soon as he saw Darius, DuPont patted at his thighs, this time with a wince. The man's aura was strong, filling the room with a warmth that made Darius uncomfortable. He ached to fix his wounds, but now wasn't the time. Instead, he came up to the officer and reached for his shoulder.

DuPont backed away and threw up his unbroken left hand to block Darius, so Darius just grabbed that instead. Skin met skin, and heat pooled into Darius's fingertips. He took a deep breath and opened the boundary between them. Their energies began to mingle.

"Sit down," he said.

He not only spoke it with his voice; he commanded it with his soul. He poured the instructions into DuPont, and for a moment, the man hesitated. Darius felt the resistance; he *felt* DuPont fighting against the order. What had Thorn told him all those months ago on their flight back from Spokane? That Influence was more challenging if you were working *against* someone's judgment or objectives?

Well, then, Darius would have to be more convincing.

"You're hurt, and you're exhausted," Darius insisted. DuPont continued to stare at him, confused and shaken, but Darius felt the pushback between them soften. "Let's sit down."

And all at once, DuPont's body moved. His knees bent, and he lowered himself into one of the two metal chairs. Darius sat in the other one, released DuPont's hand, and grabbed him on the forearm instead.

"What the hell did you just do?"

Darius ignored him. "Why did you target that woman?" he asked.

DuPont's resistance grew again, his energy pulling away from Darius's. "We didn't *target* anyone."

"What were you trying to prevent, then?" Darius asked instead. "The police don't do raids like this for no reason. Why did you need to get to her?"

Just saying the words made him feel gross, but DuPont relaxed a little. He frowned, shook his head, and rubbed his temples. Darius wondered if Virtuous Influence led to headaches the same way the Sins' did. He kept pressing.

"Tell me what she was doing."

"She was providing weapons to the gangs in Brooklyn," DuPont finally said. His eyes went a little glassy as he spoke.

Darius's brows drew together, and he glanced up at Alan, who nodded and gestured for him to continue. "What evidence do you have?"

"An undercover officer was present at a deal," DuPont said. "His written report is in the affidavit attached to our arrest warrant."

"Fabricated," Alan murmured. "Terrance Moore likely created a falsified report and Influenced the judge to issue a warrant. I will have Holly verify this."

DuPont frowned. "The commissioner didn't bribe anybody."

"What is it that drew Moore's attention?" Alan asked, crossing his arms. Darius released DuPont's arm, and the officer glanced at him, still a little dazed, before turning to Alan. "How did he identify Miss Cortez?"

"Cortez?" DuPont cut in, his disorientation giving into confusion. He shook his head like he'd had a sudden realization. "Fuck, I see what's happening. Your people got the wrong apartment. We were after Mercedes Lopez."

Alan and Darius shared a dark look. Darius turned to DuPont and said, "Mercedes Lopez *was* Elena Cortez. She wasn't a weapons dealer."

DuPont shook his head again. "Whatever the woman's name was, she *was* a weapons dealer. Your men were there. They saw the apartment."

Alan's eyes narrowed, and he stroked his neat, black goatee as he thought. "Mr. DuPont, if you'll please indulge me, what did you see inside that apartment?"

The atmosphere of the room shifted, tension building again. The man glanced at Darius's face, then at his hands, like he was aware that, *somehow*, Darius had been able to get him to talk. He thought he'd have to do it again, but at long last, DuPont said, "It was full of gang paraphernalia. There were boxes of handguns on the ground... Drugs on the tables... You can't tell me your team didn't document that in their reports?"

"His Program generates false memories," Alan breathed

quietly, turning to Darius. "I should have anticipated this. Pride used this same sort of mechanism on Jacob Locke decades ago."

"What the *fuck* are you talking about?" DuPont got to his feet again, wincing as he used the heel of his injured hand to help lift his weight from the chair. Darius stood up beside him. "I was at this apartment *yesterday*. I know what I saw."

"You know what you *think* you saw," Alan said. "What happened when your team entered Miss Cortez's home?"

DuPont looked between Darius and Alan and the camera on the far wall. His swollen mouth turned down in a frown. "We knocked and announced ourselves. Told her to come out with her hands above her head. She refused to comply. When we broke down the door, she started shooting at us. We had no choice but to respond with deadly force."

Alan took a deep breath, his nostrils flaring as he did so, and considered DuPont down the bridge of his long, sharp nose. At last, he said, "Mr. DuPont, I have many more questions I would like to ask you. If I can provide evidence that this situation is not what it seems, will you cooperate?"

DuPont took a step back, cradling his mangled hand against his chest. "What the fuck will you do to me if I *don't?*"

Alan sighed and gestured an open palm to Darius, and Darius reached for DuPont. The officer stepped back, but Darius caught him around the wrist. Energy flowed from his fingertips into DuPont's flesh. The bones on his injured hand straightened out, and the swelling on his face subsided.

After a few moments, Gabriel DuPont stood in the middle of the room, his eyes wide, his mouth dropped open, and his body fully healed.

"Jesus…"

"I will explain this as well," Alan said. "If you will work with me."

DuPont tore his eyes away from Darius to look back at Alan. Now, all traces of anger were replaced with awe. He nodded.

"Miss Silver," Alan said loudly, turning toward the camera on the wall. "Gather a set of clothes for Mr. DuPont and bring in a laptop with security footage from Miss Cortez's apartment. Let's get to the bottom of what happened last night."

Minutes later, they stood in a half-circle around the foot of the hospital bed, where Chris's laptop replayed the scene inside Elena's apartment. It was damning. No matter what Gabriel DuPont thought he'd experienced, it didn't match the level of cold, unfeeling violence Darius saw on the screen. Elena had been in the bedroom, sound asleep when the SWAT team pounded on her door with a battering ram. Just as it came smashing down, she ran into the bathroom and locked herself inside.

It had taken the cops eleven minutes to break down that reinforced door. Eleven long, terrifying, painful minutes. When they had, the two men in the lead immediately opened fire. The camera's angle didn't provide a view inside the room, but Darius didn't need to see it to know how bad it had been.

Less than two minutes later, Chris and Seth reached the apartment, trapping the officers inside until Thorn arrived.

Then the bloodbath only got worse.

Alan signaled to Chris to stop the footage, and she shut the laptop off. DuPont, now dressed in the standard Martyr gray sweatpants and white crew neck, stared at the black screen. His shoulders heaved up in a deep, slow breath.

"How do I know this footage has not been tampered with?" he asked, but his tone slipped from accusatory to nervous. He glanced at them.

"You don't," Alan said, simply and honestly. "Unless you are an expert at recognizing evidence of tampering in digital video files."

"I'm not," DuPont admitted. He raised his right hand, flexed his fingers, and then looked at Darius. Those sharp eyes considered him for a long moment. Finally, he turned fully to face Alan. With his back turned to her, Chris considered him suspiciously but curiously.

"I remember this," DuPont said, gesturing at the screen. "But not *like* this. The room, the girl—it was all the same but *different*. There were weapons. She had a gun. She *shot* at us. You could see us taking cover from the bullets!"

"Did you see bullets in the footage?" Alan asked.

DuPont hesitated. "No. What did you say earlier? Something about false memories? How can I be sure *that's* what happened?"

Alan raised a brow. "Are you beginning to believe what I have been saying?"

DuPont held his healed hand up between them. "As of ten fucking minutes ago, I don't know what to believe. I saw that woman point a gun in my face. She was *armed*. Next thing I know, my whole team is down, I get drugged and kidnapped, then I wake up here. *You* broke my fucking hand. *This guy* put it back together. This is some magical bullshit. What the *fuck* is going on? Who *are* you people?"

The words came out rapid-fire, like he was pulling a trigger and spitting them out before the situation crashed around him. He turned from Alan to Darius before finally landing on Chris. He pointed a finger at her face. "*You*. You were there. Where is my team? Did you take anyone else?"

Silence stretched between them. Chris took a slow breath and straightened her back. "They're dead."

DuPont's face paled, and his knees gave way beneath him. He almost stumbled backward onto the chair Darius had made him sit in before, staring at Chris but not really *seeing* her. His eyes were disconnected. Even they seemed to have lost their color.

Then he focused in again, and when he spoke, his voice seemed strangled. "You *killed* them!"

"You killed Elena," Chris responded, and while she tried to keep her tone even, emotion caught at the edge of it.

"We were just doing our job!"

"So were we."

More silence, heavier now. DuPont and Chris stared at each other, neither backing down, neither opening their mouths to speak again. Darius marveled at how similar they looked—how much their expressions of duty and remorse mirrored one another and how even their individual auras were equally strong and vibrant. He was struck with the tragic senselessness of it all.

In another world, Chris and Gabriel DuPont could have been coworkers. Partners. Friends.

"Mr. DuPont," Alan said, stepping forward. "We do not take lightly the lives lost in our conflicts. Our goal is to avoid this kind of situation as much as possible. Unfortunately, they are becoming more commonplace, and the last six months have been especially brutal. People are dying. I would like your help uncovering why and perhaps finding a way to stop it."

DuPont turned to Alan. The strong muscles in his throat were tight and angry, but his face wore weary, crestfallen lines. At last, he got to his feet. "If I answer your questions, will you answer mine? Because, fuck, I have a *lot* of them."

"You might not like what I have to say," Alan said.

"Yeah," DuPont muttered. "I probably won't."

CHAPTER SIX

The door to the conference room swung open, and Alan strode in. His gaze swept the table until he found his security lead. When he spoke, his voice was sharp in the silence.

"Miss Andrews," he said, and Holly's back went rigid. "All of our vehicles have been compromised."

"*What?*" Her eyes went wide behind her thick-rimmed glasses. "How?"

Alan glanced over his shoulder as Thorn followed him like a shadow and closed the door behind her. As soon as it clicked shut, he turned back and said, "Apparently, our registration pattern has been flagged by the Sins."

A leaden hush poured over the room, and Darius's chest tightened. He, along with Holly, Lina, Abraham, Mackenzie, and Chris, had been called together for an urgent meeting, and they gathered around the table as Alan stood at the head of it. He did not take a seat, and Holly stared up at him.

"That's impossible," she started after a moment, running a hand through her short, boyish hair and pulling it out of place. It sat at the top of her round face in a haphazard mess. "I've hidden our registrations in nondescript areas around the city. There's no way they can flag them!"

"That's clearly not the case," Alan said. "Something is

sending up signals."

"Signals?" Mackenzie asked, frowning, as she chewed on a brightly-painted nail. "The fuck does that mean?"

"It means," Alan snapped, taking a deep breath to steady himself, "that none of our vehicles are safe in the city. Terrance Moore has ordered every precinct to look for SUVs, sedans, coupes, and vans matching the make and model of every vehicle we have, cross-reference their registration, and target those that seem suspicious. This is why our TAC units were attacked earlier this month and how Miss Cortez was discovered three days ago. We are being hunted."

"How the hell did they learn *anything* about our car registration?" Holly asked, her face going bone white.

"According to Mr. DuPont," Alan said, "they investigated the vehicle we left behind after the incident last September." His eyes glinted furiously as he considered Holly. "Find out *what* they discovered and how to fix it. *Now.*"

Holly nodded, leapt to her feet, and rushed from the room. Abraham straightened in his chair as the door slammed behind her. "We have to get our Gray and TAC units out of New York," he said.

"They have begun emergency evacuation protocols," Alan stated.

"What are those protocols?" Darius asked.

"They are to abandon all compromised vehicles immediately," Alan said, "stash their gear in one of our security lockers within New York, and make their way to a rendezvous point outside city limits as quickly as possible. Both TAC and Gray Unit agents are commuting as we speak. When we are done here, Thorn and Jacob will assist in escorting them out. It seems his personal vehicle and her motorcycle are the only two *not* impacted by this recent development."

Lina shook her head. Her right hand wandered to her throat and gripped the silver pendant hanging there. "Thank god more people haven't been hurt."

Alan's expression darkened, and he finally took a seat.

He folded his hands on the table. "Many have been. There have been dozens of random traffic stops, arrest warrants, and no-knock raids involving civilians with vehicles matching the criteria for these police searches. Six have been killed. Police reports claim their officers were responding with appropriate force, so it has been difficult for us to prove Programming is involved. I, for one, do not believe it is a coincidence."

A brief quiet suffocated the room before Mackenzie swore. "How the hell are they getting away with this?" Her nostrils flared as she clacked her tongue piercing against the back of her teeth.

"They aren't," Alan told her. "The NYPD is claiming they are cracking down on organized crime, but the profiling is clear. The majority of these attacks have been in low-income neighborhoods. Unrest with the department is on the rise. It feels very reminiscent of the stop-and-frisk era we saw at the start of the century. The Sins have always used and abused power like this, and occasionally, people notice."

"What's their end goal?" Abraham asked with a frown. "Causing public unrest *against* an entity they control can't be beneficial."

"Public unrest is exactly how they spread their corruption," Lina offered.

"And this situation has made it more challenging for us to move about in New York City safely," Alan added. "At this point, we have successfully eliminated both Pride and Sloth, and Envy has yet to repossess a new host. They are getting desperate."

"And dangerous," Chris said.

"More so than ever," Alan said with a solemn nod. "Mr. DuPont has also informed me that the New York Police Department recently received a massive influx of funds, which has been allocated to *further* militarizing their personnel." Mackenzie let out a loose swear word under her breath as he continued. "Their weapons are bigger, better, and far more deadly, and they are hiring at an unprecedented rate. This is likely a direct result of all the incidents we had with them last year. Gluttony does not want to lose again."

"What are we going to do?" Darius asked. He rested his forearms on the table and leaned into them as he looked around the room, lingering on Thorn before settling on Alan. "This isn't just about our people. Civilians are being killed out there. Can we get rid of Gluttony's host and remove his Programming?"

All eyes in the room turned to him, hot with attention, like he was under a spotlight. Mackenzie's eyebrows raised so high that her orange bangs devoured her piercing while Lina's drew together. Thorn watched him, not angrily, but cautiously.

"Destroying the host *would* eliminate the Programming he has installed in the force," Alan said with a nod, "and while I am not against the idea, it's not so simple."

Darius frowned. "Why not?"

"Terrance Moore is the police commissioner for the NYPD," Alan said. "He is heavily protected. Getting close enough to *any* of the Sins to eliminate them without harming innocent people is a delicate balance. With Gluttony, it has always been even more of a challenge."

"I'm not saying we go in blindly," Darius argued. "I'm saying we make a plan. We've done that before." He looked to Thorn. "You've killed more hosts than anyone, haven't you? You can't tell me all those kills were pure luck."

Thorn didn't respond, and discretion rose upon her face like a shield. She pulled her lower lip in between her teeth.

"Of course we have done it before," Alan said, drawing Darius's attention back. "You will recall our disastrous first attempt to take Sloth out last year. Prior to that, the most recent *successful* strike against a host was a decade ago, and the circumstances were very different. Isla Diamandis, Pride's host before it took Derek Dane, was a renowned actress, and she was relatively easy to track. Jacob Locke spent years gathering intel for us to be able to plan an attack, and *still,* civilians were killed. Martyrs were killed."

"Civilians and Martyrs are being killed right now, too," Mackenzie said, glancing at Darius. "If taking Gluttony out would solve that problem…"

"How do you expect me to take Gluttony out right now?" Chris asked. Her tone was harder than Darius expected. "My entire fleet has to be *grounded.* We need to secure our vehicles and protect our teams before we even consider going after him."

"More people are going to die," Darius said.

Chris nodded, the muscles along her neck growing tight. "And I won't let them be Martyrs."

They watched each other in charged silence, and a disappointed bubble burst in Darius's chest.

Alan cleared his throat. "I am not opposed to removing Terrance Moore from the situation, but Miss Silver is right. Our first priority must be protecting our men and women."

"What do we do about our grounded units in the meantime?" Lina asked. She heaved a breath, her mouth sloping in concern. "We need eyes in the city…"

"We have options," Mackenzie offered, leaning her chair back on two legs. "We can always rent some cars. Not a long-term fix, obviously, and they wouldn't have the same defensive shit ours have, but it's better than nothing. Switch them out every couple of weeks."

Alan nodded. "Jacob can provide transportation assistance as well. Moving all of this forward is our utmost priority, but before we go, I have one more pressing topic to discuss." He cleared his throat, glanced up at Thorn, and his voice shifted. "What will we do with Mr. Gabriel DuPont?"

"Get 'im out," Mackenzie responded, immediately and mercilessly, gesturing a thumb over her shoulder. "We got what we needed from him."

A consensus echoed around the room from everyone but Darius and, to his surprise, Thorn. She still hadn't said a word, standing coldly by the door, her arms crossed and brows furrowed. Alan let the murmuring die down before he went on. "I'm afraid we cannot simply throw him back into New York City. The Sins will undoubtedly notice Mr. DuPont's absence. He worked in a central precinct of the police department and disappeared in a conflict where the rest of his team was killed. I'm sure the Sins suspect us. If we return him, Programmed or not, they will kill him."

Darius's stomach twisted, and Abraham frowned. "We don't have to bring him back to New York."

Alan shook his head. "The level of Programming involved to ensure he does not return to the city presents a challenge. I would have to delete several months of his life, and he would likely find his way back. I have another proposal, but I wanted to bring it to you all before I speak with Mr. DuPont again."

He paused, and Darius knew what he was going to say before he said it.

"He asked if he could join the Martyrs."

Silence. Nothing moved except the awkward shifting in seats, squeaking plastic and metal sounding so much louder than it should have, and Mackenzie's tongue piercing clacking furiously. At last, she slammed her chair forward. "This is a joke, right?"

"It is not," Alan said.

"But he killed one of our people," Chris argued. Her shoulders drew up tight.

"He was just doing his job," Abraham said.

Mackenzie rounded on him. "Are you *defending* him?"

"Think about it," Abraham reasoned. "How many people do *we* hurt doing what we do?"

Chris glanced down at the table, and Mackenzie's cheeks went pink.

"That's not the same thing, and you know it," the Irishwoman snapped.

"He had no idea who she was," Abraham said. "He had Programming that made him see her as a viable threat."

"I can't believe we're even considering this!" Mackenzie threw her hands in the air, looking desperately between

Thorn, Darius, and Lina as though hunting for someone to be on her side. "Even if he *was* just 'doing his job,' he's been working with Gluttony!"

"Many Martyrs were involved with Sins before they joined us," Alan stated, his voice measured and calculated, and he watched Mackenzie. The heat in her cheeks deepened.

"This is *different*," Mackenzie insisted as she jumped to her feet, accidentally knocking her chair backward. It clattered to the ground behind her as she paced along the wall. "He *killed* Elena! I had lunch with her less than a week ago, and she's *dead now* because of him! How the hell can you trust him after that? He's one of the bad guys!"

"He's not."

Thorn's dark voice drew attention to the front of the room. She uncrossed her arms and stepped forward a few paces, her eyes focused hard on Mackenzie. "His energy is *clean*. I don't like what he did. I don't like what he stands for. But I can't deny what I feel. DuPont has good in him. A lot of good."

Mackenzie froze, and her lips parted quietly. "You told me auras aren't always an indication of the kind of person someone is," she said, almost defensively, wrapping her arms around herself. Darius was surprised to see her light blue eyes glistening. Thorn's expression softened.

"*Cold* auras aren't," she said. "It's easier to hurt that energy than it is to heal it. People can fuck up, get better, and grow without their aura changing much, but they can't hide the fact that they fucked up in the first place. Not from me."

For several moments, no one spoke. Mackenzie's jaw was cinched so hard that her throat looked tight and painful. Lina let out a little "ahem," and everyone turned to her.

"Mackenzie does bring up a good point," she said. "Whatever his aura feels like, he *has* been Programmed."

"Programming can be altered," Alan said. "Mr. Wolfe and Miss Fulton have experience in uncovering and rewriting it. If we are successful, I believe Mr. DuPont could be an asset here."

"Does he pass the rest of my criteria for recruitment?" Chris asked.

"He does," Alan said.

Chris took a long, slow breath. Her green eyes were hard and unconvinced as she considered all of them. Finally, she landed on Darius.

"What do *you* think?" she asked him.

The room looked at him, too. He sighed and gave a short nod.

"His aura is strong," Darius said, glancing at Thorn, "and I think… I think I like the guy, as much as I hate to admit that. I like the *potential* of him. If he can be safely Deprogrammed, I say we give him a shot."

Alan nodded, and so did everyone else. Everyone but Mackenzie. She hadn't taken a seat, and when Alan put the issue to a vote, she was the only person who did not raise her hand.

"It's settled. Miss Brooks, Miss McKay, Miss Silver, you all know what to do." Alan gestured a hand out, and Mackenzie shoved her way from the room as Lina and Chris got to their feet. Thorn took quickly after her. Alan sighed and turned to Abraham.

"Mr. Locke," he said. "Prepare yourself for your upcoming sessions. Bringing a former police officer into the Martyrs will be challenging for many people here, and I want to head it off as soon as possible."

Darius glanced over his shoulder, where he could feel Mackenzie's energy, weak and fragmented in a way no other Martyrs' was, rushing down the stairs. He was sure Thorn was on her heels.

———

By the time Thorn reached her room, tucked away in the furthest recess in the eastern wing, it was already one in the morning.

She took a deep breath, slipped her key into the lock, and slowly exhaled as she opened the door to inky darkness. Sparkie vaulted from her shoulder, finding his way through the pitch-black before Thorn flicked the light switch on. Lamps on either side of her bed blared to life, filling the room with an uneven, yellow glow. Thorn shrugged her satchel off her shoulder, removed her motorcycle jacket, and hung them on a hook behind the door as she shut herself inside.

What a fucking day.

Or… three days. God, it had been three days since Elena Cortez was murdered. How much sleep had Thorn gotten since then, in broken bits and pieces from her apartment in New York? She'd been so busy covering up the Martyrs' tracks, securing their property, and personally escorting the remaining Gray Unit operatives back to the Underground that time slipped away. The numb focus had kept her from drowning in anything else.

Now that she was alone, Elena's face, lifeless and bloodied, invaded Thorn's thoughts.

The queen-sized bed was immaculately made, the beige walls empty. Beside her door, a coat rack stood, heavily laden with her wool winter jacket and a collection of black and gray hoodies. Her reflection stared back at her from a standing, full-length mirror across the room. Shadows colored the space beneath Thorn's dark eyes.

She shook her head and walked to her dresser. Sparkie wound himself into a tight ball between the white pillows. His wings were held so tightly to his body that he looked like he was wrapped in leathery, red blankets with his smooth, blue head sticking out between them. He heaved a sigh. Thorn glanced at him.

This was insane.

She grabbed her brush and started pulling it through her hair. Ripping it. Forcing it through windblown tangles woven into the strands. Cortez was dead, the Gray Unit had to be relocated, and one of the men responsible was sleeping peacefully across the courtyard. Thorn's fingers tightened around her brush handle.

And Mackenzie—god, *Mackenzie*. Thorn hadn't seen her this upset since she'd gotten clean eighteen years ago. She could still hear the Irishwoman screaming and crying her way through withdrawal. Thorn's brush caught on a snag and yanked on her scalp.

She swore, anger broiling in her stomach, as she tossed the brush onto her dresser and strode back across the room. Thorn reached into the satchel, drew out a red pack of cigarettes, and looked down at the label. She wasn't supposed to light one up in the Underground, but fuck it. What Alan didn't know…

The minute she put a cigarette to her lips, her lighter held at the ready, someone knocked on her door. Three loud, steady raps. Thorn startled and swore loudly enough for Alan to hear it. His voice filtered in from the hallway.

"May I come in?"

God damn, that man had a way of knowing the minute she got back to the Underground. She shook her head, quickly put the cigarette back in the box, and called, "Yes."

The door opened, and Alan stepped through. He'd changed from his standard slacks and button-up, now in comfortable lounge pants and a dark t-shirt—a reminder to Thorn's tired brain that *he* had been sleeping. His dark eyes moved from her face to the cigarette box, and he frowned.

"You cannot smoke in the Underground," he chided. "Our ventilation system—"

"You really came here in the middle of the night to lecture me?" Thorn cut in as she walked away. Alan's lips pressed together, his frown deepening, but he sighed and walked the rest of the way into the room. He closed the door behind him slowly; then he turned to take Thorn in.

"I wanted to see how Miss McKay is doing," Alan said.

No, he didn't, and Thorn wished he had the guts to admit he was worried about *her*. She thought about calling him out on it, but for once, she didn't feel like fighting. Instead,

Thorn shook her head, put the little red box on her dresser, and removed her gloves. The fabric grazed the *Peccostium* and sent a familiar chill up her arm, deep into her scars, and down her spine.

They could pretend this wasn't about her—wasn't about *them*.

"Not great," Thorn said, folding the gloves and putting them into a burgundy tote, which was full of over a dozen identical sets. Thorn glanced down at the *Peccostium* on her arm and the scars snarled around it before letting out a short, frustrated sigh. "Nothing ruins your day more than being reminded of all the awful shit you've done in your life."

"She was unwell," Alan said.

Thorn spun around and crossed her arms. "Does that matter? Does it fix what she did?" Alan didn't answer, and Thorn went on. "It doesn't. You know it doesn't. Here she is, face to face with a killer whose aura is one of the strongest I've ever felt in this goddamned place, and she's still cold as fucking ice. There are mistakes you can't scrub away, no matter how hard you try."

The way Alan watched her, his pale face a canvas of calm and composure, infuriated Thorn even more, if only because it reminded her how much closer he always was to fucking control. She turned away from him, stomped back toward her bed, and looked down at the nightstand.

Donovan smiled out from the photograph Darius had accidentally uncovered at Teresa's house. Thorn and her son, standing side by side, caught mid-laugh with their arms around one another. She remembered this day with bittersweet vividness. Donovan had just received a full ride to the photography program at the San Francisco Art Institute. He'd been so fucking happy. So had she. It was all over her face.

He was getting out. Leaving the Underground and the Martyrs. Finally escaping this war—this hell.

Wrath caught him seven days later.

Seeing this photo again had shaken Thorn more than she wanted to admit. After his death and the gruesome months that followed, she'd taken every possession that reminded her of him and thrown it away. Clean cut, she told herself. Start over new. Besides occasionally visiting his gravesite with Cain, Thorn tried to act as though Donovan had never existed. Up until the last couple of years, only Chris had known about him. It made it easier.

Then the photograph reappeared. She thought she'd never see his face again. Instead of filling her with rage, though, now it filled her with a longing Thorn didn't quite know how to deal with. She took a deep breath, felt the monster inside curl up on itself, and sat at the edge of her bed. Sparkie unwound from her pillows and slithered into her lap. Thorn stared at Donovan's photograph a moment longer and tried to ignore the woman beside him—a woman she didn't recognize as herself anymore.

"What do you think *our* auras are like?" Thorn murmured. She turned to Alan. His sharp face was cast in shadows, highlighting his long nose and making his eyes almost disappear in the dark. "After all we've done in the last hundred years? How cold are we?"

For a moment, Alan did not move. He considered Thorn from across the distance between them—a distance that had once felt like a canyon, and now, just a crack. Alan may have been able to control his rage more than Thorn ever could, but she could read the emotions playing out on his face as clearly as though they were her own. The corners of his eyes pinched together, and an expression of shame flashed across them before he came to sit beside her. His weight shifted the mattress, and while he leaned forward to speak, his shoulders were tense and uneasy.

"I like to believe," he said at last, "that the good we have done will overpower the evil we had forced upon us."

"I'm not talking about what we did when Wrath had the reins," Thorn said. "Maybe that's where *your* sins end, but mine…" She thought back to what Darius had said in the conference room.

You've killed more hosts than anyone.

Thorn shook her head. "After Donovan—"

"After Donovan," Alan cut in, "you *learned.*"

"So has Mackenzie," Thorn said.

Silence surrounded them again, and Alan watched Thorn with that same pained look. He glanced down at the hands she had wrapped in her lap like he wanted to reach out for them, but he held back. Still on the other side of that crack.

"When Wrath is destroyed," he said, and while his tone was somber, it was also confident, "I promise you, how your aura feels will not matter anymore."

Thorn looked away from him—down at her laced fingers, the *Peccostium* beneath her wrist, and the scars dripping from it. Then she looked at Sparkie, her Familiar, that *soul* she was so worried about...

It wouldn't matter, would it? He would be gone, and she would be whole. Warm or cold, Thorn would be complete again, and the people she'd killed along the way would still be dead.

CHAPTER SEVEN

Soft breathing filled the room with an even, rhythmic sound. Darius walked through the gym's open training area, circling two dozen men and women as they sat quietly on the padded floors. He made his way to the center of the group, his bare feet silent, and he paused to take them all in.

The Martyrs were restless today. Their tension displayed itself in subtle movements and hard faces. John pulled his knees up to his chest, his eyes closed, lips pressed together. Parker sat with her legs crossed and her back pin-straight—so straight she looked like she might snap in half. Near the door, Alexis cleared her throat and rubbed her fingers over swollen eyes. Her short, platinum blonde hair, usually perfectly styled, stuck up at odd angles. Alexis didn't typically come to this meditation session, but since losing Elena and being called back to the Underground, Abraham had instructed her and the rest of the Gray Unit to attend extra classes. He felt it would help them with their grief. Darius wasn't sure it was working.

"Check in with yourself," he said. He'd spoken softly, but a handful of people still jumped like they'd heard a gunshot. In the back corner, resting against a wall, Conrad startled awake with a snort. Darius threw him a warning look, and Conrad shuffled awkwardly. Darius went on. "Unclench your jaw. Open your palms. Let your shoulders drop toward the ground."

Bodies moved. Joints popped. People groaned. John stretched his back and sat up straighter, pulling his head from side to side and forcing his face to relax. It wasn't convincing. The corners of his mouth pulled down, and there seemed to be a permanent line between his brows where they came together. Alexis returned her hands to her lap, lacing her fingers, but her lips were tight. Conrad yawned. The sound would have been quiet in any other room, but here it broke through like a roaring wind.

"When our bodies are tense, our minds are tense," Darius instructed. "And when our minds are tense, we're disconnected from our emotions. Take a deep breath."

A great gasp filled the room as twenty-four people inhaled together.

"In for four. Focus on the count. Allow yourself to feel the air filling your lungs. Hold… and… exhale."

A gust. A pause. A hold to the tension, not relieving it, not releasing it, but keeping it tight, like a knot. Darius frowned.

"Who knows why it's important to be connected to our emotions?" he asked.

A few pairs of eyes opened, and Parker thrust her hand into the air so eagerly that her ringlets bounced around her head. Darius gestured at her, and she said, "So we can keep the Sins out?"

Darius smiled at the simplicity of the answer before he shook his head. "Yes, but it's more complicated than that. Is anyone confident that they can resist Influence?" Darius cast a look around the room before settling on John. "John? You think you've got it down?"

Heads turned toward John, and his eyes widened. He glanced to the right and left before he looked back up at Darius and shrugged. "I think I'm pretty close."

"Great. Let's test it out," Darius said, and he held out his hand.

John gave a nervous smirk as he grabbed Darius's fingers and pulled himself to his feet. Once he was standing, Darius didn't let go of him. Power rushed into his hands and connected with John, mingling with his aura as a river meets the ocean, and the ocean pushed back.

"I'm going to try to Influence you," he said. "Fight me off."

John's smile widened. "You got it."

Then Darius urged his will forward. The room collectively held its breath, the quiet around them becoming full of anticipation as Darius forced his thoughts into John's head.

First, something simple.

Touch your nose.

He felt the resistance. John's will was strong, and he grinned as he grew more confident.

Darius had assumed John would be ready for this kind of attack. So he pushed harder, and this time, he changed tactics. Instead of asking John to do something, he told John what to feel. He told him how angry he was at this whole situation, how *messed up* it was that Gabriel DuPont was allowed inside the Underground after what he did to Elena. He told him that he was frustrated with the leadership for doing something so reckless and that they were putting him and everyone he loved in danger. They were putting *Chris* in danger, and now, she would be busier than ever.

John's eyes widened, his smile faded, and his grip around Darius's fingers tightened. The ocean began to break, and Darius's energy trickled through the crack, mingling with John's, changing the texture to something blurry and indistinct. Darius didn't break contact. He held on and kept pushing.

This situation was dangerous, and you know who was to blame? *Darius.* Who made the final call? Who decided to bring this monster into the Martyrs? Darius had. *He* was the reason this was all happening. John was really fucking mad at *Darius*.

He commanded John to grab him by the throat.

John's hand ripped out of Darius's grip and wrapped beneath his chin.

The energy flow crashed to a stop as the world around them froze. Darius's mouth opened in an empty gasp as John's fingers squeezed harder. His eyes were full of a pure, hot rage, and for a numb moment, Darius wondered if he'd pushed too hard.

But just as quickly as he'd come in for the kill, John realized what was happening. His hold loosened as he stumbled back, his jaw gaping, his eyes wide and terrified.

"Holy shit, Darius, I'm sorry!"

But Darius just held up one hand while the other rubbed the tender spots on his neck. He coughed a little and shook his head. "No, no. It's fine. Are you okay?" John just stared at him, so Darius asked again. "John, you good?" He reached for John's shoulder, and the other man flinched under his touch.

"Yeah," he muttered at last.

"Did you see what I did?" Darius asked. "What I made you feel?"

John nodded silently.

"Good," Darius said. Then, at last, he looked at the rest of the room. To his surprise, a handful of people were standing, watching him and John in shock. Darius glanced around, and his stomach flipped as he spotted someone new.

Thorn.

She was resting against the wall by the double doors, her arms crossed and her eyebrows raised just enough for Darius to see she was surprised. He cleared his throat, dropped his hand, and turned back to the class.

"It doesn't matter how much you meditate," Darius said, gesturing around them. "It doesn't *matter* how well you do these breathing exercises if you don't have a grip on your emotions. These last few days have been hard on us. Really hard." He looked from one face to the next, seeing the same shock in every one of them. His eyes connected with Alexis's, and her icy blue irises glistened with a new wave of furious tears.

"But when your emotions are running high," Darius continued, "when you're bottling them up and letting them control you, you're giving the Sins a key. You need to be so in tune with what you feel that the Sins can't possibly use it against you, because that's what they do. They will use your anxiety, your sadness, and your *anger* as a way to control you." He focused on John. The other man's mouth was still open, a line of white teeth barely visible through his lips. "They will feed those feelings, and you won't even realize what they're doing until it's too late."

Darius paused, took a deep breath, and glanced at Thorn again. She watched him as an alley cat would—unblinkingly, with an intensity that felt like she could see his ghosts standing behind his back. He shook his head and spoke to the room. "Good job today. What we're doing here isn't easy, and it will take a lot of patience and practice. Take care of yourselves, and reach out to Abraham if you need support. I'll see you all next week."

The Martyrs shuffled as they gathered their things and filed out. John was one of the first to go, his face bright red as he grabbed his shoes and stalked past Thorn without putting them on. Darius walked to the weight bench at the far side of the room, sitting on it with his back to the exit while he pulled on his socks. Human warmth flowed out behind him, and the dark shape of Thorn moved closer.

"That was a fun trick," she said.

"I was just trying to show how deceptive Influence can be," Darius said, and he forced a laugh. "I didn't think John would grab me so hard, though…"

"You got the point across pretty effectively," Thorn responded. "Particularly the part about emotion. It's a lesson we could *all* hear a little more often."

He felt her watching the back of his head—saw the

shadow of her hovering out of the corner of his eye. He focused on tying his shoes. "So," he said, "speaking of meditation, you missed our session last night."

He glanced up in the mirror, tilting his head playfully, to see Thorn give him a sardonic look.

"Were we speaking of meditation?" she asked.

"We are *now*."

Darius wasn't sure she would let him get away with it, but Thorn smirked, the corner of her thin lips pulling up in short-lived levity. It faded as rapidly as it came. Her chest slowly rose and fell in a sigh. "I had too much shit to handle."

"I saw Alexis," he said as he got to his feet and turned around. Face-to-face, it was hard to pretend he didn't see the concern etched across Thorn's forehead. "The rest of your team is back?"

"All in one piece."

Darius nodded awkwardly. Since he still wasn't cleared to resume combat training, this was the first time he and Thorn had been alone together in almost a week. A *lot* had happened since then.

"How are you doing?" Darius asked. "With all this?"

Thorn's face went stony and cold, the muscles along her crossed arms tightening. Her jaw clenched together before she shook her head hard to one side.

"Not good," she said.

"Yeah. Me neither."

Quiet again. Thorn looked back to Darius, her eyes dark and a little grateful. She took a slow breath in. "Alan has Wolfe and Fulton upstairs to work on Deprogramming the new guy. He wants us there for testing."

"Testing?" Darius questioned.

Thorn shrugged. "I didn't ask."

The two of them started across the courtyard. Outside the kitchens, the dining area bustled with the lunch crowd. People gathered together, walking up to the long counter where Kenia was putting out sandwich materials. As Darius and Thorn passed, chatter ebbed. Eyes glanced up, following them as they walked by the wrought-iron tables and toward the elevator. Thorn hit the button, and Darius glanced over his shoulder. He had a weird sense of déjà vu, like he was brand new at the Underground again, and everyone was talking about him behind his back.

A few moments later, the elevator arrived with a *ding!* Thorn walked on first, Darius followed, and the doors slid shut behind them.

"People are *not* happy," Darius mused out loud.

Thorn gave a short, humorless laugh. "I get it. I'm not particularly happy, either."

Darius shoved his hands into the front pockets of his jeans while Thorn's fingers tapped impatiently on her bicep. The nearer they got to the upper floor, the more a peculiar energy movement stood out. Darius frowned as his attention shifted to the motion, and he focused on it.

"Is Jacob here?" he asked.

"Seems like it," Thorn said. Her eye-line followed Darius's, and her brows knit together. The warmth of Jacob Locke spun erratically in the vague area where Darius knew Abraham's office was—confirmed by the fact that Abraham's energy was there, too. Where Jacob was frantically darting about, Abraham was seated and calm.

"Does he have a job here?" Darius asked.

Thorn nodded. "Today's his first day helping with TAC unit patrols."

The elevator drew to a stop, and the doors slid open. They stepped into the foyer and walked down the hallway to the hospital. Just as the waiting room opened up, Jacob Locke's voice blared through it.

"It's not right. NOT RIGHT."

Thorn paused, swearing quietly under her breath as she shook her head and threw Darius a warning look. Jacob rounded the corner down the hallway that led to Abraham's office. Abraham was following on his heels.

"He *hurt people*," Jacob snarled. His hollow cheeks puffed

out indignantly as he muttered something incoherent before spinning back toward Abraham. "He fucking *killed her*, and he gets to stay?"

"We don't know if he's going to stay—"

"He shouldn't BE HERE."

"Jacob—"

Jacob threw his hands up so violently that Abraham raised his arms in defense, but Jacob didn't hit him. He just thrashed around, turned on his heels, and stormed out of the hall. As he passed Thorn, he gave her a hot look. She watched him with grim understanding as he tore the doors to the Underground open and disappeared into the garage beyond them. Darius saw his green hatchback parked by the loading area, two people seated in the passenger and back seats. Jacob got in and peeled away so quickly that the squealing of his tires penetrated the glass doors.

A tense silence overtook the waiting room. Darius looked to Thorn, then Abraham, then back out the door where Jacob's car had been. Abraham groaned, propping one hand on his hip while the other ran down his long face.

"Was that about DuPont?" Darius asked.

Abraham nodded from behind his fingers. "Yeah."

"He'll come around," Darius tried optimistically.

"I doubt it," Thorn said.

"If you'll excuse me," Abraham murmured, turning around and heading back the way he'd come. Thorn and Darius stared after him before exchanging a look.

"You don't think Jacob will change his mind?" he asked.

Thorn shook her head. "DuPont killed a Martyr. As far as Jacob is concerned, that makes him just as bad as the Sins."

He wasn't the only Martyr who felt that way. Taking a deep breath and holding it, Darius turned back toward the hospital ward, where he could feel Skylar Fulton in the same room Darius and Chris had watched Alan interrogate DuPont. DuPont's energy was to the left—alone, Darius assumed, in the same medical suite. He let out a long, slow sigh.

"You sure we're doing the right thing?" he asked. "Giving DuPont a chance?"

Thorn's teeth slammed together, and she pried them apart to say, "I fucking hope so." She glanced at him, her eyes dark and brows drawn in, before she walked across the waiting room and into the hospital. Darius followed on her heels.

When Thorn pulled open the door to the surveillance station, Nicholas was mid-thought.

"That would mean Gluttony's Programming system isn't very effective, which is fucking shocking considering how much he relies on it," he was saying. His arms were wrapped around his chest, and his lined forehead furrowed. He glanced over his shoulder as Thorn and Darius walked into the room. The rings under his eyes looked darker today.

"What makes it ineffective?" Thorn asked as Darius closed the door behind them. She looked from Nicholas to Skylar, but it was Alan who answered.

"It seems Mr. DuPont has layers of Programming that only activate once certain start-up Programs have been completed," he said, thoughtfully drawing the fingertips of one hand over his goatee. "Requiring communication to be successfully sent through *before* he takes further action could lead to missed opportunities. It is a surprising oversight."

"It might not be an oversight," Skylar said with a shrug. She half-sat on the table, one long leg holding her up while the other was crossed, ankle-over-knee. As she spoke, she absently pulled at loose threads on her distressed flats. "I'm pretty sure his Programming system is way more sophisticated than we're seeing here."

"Oh?" Alan asked.

"Think about it," Skylar said. "What happens if his cops try to engage any of us without alerting the Sins first? Our backup would get there, Moore's people would get killed, and his Programming net would be weakened. It makes sense that Subprograms to engage with us only get activated once they've contacted Gluttony."

"But that's clearly not the case every time," Nicholas argued, drawing his arms away from his chest and propping his hands on his hips. "How else do we explain what happened to our TAC team or Elena? Those cops immediately shot fucking everyone. The same is true for the traffic stops Holly found where civilians were killed."

"Elena was different," Skylar said, and her voice darkened. "That was a no-knock raid that I'm *sure* Moore knew about beforehand. But with traffic stops or police checkpoints, I'm sure they *did* contact Gluttony first, and it's pretty clear that additional Programming was at play."

"What makes you so certain?" Alan asked.

"Well, all the attacks had specific things in common," Skylar said, glancing between them before she went on. "No children, for one. None of the cars were carrying kids or seniors. The vehicles all matched a certain description with suspicious registration. Passengers were between eighteen and, say, sixty-five and wearing dark colors. Sounds a lot like our TAC units, don't you think?"

Skylar glanced at Nicholas, and he looked down at his feet.

Alan cleared his throat, drawing their attention again. "That still does not answer why that Programming would be different from what we tested this morning," he said.

"Because it's *you*," Skylar said, gesturing to Alan before swinging her open arm toward Darius and Thorn. "These random, could-be Martyrs on the streets don't matter to them. They know our people are Programmed not to divulge information, and the random killing can make moving around in New York harder for us, as we've already seen. But there are certain, let's say, 'high value' Martyrs who are worth capturing alive. Imagine the chaos we'd go through if the Sins were holding any of you hostage."

Darius felt the pit of his stomach give out, and his mouth ran dry. He looked at Thorn as she shook her head. Her eyes were narrow and calculating.

"They're Programmed to capture us?" she asked.

"Yes," Skylar said.

"How do you know?"

"We tested it," Nicholas answered.

He moved around the table as Skylar pushed off of it. Nicholas took one of the chairs, sat down, and pulled up some footage. Darius was thrown back to a few days before, watching DuPont wander the private hospital room exactly as he had on that first day. The door opened, and Alan walked in.

"This recording was our first clue that something was up," Nicholas said, pausing the video. "Look at DuPont's right hand. He's patting his thigh like he's looking for something in his pockets."

"And there's nothing there," Skylar provided. "Obviously, since he's a hospital gown away from butt naked."

Despite himself, Darius's mouth cracked a little smile at the joke, but his stomach was still up in knots. Nicholas slowly dragged the footage forward, bit by bit, as he kept talking.

"Then, when Darius comes in, he does the same thing. Look."

They watched the screen again as Darius entered. Just as he had with Alan, DuPont began to pat his right thigh for something before quietly returning his hand to his side.

"We figured he was looking for a cell phone because what the hell else do people keep in their front pockets?" Nicholas said. He closed that footage and opened up another file. The screen flashed, and suddenly the people were different. Alan walked into the room, still in his black slacks and button-up shirt, but now DuPont was fully dressed in Martyr plainclothes. Nicholas had muted the sound, so while Darius could see Alan's mouth moving and DuPont replying, he couldn't hear what they were saying. As they talked, DuPont dipped his hand into the front pocket of his sweatpants and drew out a device.

"Is that his?" Thorn asked.

Skylar nodded. "Yes, but I made it secure. I set it up to show a delivery note when he texts off of it, but no messages will leave the Underground."

"If he knows that, wouldn't it affect his Programming?"

Skylar smirked. "He *doesn't* know that. I told him it's fully functional."

Thorn raised a brow. "Who is he contacting?"

"Gluttony," Skylar said, and her eyes glistened excitedly. "He typed in a number we assume belongs to Terrance Moore. Holly is going to see if she can trace—"

She didn't finish her thought. Suddenly, the giant screen was a flurry of activity. All eyes turned toward it as DuPont dropped his phone back into his pocket and lunged at Alan. Darius gawked as the two men wrestled, but it was a quick, short-lived fight. DuPont promptly disabled Alan, pinning him to the ground with his arms wrapped behind his back in a firm hold. Then, to Darius's surprise, the cop rammed the heel of his hand against the *Peccostium* at the base of Alan's neck.

Shortly after, Nicholas and Skylar came in to pry DuPont off.

"Damn," Thorn said. "The guy's *good.*"

"I was instructed to let him carry his Programming through to its natural conclusion," Alan replied tersely, and Darius saw the corner of Thorn's lip pull up in an amused smirk. Alan ignored her. "We must understand the entire thing to delete it effectively."

"Of course," Thorn said. She glanced at Darius, her smirk a little wider now, and he smiled, too.

"If Alan hadn't let DuPont win," Skylar said as she tilted her head toward the screen, "we never would have known his Programming included going for the *Peccostium.* I bet it does for you, too."

"That's what you need us for?" Thorn asked. "To walk in there and let DuPont pin us down?"

"Do you have any better ideas to figure out what all his Programming covers?" Nicholas snapped. Thorn turned to him slowly and gave him a hard look.

"I'm assuming you've already ruled out removing the starting trigger," Thorn said. "You said this part of the Program—" she opened a hand and indicated the screen, where the footage had restarted, and DuPont was pulling the cell phone out of his pocket again "—*only* happens if he's able to successfully send Gluttony information."

"We cannot just delete the initial Program," Alan said, shaking his head. "I doubt it would break the pathway. We may discuss Programming using computer terminology, but the human mind is a very different machine. For all we know, eliminating the trigger will simply move the start of the Program to the next command."

"It's going to be more complicated to remove then," Thorn cautioned.

"A *lot* more," Nicholas agreed. He turned around in the chair and faced the room. "We haven't even fully covered his Programming around our other people or the cars in the lot. It could take up to a week to work out how to remove it all."

"And who is doing that removing?" Thorn pressed. She glanced between Alan and Darius.

"Obviously, it should be Alan," Nicholas said. "No offense, Darius, but he's got more experience."

Darius raised his palms and let out a relieved laugh. "None taken."

"We'll have to do it on the move..." Thorn's voice drifted off as she thought aloud, and Alan put a hand on her shoulder.

"We can figure out those details later," he said. "For now, we need to see how Mr. DuPont reacts to you and Darius. Allow him to disable you, and this will be over quickly."

Silence filled the room. Thorn watched Alan, her eyes hard, until she finally sighed and gave a grimace. "Fine," she said. "Get him off me as soon as you have what you need."

Alan nodded, and the two of them left the room.

Nicholas let out a snort. "There's no way she'll '*allow him to disable her.*'"

Darius glanced at Nicholas's head before turning to Skylar. "Thanks for all of this."

"It's my pleasure," Skylar said. "Security is a hot mess right now while Holly is trying to figure out how the Sins flagged our vehicle registration. I've never seen her so ticked off. Plus, it's fun to work with this guy again."

She tapped the back of Nicholas's chair, but he didn't look away from the screen. The door in the other room opened, and Thorn walked in. DuPont began to talk to her, and while he did, his hand dipped into his pocket.

Nicholas heaved a sigh and shook his head. "I'm just glad I'm doing *something* useful again," he said. Darius and Skylar exchanged a quiet look.

Suddenly, the screen was a blur of movement as DuPont lunged for Thorn. Darius's attention snapped up to it as he held his hands out, ready to grab her…

But Thorn didn't let him. She flew back with restrained ferocity, and instantly the two were locked in an awkward dance of hand-to-hand grappling, spinning in the room as he fought to get control. Her teeth were gritted behind closed lips, the muscles along her jaw tight. DuPont, on the other hand, was wide-eyed with panic.

Nicholas turned toward Darius and Skylar, his brows raised, and he gestured toward the screen as though to say, "See? I told you so." Darius let out a cold chuckle.

Then Thorn glanced over her shoulder toward the door. "Alan must've knocked," Skylar murmured. Moments later, Thorn let up. Her grip loosened, and as soon as DuPont had an opening, he twisted her arm behind her back and grabbed her *Peccostium*. Though Darius couldn't hear her scream in the muted speakers, it pierced through the hospital. He winced as DuPont spun Thorn around and slammed her body into the wall so hard the camera view shook.

Darius knew it was for a good cause, but damn, it was hard to watch Thorn lose.

"What happens next?" he asked.

The door over DuPont's shoulder opened, and Alan entered the room. He promptly disabled the cop with a few quick, professional motions that seemed way more effortless than Darius knew they should be, and when DuPont's arms were restrained behind his back, Thorn pulled his phone out of his pocket. She left the room, Alan released DuPont, and they talked. Their mouths moved noiselessly on the screen.

"Alan's interviewing him," Skylar said. "Learning what he thinks he saw. It helps get an idea of what Gluttony is putting in their brains."

Darius nodded. "There's *so* much involved in this Program."

"More that there are a lot of different Programs," Nicholas said with a noncommittal shrug. He took a deep breath, crossed his arms, and leaned back in the chair. On the screen, Alan nodded once, shook DuPont's hand, and exited the room again. The door to the surveillance station opened moments later, and Alan and Thorn strode in.

"Same story as it was for you?" Skylar asked.

"Yes," Alan confirmed. "He has vivid memories of Thorn becoming emotionally unstable enough to be a danger to herself and anyone around her."

"Basically a public mental breakdown," Skylar said, glancing at Nicholas. "Genius, really. It works in any environment, and he's less likely to play a fatal card."

Nicholas nodded. "Genius. *Great.*"

Alan passed Nicholas a dark look before turning to Darius. "Are you ready?"

Darius took a deep breath and pulled his shoulders back. "Just let him pin me?"

"Yes," Alan said. "If you do not fight him, it should be quick." Then he looked to Thorn with a mild, reproachful expression. She watched him back unapologetically. Darius glanced between them before he sighed.

"Let's get this over with."

Alan led the way, and together he and Darius walked to DuPont's room. The man's powerful aura waited like a beacon on the other side of the door. Alan said nothing as he opened it, and Darius stepped inside.

Gabriel DuPont got to his feet and looked at Darius. The door closed behind him, and DuPont dipped his hand into his pocket.

"We haven't officially met," Darius said awkwardly. "I'm Darius."

"Gabriel," DuPont said. "But I go by Gabe."

He focused on the phone in his hands and started typing. Darius watched him, the anticipation rising, the sense of danger tickling at the back of his neck, and he let out a nervous laugh. "This is so weird."

"Tell me about it," DuPont grumbled without glancing up from the screen. "I'm about to go fucking crazy on you, and I can't stop it."

Danger roared. The hairs all along Darius's neck, his back, his arms shivered as DuPont slipped the phone back into his pocket. When he looked at Darius again, his entire demeanor changed. Darius braced himself before DuPont even moved, holding his arms out to make things go as quickly as possible.

But DuPont didn't grab Darius's arms. He reached to the side, lifted a chair from the ground, and raised it above his head. Darius stared at him, his mouth agape, but DuPont's face was blank—a horrifying canvas of empty resolve.

He drove the chair down.

Darius lunged to the side, barely avoiding the thing as it smashed into pieces on the tile. When DuPont came up again, all he held was a metal leg, and he swung it like a club. Darius scrambled back, jumping to the side, ducking down, and before he knew it, his feet got tangled in themselves, and he fell backward. His back slammed into the tile.

And DuPont was all he saw. Standing over him. He lifted the rod, drawing it upward, getting ready to crash it into

Darius's skull—

Then he disappeared. A flash of black, then white, then black again as Alan tackled DuPont, the hospital room came back into focus, and Thorn appeared. Her hands grabbed either side of Darius's head.

"Darius?"

"Get him out of here," Alan snarled. DuPont fought against him, trying to pry himself out of the Forgotten Sin's grip. Thorn slipped her arm through the crook at Darius's elbow and pulled him to his feet.

"What the hell was that?" he asked.

"DuPont isn't Programmed to catch you," Thorn breathed. "He's Programmed to kill you."

Darius looked back as Thorn closed the door. DuPont stared at him through the closing gap, that harrowing coldness still stuck in his amber eyes. Darius's sense of dread didn't fade.

CHAPTER EIGHT

Thorn threw open the door to Jacob's green hatchback and flung her satchel into the front seat.

"Gluttony has people Programmed to kill him, Alan," she snarled.

Jacob was leaning against the front of his vehicle, his arms crossed and foot tapping incessantly, while Alan watched Thorn. The two of them were already wearing kevlar vests. Alan's felt awkwardly out of place on top of his red dress shirt. Thorn looked at him and propped her hands on her hips. Sparkie flew in a couple of low, swooping circles, his wings grazing the parking garage ceiling before he dove into the car and disappeared inside her bag.

"We have to get rid of Terrance Moore and wipe his Programming out from the entire force," Thorn continued. "Darius won't be safe in the city until we do."

"I understand," Alan said, "and I agree, but planning a strike against Moore will take time, and TAC is still in no place to fight. You must be patient."

Thorn swore and slammed the door shut. Jacob jumped and glowered at her. She raised a palm in his direction as a half-assed apology before rounding on Alan again.

"Fuck patience. I should go out there and get rid of him

myself." She headed toward the rear of the car and grabbed a black weapons case. She knelt down, opened it, and considered the arsenal inside, all the while aware of Alan's gaze focused on the back of her head like the site from his rifle. "We promised Darius he could go out on TAC assignments as a healer once he's passed all his assessments, but this is more than the Sins sending a couple of Puppets after him. There are over forty thousand cops in New York. *Forty thousand.* And they're all Programmed to kill him on the spot. We'll be sending him out for slaughter."

"Darius has not been approved to go anywhere yet," Alan reminded her, "and Elijah just signed off on allowing him to resume combat training yesterday."

Thorn shook her head, picked up a handgun, and checked the safety. As soon as Elijah made that call, Darius asked to start immediately. Their first session was tonight. Just what she fucking wanted—a long day stuck in a car while Alan Deprogrammed a killer only to come back to the Underground and beat Darius up until he was too tired to stand. Thorn's teeth gnashed together.

"Speak with Christine," Alan said after a moment. "Put together a proposal, and we will create a plan of attack. Once our Tactical Unit is up and running, we can put it into action."

The tension broke, and Thorn took in a slow breath. She nodded, put the gun in a holster on her thigh, and slammed the weapons case shut again. "Thank you."

Alan nodded briefly and turned to Jacob. "Mr. Locke," he said. "Miss Silver is preparing Mr. DuPont in tactical. Go get a protective vest for yourself, and we can be on our way."

Jacob hesitated, pushing off the hood of his car and flashing manic looks between Thorn and Alan. His arms were still crossed, his fingertips drumming on his jacket sleeve, and he pulled them apart to adjust his faded, orange ball cap.

"She's not coming?" he asked. "Chris isn't?"

Alan shook his head. "No."

"Good." Jacob visibly relaxed and nodded. "Good. There's no room. We'd stand out."

"My thoughts precisely," Alan agreed.

"Someone might call us in," Jacob rambled.

"I agree," Alan said patiently. "Please, Mr. Locke." He gestured a hand out for Jacob to head back to the Underground, and the man hurried away, muttering under his breath. Alan and Thorn watched him until the doors shut, and his cold energy faded. Thorn turned to her uncle.

"DuPont's Programming reminds me of what happened to Jacob," she said. "Do you really believe he has no memory of attacking Darius?"

"I do," Alan said. "He has no motivation to lie, but Gluttony certainly benefits from those memories being locked away. It keeps his officers complacent. You cannot resist what you do not know."

Thorn nodded before she turned back to the Underground. In the tactical room, she could feel Jacob beside both Chris and DuPont, whose energies were vague and indistinct. Her jaw tightened.

"Relax," Alan said. Thorn's attention snapped to him again, and he put a hand on her shoulder. "Mr. Wolfe and Miss Fulton did an exceptional job deciphering Gluttony's Programming."

"Yeah," Thorn scoffed. "And they warned us it was the most sophisticated Programming they've seen outside of what *you* can do. Wolfe flat out said he couldn't guarantee they found everything."

"No," Alan said as he drew his hand back. "But we have identified dozens of triggers that affect the Martyrs. We should be able to delete most of it and effectively cover up the rest."

"And how much time do you need?" Thorn asked.

"If you and Mr. Locke can get me thirty minutes, that will be more than enough."

Thorn nodded. "Should be doable. How do you feel

about Jacob's suggested route through Morristown? It's almost the same path we took when we worked on his Programming. It won't draw Wrath's attention toward the Underground's location, and we'll be far enough west that she wouldn't have time to get us before you're done."

"How long are we expected to be gone?" Alan asked.

"Four hours, round trip. Plenty of time alone in a car with Jacob Locke and Gabriel DuPont…"

Alan let out a chuckle and nodded. "It is, and it will ensure a safe return if the Sins attempt to find us."

Cold energy approaching made him and Thorn turn to see Chris walking up to the glass doors with DuPont on one side and Jacob on the other. Both men were wearing kevlar vests. DuPont walked into the garage first. When he saw Thorn and Alan, he instinctively patted his pockets, finding them empty. Jacob caught the motion and threw him a vengeful look.

Thorn's brows furrowed. She had a feeling getting the rest of the Martyrs to accept DuPont would be more challenging than Deprogramming him.

"Good afternoon, Mr. DuPont," Alan said, holding out a palm. DuPont took it. "Are you ready?"

"Yes, sir," he said. Seeing his hand wrapped around Alan's made a spark light in Thorn's chest, remembering how, only a week ago, those hands had tried to bludgeon Darius to death. Her teeth clenched as she and Chris exchanged a dark look.

God, this better work.

Like most "small towns" in the Northeast, Morristown was only small based on a population inside arbitrary city lines. Just over thirty-thousand people officially lived here, but as Jacob drove them north on Highway 124, they passed through at least two cities the same size. Thorn watched Morristown's welcome sign pass her window with the same bland, anticlimactic gusto that Chatham's and Madison's had. The streets moved with cold energy, twisting in paths as mankind's corruption followed them like ants. Thirty thousand was still too many damn people.

Thorn took a deep breath and glanced over her shoulder. Alan was seated behind the driver's chair. It was strange seeing him in the back of a vehicle. He seemed vulnerable. Thorn rarely thought of him this way, but she hated when he came to the surface. The Underground was better armor than a kevlar vest could ever be.

Especially when he was out here drawing Wrath right to him. The comfort of being an hour outside of New York felt a lot more secure in theory than it did on the job. Thorn's hands curled into fists, and her fingernails dug into her palms through her gloves.

"All right," she said. Jacob shifted beside her. His wild eyes darted around traffic as he meticulously merged them onto I-287, heading north. Sparkie crawled out of the satchel by Thorn's feet and climbed onto her seat, where he peered into the back. "You've got thirty minutes."

"We're starting now?" DuPont asked. His heavy brows rose high on his head. "In the car?"

"We must be on the move," Alan said. "Wrath can feel when I use my Influence, and I will be using it nonstop. She will be drawn to us, but we are well enough away to where this should not be a problem."

DuPont glanced out the window. "Half an hour is a long time to be in my head."

"I am going in with a clear goal," Alan said reassuringly. "As well as a pathway to achieving it."

"What do I have to do?"

"Relax," Alan said, "and try not to resist."

"Resist what?"

"You may have thoughts that are unfamiliar or emotions that make you uncomfortable, and your head will hurt. Just sit back and accept it all. It will go faster this way."

DuPont's jaw clenched, and his Adam's apple moved as

he swallowed. Alan gave a final, confident nod. Then he faced forward again, clasped his hands in his lap, and closed his dark eyes. His brows pulled together, and the sensation of Alan's Influence filled the car.

For a few seconds, it was all Thorn could feel. His power was immediate and intimate, so suddenly and glaringly close it took a moment for her body to acclimate to it. To Autumn Hunt, fifty miles to the east in New York City, it would be nothing more than a light on the horizon.

A light she'd come to like a moth to a flame.

Thorn rolled her shoulders, breathing in deep and even.

The first few minutes passed in silence. Thorn looked out her window, her spine rigid as her eyes swept the scenery for… what? They were so far from the city that there was nothing here to see. This wasn't like when they brought new Martyrs into New York for the basic Programming Alan instilled in all their members, where there was always the *chance* the Sins could be nearby. Now, all the way out here, Thorn wasn't sure what she should look out for.

The sheer duration of the Influence made her nervous, though. When it came to installing his Programs, Alan had become an expert. He was so adept that it took him less than three minutes to orchestrate a complicated system of Programming that prevented people from revealing the location to the Underground. Even under the stress of torture, their mouths couldn't form the words, their fingers couldn't type it… They couldn't even point to a goddamned map.

This was different. Thorn's nerves were on edge. The constant pull behind her, the icy attraction that let her *know* Autumn Hunt could feel them, that she might be figuring out what they were trying to do, where they might be, made Thorn's heart race. She glanced at Jacob. His eyes moved so rapidly around the highway it was hard for her to see what he was tracking, and his fingers gripped the wheel until they were white and the rough outline of bones shone through his knuckles.

Thorn had felt this same way with him all those years ago. It had taken Alan hours to break Jacob out of his Program-induced psychosis. Hours of driving. Hours of constant Influence. Wrath hadn't found them that time. She hadn't even come close.

Thorn breathed a deep sigh.

DuPont let out a soft, uncomfortable sound from the back of his throat, and Sparkie startled on Thorn's headrest. His wings flared up as she turned around and watched the cop—the ex-cop? Fuck, she had to stop thinking of him that way if she expected anyone else to.

"How you holding up?" she asked him.

Like Alan, DuPont had his eyes closed, and while his jaw was tight, his hands were held loosely in his lap. His posture was so impeccable Thorn thought he looked almost military. His mouth barely moved as he said, "I've had worse hangovers. I'll be fine."

Despite the tension, the corner of her mouth pulled up. She turned back toward the front of the car and glanced at the clock on the dashboard. "So far, so good. No sign of Wrath yet, and it's been fifteen minutes—"

A cold realization darted down Thorn's spine, and her voice stuck in her throat.

"Oh *fuck*," she murmured.

Jacob glanced at her, the muscles along his neck so tight Thorn could see every tendon. DuPont's eyes snapped open, coppery and dark, while Alan's voice broke the quiet. His Influence blinked out, and his voice was strained.

"She must be close."

"*Fuck*," Thorn breathed again.

"What?" DuPont asked, and he pulled himself forward. His hands gripped Thorn's chair, his fingers squeaking on the leather as Thorn grabbed the weapons case at her feet and threw it open. She drew her phone from her satchel, hit Holly's speed dial button, and turned on the speaker.

"Yo," the security lead answered, her mouth clearly full of food, as Thorn slammed a clip into one of the handguns.

"Where's Wrath?"

"I don't know why you'd think I know that," Holly said.

"I need you to look for her," Thorn snapped.

A cacophony of rapid clacking poured through the speaker. Jacob's face blanched, making him an ashy white. DuPont drew closer to Thorn. "*Wrath?*" he said.

"She hasn't used her Influence," Thorn said. She grabbed another handgun. Put in another clip.

"Isn't that a good thing?"

"No," Alan answered. "As I said, she *will* be drawn to me, and she would need her Influence to travel this distance with any hope of catching up to us. After fifteen minutes of feeling my power in full force, there is almost no chance she would not be making her way here to investigate."

"No sign of her," Holly's voice cut in, and all eyes in the car turned toward the phone sitting on the center console. "Or *anyone*. No one has triggered our facial recognition in hours, and all our regular cams have nothing. With our Gray Unit grounded, I'm flying blind."

Thorn swore again.

"What about Moore's phone?" she growled, glancing at Jacob and indicating to him to turn the fucking car around and get them out of there. His eyes were so wide Thorn could see the whole of the white around them, and his pupils constricted so tightly they all but disappeared.

"Working on it," Holly said. "I have to get into the carrier's system, tap into their towers—"

"I don't need a lesson," Thorn interrupted. "I need to know where the *fuck* the Sins are!"

"It's going to take time," Holly said.

"Call me when you know!" Then Thorn hung up the phone, punched the dashboard, and roared in frustration.

"Wrath has to be close enough that she thinks she can get us," DuPont said. Thorn turned toward him, and for a moment, he reminded her of Alan. His brows were heavy, his jaw set, but he held himself with a calm in the storm that spoke of experience. "We need to get out of town."

Thorn shook her head. "What? Why?"

"When she *is* close enough, she's going to Puppet this city," DuPont said. Thorn's mouth dropped open in surprise. DuPont kept talking. "We need to get as far away from other people as possible."

"No." Jacob shook his head erratically—so much so that the car swerved. "No! Rural means remote. No freeway. No *escape*. We need to move *fast*. We need to outrun them!"

"We can't outrun them," DuPont said.

"Not if all four of the Sins are after us," Alan agreed.

Thorn glanced at him. His black eyes were a little weary, but he locked onto Thorn with a rigid determination.

"How far into the Deprogramming did you get?" Thorn asked.

Alan shook his head. "Not far enough."

Thorn swore and turned to DuPont. "You're a quick study," she said. Then she held one of the pistols out to him. "I hope you're a quick shot, too."

DuPont hesitated. His eyes widened as he looked between Thorn's face and the gun in her hand. "Are you sure?"

"Take it."

"I tried to kill your Virtue."

"*Take it,*" she insisted, and she thrust the weapon into his palm. "You can make it up to me by trying to kill something I actually want dead. Locke." While DuPont stared at the back of her head, shocked, Thorn turned to Jacob. "Get us the fuck out of here."

Jacob's mouth dropped open, then slammed shut, then opened again. "No—NO. You can't *trust him*! He's been compromised! He's been—"

"Stop," Thorn yelled, but Jacob shook his head.

"He *killed* a Martyr! He'll kill more!"

"JACOB."

They were barreling down the highway, swerving around cars. Jacob hardly seemed aware of their surroundings now. His manic focus, his panic, his terror was fixated on the man in the back of the car. He shook his head so violently that Thorn reached out for the wheel. They swerved again, and her belt pulled tight against her collar.

"Jacob, listen to me," she said firmly. She had one hand guiding the car while the other gripped tightly to his shoulder. "I understand your concerns, okay? I do. But we need to get out of here, and I need you to help me. You're the only person I trust to get us out of this alive. The only one who can do it."

Jacob didn't respond, and his body didn't relax, but his focus shifted away from the rearview mirror and onto the road. Thorn breathed a hot sigh of relief, but it was short-lived. Jacob's eyes widened, and he swallowed hard.

"Too late," he said.

Then Thorn felt it. Not the Sins. Not Wrath's Influence. *People.* The vehicles on the road ahead slowed. The ones to the right and the left veered toward them. Cold, human essence drew in closer until civilian cars surrounded them on all sides. Thorn looked through her window at the driver of a massive, silver pickup truck beside her. The man's face was plastic and expressionless.

The car went silent. Thorn's phone began to trill. She answered the call, and Holly's voice blasted into her ear.

"Thorn, he's—"

"Here." Thorn's empty chest concaved, and she took a long breath. "I know. I'll call you back."

She hung up the phone, dropped it into her satchel, and grabbed the second loaded handgun from the case. She handed it to Alan, and they shared a dark look.

The other cars crowded in even closer—so close that Thorn could touch the truck to her right when she rolled down her window. She hit the button, and wind roared into the cab. As she squinted into the gust, Sparkie leapt through. His wings caught air, and for a disorienting moment, he spun wildly before finding a draft and lurching into the sky. Thorn rolled the window shut again. Jacob was muttering incoherently under his breath, sweating so much it soaked his t-shirt, and the sour stink of it hung heavy in the cab.

"What's your plan?" Alan asked.

"Not dying," Thorn growled. She grabbed the pistol from her holster before she looked back at DuPont. "It's them or us," she said. "All that matters is getting the fuck out of here. That might not look pretty. Do you understand?"

DuPont nodded. Thorn pulled her hair into a tight ponytail at the base of her head.

"Locke," she said, rolling the window down again, yelling over the roar of wind barreling into the cab. It whipped around her, assaulting her face with brisk, spring air. "Get ready."

Thorn unbuckled her belt, knelt on her seat for a better angle, and pointed her gun at the truck's front left tire.

She pulled the trigger.

A deafening *pop!* then the truck swung violently left, right, and left again—glancing off their vehicle twice before it spun out and slammed to a stop on the side of the highway. As Jacob swiftly turned them into the empty spot, Thorn was thrown onto the center console. She pulled herself out the window and aimed at the cars ahead.

Another shot. Another tire blown out. This time, the rear right on a black sedan. It skidded, dragging a blackened trail of burned rubber on the asphalt behind it. Jacob threw them onto the shoulder of the road. They sped around it, past the next two cars, and—

They were out.

But not safe.

Sparkie hugged his wings close to his body and torpedoed toward the highway, his keen eyes sweeping the swarm of vehicles falling into place behind Jacob's green hatchback. They moved as a unit, connected to a twisted hive mind.

He spotted it.

At the back of the horde, a sleek, black vehicle with NYPD plates. The unmarked cruiser hovered just far enough to where Thorn couldn't easily feel the energies of the people within it, but she didn't need to.

Terrance Moore.

And she knew, without a doubt, Autumn Hunt was with him.

Thorn's stomach broiled as she spun toward Alan and DuPont. "Gluttony and Wrath are about a quarter mile behind us," she said, climbing into the back and jamming between the two men so she could see out the rear window more clearly. "We've got to disable them. Alan, get any cars ahead of us out of the way. Force them to stop so the Sins can't pick them up."

Alan moved silently into place, squeezing his long body through the two front seats until he was positioned beside Jacob. Jacob threw him a horrified, anxiety-ridden look. His mouth parted, his lips so dry that no matter how often his tongue darted out to wet them, they still looked chapped and painful.

"DuPont." Thorn turned to him. "Help me get rid of these drivers."

DuPont's tan face was pale, but he nodded, unclipped his belt, and rolled his window down. Thorn took a deep breath and did the same.

"Aim for back tires," he shouted to Thorn over the noise. "We're less likely to flip cars and kill people that way."

"You got it."

Then they shot, firing round after round into the long wake of cars behind them. Thorn caught glimpses of faces through windows. Children, sobbing to a vacant mother while their van spun out of control. A man, frantically shaking his cabbie, fighting for the wheel. Solitary drivers, unrestricted by anyone and anything as they plowed forward. They all disappeared as Thorn buried bullets in rubber, zipping away so quickly that she had no time to tell if they survived.

Behind her back, Alan's Influence blared to life again. Soon, the side of the Interstate was full of vehicles—ones with blown tires and others that had pulled over so quickly they left behind smoking signals of hot asphalt and dust. Cold points flashed by Thorn as quickly as headlights. Human energy, there and then gone again, too slow to be of any use to the Sins.

She could see them now. The unmarked cruiser pulled forward closely enough for Thorn to feel two familiar points of cold energy. Wrath was behind the wheel, her face pulled tight in a horrifying smile, while Moore sat to her right, putting all his focus on the two Puppetted cars left between them. As the Sins sped forward, Thorn leaned out the window and raised her weapon.

Wrath's Influence filled her brain with cold, crackling static.

Surrounded on both sides—Alan ahead, driving people off the road, and Hunt behind, pushing forward. Who the fuck could she be Influencing out here?

A chill rushed down the back of Thorn's neck, and she turned to Gabe DuPont.

He'd stopped shooting. Drew into the car.

And he was staring down at the gun in his hands.

"DuPont?" Thorn said.

He glanced at her and winced as he began to rub his temples with the fingers of his left hand. His right was still wrapped around the pistol. Thorn looked at it. She looked at him.

"DuPont," she said again. "Fight her—"

"Thorn, get the gun!" Alan exclaimed.

DuPont suddenly roared and threw the weapon out his open window. Thorn stared at him, her mouth open and eyes wide. He shook his head and waved in her direction.

"I'm good," he said. "Get rid of them!"

Thorn spun back around.

Wrath was still forcing her will forward, trying to contort DuPont into a monster. The pinging evil of her Influence gave Thorn a clear direction. She propped her elbow on the window frame and pulled the trigger.

Miss.

Hunt's Influence intensified. DuPont grabbed the sides of his head. Alan abandoned his station and turned around. Suddenly, Thorn felt his Influence beside her, pushing into DuPont, fighting Wrath for control. DuPont let out a haggard, wordless sound.

They were going to fucking kill him.

Sparkie descended. He slammed into the driver's side door of Moore's police cruiser and tightened his wings against his tiny body. They were close enough now that Thorn could see Gluttony's broad face set into hard-lined determination. Autumn Hunt's manic, gray eyes, her brown hair long and wild around her shoulders. She cackled. Thorn couldn't hear it, but *fuck*, she felt the joviality. The *thrill*. It made her sick. Her chest lit with fire as Sparkie pulled himself up, battered by the wind, disoriented—

And he positioned himself right behind Hunt's head.

Thorn locked onto her Familiar. Onto *herself*. The purest aim. A straight line from one fragment of her broken soul to the other.

She pulled the trigger.

The bullet crashed through the windshield, sending a spiderweb of black cracks through the glass, and hit Hunt in the shoulder. Sparkie unfurled his wings and caught the wind. He shot upward as the Sins' car smashed onto the side of the road.

And all at once, they were gone. Gluttony. Wrath. The cars they had Puppetted. Every energy disappeared in a flash as Jacob Locke tore down the highway at eighty miles an hour.

CHAPTER NINE

The atmosphere inside the parking garage shuddered with anxious anticipation. Darius stood outside the glass double doors, arms crossed, as he watched the soft glow from headlights above fill the concrete cavern with an eerie, yellow shine. Chris was to his left, dressed in her Tactical best, a pistol clipped to the belt in her beige cargo pants. Darius glanced down at his watch. It was almost eight p.m. Two hours later than Thorn and the others were supposed to be back.

"How did the Sins find them?" Lina murmured. Her voice disappeared in the chamber, overpowered by the rumbling of an unfamiliar engine.

Abraham let out a sigh. "Maybe Jacob's car was being tracked, too."

"DuPont didn't have any reaction to Jacob's car when Skylar and Nicholas tested him," Chris said. Her shoulders squared as a gold minivan pulled up outside the loading area. "But I guess it's possible."

The vehicle squealed to a stop, its noisy brakes sending a shrill tone into the garage that echoed back so loudly it made Darius's teeth ache. Thorn stuck out like a black smudge inside the thing, her dark hair and clothes a stark contrast to the fluffy, pink decorations dangling from the rearview mirror. A decal stretched across the back window, showing a string of cats stretched along the phrase, "Life is Purrfect."

Darius couldn't help it. As Thorn stepped out of the driver's side, he let out a short, desperate laugh. She was okay. They were all okay.

"I like the van," he said.

Thorn threw him a look, her eyebrows rising in a humored way as she walked around the front of the vehicle.

"What happened to Jacob's car?" Lina asked.

"The Sins saw it," Thorn said with the mood of an overworked parent who accidentally lost their child's security blanket. She shook her head. "We had to leave it behind."

Darius looked over her shoulder. Jacob sat in the front seat of the minivan, rocking back and forth and anxiously gnawing on his cuticles. The nails themselves were already chewed right to the bed. Lina hurried to him as Abraham crossed his arms.

"Did you finish the Deprogramming?" he asked. When Thorn nodded, he raised his brows. "And? Did it work?"

"I don't fucking know, Locke," Thorn snapped. "We didn't have the chance to test it." Then she looked at Darius. "Until now."

Alan opened the van's large, sliding door and stepped into the lot, DuPont directly on his heels. Darius's stomach twisted nervously, and as soon as DuPont looked up, Chris drew closer. Her hand instinctively reached for the gun on her belt.

But DuPont didn't do anything. He didn't pat his pockets. Didn't search for a phone. Didn't rush across the space between them to wrap his hands around Darius's throat.

The six of them stood in silence. Darius paid close attention to his body, waiting for a warning call, but it never came.

"Well," DuPont said at last, breaking the silence—and the tension. He threw his thumb back at the minivan. "*That* was fucking insane. Is that always how it goes?"

A nervous laugh echoed through the emptiness around them. Chris's hand relaxed, and her face broke open in a smile. Even Alan's thin mouth pulled into a smirk.

Thorn, however, didn't soften. "No," she said. "Sometimes, it's worse."

The levity drained from DuPont's face, and his throat went rigid.

"We are fortunate Mr. DuPont was there to assist us today," Alan said. "Miss Silver, please escort him back to his room. Tomorrow morning, we will run tests to determine how effective our Deprogramming has been. Until then, I want a guard posted at his door." Alan nodded briefly in DuPont's direction. "I hope you understand."

"I do," DuPont said.

"Assuming everything goes well," Alan added, "we will set you up in our TAC training classes."

"Yes, sir."

Then Chris and DuPont left. As soon as they were gone, Abraham's voice broke the quiet.

"How's Jacob doing?" he asked.

"He has been rather shaken by the entire event," Alan said. They glanced at the car, where Lina spoke to Jacob in soft, hushed tones. "I would like him to stay in the hospital ward tonight for observation. We can provide medication to calm his nerves."

Abraham watched him with a frown, his lips tight, as Lina returned to the group. "God, this has been so triggering for him," she murmured. "He's terrified of the Sins."

Alan bowed his head in her direction. "Understandably so. Miss Brooks, would you ask Elijah to ready one of the private suites? Abraham—"

Abraham raised his hand to silence Alan and drew closer to the van's passenger door. Jacob was still huddled over his knees, shaking and muttering something unintelligible to himself. Thorn and Darius exchanged a look, and he gestured his chin back into the Underground. Thorn nodded, and the two of them slipped away.

As soon as the glass doors shut behind them, Darius turned to her.

Compared to the other fights he'd seen Thorn come home from, she looked put together. No blood. No fading bruises. No bullet holes closing themselves up.

But her shoulders were so tight and angry that Darius felt like she was one wrong word away from hitting something.

"It's been a long day," he observed.

Thorn scoffed and led them into the hallway. "Thank god it's fucking over."

Darius's heart sank as they reached the foyer outside the elevator. Thorn flipped open her satchel, and instead of hitting the button to go down, she started toward the stairwell.

"So," Darius said as she opened the door. "We'll get back to training tomorrow?"

Thorn groaned and pinched the bridge of her nose. Sparkie poked his head out of her bag. "Fuck, Darius. I totally forgot."

He chuckled. "I figured. It's fine, really. I've waited two weeks. Another day won't kill me."

And he tried to smile, to convince her he wasn't as disappointed as he really was, because he'd been looking forward to getting back at it. His insomnia had only gotten worse since they'd stopped. The muscles in Thorn's jaw tightened as she watched Darius for a moment. At last, she shook her head.

"I'm sorry," she said. "It's not a good idea right now."

She didn't want to hurt him. That's what her eyes told him. Her brows turned down, and the half-empty blackness filled with remorse. He nodded, but his stomach was in knots.

"I understand," Darius said. He reached out and hit the down button.

Then they stood in awkward quiet. The elevator hummed as it slowly rose to the first floor. Darius glanced at his watch again. It was too early to go to bed, too late for dinner—not that he was hungry anyway. Maybe he'd run to the kitchen, make a pot of coffee, then come back up to the R&D headquarters to look for more Virtues. God, he was so behind—

"I'm going to get some fresh air," Thorn said suddenly. She was still holding the door open, one foot poised to step into the stairwell. "You look like you could use some, too."

The discomfort broke in a grateful wave. Darius smiled.

"I wouldn't want to intrude," he began, but Thorn cut him off.

"Shut up, Jones," she said. "You're keeping me from my cigarette. Let's go."

There were only two ways in and out of the Underground. The primary entrance into the garage was accessible through a carwash attached to the southern wall of a Martyr-owned gas station. The other was up a long flight of stairs, hidden in a secret room at the back of a storage closet inside the store. While all Martyrs had an access card to the carwash, only a select few could enter or exit through the building.

Thorn typed her code into the door handle. A light on the keypad flashed green as the mechanical lock whirred to life.

It looked like every other storeroom Darius had ever stepped foot in. It was filled with boxes of paper goods, old packing materials, and indistinct containers filled with miscellaneous items that had long since been stocked for safekeeping and forgotten. Thorn closed the door behind them, and it all but disappeared into the wall. The seams were so closely cut that they merged with the painted concrete, and the exterior handle was hidden inside a nondescript electrical box. It locked automatically as Thorn strode through the closet and walked into the shop like she owned it.

"Oh," Darius heard a voice say at the far end of the room. "Uh, good evening."

A surprised clerk—or someone who dressed and played

the part of a clerk—stood behind the counter. All the employees here were specialized TAC members, trained both in managing the station and emergency procedures in case the Sins ever attacked. As far as Chris was concerned, they had the hardest job in the whole Underground.

Customer service was worse than facing the Sins, she'd joked with Darius once.

The clerk, a man named Stefan Brandt, glanced at Darius in surprise as he came around the corner, too. He looked between Thorn and Darius like he wanted to ask if this was allowed before he shrugged and got back to scrolling his phone. Thorn pulled a red box of cigarettes out of her satchel and walked through the glass door. As soon as she was out, Sparkie vaulted into the sky. His blue body disappeared immediately in the dusk.

Cool, evening air blew against Darius's face, and he closed his eyes to take it in. It had been a long time since he'd come above ground. Not since his last mission with the Recon units into the city a few months ago. He couldn't help but think how lucky he was that their car hadn't been caught at one of the police checkpoints. If it had, he'd probably be dead.

Thorn seemed to be thinking the same thing.

"We've got to kill Moore," she muttered.

She put a cigarette to her lips and struck the lighter. The flame cast her in a warm glow that blended the highlights and shadows of her face with the navy and orange sunset shining above the trees. In the evening, distant frogs croaked and crickets sang, a testament to spring they never experienced below ground.

Darius didn't say anything as Thorn drew a lungful of smoke in deep and exhaled it through her nose. It obscured her face for a moment but not long enough for Darius to miss the sharp, thoughtful anger tight across her forehead.

"Was there a problem with Gabe's Programming?" Darius asked.

Thorn shook her head. "No. At this point, I'm more

worried one of our guys is going to kill *him* than I am about DuPont hurting anyone else."

"So, what's wrong?" Darius pressed. Thorn glanced at him. "You seem really worked up."

Thorn turned away, her jaw clenched, and she pried it apart as she held her cigarette to her mouth again. Instead of smoking it, though, she absently ran the top of her thumbnail against her lower lip. "It's just really fucking sophisticated," she said at last. "According to Wolfe and Fulton, Gluttony had Subprograms buried beneath criteria they've never seen before, and it's *everywhere*. Every damned cop in New York City. We can't Deprogram them all. A lot of people are going to die…"

Her voice drifted off, and while Darius nodded, his stomach twisted up in knots. "Maybe not," he said. "Once I pass my assessments, I'll be able to heal people out on the field."

Thorn cast him a grim, sidelong glance. Darius's breath caught in his throat. After a moment, Thorn shook her head and turned back to the street. An isolated little road connected the Martyrs' gas station to Highway 9, less than a mile away. The sounds of passing cars whispered through rustling leaves, fading and growing like the wind. "That's right," she said. "Unless I kill Gluttony first. And from what I've heard about your shooting classes, I probably will."

The shadow of a smile pulled at her mouth only to die before it could fully spread across her lips. With a sigh, she lowered herself onto the curb of the abandoned parking lot. Darius sat beside her.

"You're serious?" he asked. "You're going to try to kill Gluttony?"

"Yes," Thorn said plainly. "Alan gave Chris and me the go-ahead to start planning our attack."

Darius nodded. "Good," he said, but the word felt strange in his mouth. Gluttony was a problem, but there was a man trapped beneath that evil.

"Yeah," Thorn agreed bitterly, raising her cigarette to

her lips. "Good."

For the next few minutes, they watched the sunset fade in silence. The vibrant, warm hues dissolved to a deep, cold blue. Thorn and Darius's shadows grew on the asphalt, stretching out in front of them, dark pillars in a halo of bright, yellow light. Every so often, a furl of smoke clouded Thorn's silhouette, like she herself was on fire.

"Jones! Wait up!"

Mackenzie's indistinct, lukewarm aura rushed at Darius from around the corner as he left the R&D headquarters. He turned to see her waving enthusiastically, a grin across her face, her brightly painted nails and vibrant orange hair adding a welcome dose of color to an otherwise beige hallway.

"Heading down to class?" he asked as she sidled up beside him.

"Yeah." She waved her hand, clearly having another agenda. "Hey, are you still good to go out on scouting missions with the recon units?"

Darius frowned. "Yeah. I think so. I better be." That came out harsh, and Darius cleared his throat as Mackenzie cast him a wide-eyed look. "But I thought those were on hold since our fleet is grounded."

"Well, we're ungrounded," Mackenzie said. "Kinda. We *finally* got a couple of rental cars allocated for our guys, so we can start doing runs again. I have a whole backlog of day-trip missions we'd like you to go out on. You know, to put that Virtue sense to good use." She winked and elbowed him in the side.

Darius chuckled. "When?"

"Soon as possible. John and Nicholas are gonna go out tomorrow."

"To New York?"

Mackenzie blew a huff of air through her lips. "Pfft, no,"

she said. "Local-ish, but nothing in the city proper, so hope-fully Thorn won't have an aneurysm about a cop spotting you. Can she even *have* an aneurysm, you think?"

"I have no idea…"

"Anyway." Mackenzie waved her hand again. "It's all suburban stuff, nothing too dangerous, but we've got to get back on top of it."

A guilty surge sent a warm flush across Darius's face. "Yeah, sorry. I've been doing so much other shit—"

"I'm not blaming you," Mackenzie corrected quickly. "The whole place has been kinda fucked in the last couple of months, but I don't want it to get *more* fucked, you know? I'll chat with Lina, and we'll make a plan for getting you back out there."

They reached the foyer, and Darius paused. A cluster of warm energy was gathered at the bottom of the stairs. He let out a sigh. "Looks like Chris is running late."

Mackenzie shook her head and grinned. "What'd I just say? The whole place is fucked."

The two of them started down the stairwell. Voices from their class echoed upward in a soft drone. Something felt off, though. Darius counted four auras. That was strange. With Elena gone and Nicholas empty, the math didn't add up. He focused on them a little closer, and his stomach dropped.

"Oh, man," Darius murmured.

Mackenzie looked over her shoulder at him from a couple of steps down. "Hmm?"

"DuPont is here…"

Mackenzie froze so suddenly that Darius almost fell onto her. He caught himself on the railing as Mackenzie spun around and glared at him, her face pale and rigid.

"He's in *this* class?" she hissed.

Darius shrugged. It had been a couple of days since DuPont's Programming had been removed. The tests had gone well, and all the Martyr directors were starting to inte-grate him into the Underground—all but Mackenzie.

"I can't fucking *believe* Chris assigned him to this class," she went on. "Elena is *dead* because of him!"

"I'm sure she just—"

"She wasn't fucking thinking!" Mackenzie yelled. Her words roared through the stairwell with all the subtlety of a freight train, and the murmuring voices quieted. Mackenzie's nostrils flared as her blue eyes filled with furious tears.

"Hey." Darius grabbed the Irishwoman by the shoulder and hurried around her, stopping on the step below to look her in the face. "If you need to take today off, that's fine."

"I don't need a day off," Mackenzie said.

"Okay," Darius said, "then we need to lead by example—"

"Fuck this," Mackenzie cut in. She threw her hands up, tearing herself away from Darius, and stormed down the stairs. He groaned and followed after her. He couldn't believe such a small woman could sound like a stampede.

When they reached the bottom, Darius found a stunned, silent crew waiting for them.

Five people gathered outside the locked door. To the right, Caleb, Nicholas, and John leaned against the wall, almost universally set into firm, unapproachable moods—arms crossed, mouths tightly shut. Conrad stood by the door, one of his thick hands wrapped around the handle and jostling it impatiently.

"'Bout damn time," he grumbled as Mackenzie and Darius hit the landing. "Silver's running late. *Again.*"

He threw a hot look across the room, where Gabriel DuPont stood alone in the other corner. Mackenzie ignored him as she stomped to the door and shoved Conrad's hand away.

"This is fucking ridiculous," she muttered as she started to punch her key code into the lock.

"You're tellin' me," Conrad said. The light on the handle glowed red, and Mackenzie swore before she started the code a second time.

Darius shook his head and turned to DuPont. DuPont's

attention darted toward him, his whole body tense and ready. When Darius smiled and held out his hand, DuPont's eyes widened.

"You go by Gabe, right?" Darius asked. "Welcome to shooting class."

A flood of visible relief poured through Gabe's shoulders, and for the first time since watching him on the camera in that hospital room, Darius saw him smile. It was a little crooked, pulling more to the left in a way that made him somehow charming. He grabbed Darius's palm and shook it firmly.

"Yeah," he said. "Thanks."

"Fuck!" Mackenzie snarled after hitting the wrong buttons again. John, Caleb, and Nicholas cast her a quiet look. Gabe's spine drew tight, and Darius forced a smile.

"You found your way down here okay?" he asked.

"I got a little lost," Gabe said, "but I managed."

"It's a big place," Darius said. "Don't worry. The Influence classes are a lot easier to find."

"Yeah? I have one of those tomorrow morning."

"Great," Darius said with a nod. Gabe nodded, too, and a tense silence fell. Darius cleared his throat. "Have you met everyone?"

Gabe shook his head, so Darius gestured around the alcove, indicating every person by name and position in the Underground. John and Caleb both gave self-conscious nods while Conrad grunted, and Mackenzie didn't look back from the door she had finally managed to open. She stomped through it as Darius turned to the last man he had to introduce. "And this is Nicholas Wolfe."

Then he paused. What title should he give Nicholas? Technically, he was John's partner in Research and Discovery, but it didn't feel right to ignore everything else Nicholas had done for the Martyrs.

Everything he'd sacrificed.

After the silence stretched on for long enough to be awkward, Nicholas watching Darius with his eyebrows high,

Gabe said, "We've met. You're the guy who got rid of Sloth, right?"

Gabe held out his hand, and Nicholas's mouth opened slightly in surprise. He reached out, grabbed DuPont's palm, and said, "Yeah."

"I read the reports," Gabe said. "Amazing."

Nicholas frowned. "They let you read the reports?"

"Not all of them," Gabe admitted. "But I wanted to get up to speed."

Nicholas's frown didn't fade, but he nodded thoughtfully. Then Darius walked through the doors and led them from the empty stairwell to the shooting range. Ahead of him, he felt Mackenzie and the others already inside the control booth and, beyond her, another energy at the edge of his cerebral map.

"Chris is at Holly's," Darius said.

"Well, go grab her," Nicholas said as they approached the range doors. He opened them, and Mackenzie's voice poured into the corridor.

"—shouldn't be here!"

Darius, Nicholas, and Gabe paused, and Darius rubbed his fingertips against his eyes.

"Yeah," he said. "Okay. I'll be back soon."

Darius took off at a jog. The security office was at the furthest edge of the basement, tucked around a corner and down a long, dark hallway. A bright light from the door's window lit up the corridor. He cracked it open.

"Son of a *bitch*."

Darius peeked his head into the room, a blast of cool air harsh against his skin. Holly and her team of security agents were hard at work, diligently typing away at their desks around the small room. Four of them were set up at the back beside a sleek, black server adorned with hundreds of neatly organized cables. Holly's desk was right by the entrance, and as she swore again, Chris rubbed her eyes with the tips of her fingers.

"You're late," Darius said.

Chris jumped at his voice and spun around in her chair. Her bright eyes were tired, and faint shadows raised beneath them. As soon as her focus landed on him, it darted to her watch.

"*Fuck*," she said.

Darius laughed. "What are you doing?"

"We're looking into our vehicle registration to see what the Sins might have figured out," Chris said. "I completely lost track of time."

"Any ideas?" Darius asked, opening the door further and slipping fully into the room.

"About *seventeen*," Holly said. She didn't look at him as she typed away. Her short hair was pulled into a messy disaster on top of her head, like she'd run her hands through it so often it figured it might as well stay up.

Chris sighed. "We're working on narrowing it down."

"*I'm* working on narrowing it down," Holly said. Chris glanced at her. "Go on. Get out. Do something else for a while, so maybe *one* of us doesn't want to smash our face through this monitor."

"Keep me updated," Chris said as she got to her feet.

"Always do."

Darius and Chris stepped out of Holly's office, tucking the cold air away with a sharp snap as the door sucked closed. The second they were alone, Chris breathed a whole week's worth of stress out in a single sigh.

"I'm sorry," she started, but Darius cut her off with a wave of his hand.

"It happens," he said. "It's been crazy around here."

Chris scoffed. "And it's just going to get crazier."

They turned the corner, and she glanced down the corridor, where the shooting range doors stood out under dim, yellow light. She drew another breath that raised her shoulders, and they refused to come back down. Darius cleared his throat.

"So, I wanted to ask about Gabe…"

"Gabe?"

"DuPont," Darius clarified. "Him being here is making people uncomfortable. What if we gave him private lessons instead?"

Chris shook her head. "No." The word shot through the room, echoing off distant concrete walls. "If he's going to join the Martyrs, he has to *join* the Martyrs. Keeping him separate won't help. If anyone has a problem, they'll have to deal with it."

She spoke with such a sense of finality that Darius knew there was no point arguing with her—and he didn't disagree. He nodded, watching the shooting range as it drew closer. DuPont's energy stood apart from the rest.

"Besides," Chris went on after a moment, a little gentler. "These classes are just a formality. He has to have one session on the VR, one with real weapons, and then he can test. I'm sure he'll pass."

"That's true," Darius agreed.

"And," Chris added as she cast Darius a sly smile. "If I were going to give anyone private lessons, it'd be someone who needs it… Like *you*."

She chuckled as she reached for the door, but Darius was struck with an idea. "Actually," he said, "what's your schedule look like this week?"

Chris's brows drew in, but at the smile on Darius's face, her lips toyed with one, too.

"You're doing *what?*"

"Giving Darius private lessons," Chris repeated. She sat behind her desk, not looking up at Thorn as she worked. "On top of our normal classes. He wants to get on the field as a medic, and I want him out there to heal our people. This will get us there faster."

Thorn crossed her arms, and a tense pause filled the room. When she didn't speak for several moments, Chris finally looked up, and the expression on Thorn's face made her stop. With a sigh, Chris leaned back in her chair.

"Is there something specific you wanted to ask me?" Chris asked—almost challenged—and she raised her brows.

"I just don't think Jones needs special accommodations," Thorn snapped.

"I think he does," Chris said. She focused back on the computer screen. Thorn could see her open calendar—every hour of Chris's life planned out in color-coded blocks. Red for duty shifts. Blue for training. Green for meetings. White for downtime.

There was hardly any white. Chris clicked on one of the open slots, and Thorn watched her type "Darius" into the space. Her teeth gnashed together, and Sparkie shuddered from his hiding place behind her hair.

"You're stretching yourself—"

"Look, Thorn," Chris said, exasperated. She pressed her fingertips to her eyes and sighed. "I watched Jeremiah run this department for twelve years, and you never got on his case like this."

She dropped her hands and peered up at Thorn. The light from her screen illuminated her face, casting shadows beneath her eyes that Thorn knew were deeper than they looked. She considered Chris for a moment before gazing around the rest of the room—a room that had once belonged to Jeremiah Montgomery and, in many ways, still did. Chris had done very little to make the space hers when she'd taken the job. It was as much of a blank slate as it had been before. One desk. Two chairs. A bookshelf filled with tactical reports, firearm manuals....

And a single, dusty photograph of a young man wearing a purple graduation cap. Jeremiah's son. Noah and Chris had grown up together, children of a war they didn't understand, but where Chris had decided to join the Martyrs, Noah left as soon as he turned eighteen. Alan wiped his memories of the Underground so the kid could pretend his childhood had "normal" trauma. Abandonment. Illness. Foster care.

Instead of the real horror of Gluttony ripping his mother to shreds when he was nine and the anxiety of wondering if his father would be next.

"Jeremiah slept more," Thorn stated at last, knowing it was weak, knowing Chris could sense the lie, but refusing to admit she was treating her any differently.

"You asked me to do this job," Chris said. "So let me do it."

Their eyes locked again, and Thorn's jaw clenched. She wanted to argue further, but what could she do? Yell at Chris for doing exactly what *she* was doing: throwing herself into work, closing the rest of the world out, and burying her horrors in things she could control because, fuck, it was easier than dealing with them. Thorn opened her mouth, trying to find the words to tell Chris how worried she was, but an aura down the hall stopped them in her throat.

"Claytor is here," she said instead. She could never give Alan shit for not speaking what was really on his mind again. Thorn ran her tongue along the bottom of her teeth as she opened the door. Alexis Claytor stood on the other side, one arm upraised, ready to knock. Her icy blue eyes moved from Thorn to Chris as she held up a massive binder.

"I have all my intel on Terrance Moore," she said.

"Perfect," Thorn said, ushering Alexis in. She pulled up one of the chairs and slammed herself into it. "Let's take this fucker down."

Because that's what she needed. Something else to hide behind.

CHAPTER TEN

The courtyard bustled with more energy than Darius was used to. He sat with Nicholas at a table near the far edge of the dining area, ignoring a half-eaten plate of roast chicken as he sorted through a folder of old files. Martyrs came and went around them, the tail-end of dinner catching stragglers as they went to get their meals. Darius made a habit of eating this late because it was never busy. Today, that wasn't the case.

He glanced up as Conrad Carter and Liz Wright sat down at a neighboring table, plates in hand. Conrad grumbled something incoherent but frustrated, and Liz nodded in agreement. Then, Conrad's eyes met Darius's, and they darted back to his food.

In the weeks since the Martyr fleet had been grounded, they were relying on a network of rental cars from local towns, keeping each for no more than five days before returning it and picking up a replacement from a different location. The result was a compound full of pent-up TAC members who couldn't go on duty, Recon units who couldn't leave the city, and in-house staff who suddenly had a lot more people in their space than usual. According to Chris, only one-third of their standard Martyr presence was in the city. The rest were here.

"I don't see why you wanted my help," Nicholas said, scratching his stubble-speckled chin. "I'm not exactly an asset anymore." Bitterness laced its way into the words.

Darius glanced up from the papers sitting in front of him. "Of course you are," he said. "You've done *so much* down here."

"Yeah," Nicholas said. "I *did*—back when I was a Virtue. It's a little different now, isn't it?"

He looked back down at the table, where piles of old articles sat beside two half-eaten plates of food. Darius sighed and picked up one of the stacks. "Just because you aren't a Virtue doesn't mean you aren't valuable. You found these leads. Maybe you'll remember why they stuck out to you."

Nicholas let out a harsh huff of air as he mindlessly thumbed through a handful of black and white printouts. His baby blue eyes were dull and listless. "Nope," he stated. Darius fought the urge to dip his face into his hands and groan.

For a week now, he'd spent his days trapped in a car with Nicholas, John, and whatever TAC team was assigned to them as a security detail, tackling Mackenzie's backlog of "local-ish" leads. Every morning, they climbed into a different rental (for security, as per Thorn's orders) and drove around upstate New York, Eastern PA, and Connecticut with the desperate hope that, eventually, Darius would be close enough to a Virtue to sense it. All he felt, though, was the cold disappointment of wasted time.

"These stood out to you when you were a Virtue," Darius insisted, glancing at another sheet. In his first few months at the Underground, before he'd sacrificed Diligence to destroy Sloth, Nicholas gathered over seven hundred articles, claiming all of them "felt right." Virtues were graced with a sixth sense that drew them to one another, and Teresa had used this sense to find Virtues in the past by just reading through the news. Darius knew it worked because it had led him to Nicholas in the first place.

Nicholas leaned back in the cast iron chair and gestured a broad palm at the five stacks of files on the table. "Clearly, I was never great at this part of the job. No way these are all legit."

Darius's resistance failed him, and he pressed his fingertips into his tired eyes.

"It's better than mindlessly driving around the whole Tri-State area," he said. "At least these leads had *some* Virtue intuition backing them up. Just help me sort them."

Nicholas raised his eyebrows, his forehead transforming into a sea of weary creases and canyons. He was in his late forties, but Darius felt like Nicholas had aged a decade in the last six months. The former Diligence slowly rearranged articles into stacks. There were large piles for New York State, Pennsylvania, Vermont, and Georgia and a smaller one for miscellaneous leads in other parts of the country. Darius took a long breath, lifted the stack for Georgia, and started to flip through them, hoping, maybe even goddamned *praying*, he felt something.

They worked in silence for a few minutes, Nicholas moving articles into their respective categories while Darius read through headlines, glanced at pictures, and divided them into two piles: definitely nothing and maybe something. So far, none of them jumped up and screamed, "There's a Virtue here!" Just the occasional inkling of possibility. He was starting to worry these inklings were borne from desperation.

"You know what you *don't* need Virtue senses to see?" Nicholas said suddenly, drawing Darius's attention away from an article about some flea market outside of Sandersville. Nicholas had stopped sorting, and instead, he watched the elevator. Darius turned, but he knew, from both the warm aura and Nicholas's tone, that he would see Gabe DuPont.

When the ex-cop stepped into the courtyard, a hush poured through the dining area on a wave of tension.

Nicholas threw Darius a look.

"Did you see him in the news?" he pressed on. He only had a few more papers to sort, and he quickly threw them into their respective stacks. "His whole SWAT team is being hailed as fallen heroes. Load of bullshit."

"Yeah, I have," Darius said with a sigh, turning back to his articles and putting the one he'd been looking at in the meager collection of "something" leads. "It's all any of the stations are talking about."

"Lina thinks the Sins are trying to create even more civil unrest," Nicholas said. "Praising some fallen cops while they ignore the woman they killed in this no-knock warrant, not to mention all the other civilians the police have murdered in the last few months. It's pissing a *lot* of people off, and not just in the city. Down *here*, too."

Nicholas looked around, where the gathered Martyrs were still quiet, still tense, as they observed DuPont getting his meal together. Darius glanced up, drew a deep breath, and sighed.

"Well, *our* people will get used to him," he murmured. "Eventually."

"Where are you planning on putting him?" Nicholas asked.

"Chris wants to test him for TAC," Darius said. "You've seen how well he's doing in the shooting classes."

A sudden laugh from the neighboring table made Darius and Nicholas turn. Conrad shook his head and said, through a full mouth, "Of course he's gonna pass all the damned tests. He's a fucking cop! Son of a bitch will never get a spot on the team—"

"That's not up to you," Darius cut in, moving another article to his "something" pile without even looking at it.

Conrad threw Darius a hot look and busied himself by aggressively slicing his chicken into thick hunks. Darius glanced over Conrad's shoulder, where Liz was staring at him, and as soon as their eyes met, she quickly averted her gaze. When the tension settled, Darius sighed and turned back to the table to find Nicholas leaning over it.

"You really think she'll let an ex-cop in?" he asked with a frown.

Darius didn't respond right away. Gabe's energy, still so robust that it made Darius pause every time he felt it, was approaching the only empty table in the courtyard—one right beside Darius. Conrad's flat mouth was curled into a snarl as he passed, but Gabe ignored him. As he reached where Darius and Nicholas were sitting, he glanced up and nodded. They nodded back.

"I think," Darius replied slowly, knowing Gabe could likely hear him, "Chris is going to do what's best for the Tactical Unit."

Nicholas shook his head. "I fucking hope so," he said. Then he got to his feet. "Well, I'm done. Good luck with… *this* mess…" He gestured widely around them, said some half-hearted goodnight, and walked away. As soon as he was gone, Darius sighed and started flipping through the Georgia leads again. It seemed Nicholas's foul mood had taken a toll, and suddenly Darius wasn't getting *any* positive vibe from the articles anymore.

He worked quietly for a few minutes before a voice behind him made him jump.

"Hungry?"

Darius spun in his chair to see Thorn standing there, her black hair damp and a gym bag slung over her shoulder. One eyebrow raised as she indicated the table, where Darius's and Nicholas's meals were still sitting. He chuckled and scratched the back of his head.

"Nicholas just left," he said.

Thorn came around the table and took the empty chair beside him. She smelled lightly of vanilla, sandalwood, and a hint of chlorine. As she placed her gym bag on the back of her chair, Sparkie slithered out from within it to sit on her lap.

"What are you doing?" Her dark eyes moved from one stack of papers to the next. Aside from the two plates of mostly uneaten food, paperwork took up the entire surface of the table.

"Looking for better leads," Darius sighed. "The day trips Mackenzie is sending us out on aren't going anywhere."

"Disappointing," Thorn said with a half-shrug, "but not surprising." She picked up the pile Darius had just sorted through and fanned it out. Sparkie peered up at him from Thorn's knee, his beady, black eyes alert. Thorn frowned. "Where did these come from?"

"Nicholas found them last summer," Darius said, leaning back in his chair. "I was hoping his Virtue senses pointed him in the right direction… I'm just so sick of coming up empty."

Thorn's eyes darted up at him. "Coming up empty?"

"I mean, yeah," Darius said, his cheeks flushing with warmth. "It's been over nine months since I've had any good feelings about a lead."

For a moment, Thorn just watched him, her face relaxing, her thin lips slowly curling into an amused smile. At last, she let out a laugh and shook her head. "Before *you*, we hadn't seen any real sign of a Virtue for seventy years."

Her smile widened, and he couldn't help but laugh, too.

"Maybe I'm being a little impatient," Darius said, raising his hands. Thorn's brows, if possible, moved even higher. "All right. A *lot* impatient."

"Good thing that isn't your Virtue," Thorn said, but her smile softened as she looked back down at the table. A little bit of that concern she tended to wear lately shadowed her expression, and she shook her head. "And neither is Diligence. You need to take a fucking break. This is some Nicholas-Wolfe-level shit."

Her attention turned back to the papers in her hands. Darius shook his head. "I'll take a break when—what?"

The look on Thorn's face stopped his thought before it had fully formed. She suddenly sat rigid in her chair, her eyes sharp as she squinted at one of the articles. Darius leaned over to read it. It was the one about the flea market.

"They had a record-breaking turnout for some raffle," Darius murmured with a noncommittal shrug.

Thorn shook her head. "It's not that. Look. Is that what I think it is?"

She pointed to the photograph at the top of the page. It was small, printed in black and white, showing three women smiling for the camera. Behind them, a man hoisted a box onto his left shoulder. It obscured his face, but his right hand swung past his hip.

The *Peccostium*, camouflaged against his dark skin, sat below his wrist joint.

Darius gawked, amazed Thorn had noticed it at all. A spark of apprehension made his stomach uneasy, and his chest felt carved out. "Do you think it's Envy?"

Thorn shook her head as she put the file back on the table. "I don't know… It would be really quick for a possession, but this *is* where Envy's *Peccostium* would manifest." Almost subconsciously, she moved her fingertips to her left wrist, pressing down on the spot Darius knew her mark was hidden behind long sleeves. Then she got to her feet and swiped her bag off the chair. "We need to go talk to Cain."

"What?" Darius asked as he stood up, too. Thorn kept moving, so he frantically scooped up his papers. The Georgia stack slid off the top, sending a handful of articles fluttering to the ground. He swore as Gabe leaned around his chair to grab them. He glanced at the photograph from the flea market before handing it back over.

"Here you go," he said.

"Thanks," Darius said, throwing the pages back into his stack before he chased Thorn. He reached her right as she called the elevator. "Why do we need to see Cain?"

"Because he'll know if Envy's taken a new host," Thorn said. "And if it hasn't, there are other things I need to ask him."

"Can't we just call him?"

Thorn threw Darius a humored smile. "He'll want a visit."

Landscape flashed by as Darius sat in the back of a rented SUV with Jacob Locke behind the wheel. The noon sun sat high above green fields and full, flowery trees. Jacob refused to let them roll down the windows, but Darius could almost imagine what the full-bloom fragrance of spring smelled like just beyond the glass.

"Turn here," Abraham said from Darius's left.

"I remember the way," Jacob snapped.

Darius glanced at Abraham to see his cheeks fill with a breath of exasperated air. In the distance, Cain Guttuso's ghost of a house looked down at them from the top of a long, unpaved driveway.

"Thanks for driving, Jacob," Lina said gently. She sat shotgun and reached across the center console to grab Jacob's shoulder. His fingers were so tight on the wheel that his knuckles shone pale against his skin. At Lina's touch, they relaxed, and he grumbled something Darius took as a variation of "you're welcome."

In light of their vehicle situation, nonessential trips outside the Underground had been postponed, which meant Lina and Abraham hadn't been permitted their weekly visits to the Martyrs Memorial Garden. When they'd learned about Thorn and Darius's business here, they'd tagged along for the ride—all for the sake of visiting the dead.

Moments later, their car turned up the driveway, and Cain's house loomed over them. White paint chipped free in massive flakes around dusty trim, and several shingles from the roof had blown off in a recent storm, littering the drive like breadcrumbs. It was modest and unassuming, but behind the tall, wooden perimeter fence, Cain had a garden full of graves.

"All right," Lina said, a bittersweet lightness to her voice, as Jacob parked outside the faded garage doors. She turned around in her seat and smiled at the three of them. "We're here."

Jacob cut the engine, and Abraham stepped out, his loafers crunching bits of shingle into the gravel. Darius looked up at the house again as a face peered out from the living room window. The moment Darius noticed it, it disappeared in a fluttering of sage curtains. He suddenly felt nauseous. He hadn't been here since Eva's burial, and frankly, he hadn't intended to return so soon.

Thorn's voice cut through his fog. "Jones?"

Darius glanced back to see her waiting for him to move so she could get out. Her brows, though, were drawn together perceptively. Darius unbuckled his belt, opened the car, and leapt out.

"Sorry," he said. Thorn pulled the lever, folded the seat forward, and climbed out of the vehicle. Somehow, she made even this awkward movement look graceful. As she stood to her full height, the screen door to Cain's house creaked.

"Good afternoon," Cain's silky voice crooned from his front porch.

Before Darius turned around, Cain's Familiar, a beautiful, brown tabby, was standing by his feet, staring up at him with bright, orange eyes. He looked up to find Cain watching him over the top of Lina, Abraham, and Jacob's heads. The old Forgotten Sin had clearly put himself together. His salt-and-pepper hair was longer than the last time Darius had seen him, and he'd styled it handsomely away from his face. He had a freshly-ironed, white v-neck shirt half-tucked into the waistband of slim slacks, and even his leather shoes looked shined. Cain caught Darius's eye, smiled, and raised a glass of wine in welcome. His teeth were crowded and his lips lightly stained from merlot. Darius provided an awkward wave, and Cain looked back to the others at last. "Lina, my dear. Abraham. And Jacob, my, how long has it been?"

Cain held out a hand, which Jacob watched with leery eyes. He quickly grabbed Cain's fingers, gave a hard shake, and returned his clenched fists to the front pocket of his sweatshirt. Cain's smile tightened upon his face as he bowed his head.

"It's so good to see you again, Cain," Lina said, smiling as she climbed the steps and put an affectionate hand on his forearm. "I'm sorry it's been so long. With everything happening at the Underground…"

Cain waved her worries away with a delicate flick of his wrist. "I understand," he said, grabbing Lina's fingers in his and raising them to his lips. "I'm sure you all have your hands *very* full down there."

Abraham let out a loose laugh. "Like you wouldn't believe."

Cain's eyes crinkled up in an indulgent smile, but he said nothing else as the group filed past him and into the house. He looked back toward Darius again, who glanced at Thorn. She'd slipped away from him and was leaning against the back of the rental car, a smoldering cigarette sending ribbons of smoke into the air. Darius sighed and walked up to the porch. Cain was waiting there for him, one hand clutching his wine glass while the fingers of the other tapped anxiously against it.

"Darius," the Forgotten Envy said as soon as Darius hit the top step. He reached out, thought better of it, and returned to his glass. "It's a pleasure to see you again."

Darius smiled and extended his own hand, which Cain took gratefully. Tension loosened across the man's shoulders, and his grin became more natural. It wasn't Cain's fault that Darius's Virtue made the void in his chest feel full, and though it was uncomfortable, Darius made a conscious effort not to let it affect how he treated him.

"Thanks for agreeing to help us," he said, gesturing over his shoulder to Thorn. He glanced back and, to his surprise, found Cain's cat had not followed him up the stairs. Crescendo perched on top of the rental car above Thorn's head. Darius frowned as Cain cleared his throat.

"You are very welcome," Cain said. "Please, come in. Make yourself at home. There is wine in the kitchen…"

He opened his screen door, beckoning Darius inside, but

when Darius walked through, Cain didn't follow. Darius waited in the doorway, watching as Cain approached Thorn's side. The two of them exchanged a few quiet words Darius couldn't hear, and then…

Then Thorn hugged him.

She wrapped her arms around Cain's shoulders in a familiar, comfortable embrace. The hard lines of her face relaxed, and her body shook in a deep, genuine laugh. Sparkie crawled from Thorn's satchel and leapt up, bounding in excited circles around Crescendo. The cat followed his movement with bright eyes, his tail flicking.

For a second, Darius stood, surprised. He hadn't known Thorn and Cain were close, and suddenly he felt like he was lingering in a moment that didn't belong to him.

Darius walked through Cain's living room and into the kitchen. Unsurprisingly, the drying rack beside the sink was full of stemmed wine glasses and nothing else. Darius grabbed one and filled it from the tap just as the screen door creaked open again.

"I have regular cups in the cabinet," Cain's voice hummed from the hall. Darius glanced back to see him standing with one hip propped against the doorframe. His lips turned into an amused smile as he brought his wine back to them.

"You don't mind?" Darius asked. Cain shook his head, smile widening, as he strode into the room. He took a seat at an old table by the window. The dusty blinds were closed, but the afternoon sun beat down on them enough to illuminate the room in soft, warm light. Darius took a sip of his water, which felt strangely imbalanced in the wine glass, and sat across from Cain. Thorn walked into the kitchen and helped herself to a whiskey tumbler and a bottle of scotch. She smoothly poured herself three fingers' worth, swirled the amber liquid, and tilted a splash into her mouth. At last, she came around to the table and pulled out a chair beside Darius.

"So," she began, but Cain held up a hand immediately.

"This man isn't Envy," he said, passing Thorn a teasing, offended look. "And, I must say, I am *hurt* that you think I wouldn't tell you as soon as I sensed the Sin had taken a new host."

Thorn raised her brows and lifted her drink to her lips while Cain's eyes glittered. Darius was struck with the immediate thought that this whole damned ordeal could have been an email, but he just placed his glass on the table and asked, "You're sure?" A relieved, almost guilty knot wrapped itself around his windpipe.

Cain looked him over quietly before he nodded. "Certain," he said. "Envy hasn't used its Influence."

Darius frowned. "Isn't it possible that it repossessed and hasn't used Influence yet?"

Cain gave a wry, permissive smile. "Possible, but unlikely. The article was written over seven months ago, and very few Sins have the restraint to go so long without it. Besides that, there are other hints. The location, for one. Why in the world would Envy choose a host so far from where it already has power? There are also the scars."

Darius shook his head, confused, but Thorn's eyes narrowed in a sharp, cold motion. "Scars?" she repeated. "What scars?"

"On his wrist," Cain said. He set his wine down, grabbed his phone from his pocket, and scrolled through it. "When you told me about the picture, I took the liberty of searching for it myself. It was difficult to find… some tiny publication last *July*… Ah, here it is."

He pulled up the article and laid his device on the table. The photograph was much crisper than the black and white printout Darius and Thorn had seen, and while it was still somewhat out of focus in the background, it was unmistakable. In color, Darius could see the black mark more clearly against the man's warm, umber skin. Where the *Peccostium* itself was smooth and unmarked, thick, fibrous lines cut across it like someone had come at it with a blade.

Darius glanced at Thorn's left forearm, which she

reflexively pulled beneath the table. She didn't look at Darius, but Sparkie peered at him from behind her veil of dark hair from his spot on her shoulder. Darius quickly focused back on Cain.

"What do scars have to do with anything?" he asked.

A cloudy pause filled the kitchen. Cain looked between Thorn and Darius before he sighed, got to his feet, and stepped his right foot onto his chair. Darius leaned around the table as Cain rolled his pant leg up and pulled the sock down, revealing his *Peccostium*. The mark sat on a circle of smooth skin surrounded by brutal, pocked scarring.

"When the *Peccostium* is damaged severely enough," Cain stated, "it disrupts our link to the Sin. Not enough to free us, unfortunately, which is what most of us were attempting to do, but enough to temporarily interfere with our abilities. Naturally, this includes our healing powers, and we're often left with scars to remind us what a positively *stupid* thing we did."

His face fell, his bright eyes duller than usual. Even Thorn seemed unusually cold. Darius glanced at her as Cain pushed his pant leg back down, but she didn't meet his eyes. Her fingers tightened against her glass, rigid and bone white.

"I'm sorry," Darius said, but Cain took his seat again and silenced Darius with a wave.

"In all my years, I have never seen scarring like this on a Sin," Cain said, lifting his wine again. If Darius wasn't mistaken, his hand was shaky. "But I *have* seen it on many of us. *Oblitus Peccatum* may not be human, but we are not without human failings."

"How many Forgotten Sins have you met?" Darius asked.

Cain smiled sadly. "Dozens throughout the centuries. Most came and went, but occasionally we stuck together. The original Martyr founders were all Forgotten Sins, in fact. There were six of us then."

Darius frowned. "What happened to them?"

"Wrath," Thorn stated plainly, and she took a sip of

scotch. Her eyes glistened with a mixture of fury and remorse.

"It doesn't matter," Cain said. "Now, it seems, we may
have stumbled upon a new one. I assume you plan on paying him a visit?"

Thorn nodded. "Do you want to come? This is the first
time I've ever had to explain this kind of shit to a new Forgotten Sin, and I could use the help."

Darius's eyes widened, and he suddenly understood why
they'd driven out here. Cain seemed to genuinely consider it
for a moment before he wrinkled his nose and shook his
head, attempting a smile. "Thank you, but no. That's not
where I belong anymore. Besides, who would tend to my
garden?"

"Any insights, then?" Thorn asked as she leaned forward, clutching her scotch with two hands.

Cain sighed. "He's most likely confused, but he is probably over a century old, considering we've kept close track
of the Sins' lost hosts over the last hundred or so years, and
he hasn't come to our attention until now. He's had time to
accept what life's done to him, even if he doesn't understand
it."

Thorn shook her head. "How do you know that?"

Cain chuckled. "My dear, did you even look into the
man?"

He winked at her, and Darius saw the familiarity between
them again. Cain's expression was kind and warm. Thorn's
face relaxed, and she raised a brow, challenging him to continue.

"Well, *I* did," he said with a dramatic drawl. "The box
he's carrying has a name on it. You see?" He indicated the
phone. *"Reflection Farms"* was stenciled across the wood slats
on the crate the man was holding on his shoulder. "I dug
into this little farm, which was a tedious affair, I might add.
They're very private. I could only find an address, a single
phone number, and a handful of articles referencing local
markets around Central Georgia. He clearly wants to keep a

low profile. I'm sure he will be *very* curious about you."

Thorn slowly nodded. "So, just tell him everything?"

Cain's smile flickered. "That has always been *my* philosophy," he said. Then he downed the rest of his wine in one smooth gulp.

"That's easy enough," Thorn said.

"Isn't it?" Cain stood and walked back into the kitchen. He grabbed a half-full bottle off the windowsill and pried the cork off. "When are you going?"

"I'm not sure," Thorn said. "I have a meeting with Alan when we get back to the Underground."

The muscles along Cain's jaw tightened. He poured the wine until the bottle was empty and his glass was full to the brim. "Splendid. I won't be keeping you, then, but—" he cleared his throat and turned to Thorn just as Darius brought his water to his lips "—I did gather flowers for Donovan this morning. If you would rather not…"

Darius choked, coughing into the back of his fist, and looked to Thorn. The last time he'd heard anything about her son was when the two of them talked by his gravestone after Teresa had died. Since then, it was as if Donovan Rose had never existed. Now, though, when Darius watched her, all he saw was the familiar pain of a mother who had lost more than just a part of her soul—she'd lost the whole damned thing.

"I would," she said. Her deep voice constricted with the tiniest emotion, and Sparkie disappeared down the back of her tank top as she stood.

Cain nodded as he came around the island and opened the door. Thorn poured the rest of her scotch down her throat with the same smoothness she'd poured it from the bottle. Then she set the glass onto the table and strode outside. Cain turned to Darius, who was still sitting, dumbfounded.

"I gathered enough for your family, as well," he said. Darius's heart clenched with bittersweet gratitude. He didn't know what to say. So he said nothing as he got to his feet and followed Cain onto the back deck.

Thorn had already disappeared around the corner to the side of the house where Donovan Rose's headstone stood alone. A modest collection of freshly picked flowers laid across a weathered patio table. A few bundles had been taken already: one for Donovan and another for Stella. Darius could feel Lina, Abraham, and Jacob through the lush foliage of Cain's estate, their warm energies the only sign of human life in this stunning boneyard.

Crescendo trilled at his feet, and Darius jumped. The Familiar wound his way around Darius's ankles once, his lamp-like eyes bright and knowing, before he pranced over to Cain, who had grabbed the remaining flowers up in one arm. He gestured his head toward the path. Darius followed him, and as they disappeared into the trees, he cast one final look back. From here, he could barely make Thorn out. She stood, a gloomy shadow against the greenery, with one hand laid across her son's name.

"Hey, Cain," Darius asked, spinning around again. The Forgotten Sin glanced over his shoulder. "Did you know Donovan?"

"Know him?" Cain repeated, and his voice trailed off. "I *adored* him."

They made their way down the path. The trees were in full bloom—a dazzling mosaic of pale purple, snow white, and vibrant magenta flowers cast the walking path in vivid light. The first time Darius had come to the Martyrs Memorial Garden, shortly after the Sins had decimated his orphanage, it was autumn. Cain had lamented then that Darius wasn't there in the spring. Now, he understood why.

"Do you want to talk about it?" Darius murmured.

Cain paused, pain etched into the lines of his face, and Darius thought for a moment the topic was too tender to touch. Then, the old Forgotten Envy let out a sigh.

"Thorn joined the Martyrs several years after she escaped possession," he said. His voice felt loud in the stillness around them. Crisp and clean like spring itself.

"Donovan was not even a year old. Wrath had killed his father, and Thorn knew the only place she could safely raise her son was with us. Of course, 'safe' is a relative term, especially within the Martyrs…"

A bite stung Cain's words. Darius watched him for a moment before he asked, "What was he like?"

"In a word? Remarkable. From the minute that little boy walked into the Underground, he had me wrapped around his finger. He was endlessly curious, joyous… irenic to a fault. His giggling filled the whole courtyard with music." Cain's lips pinched up in a somber smile. "Uncle Cain, he called me, and he knew if he asked Uncle Cain for something, I was powerless to say no. I would have done anything for that child." His voice tightened, and he took a slow breath. "I would have died for him."

More silence. Cain stared down the path, his bright eyes glistening, as they passed by a small pond. Darius glanced down as a turtle surfaced in the water, its beady eyes and tiny nostrils visible for only a second before it dove down again. "Is that why you left the Martyrs?" he asked. "Because Donovan died?"

"No," Cain said, shaking his head. "I left, oh, a decade or so before. Let's just say there was some… conflict… within the Martyr leadership about how things should be run." Darius opened his mouth to ask more, but Cain must have anticipated him because he quickly went on. "Donovan's death *is*, however, why I returned. Before Donovan, Martyr dead were left behind, unceremoniously laid to rest in unmarked graves by the city. I couldn't bear the idea of my sweet, little—"

His voice cracked. Cain cleared his throat and shook his head.

"Yes," he said after a tense, quiet moment. "I knew Donovan. After six and a half centuries on this massive, spinning rock, I have met thousands of people. Tens of thousands. Only a handful of them made a lasting impression on me… Donovan Rose was one of them. He has been gone for nearly seventy years, and sometimes, it feels like we lost him just yesterday."

At last, they rounded a final bend to where the trees opened to a small glade. In the center of the grassy area, a beautiful gazebo stood amongst blossoming maples, their gray bark and yellow-green flowers highlighting the ashen wood. For a moment, Darius felt like he was inside one of the storybooks he used to read to the kids at the orphanage. Cain led him up the stepping stones to the structure. Thirteen trees surrounded it, while four lined this path now. These were newer. Planted in the last six months.

When Saul, Juniper, Lindsey, and Eva had been laid to rest. Darius paused and touched one of the slender, woody trunks, and he wondered…

Would he still mourn them when his whole life felt empty the way Cain and Thorn mourned Donovan?

———

Alan sat behind his desk, a pair of glasses perched at the end of his long, sharp nose as he read the report Thorn had set down moments before. She was situated in one of the two cushioned chairs he kept for guests, her arms crossed, foot tapping impatiently on the plush, burgundy carpet while Sparkie kneaded the exposed skin on her shoulder. The room around her felt so distinctly *"Alan"* that it was almost suffocating. Proper, professional, and put together. All the books, artifacts, and other timeless paraphernalia the six Martyr founders had gathered in their combined thousands of years of life were collected here. Thorn's eyes passed over them.

She wished Alan would pack this shit away and leave the past in the past. Sometimes, she wondered if he put it on display to cope with his guilt—to honor the fallen Forgotten Sins Wrath had cut down when they tried to free Thorn from its grasp. Her jaw tightened.

Alan had been willing to sacrifice too much, and this was

all just a constant fucking reminder of the ocean of blood she'd spilled. She was drowning in it.

"Cain is certain this Forgotten Sin isn't a risk?" Alan asked, drawing Thorn's attention. He frowned behind his goatee as his eyes darted up to her.

"He didn't seem concerned," she said. "He thinks he's laying low."

Alan nodded slowly. "I suppose he would know. He is much more versed in this than I am…"

His voice drifted off, and Thorn's foot stopped tapping. Alan didn't look up at her, but the crease between his eyebrows drew closer. While Cain had brought all the founders together, Alan had only ever helped with one Forgotten Sin: Thorn herself. The memory of that night made her hollow chest feel emptier. The pain. The terror. The leap, and regretting that leap every second of the fall until she crashed against a body of water as solid as stone—

Thorn shook her head and glowered down at the ground. Suddenly, she felt like she was underwater again, her lungs somehow full and empty all at once as she sank into the dark.

"I expect he's going to ask a ton of questions," she said. When Cain had dragged her out of the East River and breathed the life back into her, that's what she had done.

"If he has not left," Alan stated, removing his glasses and putting them on the desk. Rae was sitting, still as a statue, to his right. The wolf's keen, blue eyes watched Thorn intently. "Forgotten Sins are often on the move. Otherwise, they may be exposed as immortal."

He had a point, she realized. God, she probably needed to disappear soon, too. Forge a new life. A new name. Finally retire the moniker Mackenzie had so happily given her. Teagan Love was one of the longest-lasting aliases Thorn had at this point. As much as she hated the name, she'd lose a lot when she gave it up.

"How do you plan on traveling?" Alan asked.

"By car. After the Sins found us in Washington State,

I'm not taking chances on a flight."

Alan nodded. "When do you plan on leaving?"

"As soon as I can," Thorn said. "On the drive back from Cain's, Lina and I talked about Friday, but I'd like to bump it a day or two earlier."

Alan frowned. "And you talked with Miss Brooks because you want Mr. Waters and Mr. Wolfe to do reconnaissance for potential Virtues in the area, correct?"

"Yes," Thorn said, straightening in her chair. The look on Alan's face was telling, like he had a point he was waiting to make. She gestured at the paper he'd just put down. "It was in the report."

"So I read," Alan said. "What your report does *not* say is that you want Darius to go, as well."

Thorn's teeth clenched together. A hot flush rushed to her face.

"How did you know?" she asked.

"I know *you*," Alan stated.

Her fingers tightened against her biceps. "Let's just get to the part where you tell me it's a bad idea."

"It is *not* a bad idea," Alan said, his voice level. "You bring up some fine points. Mr. Wolfe did collect a decent number of leads in central Georgia, and Darius himself felt hopeful about some of them. It makes sense to spend time looking for a Virtue there. Logically, Darius should be involved."

Thorn didn't speak right away. She watched Alan with narrow, suspicious eyes.

"Right," she said, waiting for the trap to fall.

Alan considered her a moment longer. "Seeing as you did not put this request in your *public* report, I presume you have not asked Darius yet?"

Thorn paused. Then, she shook her head. Alan frowned. "Why not?"

"I thought you'd deny it," Thorn said. She pried her arms away from her chest and pushed her fingertips against the sides of her nose. "I didn't want to get him worked up if it didn't matter."

Alan watched her, his gaze steady, piercing, and curious. Thorn stared back, not willing to be the one who backed down first, but there was a reason Alan's Familiar was a damned wolf. The man was borderline unshakable. Thorn was about to open her mouth to defend her reasoning further when he finally spoke again.

"I worry about him," he said at last. A shocking rush of relief made Thorn blink. "Both Miss McKay and Miss Brooks have expressed concern for his well-being. I suspect you feel the same?"

"Yeah," was all she managed to spit out at first. "He took Eva's death hard."

Alan slowly nodded. "Some losses are more difficult than others," he said. "He will recover in time. Until then, giving him a break from the Underground may be to his benefit. Get your affairs sorted and your units tasked out. My only stipulation would be that Darius is not left without a guard. Seeing as Mr. Wolfe and Mr. Waters have not yet passed their TAC assessments, that means he is in your charge."

Thorn wasn't sure what to do with herself for a moment. She'd been so ready to fight that she just sat there, stunned. This feeling was unfamiliar. At last, she got to her feet.

"Sounds good," she said as she turned to leave the room. At the door, she paused. Alan had returned to the various paperwork on his desk, his reading glasses in place again. Thorn felt a surge of emotion for him. Of gratefulness at his support and guilt that she didn't always anticipate it.

"Thank you," she said.

He looked up and smiled. "Of course."

Throughout all they'd gone through together, throughout the bickering and disagreements and hurt feelings, Alan was the one consistent thing in Thorn's life—the only person who was still there when she woke up from being a monster. Every time she'd woken up.

CHAPTER ELEVEN

Georgia's sweltering, humid air felt like being dunked in a vat of hot soup. After nearly eleven hours on the road, their rental car's air conditioning started to fail. Darius pulled at the neckline of his shirt as he watched the landscape roll by on a rippling tide of thick trees and smooth farmland. "How much further do we have to go?"

"We just passed Sandersville," Thorn said. Sparkie wedged between the nape of her neck and her headrest and poked his face through her hair to watch him. "Reflection Farms is another ten, fifteen minutes. Fuck, I hate these rentals."

She toggled the controls. Air came out more forcefully but no cooler. She swore under her breath.

"Holly's close to figuring out how the Sins tracked our vehicles," Darius said. "Then we should be good to go."

"It might not matter." Thorn gave up on fixing the air and focused back on the road. "Now Chris wants to replace our fleet. Part of it, at least. Between creating a more secure registration system and acquiring new vehicles, it could be a while before we're back up and running."

Darius frowned. "Why does Chris want to replace them?"

"Because of Jeremiah," Thorn said.

A flash of memory made Darius's stomach flip. Gunshots bursting the window of their old SUV. Blood blossoming through Eva's shirt. Jeremiah Montgomery's energy blinking out. One of the last things Darius remembered was seeing the TAC director's lifeless body slumped over the steering wheel as their car veered into oncoming traffic. He took a deep breath and swallowed hard against his dry throat.

"The only fully fortified vehicles we had before were our specialized combat units," Thorn continued. "They're expensive to replace, so we didn't have as many, and we only sent them out on planned strikes. Now that we're seeing more Sin activity, though, Chris is fighting to make sure every single car in our lot has more than reinforced doors and framing. She wants extra munitions storage, AI navigation systems, bulletproof glass… They need to be invincible, especially if we're going to take Terrance Moore down."

The thought made Darius uneasy. He shifted in his seat. "How's that plan going?"

"It's… slow," Thorn said through a sigh. "I just want to see some fucking *movement*."

Darius let out a cold laugh. "Yeah, I know what you mean."

Thorn's keen eyes darted to his face before turning to the road again. She tried on a smile that didn't reach her eyes.

"Don't worry," she said. "We'll head up to Augusta to help Waters and Wolfe look for Virtues as soon as we're done here."

Darius's stomach churned, and he looked out his window, watching fields of young corn and freshly plowed earth fly by in silence. He didn't have the heart to tell her that wasn't what he'd meant. He hadn't wanted to go on this wild Virtue hunt in the first place. The Martyrs needed him more as a healer right now, and he wished he was back home training for his position on TAC.

"Hey." Thorn's voice drew his attention, and she stole a look at him while she drove. Her eyes were softer than he was used to. "You okay?"

"Just tired," Darius said, not lying. Not really. He ran his hands down his face, feeling the ache of fatigue in his muscles. "You're sure we should try to talk to this guy today?"

"Yes," Thorn said. Her grip tightened on the wheel. Darius watched her profile for a moment. Her back was straight, her mouth set into a hard line.

"Are you worried?" he asked.

Thorn shook her head, and the motion made a strand of hair fall out of the loose ponytail at the base of her skull. She pulled it behind her ear. "He's going to have a lot of questions," she said, "and I want to make sure I have enough time to answer them. Hell, I hope I *can* answer them."

She took a deep breath, and Sparkie disappeared down the back of her top. Darius opened his mouth to pry but decided against it. Instead, he took in the momentary quiet, the deceptive sense of peace, and looked out his window again. Tall trees lined the road, their branches overhanging it so much that he could hardly see the forest floor at their roots. When Thorn spoke a few minutes later, her voice was so sudden it made Darius jump in his seat.

"We must be getting close."

"What do you mean?" he asked.

She gestured her chin out his window. "Can't you feel them?"

Darius focused in the direction she'd indicated, and suddenly he realized the warmth he was picking up wasn't from the rental's grumbling air conditioner. It was people. Thorn pulled off the highway and stopped by a green cattle gate. A weathered sign dangled lazily from its bars.

"Reflection Farms," Thorn read out loud, and her eyes narrowed on the hand-scrawled line beneath the name. "*Where Broken Souls Reconnect With God.*" She turned to Darius, her frown deeper.

He shook his head. "A *Forgotten Sin* in a Christian community?"

"It's not what I was expecting, but it makes sense," Thorn murmured as she parked the car.

"What do you mean?"

"This man's got half a soul," Thorn said, opening the door and letting the heavy, Georgia air in. "A gnawing emptiness in his chest. Probably at least a few memories of the horrible shit he did before he escaped possession. Christianity promises forgiveness and redemption. All you've got to do is pray to the right god. I wish it were that simple."

Her voice gave way to a familiar, caustic silence. She shut the door behind her and walked around the car to open the gate so they could drive through. If Darius thought Thorn looked misplaced in a white sedan, it was nothing compared to how much this city woman stuck out in the woods. Her boots immediately attracted a fine layer of dust, and her black clothing and hair made her look like a smudge of ink splashed against a painting.

The drive from the road to the farm brought them by a pasture full of sheep, another with a handful of cattle, and crop fields boasting rows of young vegetables. They rumbled past a line of greenhouses so full of plants that the windows themselves were brightly colored in a splattering of greens, purples, and oranges smashed against the glass. Small, simple houses dotted their right, leading to a quaint community square with a single parking lot. Thorn pulled them beneath the shadow of the tallest building in the place: a simple, wooden structure with arched windows, a pointed steeple, and a cross carved across the doors. Darius's jaw tightened.

Sparkie slipped into Thorn's satchel as she and Darius stepped out of the vehicle and looked around. A mosaic of different people filled the square—young and old, heavy and small, with hair and skin and eye colors of every shade and tone. For a bittersweet moment, Darius was breathlessly reminded of the Williamsburg Street Market. Men and women from all walks of life working together for a common goal. Here, though, it wasn't about survival. It was about something less tangible—something more spiritual.

As they walked toward the church, people took notice of them. Everyone was dressed in the same modest style—simple trousers, flowing tops, and wide hats to protect them from the sun—and they offered warm smiles. A giggling swarm of barefoot and dirty-cheeked children chased a red squirrel along the side of the building. They stopped as soon as they turned the corner and saw Darius and Thorn standing there. The poor animal clambered up a nearby tree as the kids grinned and waved enthusiastically.

Darius was waving back when an energy behind him drew his attention. A woman came from a nearby shop, holding a basket of fruit against one hip. She was older than Darius, perhaps in her early forties. A silk scarf covered her braided hair, and her face was dark from working long hours in the sun. When she smiled, it was vibrant and welcoming, like a freshly bloomed flower on the first day of spring.

"Hello," she said earnestly, adjusting her basket to hold out a hand. They shook it; her palms were calloused and her grip strong. "Welcome to Reflection Farms! My name is Gloria. Are you here for the initiation service tonight?"

Darius glanced at Thorn, his brows raised, but Thorn just smiled at Gloria and shook her head. Whatever front Thorn put on for people who were not in the Underground came up like a mask. Even the pitch of her voice raised as she said, "I'm sorry, no. We're actually looking for someone, but I'm not sure he's still here. He's an old friend of mine, has a tattoo that matches this one..."

She grabbed her left glove, pulled it down, and exposed the *Peccostium*. Gloria looked it over with a curious frown. If Thorn's heavy scarring disturbed her, she didn't show it. "Oh, Leroy? He's our founder's husband! I believe he was putting things away in the old tractor barn. I can walk you down."

"Oh, no," Thorn insisted sweetly, pulling her glove back

on. She gestured to the basket in Gloria's arms. "You've got your hands full. We can manage on our own."

Gloria shook her head. "Don't be silly. It's a short walk. Give me just a moment to drop this off…"

She briskly walked away. When her back was turned, Darius frowned. "He's married? How does that work?"

"It doesn't."

Thorn's eyes darkened, and her mouth tightened into a fine line. Darius glanced at her, a little surprised, but she didn't meet his gaze. Gloria appeared again, brushing her hands on the front of her skirt.

"All right," she chirped. "Let's go find him, then."

Thorn graciously thanked her, showing no signs of the annoyance Darius knew she felt at being escorted, and the two of them followed Gloria back down the road.

"How do you know Leroy?" Gloria asked, glancing over her shoulder as Thorn strode up beside her.

"We shared the same group of friends," Thorn said smoothly, her cadence precise and practiced. Darius fell into step behind the two of them, his heels crunching on the dry soil beneath his feet as they walked.

"I wish I could say I'd heard of you," Gloria said without any indication that she caught onto the lie, "but he's a very private man. Doesn't talk about his time before coming to Reflection Farms much."

Thorn nodded as though that made perfect sense, and Darius supposed it did. She watched Gloria with a sharp, curious focus. "This is the last place I expected to find him," she said.

"I think this is the last place many of our residents expect to find themselves," Gloria said, and she laughed. "Reflection Farms is a refuge for the lost and broken. God has a way of leading them here when they need us most."

She cast Thorn and Darius a soulful look that made his stomach uneasy.

"How do you fix them?" he asked. Thorn's eyes darted back in a way that let Darius know he wasn't hiding his skepticism for this place as well as she was. He cleared his throat. "Er, help them? The lost and broken?"

Gloria's smile widened. "Reflection Farms is all about disconnecting and recharging. We've given up our material possessions, living purely off what we can grow or nurture here, and our needs are paid for by our work at markets all across the state. Our only link to the outside world is through traditional mail or, for emergencies, the phone in the church. This way, we get to focus on fostering our relationship with God without any distractions. We have healed hundreds of souls and helped people find a new purpose for living."

Though Thorn didn't move, Darius saw the distinct, irritated rustling of something inside her satchel. Out loud, she said, "That sounds incredible. How many people live here now?"

"We have forty-three residents today," Gloria said. Darius looked around. He could feel them mainly concentrated at the community center, but dots of hot energy peppered the fields. "Ten of us are here to stay, but the rest are only with us until they feel ready to go back into the world." She considered them again, her eyes gleaming. "We always have room for more."

She turned back to the path. Darius and Thorn shared a quick look behind her back.

From there, Gloria spoke less about the godly part of Reflection Farms and more about the work. She pointed out a community kitchen, outdoor dining areas, and storage facilities for all kinds of goods produced here. There were chicken coops, hay lofts, a small grove of olive trees, and a cluster of fertile greenhouses. She turned up a path between them, where Darius spotted an old, red barn jutting over the glass roofs.

"This is where we store our tools," Gloria said. "I'm sure Leroy is just inside."

But before Gloria took another step, she paused. Her expression shifted briefly, almost confused, and she closed her eyes. Then she let out a little groan and pressed her fingertips into her temples.

"Oh, *no*," she said. "I'm so sorry. I forgot I have rehearsal with Reverend Weston for tonight's service. Can you find your way from here?"

"I think we can manage," Thorn said with a smile. "Thank you."

"It's my pleasure. I hope to see more of you!"

Gloria beamed, turned away, and headed back up the road. Thorn waited until she was a good ten yards out before the smile died upon her lips with a sigh.

"Thank god. Let's go."

The barn was the oldest building Darius had seen on the property. The paint wilted along the planks, and the roof looked like it had seen one too many heavy rainfalls to survive another, but it was all still standing. He and Thorn stopped outside the door and took it in. Sparkie squeezed out from her satchel, scurried up to her shoulder, and launched himself skyward. When her Familiar was nothing but a dot in the clouds, Thorn glanced at Darius. "Ready?" He nodded, and she pulled the barn door open.

It groaned on old hinges, the metallic sound echoing through the hollow, wooden building like an antique instrument that hadn't been tuned. Darius squinted into the darkness. Beams of light from high windows cast long, yellow lines across the room, catching a golden fluttering of dust as it settled back to the ground. Thorn stepped inside and slowly looked from right to left. All Darius could see was a wall full of tools and a bright orange tractor.

"Hello?" he called.

Nothing. He and Thorn exchanged a look, and Darius shrugged.

"Maybe he left?"

"Maybe..." But Thorn's frown deepened, and she took another step into the building. She began to make her way around the side of the tractor, but Darius paused. There were too many dark corners his eyes hadn't adjusted to yet, and something felt off. "Or maybe we surprised him. He can't feel our—"

"Thorn, wait."

She had almost reached the back of the rig, and Darius's stomach felt sick. The hairs on his arms began to stand on end. She stared at him from across the room, and they listened. Silence. Then a shuffling by the window. Darius glanced at it, but Thorn didn't move. The sense of uneasiness grew… When Darius turned back, he saw something shifting in the darkness behind her. She seemed to sense it at the exact same moment. Her eyes widened as she turned around—

A man leapt from the shadows, driving a pitchfork into her stomach.

Thorn grabbed the fork the second it came at her, but she wasn't fast enough. Four hard, sharpened points slid into her flesh with a sickening *thch*, and Thorn gasped. The man was built like an ox—as tall as Darius but easily carrying fifty extra pounds of pure muscle. He tried to force the weapon further in as Thorn pushed against it. She had it by the two outer tines, and she held firm while he took a step forward. The muscles in her arms and shoulders hardened, and her legs widened in a braced stance as she tried to force the thing out, but her feet slid on the dirt floor. The Forgotten Sin snarled furiously and tried to twist it deeper. Thorn cried out.

And the sound of her voice froze Darius where he stood. His heart lodged in his throat, suffocating him, as memories of Eva assaulted his brain. The bullet. The blood. The way she screamed… Sparkie landed on him from above, but Darius hardly felt him—hardly had the sense of self to hear the man's next words.

"You!" he screamed. "You should be *dead!*"

He thrust the fork forward. Thorn gritted her teeth and let out a low, painful grunt as the force of it made her feet slide backward again. Her heels tore deep trenches through the earth. She pushed against the tool with everything she had, keeping the points from digging deeper. They were already embedded two inches into her gut.

"I know!" Thorn shouted back. Sparkie let out a harsh cry from Darius's shoulder, and the world rushed back at him, but he still couldn't move. *Why couldn't he move?*

"I shot you!" the man went on.

"I know!"

"In the *head!*"

"Goddamn it, *I know!*" Thorn yelled. "Clarke, if you would just—"

"Don't *call me that!*" The man shrieked, taking a step forward, forcing Thorn back another foot. Her back slammed against the wall. The inside of her mouth was coated in red.

"Christ, *Leroy!*" Thorn corrected frantically. "Leroy! I'm sorry! Fuck, I'm here to help you!"

"No!" Leroy growled. "You're here to finish the job!"

The Forgotten Sin hadn't even looked at Darius—his focus was entirely on the woman at the end of his pitchfork. His brown eyes filled with such a terrified loathing that Darius was sure he intended to murder her. She kept pushing against the tool, but with nowhere else to go, she started to lose. The tines slid another centimeter into her gut, and Thorn cried out again. Her eyes flashed to Darius.

And Darius ran to her. Sparkie fought against him, frantically digging his tiny claws into Darius's hair, using his wings to block his vision, but Darius swatted them back.

"Stop—STOP!" Darius yelled, and he raised his hands. "You don't want to do this."

Leroy's jaw clenched shut, and his eyes darted from Thorn to Darius to the animal on Darius's head. The loathing began to fade, but the terror didn't. His broad hands shook on the wooden handle.

"Are you like me?" Leroy asked. "Like *us?*" He twisted the fork again. Thorn gasped, and Darius's chest clenched desperately.

"No," Darius said, laying a hand on Thorn's shoulder. Her muscles were so rigid that they quivered under his touch. Sparkie quaked, too. He could feel the lizard's wings shivering against the nape of his neck. Now that Darius was this close, he could smell the metallic sweetness of Thorn's blood. His stomach felt sick. "I promise I'll explain, but you've got to stop. You don't want to hurt anyone."

His grip tightened on Thorn as he reached for the neck of the tool, just above where the wooden shaft met the fork. Her dark eyes drilled into Leroy's as she continued to push against the points digging into her abdomen, her teeth grinding together, her nostrils flaring. Leroy held on for a moment longer.

"If you try anything funny—"

"You'll fucking kill me," Thorn growled. "I got it."

Leroy nodded once, glanced at Darius, and stepped back, ripping the fork out. Sparkie shrieked as Thorn grunted and fell to her knees. She pressed her hands against her stomach; blood coated her pale fingers. Her Familiar practically fell off Darius's shoulder and into her lap as he knelt beside her. Leroy glowered at them before jamming the fork into the dirt floor so hard that the metal points bent.

"My house," he said. "You can clean up there."

Then he walked away. Thorn glared after him.

"Thorn, are you okay?"

Darius stood in the hallway of a tiny, one-bedroom rancher, his hands shoved deep in his pockets as he waited outside the bathroom door. As soon as Leroy had let them in, Thorn shut herself inside. The house was quiet except for the occasional sound of Thorn vomiting into the sink. It made Darius nervous. This whole damn situation did.

"C'mon," he said, reaching for the doorknob to find it still locked tight. "Let me in. I can help."

He glanced into the living room, where Leroy sat in an old armchair. The Forgotten Sin watched Darius with his arms crossed and mouth curled up in a sneer. Darius sighed and turned back to the door.

"Thorn—"

The lock clicked open, and Darius let out a breath of relief as he let himself in.

Thorn didn't seem to have moved. Her back was to him, and her hands braced on either side of a pedestal vanity. Sparkie was wrapped around the inside handle, and he fell to the floor in a heap as Darius shut the door behind him. "See," he said as he crouched down and picked the Familiar off the floor. Darius placed him on the back of the toilet tank, where he stumbled awkwardly. "Part of you wanted my help."

"Shut it, Jones," Thorn grumbled. She lurched forward and heaved a mouthful of red, syrupy acid into the sink. Darius quickly pulled back her hair, holding it behind her head as she wiped her mouth with the back of her hand. Her skin was clammy and broken out in cold sweat.

"What's going on?" Darius asked.

"This can happen when my stomach is punctured," Thorn said through a shaky breath. After a pause, she shook her head and stood a little straighter. "As it's healing, it fills with fucking blood, and then—"

Thorn's abdomen bucked again, sending her curling forward as another wave of nausea flooded through her. This time, there was more bile than blood in the slurry swirling down the sink.

"Fuck," Thorn breathed. She lowered herself onto her knees, resting her forehead against the cool, porcelain sink. When she was still for several seconds, Darius released her hair and sat on the floor beside her. Her lips were tinted with pink, and Darius noticed the wounds in her stomach were still bleeding. Her black tank top was saturated.

"You good?" Darius asked.

Thorn nodded.

"Then let's get you cleaned up."

For the next fifteen minutes, Thorn and Darius quietly

put her back together. Thorn removed her blood-soaked gloves and rolled her ruined shirt up to the base of her rib-cage. Darius winced. Four ragged, weeping puncture wounds dug so deep into her flat stomach they looked black at the center. Using an old, seemingly unused first aid kit they found in a cupboard, Thorn cleaned and dressed the injuries while Darius sat on the closed toilet seat lid and cut the gauze and tape for her. He was clumsy with this kind of healing. By the fourth one, Thorn was sick of waiting for him.

"You need practice," she said as she grabbed the gauze and took over. The other three wounds were already beginning to bleed through their bandaging.

"Or you could just not get yourself stabbed," Darius said.

Thorn raised a brow as she ripped the medical tape with her teeth. "Are you blaming the victim, Jones?"

He laughed as she secured the final gauze pad against her skin before she returned to the sink and started the tap. Using a white towel, she washed the blood away. Darius watched her.

"So," he said. "Who is he?"

Thorn glanced up in the mirror and met his eyes before her attention darted back to her work. She was clean now, and she pulled her top back over her stomach. He considered going back to the car to grab a new shirt for her, but he didn't want to leave her alone here, considering the man in the front room was the reason she was covered in blood in the first place.

"He *was* Jeremy Clarke," she said at last. "Gluttony's host back in the early 2020s. Alan killed him in April 2025. Or, at least, we assumed he had."

"I thought his name was Leroy?" Darius asked with a frown.

"It is now," Thorn said, a bitter sting in the words. "I'm sure he hated being called by the same name he had as a Sin. I fucking did."

Silence fell. Darius watched the side of Thorn's face as she wiped down the sink.

"And he *shot* you?"

"As Gluttony," Thorn said with a nod.

"Yeah, that's a story I'm gonna need to hear."

Thorn looked up at him. While the side of her mouth drew up in a smirk, there was no humor there.

"Another time," she said. "It's a long one, and we have other shit to deal with right now."

"Like Clarke—"

"Leroy," Thorn corrected sharply.

"Right, Leroy," Darius went on. "Are you ready to talk to him?"

Thorn turned around, took a deep breath, and threw the bloody washcloth into the trash. "Yeah. As long as the son of a bitch doesn't fucking stab me again."

CHAPTER TWELVE

"Explain," Leroy said as Thorn and Darius stepped into his living room. It was minimalistic in a way that made the Underground feel warm and inviting. The walls were bare besides a single wedding photo above the fireplace and painted an off-white that was somehow worse than being bright and blinding. Leroy's easy chair was positioned in front of the hearth, and the poker from the rack was currently sitting across his thighs. Thorn paused at the threshold, glaring at the iron rod before she focused on Leroy's face.

"Put it back," she said firmly.

Leroy's brows drew together over his dull, brown eyes. "No."

Sparkie's wings flared dangerously. He clutched Thorn's shirt, the length of his body and tail following the line of her shoulder blade. Thorn crossed her arms.

"If we can't talk like civilized people without weapons, then we're not talking."

"Fine," Leroy growled. "You can leave."

Though Darius's Virtue sense of danger had calmed down, Leroy was still wound tight and ready to snap. Thorn opened her mouth to speak again, but Darius gently touched her arm and stepped forward.

"If you wanted us to leave, you would have made us go a long time ago," he said, throwing Thorn a look and nodding in her direction. "And if you wanted to kill us, you would've tried already."

"I *did* try," Leroy said. His teeth ground together. "How did you find me?"

Thorn held out her left arm, fist closed, with the inside of her wrist facing the ceiling. Her *Peccostium* and all the scars around it opened up to the room. Leroy glanced at his own. "I saw it in a photograph," Thorn said. "I wasn't looking for *you*. I was looking for someone like you. Like me. To be honest, I thought you were dead, too."

"That other man shot me," Leroy said, like he just remembered it. Thorn nodded. Leroy took a slow, steady breath. "What do you mean like us? What in God's name *are* we?"

Thorn gestured to the poker still clenched in Leroy's palm without saying a word.

Silence. The dread in Darius's spine ebbed even further, and after a few moments, Leroy lifted the iron tool, shifted it behind his back, and hooked it onto the stand. He never looked away from Thorn.

"Okay," he said. "*Now* explain."

It took half an hour for Thorn to work through the phenomenon of Forgotten Sins. From the evil energies that make up the Sins themselves to the possession, from hosts being abandoned before death or after attempting to commit suicide, Thorn outlined everything she and Alan had explained to Darius over a year ago. She did not, to Darius's disappointment, discuss what had happened to Leroy.

And, while Thorn talked, Leroy didn't move. He didn't make comments, ask questions, or take his eyes off Thorn's face. When she finally quit speaking, he just continued to stare at her. Thorn stared back.

Darius, on the other hand, looked out the window, where he could see a squirrel climbing up an old oak tree, or at the photograph hung above the mantle. Leroy on his wedding day. His bride was much shorter than him and appeared to be at least fifteen years younger, but Darius knew it was more than that. He frowned and looked over the woman's pretty, brown face and dark eyes, wondering what she knew about the man she married.

When Leroy's deep, rough voice broke the silence a few moments later, it was so sudden that Darius almost jumped.

"So, I *was* possessed." He said it almost like a question but with a cadence of understanding—like finally having a suspicion confirmed after years of wondering. "Which one?"

"Gluttony," Thorn said. She and Darius were situated on a stiff, beige couch across from Leroy, and she leaned toward him, resting her arms on her knees.

"Can it get me again?" Leroy asked, this time with a hint of panic. "Will it come back for me?"

Thorn shook her head. "No. From what we've gathered, Sins can only attach to *uncorrupted* energy. Now that your soul has been tainted by a Sin, they can't get back in."

Leroy nodded slowly, but his expression didn't relax. The creases in his face spoke to decades of frowning. If Darius had to guess, his possession had been completed when he was in his late forties, forever freezing him at that age. He wondered what had made Jeremy Clarke so unhappy before Gluttony took him.

"And that's what you were trying to kill," Leroy said. "All those years ago? It wasn't me. It was never about me. It was that demon inside me."

Thorn nodded. "Destroying a Sin's host is hard," she said, "but freeing them is almost impossible. It might seem cold, but we don't try to rescue hosts. We try to kill them to halt the Sin's progress."

"Dying sure as hell beats being Satan's puppet," Leroy growled, and for the first time, he looked away from Thorn, down at his hands. They'd balled into fists again, and the *Peccostium* on his right wrist shifted as his muscles moved. In person, the scarring was more apparent. Deep slices. Three of them. Hard and desperate. Like he'd tried to carve the thing off only to find it growing back again.

"I agree," Thorn said, her voice low and somber. "Darius and I are part of an organization called the Martyrs, and our primary focus is weakening the Sins by eliminating their hosts."

Leroy cleared his throat and looked back at her. "From what I remember, you eliminated a lot of them all on your own."

Thorn's eyes darkened. "How much *do* you remember?" she asked.

"Not a lot," Leroy said with a sigh. "Bits and pieces, here and there. I lost almost eight years of my life. *Eight years.* I mostly remember the bad things. Really bad things." Leroy's voice faded for a moment, and he rubbed his eyes with the tips of his fingers. "And I remember *you.* You were hunting me."

Thorn's expression was a hard front of stoic coldness that didn't let out the light. Or the dark. Darius watched her, curious, but Thorn just nodded. "Some Forgotten Sins remember more than others," she said. "Consider it a blessing you lost those eight years."

"How long were you possessed?" Leroy asked her.

"Two decades," Thorn said. "By Wrath."

"You remember it?"

Thorn didn't respond right away, and when she did, her voice was quiet. "Almost everything."

Darius's eyes widened, and so did Leroy's. Thorn said nothing more, content to let the room feel as tense and painful as Darius was sure she felt. He opened his mouth to change the subject when something stopped him.

A *pull.*

A magnetic draw in the distance, tugging at his soul. His chest fluttered with a hope he didn't dare let himself believe in.

"Darius?"

Darius looked down. He was on his feet, but he didn't remember standing, and Thorn stared up at him from her spot on the couch. Leroy was standing, too, looking at the front door.

"I hope you're ready to tell that whole story again," he said. "My wife *knew* it had to be something like this…"

"Your wife knew?" Thorn repeated. She got up, and Darius grabbed her shoulder.

"Thorn," he murmured. He was only vaguely aware of Leroy now. The magnetic sensation was quickly drawing closer, and the closer it came, the more Darius ached to move toward it. His mouth broke open in a wide smile as Thorn stared at him, her striking, black eyes narrow. "There's a *Virtue* here."

Gravel crunched in the driveway outside. A car opened and then shut. Darius and Leroy stared at the door until it swung open.

A woman walked into the room. Darius stared at her, shocked, and she stared back. For a few precious seconds, she was all he could see. He was struck with the odd realization that, if not for the Virtuous pull drawing him to her, he never would have picked her out of a crowd. The woman was short, her silky black hair pulled neatly into a clip behind her head, and her khaki capris and burnt orange top made the deep, golden brown of her skin look rich and vibrant. As she watched him, her dark eyes glistened in reverence.

"You!" She breathed the word, walking right past Leroy as she came upon Darius and grabbed his hand in both of hers. Her touch was firm and comforting. "You're one of God's chosen, aren't you?"

A cold rush doused the excitement in Darius's chest, and he shook his head. "What? No." He glanced at Thorn. Her mouth had opened a sliver, astonishment written in the lines of her face.

The other Virtue's smile faltered a bit. "But I can sense it in you." Leroy stood behind her, gawking at Darius as though seeing him for what he was for the first time. "God's grace. You *must* feel it, too! It's bright and warm and… and…" She pulled one of her hands away from Darius's fingers and pressed her palm flat against her chest in the exact spot where her Virtue drew on Darius's.

"Magnetic?" he ventured.

The woman nodded, reinvigorated, as she gripped Darius even tighter. "Yes! Yes, exactly! Magnetic!" Her smile widened again, drawing the tip of her long nose down a little.

Darius let out a laugh. "Yeah, I feel it, too," he said. "But it's not God. I'm a Virtue. *You're* a Virtue."

The woman's eyes narrowed. "To live in virtue is to follow the principles He empowers us to live by," she insisted. "Whatever you call it—His grace, His gift, His *virtue*… It's all the same. He has blessed us. We can feel the souls of those around us—heal the sick and wounded!"

"I… yes," Darius stammered. "That's true—"

"Then why do you deny God's presence?" she asked, the knit between her brow tighter.

Darius stared at her, his mouth open. "Because I don't believe in God."

The veneration she'd had for him dissolved into confusion. She released Darius's hand and took a step back. "What do you mean you don't *believe* in God? Your gift is proof of his mercy!"

"None of this is about God."

Thorn's voice startled the woman, and she spun around like she just realized another person was in the room. Her eyes moved from the reptilian Familiar on Thorn's shoulder to the puncture marks tearing through her bloodied tank top before finally landing on Thorn's *Peccostium* and all the scars around it. She stepped back again, and her gaze snapped up to meet Thorn's eyes.

"You're—"

"A Forgotten Sin," Leroy said. He walked up to her and put his hands on her shoulders. She jumped a little at his touch before reaching up and placing her fingers on top of his. "Apparently. Samira, this is Thorn. I knew her from my time before… ah… well, you know. Can't say we were exactly friends…" He sent Thorn a hard look but didn't say more on the matter. "And this is Darius."

Leroy gestured a hand toward him, and Darius smiled awkwardly.

"So, you know about Leroy, and you know about your gifts? Your Virtue?" Thorn asked. A line of subtle panic tightened the words. When Samira nodded, Thorn gestured an open palm toward her. "Who else knows?"

Samira frowned. "Only our inner circle. There are just six of us. When my gift first manifested, I counseled with our reverend, who advised me not to practice openly outside of our community or to speak of it beyond our church walls. We did not want to draw the wrong crowd—people who crave power, not those who seek connection with God."

Thorn and Darius glanced at one another. That was probably the only reason they hadn't found her before—and the only reason she was still alive today. Thorn turned back to Samira. "How did you figure it out?"

"I'm sorry?"

"Virtues aren't born with power," Thorn said. "They don't know what they are or what they're capable of until they learn about and accept it. You've clearly done both." Thorn's eyes narrowed, confused. "How?"

Samira considered the question. "I was raised to be a woman of faith," she said at last. "But Leroy is the one who helped me discover God's plan for my life. Four years ago, he came to my farm for spiritual healing. Six months in, I learned about his condition."

"What condition?" Thorn pressed.

Samira blinked and shook her head. "His spirit has been broken," she said, holding her hand out graciously in Thorn's direction. "As I feel yours has been."

Thorn glanced up at Leroy, her frown deeper, but Darius caught a curious glint in her eye. "You couldn't feel that before you gained your power, though," Thorn said, turning back to Samira again. "How did you know about Leroy's spirit?"

"He told me that my presence was healing to him," Samira said. "I realized I was blessed with something greater than myself because I could fill his emptiness. I'm sure it's the same for you."

She gestured between Thorn and Darius, and a stone crashed into the pit of his stomach. He and Thorn shared a dark look before he turned to Samira. "You're Temperance, aren't you?"

Samira's mouth dropped open. "That's the name the Lord gave me, yes… How could you possibly know that?"

Leroy's hands tightened on his wife's shoulders, and he glowered at Thorn and Darius with a primal, protective wariness. It was more than protective. It was almost possessive. And Darius understood why now.

Because Samira's Virtue made Leroy feel whole again—and she was the only one in the world who could.

***

The kitchen table was only large enough for two people, and the women took the chairs. Leroy seemed uncomfortable with their closeness. He positioned himself right behind Samira and watched Thorn like she was an aggressive dog without a muzzle.

Darius stood off to the side, leaning against the countertop with his arms crossed as he looked around. Like the living room, this one was bland and uninviting. The only "decor" was a map of central Georgia, a calendar depicting religious stories, and a single, simple cross hanging above the window. Darius frowned at it.

"When the Sins possess a host, they rip their soul to pieces," Thorn was saying. Darius turned back to see her arched over the table, her bare hands clasped on the oak surface. "It's ejected from the body, and the Sin moves in.

That displaced energy hovers around the host, trying to get back in, but it can't. When someone is possessed by a Sin, you can feel that energy as a false aura."

Like Leroy, Samira listened to Thorn explain Virtues, Sins, and Forgotten Sins in silence. While they did, Darius couldn't help but watch Samira, and a lightness fluttered through his chest.

He couldn't believe they'd found her.

The new Virtue's lips pressed together while Thorn's rich voice filled the space in a consistent, almost hypnotic cadence. As Thorn got into what happened to abandoned hosts, Samira's pretty eyes glistened sadly. Leroy placed his strong hands on her shoulders.

"And when the Sin leaves, the ejected soul just dies off?" Samira asked, wiping tears away with her knuckles before she reached across her chest and gripped her husband's fingers. "I can't feel Leroy's soul at all, so it's... it's just gone?"

Thorn shook her head. "No. It's been pulled together into a physical form. A Familiar. Like this." Sparkie, still clinging to Thorn's back, poked his head out at the crook of her neck. Samira frowned, and Thorn went on. "Most Familiars are more ordinary. Mine is like this because—"

"You have a Familiar?" Samira asked abruptly, cutting Thorn off as she spun toward Leroy. To anyone else, Thorn's face may have seemed inscrutable, but Darius saw her eyes widen ever so slightly.

Leroy's mouth opened, then closed, then opened again, and he stammered, "I-I don't know. I guess I had one. Once. A little, furry thing—"

"You *had* one?"

Samira's brown cheeks darkened in a hot flush, and her lips pressed hard together. Thorn cleared her throat, and both Samira and Leroy turned back to her. "He didn't know what it was," Thorn defended. "It's common for Forgotten Sins to reject their Familiars for a while, especially if they're trying to live a normal life again. Our Familiars are our *souls*. They know us better than we know ourselves. If you're rejecting it, it's keeping its distance… Maybe even blocking the connection between you."

"They can do that?" Darius asked, taken aback. Thorn glanced at him, her expression heavy, and she nodded. Before Darius could say anything else, she faced Leroy again.

"Your Familiar is probably keeping close," she said, "waiting to be a part of your life again, when you're ready."

Leroy's mouth pressed together, and he nodded as he looked down at the top of Samira's head. She watched Thorn with an expression that blended horror and amazement.

"Can he ever become whole again?" she breathed.

"Not easily," Thorn said. "When the Sins leave, some of their corruption lingers and keeps us trapped. Our ejected human energy can't reconnect to the tainted energy inside that keeps us tied to the Sin's life force. We get the power but at the cost of our souls. That's why we feel that aching emptiness—" Thorn gestured up at Leroy with her right hand while her left pressed flat to the spot just between her lungs "—because we *are* empty."

Samira nodded and then shook her head so quickly that her hair began to fall from its clip. It cascaded over her shoulders in messy, black waves. "So, what brings it back together?"

Thorn glanced at Darius, and Samira did, too. He tried on a smile and said, "You do."

A restless pause shuddered through the kitchen as Samira's mouth dropped open. Leroy's brown eyes narrowed. "How?" he asked.

"You feel whole when she's around because of her Virtue. It's masking the emptiness," Thorn explained. "She doesn't have that effect on me. Neither does Darius, because they are not the Virtue that can free me. But Samira is Temperance, and you used to be Gluttony. Temperance is meant to destroy Gluttony, and if she does, the corruption in your soul will burn away. You'll be whole again."

Tears glistened in Samira's eyes, and she grinned so

broadly it pulled her nose up, too. "Really?"

Darius's smile widened, and he nodded. "Yeah. More than that, though. You'll wipe out all of the corruption Gluttony has been spreading. All his Programming. It's not just about helping your husband. You'd be helping the world."

Samira's head tilted back in a joyous laugh, but when she turned to Leroy, that joy softened. If possible, Leroy's eyes had grown even narrower.

"What's the catch?" he asked, crossing his arms. "There has to be a catch. She gotta die? Is killing Gluttony gonna kill her, too?"

All at once, Samira's smile shattered, and she spun to look at Thorn and Darius again. Darius's expression fell, and he took a deep breath. "No, but there is a cost. She'll have to give up her Virtue."

Another silence. This time, it was heavy and suffocating. At last, Samira said, in a tight voice, "My… Virtue?"

Darius nodded. "You'll lose your power and half of your soul. The emptiness Leroy feels when you're not around… you'll feel that. For the rest of your life."

That hung in the room for several long, aching moments. Darius didn't look away from Leroy and Samira, and out of the corner of his eye, he could tell Thorn was doing the same thing. Waiting. Wondering.

"Fuck this," Leroy murmured at last.

"Leroy!" Samira admonished, but he shook his head.

"You're telling me," he said, his voice rising, the muscles in his neck tense and rigid, as he paced between the hall and the table, "that for *me* to get my soul put back together, Samira has to give hers up? No." He shook his head. "No. No. NO. It's not worth it."

"Baby, I could destroy this Gluttony," Samira started, but Leroy threw his hands into the air.

"I don't *care* about Gluttony," he snarled before he turned toward Darius, causing a nervous tickle to run down his spine. Leroy kept raging. "I care about my *wife*. She is not selling her soul for mine. This emptiness is my hell—it's *hell*—and she doesn't deserve to live in it!"

Leroy stormed from the room, grumbling under his breath as he thundered down the hallway, turned a corner, and slammed a door behind him. Samira leapt to her feet.

"Excuse us for a few minutes," she muttered, pulling strands of her hair behind her ear as she stepped away. Darius tracked Samira's magnetic allure until he heard the door open and close again. Thorn sighed. She was still sitting, her elbows propped on the table in front of her while her steepled fingers pressed thoughtfully against her lips.

"What's wrong?" Darius asked as he took the chair across from her.

"This isn't working," Thorn murmured against her fingertips. "I'm just pissing him off."

"To be fair," Darius reasoned, leaning toward her. "I'm the one who pissed him off." He raised his brows and chanced a smile. Her lips parted in a quiet chuckle. Darius went on. "We can't hide the truth. It won't help."

Darius's smile faded, and he cleared his throat as he glanced down. Thorn's attention stayed on him. He could feel it, hot and pointed.

"I agree," Thorn said after a tense moment. Her voice filled with old bitterness, dredged to the surface. Darius looked up to her, finding her eyes hard and sincere. "We don't have any other choice, but fuck, I didn't want this to be like…"

Her voice drifted off, and she angrily pulled her lower lip between her teeth. Darius frowned.

"Like when *you* learned about being a Forgotten Sin?"

"After Cain explained what happened to me, I lost it," Thorn said. "I was only six hours out. I still hurt from the detachment. Every muscle, every bone, felt like it was on fire. I just wanted out, so I ran." She gazed over Darius's shoulder, down the hallway Samira and Leroy had disappeared into. "But Leroy's been a Forgotten Sin for almost seventy years. I was hoping he'd be sick of running."

"We did just tell him his wife has to tear herself to pieces for him to be whole again," Darius said. "That's hard to hear. Don't worry. They'll come around."

Thorn's brows furrowed. "How do you know?"

"Because she's a Virtue," Darius said, and his smile came back. "It's what we do."

Thorn nodded, but her eyes moved past him and went distant. The movement of Samira's Virtue made Darius turn around just as they heard the door open. Seconds later, she and Leroy appeared in the hallway, Samira leading the way while he absolutely towered behind her. His face was set into a stony determination, but Samira's eyes filled with quiet reserve. She looked at Thorn first, and when she turned to Darius, his heart sank.

He got to his feet, and Thorn snapped up with sharp, subtle aggression. She walked around the table to stand at Darius's side as Samira and Leroy stepped into the kitchen. The air steeped in tension that made Darius's stomach twist.

"I'm so sorry you've had to come all this way," Samira began, but Darius shook his head and held up his hands.

"You're staying here?" he asked. "Why?"

"This is where God has sent me," Samira said.

Darius's chest constricted even more. His lungs felt shallow and empty, and he swallowed through a tight, dry throat as he glanced at Leroy.

"Is this your decision," he asked, "or his?"

"It's *ours*," Samira said. Leroy came up behind her like a mountain. "My purpose is to help these people here."

"Help them?" Darius stammered. "Help them do *what*? Disconnect from the rest of the world? So they can live in this… this *fantasy* that everything is fine?"

"This isn't a fantasy," Samira defended, and while her voice shook, she held herself high. "It's a refuge! Reflection Farms is a place for the lost and broken to find meaning again. What we do *is important* for so much more than the family we've built. I've dedicated my life to them, and I can't leave. I've saved hundreds of people—"

"But you could save *millions*," Darius breathed. He

hadn't noticed how fast his heart was beating until he felt it pounding in his fists, erratic and furious. He was vaguely aware of a movement over his shoulder, but his focus was glued to Samira. Everything beyond her felt fuzzy and gray, like it didn't matter. None of it mattered.

"I'm sorry," Samira said again. Even her voice felt blurry. "Perhaps it is God's will for the next Temperance in the line to destroy Gluttony."

Darius's ears were ringing as he stared at Samira in disbelief. He reached up and pinched the bridge of his nose. "You think your *God* wants you to let this evil live in the world? I can't believe you can sit there and preach about kindness and compassion when you're asking us to wait another lifetime. Who knows how many more lifetimes? Most of us die before without ever knowing what we are!"

"Darius." Thorn's voice barely cut through. He shook his head and kept talking.

"What about all the people Gluttony is going to kill? All the lives it can destroy? What about your *husband?*" Darius held a hand out and took a step forward. Leroy put his palms on Samira's shoulders and glared at Darius. "He'll watch you die. He'll live *forever.* You don't even want to save *him?*"

"You don't know it would save me," Leroy snarled. "For all you know, destroying Gluttony will burn me up, too."

Darius shook his head. A hand wrapped around his forearm, but he pulled away. His mind filled with the faces of people he'd lost. Thad and the kids at the orphanage. Saul, Juniper, and Lindsay. Eva. People he could have saved—should have saved. How many countless others had died because Darius hadn't been there? And Samira didn't *want* to be there! A fluttering as something climbed onto Darius's shoulder. He shook his head. "What kind of god would expect you to choose this?"

"With all due respect," Samira said quietly, crossing her arms as though putting up a barrier between herself and Darius, "it's not our job to question what God asks of us. It's our job to follow the path he lays out. I'm sorry you don't understand."

"What I don't understand is how you're willing to let whole generations of people *suffer* because it's 'God's will,'" Darius exclaimed. "You're *wasting* your life. You're wasting your Virtue!" He threw his hands in the air. Leroy stepped around Samira and got in Darius's face. Sparkie spit furiously, snapping at Leroy's fingers as he tried to grab Darius by the shoulders.

Then Thorn was in front of him, and she shoved Leroy backward so roughly he almost stumbled over his own feet.

"That's enough," she commanded. Her deep voice boomed through the room and marshaled Darius's senses back into order. He stared, realizing now how close he'd come to Samira. She had backed up nearly to the wall, her eyes wide with hurt. Leroy stood in front of her, a tower of muscle and rage. Thorn squared up to him. Leroy had almost four inches on her, but Thorn's poise was unshakable. She didn't look away from Leroy as she said, "It's been a long day, and I think we all need some time to cool down. Can I come by again in the morning?"

That question had been directed at Samira, but Leroy answered. "No."

Thorn took a deep breath. The corners of her lips flared up dangerously.

"Fine. Then take this." She reached into her satchel and pulled out a red card and a pen. The card had nothing but a phone number, and Thorn scribbled something onto the back. "This is my number, and this is where we're staying tonight—that little motel right off the main highway. If you decide you want to talk, you know where to find me."

She held the card out. Leroy swiped it from her fingers, never breaking eye contact.

Without another word, Thorn grabbed Darius by the crook of his elbow and led him from the house. They moved through the kitchen, into the hallway, and Darius glanced over his shoulder to see Leroy open the trash bin by the back door and throw the card into it.

When they reached the road, Thorn released Darius's arm and swore loudly into the hot Georgia air. They walked to the car in silence, Thorn's anger emanating off her in waves. People didn't seem as happy to see them as they made their way out.

Thorn turned the car on, put it into reverse, and pulled out of the gravel parking lot. Hot, stale air poured from the vents as Darius stared out the window. A red squirrel perched on top of a nearby fence post and watched them drive off.

Suddenly, without warning, Sparkie let out a restrained growl. Darius turned around. The lizard was sitting on Thorn's shoulder, his wings frazzled behind him as his claws kneaded into her skin so hard it looked like he might puncture it. Thorn's fingers were tight on the wheel, her mouth a fine line of fury. Her black, half-empty eyes glistened with bitter regret.

CHAPTER THIRTEEN

Sandersville wasn't large enough to accommodate fancy lodging. The most they could hope for was a crappy motel, and the room they shared didn't have much beyond a tiny table in the corner with a single chair, a couple of lumpy beds, and a wall-mounted air conditioning unit with two settings: arctic wind or off.

A frigid gust from the AC hit Darius as he walked through the door. He paused, looking around the space with numb indifference before making his way to one of the double beds. As he sat down, Thorn slammed the door behind her and pulled open the curtains. Bright light from the setting sun blared through their window.

She grabbed her phone, hit a few icons, and held it to her ear.

"Waters," she said. She tossed her satchel onto the bed and turned back toward the window, a silhouette of rage as she braced one hand against the frame and stared outside. Sparkie leapt from her shoulder and tucked himself inside the bag.

"Yeah, we found him," Thorn said. "And a Virtue."

A cold stone formed in Darius's chest, and he drew his own phone out of his pocket just to give him something to do. Mackenzie's face stared up at him from his lock screen. Months ago, she'd replaced the default background with some silly selfie. Usually, it brightened Darius's day. Not now.

"Yes," Thorn went on. "The Virtue you and Wolfe are looking for. It's a long story."

The stone grew heavier. Darius took a deep breath to dislodge it, but it stuck stubbornly, almost painfully. His inbox was full of messages. Chris, confirming the date for their next one-on-one training session. Mackenzie, sending him funny videos of cats getting spooked by vegetables. Gabe, asking for advice on a meditation technique Darius covered last week. He didn't respond to any of them.

"No," Thorn stated. "There's no point in sticking around." She paced by the window, her figure blocking out the sun and darkening the room once. Twice. Three times. "Head out in the morning. We'll see you back at the Underground."

Thorn stopped pacing, and Darius glanced up. Her back was to him, but the tension in her spine extended all the way down her arms, and her fingers gripped her phone so tightly that Darius wondered if it would snap.

"They're not coming," Thorn said at last.

She went quiet for a moment. Darius's whole body felt cold and disconnected as he watched her shoulders rise and fall with a slow, silent sigh. She shook her head.

"Sounds good. Let me know when you leave."

Thorn hung up, tossed her phone onto the hideous, paisley duvet with a surprisingly hard *thump*, and ran her tongue across the bottom of her front teeth. Then, without warning, she slammed her open palm against the wall. The slap was sharp in the room. She pulled her fingers through her long, black hair and groaned.

"Fuck!"

Darius glanced down at the bed between them. Her shadow fell long across it, ending right at Darius's feet. Thorn's whole body heaved with hard, angry breathing.

Darius shook his head.

"I'm sorry," he said. "I fucked up."

Thorn's attention snapped to him, her jaw hard, brows drawn together. "No," she said softly. "You didn't."

"I was way out of line."

"She needed to hear it."

"I should've been nicer about it," Darius said. "Maybe then she *would have* heard it."

"She did." Thorn still stood across the room, but the tension in her shoulders began to let up. Sparkie peeked his head out from the opening in her satchel, his beady, black eyes moving to Darius. "Samira might not have listened, but she sure as fuck heard."

Darius nodded, but he didn't feel better. Did it matter that she heard him if she refused to do anything about it? If she was happy to live in her perfect little bubble while Gluttony killed hundreds of people in New York? Darius's stomach began to broil as he thought about Gabe DuPont and all the Programmed cops in the city hunting down the Martyrs and anyone unlucky enough to look like them.

"I don't get it," Darius grumbled.

Thorn shifted, and the light shone brighter as she moved away from the window. Even though she didn't have an energy he could feel, he sensed her closeness, her concern, as she drew up beside him.

"How the hell can she want to stay here now?" Darius went on. "How is she just... *okay* with letting this happen? With letting more people get hurt? How can she be so... *selfish?*"

Thorn didn't respond right away. For a few quiet moments, she and Darius watched each other. The sun dipped beneath distant tree lines and buildings, and shadows fell across the floor as Thorn finally shook her head.

"She's scared."

"Scared," Darius scoffed. He got to his feet, throwing his hands up. "Well, *I'm* scared, too! Scared we're going to lose this war because of people like this—people who won't step up and do what it takes. Gluttony is *killing* people, Thorn—"

"I know he is."

"—and we found the Virtue who can stop it forever." His heart pounded hard against his ribcage, like it was trying to break free. Thorn stood still as stone, her face statue-like in its stern expression. "She could do something *truly* god-like, but she won't. She *can't.* Leroy won't let her—"

"He's even more scared than she is."

"Only because he could lose the only thing that makes him feel whole."

Thorn's lips parted just enough for Darius to hear the soft brush of air she drew in.

"She's his *wife,*" Thorn said, a tinge of offense crackling like embers.

With a sigh, Darius shook his head. "Why are you defending them?" He tried to keep his tone more even now. "This isn't right—"

"I never said it was," Thorn snapped, raising her hand. "I'm saying I understand. At least, I understand Leroy. I *was* Leroy once. I might have been worse."

Darius shook his head and looked down at Thorn's palm. Her scars extended to its heel, and the *Peccostium* stood out as dark and crisp as fresh ink. Sparkie climbed out of her satchel, and he edged closer to them curiously. His shining, blue scales seemed somehow brighter framed by the orange duvet. He tilted his head at Darius, and Darius frowned.

"You rejected Sparkie like Leroy rejected his Familiar, didn't you?"

Thorn's jaw clenched, and her throat went rigid.

"For seven years," she said, her voice low and steady. "From the minute I escaped Wrath until I joined the Martyrs, and even after that, I didn't really accept him. Not until Donovan did. Fuck, Donovan is the one who *named* him. He was three."

Thorn looked at Sparkie and held out her hand. The

animal fidgeted on the bed, shifting from the right to the left, before he vaulted from it, flapped his wings once, and landed deftly on Thorn's arm. He scurried up to hide behind her hair. All Darius could see now was the lizard's long tail draping around the slender curve of her neck.

"It wasn't like Leroy, though," Thorn went on. "I knew what Sparkie was… What *we* were. Cain told me everything the night I got out."

"Then why did you reject him?" Darius asked.

"Because I didn't want to have anything to do with this war," Thorn said. "I didn't want to be a Martyr. I didn't want to fight the Sins. I didn't want *any* of it. I wanted to be normal. Just like Leroy."

The sunset was in full bloom now, sending a stunning array of orange and yellow light through the window. It cast Thorn's face in a harsh contrast—half dark, bruise-purple, and the other a vibrant and shining marigold. She shook her head.

"But we can't be normal. Leroy knows that. He's been a Forgotten Sin for almost seven decades. This isn't the first life he's built for himself, and it's only a matter of time before this one falls down around him, too. When it does, he knows who to call."

"He threw your card away," Darius mentioned, and to his surprise, Thorn smirked.

"I guess I'll have to drop off another one."

Darius chuckled and glanced down at his feet, suddenly aware of how tired he was. His legs felt weak, and his mind was weary. With a soft groan, he sat back on the bed and stared out the window. A streetlight had come to life at the corner, trying to shine through the last orange glow of day. The bed shifted as Thorn sat beside him.

"You know, I didn't even want to come on this trip," Darius admitted. He felt Thorn watching him as he looked down at his hands. His right thumb absently tapped against his fingertips, from pointer to pinky and back again, as he tried to ground himself. "I've been feeling so burned out by the Virtue hunt… Then we actually found one, and it went *so* badly."

Thorn nodded. "Today was shitty." Cars passed by on the road outside, their headlights flashing across her dark, thoughtful eyes. "When people are faced with hard situations, with hard truths… sometimes they make bad decisions. But Samira won't change her mind because we force her to. She has to come to it on her own."

Thorn reached across the space between them and caught his fingers. His tapping quieted within her tight, comforting grip.

"We're not done here," she said, leaning into him. Her body felt cool against his side. "We found her. That's half the battle. We have to look at today as a win, even if it didn't feel like one."

Darius glanced down at their hands. In the dark, Thorn's looked especially light inside his. He squeezed her gratefully. "You're right," he said. "Thanks."

Thorn's thin lips pulled into the shadow of a smile, but she quickly cleared her throat, released Darius, and got back to her feet.

"We haven't eaten all day," she said as she headed back across the room. Sparkie peered through Thorn's veil of dark hair and watched Darius as she turned on the lights. The sudden brightness was almost blinding. "Let's grab some dinner."

Then Thorn disappeared into the bathroom, and the door shut and locked with a click. Darius's shoulders relaxed. Somehow, the room felt warmer.

Thorn and Darius took turns showering and changing into comfortable clothes while they waited for their dinner to arrive, and now they were eating Chinese food in silence on the rough carpet at the foot of Darius's bed. A collection of opened paper boxes between them sent rich, savory smells into the air. Thorn had ordered an array of dishes: Kung Pao chicken, fried rice, chow mein, and a couple of things Darius didn't recognize. It didn't matter. It all made his mouth water and his stomach rumble. He opened his chopsticks as Thorn scooped some chow mein onto her plate. When he put them between his fingers, she paused.

"What are you doing?" she asked.

"Uh… eating?"

Thorn's brows pinched together, and she pointed at his chopsticks with her own. Her lips teased at a smirk. "Not holding those like *that*, you're not."

Darius let out a laugh. Thorn inched forward. "Pinch the bottom one with your thumb joint," she instructed, holding hers out to demonstrate. Darius did so. "And the other, in your fingertips. Yeah. Try that."

For a few graceless minutes, Thorn silently ate her meal while Darius managed to get exactly one piece of chicken into his mouth by finally stabbing it in frustration. He looked up at her and shrugged. Thorn shook her head, put down her plate, and held out a hand. "Give them here."

Darius dropped his chopsticks into Thorn's open palm and watched as she rolled a long strip of the wrapper into a tight cylinder. Then she pulled her dark hair out of its ponytail. It cascaded over her bare shoulders, and she flicked it out of her way with a smooth, elegant motion. With the paper and elastic band, Thorn fastened Darius's chopsticks together to create a hinge on one end. Her fingers moved quietly. She hadn't put her gloves back on, and her strong hands seemed more delicate than Darius was accustomed to. He was still watching them when Thorn held the chopsticks back out.

"Try that," she said, and her eyebrows raised. "Or give up and use a fork."

Darius snatched his chopsticks back with a grin. "Keep it up, and I'll stab *you* with a fork."

Thorn laughed. It was deep and rich. "Watch it," she said. "This time, I can stab back."

A chuckle grew in Darius's throat, but it died there as the memory of Thorn at the end of Leroy's pitchfork flashed in his mind. His stomach twisted at the thought of the blood staining her lips and dribbling into a bright, white sink. She glanced at him, her eyes still glittering with humor, but as soon as she saw the look on his face, hers fell.

Darius cleared his throat and focused back on his dinner. Thorn's trick worked perfectly, and he easily grabbed a piece of meat he no longer had the appetite to eat. He tried anyway, and it sat dense and tasteless in his mouth.

"I really thought he was going to kill you," Darius said after a moment. He considered Thorn from over his meal. She wasn't looking back. She focused on moving the rice around her plate as Sparkie fidgeted on her lap. Wrapped in his leathery, crimson wings, the lizard blended into the deep red fabric of her lounge pants, and as Darius continued to watch Thorn, the Familiar grew more restless. He unraveled himself and dove out of sight beneath her legs. At last, she nodded.

"He was trying to," she stated.

Darius put his dinner down and leaned forward, resting his forearms on his knees.

"What happened?"

Thorn stopped moving. Her left hand hovered over her meal, the chopsticks held tight in stiff, white fingers. She clenched her jaw and swallowed.

"He shot me," she said.

"I got that."

"In the head."

"Thorn—"

She sighed and dropped her plate back onto the ground so forcefully that rice flew off of it. Thorn closed her eyes and pressed her fingertips against them.

"Does it fucking matter? It was a long time ago."

"Right," Darius said. "Seventy years." Thorn moved her hands away from her face. The way her eyes sparkled with something closer to pain than anger made him think she knew what he was about to say. He took a deep breath and pulled his lips in between his teeth. "I talked to Cain about Donovan. That happened seventy years ago, too, didn't it?"

Thorn's expression became stony. She wrapped her arms around her chest, and for the first time since walking into this cold motel room, Darius saw goosebumps rise on her pale arms. She didn't look away from his eyes, her focus intense and piercing. After a moment, she said, "You wouldn't believe it was a coincidence, would you?"

Darius shook his head. Thorn shook hers, too, before she sharply turned away from him and glared at the carpet, stewing in whatever internalized torture she was reliving.

"I'm sorry," Darius said. "I shouldn't have—"

"Don't," Thorn said, holding up her hand. "You didn't do anything wrong. It's just…"

She gently bit her lower lip, and her eyes shifted around Darius's face, from his mouth to his eyes and back again, like she was looking for a clue there.

"Fuck, Darius," she said at last. "I don't want you to think I'm some kind of monster."

The cold shock of Thorn's openness stunned Darius for a moment. "I could never think you're a monster," he said. Thorn's face didn't shift, didn't show any signs that she believed him, so he leaned in even closer. "You said it yourself. Sometimes we make bad decisions—"

"Bad decisions don't include killing people," Thorn snapped.

"In the Martyrs, they might. People get hurt—"

"That's not what I said," she interrupted again. She pulled her knees up beneath her, and her fingers dug violently into her bicep. Sparkie darted behind Thorn's back. As her mouth tightened into a hot line, her nostrils flared dangerously. She didn't say anything else, but she didn't need to. It dawned on Darius, and his chest constricted—not out of horror, but because the subtle, terrified look in Thorn's dark eyes felt like a punch. He slowly nodded.

"What happened?" he asked again.

She stared at him for a few leaden moments. At last, she said, "The Sins captured my son. Tortured him… Then they killed him."

A pool of water brushed behind Thorn's eyelashes, and she furiously blinked them away.

"So, I decided to kill them, too," she said, her voice grinding with forced control, like two tectonic plates gnashed together. "After three months, Jeremy Clarke and Autumn Hunt were the only two left."

Darius's eyebrows went up. "You killed five Sins in three months?"

Thorn's shoulders went rigid. "Five Sins," she confirmed solemnly, "and ninety-two innocent people. Ninety-fucking-two."

The entire time she'd talked, Thorn hadn't looked away from Darius, and she didn't look away now. He held his ground. After a few seconds, the tension in her face relaxed a little. She pinched the inside of her cheek between her teeth.

"Simon Reed, the doctor in the Underground at the time, thought the whole thing was part of some violent psychosis episode," Thorn said as she uncrossed her arms, instead leaning onto them as she drew her knees closer to her chest. "Makes sense. I wasn't thinking clearly. I was so consumed with hurting the Sins that I wasn't thinking at all…"

She sighed and shook her head. "Anyway, Alan tracked me down while I was on this… this rampage. Right before I went for Gluttony. Thank god. That attack would have put my body count over one hundred people…" Her voice drifted off, and she stared in the distance behind Darius's head.

"What did Alan do?" Darius asked.

"He told me I was no better than Wrath," she scoffed. "And he was right. Focused on… *violence*, with such a blind disregard for human life…"

She paused and glanced out the window. The sky outside was black, but it glistened with stars Darius never saw in

New York City—a splattering of white, twinkling lights against a midnight canvas. Thorn watched them, her brows drawn together.

"When I was possessed, I was a *fighter*," she said after a few seconds. "I grappled for control more times than I could count before I finally pushed that fucking thing out of me." She didn't look at him, and her voice was low—so low Darius felt like he had to hold his breath to hear it. "So Wrath was really careful. It stopped carrying guns or anything I could use to hurt myself, and it tried not to get directly involved in shit that would trigger me to fight back. Less personal violence. Instead, it used me to… organize violence. From a distance. So this revenge spree? It was bloodier than almost anything I did when that Sin was pulling the strings. I wasn't just *like* Wrath. I was *worse* than Wrath. It took a pile of bodies and Alan screaming in my face for me to see it."

Thorn's jaw slammed together, and she swallowed. The muscles in her slender neck hardened for a moment. Then she turned to him.

"After that, I don't remember much," she admitted. "I completely dissociated and spiraled from there." She cleared her throat and ran her tongue across her lips. "Alan filled in the blanks. I got away. Went to some lab supply warehouse. Stole a bottle of sulfuric acid… Did this."

She held out her left arm.

Darius followed the line of scars, from the fine points near her elbow to the tangle wrapped around the *Peccostium*, and he imagined what they'd been like fresh. Dripping, blistering wounds of melted flesh and blood, flowing on a river of caustic self-loathing. His chest ached, and he wished more than ever before that he could heal old wounds—that he could heal Thorn at all.

"I guess I thought if I dug in deep enough," Thorn went on, "if I poured acid right to the core of the fucking thing, I could burn it off." She gave a wry, humorless chuckle. "Obviously, it doesn't work that way, and it left me defenseless in some alley. Clarke—Leroy—fucking *Gluttony* found me first, and he put a bullet in my brain."

Thorn pulled her hair up just above her right temple. Darius could barely make out a tiny, circular scar there, too. He shook his head.

"Wouldn't Wrath have come after him for trying to kill you?" he asked.

"I'm sure she would have," Thorn said, drawing her long hair around one shoulder. She pulled her knees into her chest again and wrapped her arms around them as though they might try to escape. "But Gluttony panicked. He was right to panic. He wouldn't have been able to stop me. So he decided to act first. Didn't matter, though. Alan got there before he finished the job."

"What happened after that?" Darius asked.

Thorn pinched her lips between her teeth, shrugged, and shook her head.

"My powers were disrupted," she said. "My healing slowed to practically human rates. Alan barely got me to the Underground alive, and Reed hooked me up to some machines to keep me stable. They had no idea what to expect. I guess Reed wanted to pull the plug—said I was suffering, and it would be compassionate to let me go."

Darius's eyes widened. "What did Alan say?"

"I don't know," Thorn admitted, "but I can guess. When I woke up, the plug was still in, and Reed was gone. I never saw him again."

"How long did it take you to wake up?"

"Thirty-four days," she said. "I was in a coma until the *Peccostium* healed and my link to Wrath's power recovered. Then my body pushed the bullet out of my brain and—did you know the brain doesn't scar? I didn't know that until I woke up. So when my power came back, the necrotic tissue healed like nothing had ever happened. Scarred skin." She glowered at her arm. "But a perfect fucking brain, so I couldn't forget what kind of goddamned monster I'd become."

Her eyes didn't move away from the mark of the Sins. Darius had never looked at her *Peccostium* this closely before, and he could see the details of her injuries more clearly now. A perfect patch of circular skin beneath the symbol, while the rest of her arm dripped in thick, ropy acid scars. The inside of her forearm was covered with them, and tiny tendrils wrapped onto the heel of her palm and around her thumb joint. Thorn ran her fingers over them absently.

"You're not a monster," Darius said after a moment.

He looked away from her scars to find she was already watching him, her face dark and cynical.

"I'm not sure what else you would call it," she began, her voice full of old venom.

"Thorn, they killed your son," Darius said, shaking his head. "That would make anyone break down. Show yourself some grace." A fresh brush of tears glistened in Thorn's eyes. Darius reached forward and gently grabbed the back of her wrist. She seemed surprised but didn't pull away as he turned her arm around to expose her scars to the room again. His thumb brushed against the side of her *Peccostium*, and a shiver whispered through Thorn's body.

"This thing?" he said with a frown. "And the thing it's attached to? That's the monster. And you didn't just escape it once. It's still there. You have to fight it every single day."

Thorn stared at Darius, her eyes wide, her lips gently parted. Sparkie climbed up Thorn's back; his tiny head crested her bare shoulder, and he watched Darius from behind her veil of long, dark hair.

"Maybe it was winning for a while," Darius said, squeezing her arm for emphasis. The taut fibers of her scar felt smooth beneath his fingertips. "But the monster was *never* you. And, as long as you never stop fighting it, it never will be."

The tension in Thorn's expression softened even more, and she took a long, slow breath. Darius smiled again. Thorn didn't. She opened her mouth, about to speak—

Something rattled against the window, and they both

jumped. Thorn leapt up, pulling her wrist out of Darius's grip. The bare soles of her feet were silent against the carpet as she cleared the space between the bed and window in four strides. Sparkie vaulted to the top of the curtains and clung to the fabric as he and Thorn looked out at the street.

"Anyone out there?" Darius asked. He sensed the warm energy of other visitors in the rooms around them, but he hadn't felt anyone moving on the walkway outside. Thorn's eyes narrowed as she looked into the darkness. After a moment, she took a deep breath and shut the curtains. Sparkie went along for the ride until they met in the middle, where he fell back to Thorn's bare shoulder, his claws catching to her flesh to keep him standing.

"No." She turned back to Darius, looked him over. "We should finish eating and get to bed," she said as she walked back and sat across from him again. "It's a long drive back to the Underground."

Thorn picked her plate up, and Darius did the same. While they ate, Thorn expertly handling her chopsticks as Darius switched to a fork, he occasionally looked up at her. She was still stoic, but her shoulders relaxed toward the ground like a heavy weight had been lifted off them.

***

It was quiet and cold. As cold as it could get at three in the morning in The-Middle-Of-Nowhere, Georgia, at the beginning of May. A streetlight threw dim, orange light across the parking lot outside their motel. The town beyond it soundly slept. No cars busied the roads. No lights flickered in distant windows. No energy moved. The only sign of life at all was the quiet song of crickets chirping into the wind.

Thorn lit a cigarette, holding the end between her lips while she drew bitter smoke into her mouth. It coated her tongue and burned against her throat, hot all the way down until it reached her lungs. She leaned against the railing and closed her eyes as a breeze tugged gently at her hair. When she exhaled, spiraling, gray ribbons floated around her head.

God, what a day.

Leroy's face and the horrified snarl contorting it flashed through her mind. She never thought she'd see him again, let alone on the other end of a pitchfork buried three inches into her stomach. Just thinking about it made her body tighten, ready to fight. Leroy brought up a lot of old complications, a lot of bad memories… Things no one knew about her. No one but Alan. Cain. And now, Darius.

She glanced at the window behind her to the room where Darius had finally fallen asleep. Sparkie was still inside, and he perked his head up from Thorn's pillow to look at the Virtue—an indistinct blob under ugly, orange covers. For hours, Thorn had listened to him fight for sleep. Restless. Like he didn't know what to do with his body when it was finally time to lie down and give the thing a fucking break.

She took a deep breath and realized her teeth were clenched so tightly she probably could have bitten through bone. She closed her eyes, felt the bubbling fire in her belly broil a little, and exhaled slowly. It simmered down, and the tension melted from her jaw.

The monster wasn't winning tonight.

A brief, warm surge echoed through the empty pit in Thorn's chest, but that warmth was quickly doused by icy guilt.

What was it about Virtues, putting everyone else before themselves, letting their own health and happiness deteriorate because they were so goddamned *concerned* with the people around them? Darius had enough to worry about without adding Thorn's sins to the list.

She shook her head, propped her cigarette between her lips, and drew her phone from her pocket.

Maybe it wasn't a *Virtue* thing, she thought as she opened her reporting app and flicked through the notes until she found Samira's name. Thorn frowned. It was a *Darius* thing. She could just imagine what this new Temperance would have said about her past. Nicholas, too. And Teresa—

A poisoned stone sunk into Thorn's gut.

Teresa would have understood because Teresa had known Donovan. Loved him. Been loved *by* him.

Thorn swore under her breath. So much for beating the monster. She slammed the touchscreen keys, adding an update that she planned to drop off another card at Reflection Farms before they headed back to the Underground. As she lowered the device, it rang in her palm. Alan's face looked up at her.

Thorn drew in a fresh mouthful of smoke and answered the call on a nicotine cloud. "You're up late."

Alan chuckled. His deep voice was a source of familiar comfort. Thorn relaxed into it. "I wanted to check in after your... eventful afternoon."

"You worry too much," she said as she flicked ashes over the railing, her lips pulling into a half-smirk. This was the closest Alan ever got to sentimental.

"I believe I worry exactly the right amount," he countered. "You were stabbed, if I read correctly, by a man I killed nearly seventy years ago. How are you doing?"

Thorn pressed a palm flat to her belly. Even though the wounds had healed, she could still feel the ghost of them, and the acidic, iron-laced taste of blood and bile lingered in her mouth.

"It's not a shot to the head," she said at last.

Alan paused, like the very thought of that disconcerted him enough to steal his train of thought. After a few seconds, he said, "You are returning to Reflection Farms before you leave?"

"Yes." Thorn brought her cigarette back to her lips but stopped just short of drawing on it again. "Leroy threw my card away, so I wanted to get one to Samira—if I can. She seemed more receptive to us than he was."

As she sucked in another hit, Thorn could practically feel

Alan nodding—almost see him stroking his goatee the way he always did when he was thinking.

"Is it possible she could be persuaded to join you?" he asked at last.

"I doubt it," Thorn said. "Leroy made it pretty damned clear he wanted nothing to do with us, and she won't come without him."

"Ah." Disappointment dampened the word, and Alan sighed. "We will keep in touch. She may change her mind in time. For now, we should be grateful we found her at all. To be honest, I can't believe we have."

"I can't believe *Leroy* found her," Thorn scoffed bitterly. "One Virtue in this whole damned world who can save his soul and he fucking married her."

Another pause. This one felt heavier, laden with resentment at the fact that she had never experienced relief from the pit in her chest. Thorn tried to fill it with another lungful of cigarette smoke. It didn't help.

"How do you think that works?" she asked. Her throat tightened, and her voice sounded strangely loud in the country air.

"What?"

"Their marriage." Thorn swallowed hard, and her jaw ground together. She rarely let herself explore the possibility that she might meet Patience one day—couldn't be let down if she didn't hold onto hope in the first place—but when she *did* explore it, never once had *this* scenario played out in her mind.

"Besides the fact that he's immortal and almost a century older than she is," Thorn went on when Alan still hadn't spoken. Darius's words rang out in her head, and somehow, she felt emptier than usual. "She's the only thing that makes him feel whole. Can we even call that love?"

Alan took a long breath. It rattled through the speaker like a wave pulling away from shore. "We can," he said at last.

"But she's Temperance."

"Her Virtue might have drawn him to her, but we know nothing about what holds them together," Alan said. The words were sharp and quick, almost defensive. "It is certainly more complicated than that."

"How do you know?" Thorn asked.

"Because you and I are not driven solely by our emptiness," Alan said. "Nor is Cain or any of the other Forgotten Sins I have met. Why would this man be any different?"

Thorn nodded, but the tightness in her jaw didn't loosen, and she practically had to pry it apart to bring her cigarette to her lips again. She drained the thing down, dragging the flame through packed tobacco until all that stood at the end was a hot column of gray ash. As she exhaled, she flicked it over the edge.

"You're—"

Something moved to her left.

Thorn snapped around, a creeping anticipation trickling down her spine. Sparkie, suddenly alert, leapt to the window and slipped beneath the curtain to press his face against the glass.

"Thorn?" Alan asked.

She didn't answer. Her ears strained, and her skin tingled as she searched for anything that didn't belong, but she was alone. No movement. No shadows. No cold human energy anywhere within thirty feet. In front of her, the concrete walkway stretched out, ochre doors dotting the wall. She took a deep breath, shook her head, and opened her mouth to speak...

Something scampered up the top step—a small, furry thing—and made a straight line right toward her. Thorn's eyes shot wide open.

"Fuck," she muttered. "I think it's Leroy."

"*What?*"

"I'm going have to call you back," Thorn said, and she hung up. A frantic red squirrel skittered to a stop just out of kicking range. It barked, spinning on the cement, its bushy tail so frazzled it looked as though it had stuck its paws in an electrical outlet.

"Something happened," Thorn said—she didn't ask it—and the animal spun faster. "Fuck."

She burst back into the room, and Darius sprang up in bed like he'd already been awake. He flicked on the bedside lamp, and yellow light flooded the room. The squirrel ran in circles at Thorn's feet, chattering helplessly as it looked between her and Darius. Sparkie leapt down to catch it, but the squirrel scampered away only to spin and chirp some more.

Darius gawked at it.

"What the hell is going on?" he asked.

"It's Leroy's Familiar."

"What?" Darius jumped to his feet. "What's it saying?"

"I don't know," Thorn said, grabbing her clothes and sprinting into the bathroom. She didn't shut the door all the way, and she shouted through it as she dressed. "But it's not fucking good. I've got to get over there."

"I'm coming," Darius said.

A snake of dread coiled in Thorn's gut, and she strode back into the room, where Darius was buttoning his jeans. She stopped to glare at him as he grabbed a shirt from his bag and threw it over his head.

"No," she snapped, pulling her gloves on. "You stay *here*."

"You stand a better chance at finding Samira with me," he said as he dropped back to the mattress to put on his shoes. His voice held the same drive he'd had when he'd run into a building full of dead children and gotten himself thrown out a window.

Thorn worried he was doing the same thing now. Darius had come a long way since he'd walked into that nightmare and his world had been blown to pieces, but this life was wearing on him. His deep, olive skin seemed more gray than golden, and in the last few months, dark circles made his green eyes somehow look both bright and sick at the same time. She stared at him, her teeth gnashed together, and an anxious pit opened between her lungs.

Darius got to his feet, grabbed his bag, and walked to the door. "Let's go."

Thorn's lip curled up. She felt trapped, and nothing made her want to lash out more than being backed into a fucking corner. Her hands wrapped into fists. "You listen to me. Whatever I say. You got it?"

His jaw clenched, and his Adam's apple moved down his strong throat with a hard swallow.

"Got it."

"Good," Thorn said, but she felt anything but good about this. "Let's go."

She grabbed her satchel, once again wishing she had more than a goddamned handgun to go into whatever situation they were about to find, as Darius opened the door. They rushed to the car, and both Familiars—Sparkie and Leroy's red squirrel—leapt into the back seat as Thorn turned on the ignition. At 3:00 a.m., the people of Sandersville were as cold and still as corpses.

CHAPTER FOURTEEN

Thorn felt the people first.

Cold energy buzzed like a swarm of hungry cicadas in the distance, just close enough for Thorn to catch it. She pulled up to the green cattle gate. It was left open, swinging out into the road. Thorn's stomach dropped.

"It feels like a lot more people than before," Darius said. The dim lights from the dashboard reflected in his eyes, casting shadows upward and making his face look haunted.

Thorn's teeth gnashed together. The sedan's tires bumped along the rough terrain as she pulled off the road and parked under low-hanging branches from leafy trees. It wasn't impossible to spot in the dark, but it was harder, and it would have to be good enough. Sparkie sat behind Thorn's hair and kneaded the nape of her neck with tiny, sharp claws. Leroy's squirrel scampered back and forth across the dash, its tail a constant flick of movement. Thorn turned off the vehicle and pulled out her satchel. She attached her thigh holster and slipped a blade into a sheath at her calf before handing Darius a pistol.

"What's the plan?" Darius asked as he strapped the weapon around his hips.

Now shrouded in total darkness, Thorn couldn't make

out his features, but his deep voice was steady. Ready to go. He was always ready. Always on board for whatever fucking shit-show she dragged him into. She admired that about him just as much as it drove her insane.

"We walk," she said.

They kept to the trees, fumbling through underbrush and low branches as they came upon the little community square. Leroy's familiar darted ahead of them while Sparkie watched from the sky. To their left, fields were empty, illuminated only by a sea of stars, a waxing crescent moon, and a splattering of lit windows in nearby homes. In the distance, cold energy encircled the buildings. A brutal scream broke the silence, and a small piece of that energy blew out like a candle flame.

"Fuck," Thorn whispered. They reached the turn in the road where it meandered by the greenhouses and up toward the church. Thorn crouched behind a large crop of thick blackberry bushes, and Darius knelt beside her. Ahead of them, men and women walked the property. Sparkie watched them move like black ants on dark paper, and their energy extended as far as Thorn could feel. Behind the greenhouses. By the buildings in the town square. Inside homes.

Someone roared furiously—a familiar, nauseating sound that rolled in deep vibrations through the village like thunder. A huge figure stomped out of an empty house. The open door filled with a dangerous, flickering light, and smoke billowed through the gap.

"Is that..." Darius began to ask.

"Terrance Moore," Thorn confirmed with a snarl.

She couldn't see his face, his dark features all but obscured in the blackness around them, but when she focused on his aura, she recognized it. Gluttony stormed away from the house and headed toward another. Behind him, a blank-faced man with a thick neck and thicker arms ambled into the yard. He followed Moore like he was being led on a string.

"Puppets," Thorn said. She glanced back up the road, where she could feel more than sixty people spread throughout the complex. "They're all Puppets. It looks like he brought people from the town. Fuck, there are so many of them…"

Too many. Gluttony shouldn't have had enough power to keep this large of a group under his thumb at once…

"Samira's still alive," Darius whispered breathlessly to Thorn's left. His forehead glistened, beads of sweat dripping down the side of his face as he ran a hand across his mouth. "It feels like she's by the store outpost. Not so far as the church."

Thorn looked back to the road. Along the right were the greenhouses, sheds, and the barn she had been stabbed in. Across from them, houses. Dozens of tiny, ranch-style structures set up in a quaint, grid-like pattern. Some were full of terrified, huddled energies trapped in back bedrooms, but others were empty. Mostly empty. From this distance, Thorn could barely make out the flashing of fire in glass windows.

She glared at Moore as he walked toward another house. Darius shifted beside her, and Thorn glanced over to see him drawing his weapon.

"What the fuck are you doing?" she hissed. She laid her hand on the top of his gun and forced it toward the ground.

"We could get rid of him," Darius whispered. "Break his Programming in the NYPD right here."

"What the hell do you think will happen if we miss?" Thorn challenged. "It's dark, and he's over fifty yards away!"

Darius's jaw tightened, but he holstered his weapon all the same, and Thorn breathed out a sigh. "Follow me," she said, "and stay low."

They kept close to the ground and tucked into the tree line until they were behind the greenhouses and old tractor barn. A cold energy turned their way, and Thorn stopped. She grabbed Darius's arm, pulled him backward, and hid under the dense shadow of a giant maple. A man rounded the barn, sweeping a flashlight left and right, his disconnected eyes searching for something. Thorn drew her knife from the sheath on her thigh, holding it low and ready. The man never turned to the trees, though. While Thorn held her breath, he passed by without a glance.

When he was far enough away, Darius murmured, "Why don't we cut them off?" Thorn slipped her knife back into its place and turned to look at him. "Just hit them hard enough, and they'll drop, right?"

"Yes," she whispered, "but Sins feel when Puppets are severed from them. I don't want Moore to know we're here."

Darius's eyes darkened. Thorn could barely see them, but his brows drew together, making the shadows on his face even deeper. "People will get hurt."

"People are already getting hurt," she hissed. "And we can't help any of them if we get ourselves killed." Thorn turned back to the greenhouses, felt that the nearest patrol was several dozen yards away, and gestured for Darius to follow her. As they stalked along the trees, Thorn kept track of Moore's aura. She could feel him walking. Pausing. Someone new screamed, and further toward the township, another cold spot flickered to nothing.

They had to stop three more times as Puppets moved along the farm's perimeter. The last, a young woman in silky pajamas, came so close that Thorn was sure she'd have to disable her. She pressed Darius backward, feeling his body hot against her back as she grabbed her knife again, but just like every time before, the Puppet passed without incident. When she walked away, Thorn let out her breath in a long, slow stream.

"I wonder what they're looking for," Darius muttered.

They had almost made it to the farm's main square. More energy was gathered here, most of it inside the church. Thorn could barely make out the building through the trees, but she saw two Puppets standing guard at the front doors. They were armed with a crowbar and wooden bat. Both weapons glistened with blood in the moonlight. As Thorn went to take another step, her shoe caught something. She looked down at a body—

Thorn threw out a hand to keep Darius back. He ran into her palm, hesitated, and leaned further into it as he tried to see what she'd stopped for. His chest widened under her outstretched fingers as he sucked in a harsh breath.

A man sprawled in the underbrush, his skull so thoroughly crushed that his face was all but indistinguishable. A pool of blood around his head slowly sank into the soil at the edge of the forest. He wore a white nightshirt that extended to his ankles, and it was splattered in crimson droplets. Thorn's jaw clenched, and a fire blossomed between her lungs.

"They're making sure no one gets out," she said.

"We have to stop him," Darius breathed.

His eyes were glued to the man on the ground, disconnected, like he wasn't here anymore. A chittering at Thorn's ankle drew her focus, and Leroy's Familiar tapped her shoes with little forepaws. Thank fucking god for Leroy. Thorn wrapped her fingers around Darius's forearm and dragged him forward.

"We need to find Samira," she said. "Where is she?"

"Close," Darius muttered. "We've got to go into the village now, though…"

Leroy's Familiar squeaked again, like it was agreeing with him, and darted into the open. It disappeared behind a distant shed, and when Thorn and Darius didn't immediately follow, it poked its head out from around the corner and watched them with beady, eager eyes.

Thorn's gut twisted into knots. There were more people—and more Puppets—in the village.

Together, they made their way through the structures built at the outer edge of Reflection Farms. Following a bushy, orange tail, they wound between grain sheds, rain barrels, and poultry coops until they reached a community kitchen. There were people inside. Thorn paused beneath a window, Darius pressing up beside her, as a cold point shifted by the door. All her senses were on fire, her fingers wide and ready to grab the gun strapped to her leg. Her body filled with a furious need to get them the fuck out of there by whatever means necessary. She took a deep breath.

"We're practically on top of her," Darius whispered. Light from the window highlighted his face as he frowned. "She's... underground?"

The squirrel called to them again. It had climbed on top of a tattered brown rug at the backside of the trading out-post and began to claw at it. Thorn glanced at the window before she sped over, Darius following behind her. They pulled at the rug, and the scraping sound it made as it slid against the packed gravel made Thorn's heart pound in her ears. She looked over her shoulder, feeling for the human coldness in the kitchen, waiting for a reaction—

"There's a door."

Darius's voice made Thorn spin around. An old cellar door lay at her feet. Darius leaned down to pull it open, but it swung on its own before he got there.

"Hurry!" Leroy whispered, waving his arms. Thorn allowed Darius in first before jumping down herself. Leroy carefully shut them inside, the wood closing with a soft *thump*. Sparkie dove from the sky and helped Leroy's squirrel smooth the rug over the door again. Once it was sufficiently hidden, both Familiars rushed up to the rooftop, and Thorn breathed easily for the first time in what felt like hours. A light flickered to life.

Samira was sitting on a crate across from them, an electric lantern between her quivering hands. Wet tears streaked down her face, leaving glistening rivers across her cheeks.

"Thank God you've come," she whispered, the words rattling like they were being shaken from her mouth. "They—they—"

"They found you," Thorn murmured, and she glanced up at Leroy. His broad arms were crossed around a nightshirt like the one they'd seen on the dead man in the trees.

A thick line of sticky blood dribbled from his dark cheek onto the shoulder, staining it crimson. His eyes were wide, but his jaw clenched.

"Gluttony?" he asked.

Thorn nodded.

"They're killing everyone!" Samira was almost frantic, her words gaining volume and pitch as she shook her head. The light on her lap flickered around the cavern, bouncing off wooden boxes, dusty sacks, and old, glass jars. "I can feel them disappearing. Dying. Oh, God. Mikael. Susanna. Liam!"

Samira dipped her head and sobbed. Leroy knelt by her side and put his hands on her shoulders. As he hushed her, murmuring quiet words of comfort, Thorn frowned. "They?" she asked.

"There's two," Leroy confirmed. He got to his feet and turned around, but one of his strong hands still held tightly to Samira's shoulder. Her crying was quieter now, but her body still rocked with hard sobs. Leroy talked over her. "Little man. Smaller than Gluttony. Brown hair—"

Thorn swore under her breath and looked at Darius. "Ruiz," she said.

"Who?" Leroy asked.

"Carlos Ruiz," Thorn said. "Lust." Rage snaked its way up Thorn's spine, and her fingers clenched. "That explains how they can have so many fucking Puppets here." Leroy squinted in confusion, and she sighed. "Moore has only been a host for seven years," Thorn explained impatiently. "He doesn't have the power to control this many people. But Ruiz can. He's been Lust for almost two decades. And if he's here…"

Thorn's rage broiled. She turned her back and walked away from the others, propping her hands on her hips while she tried to figure out how the fuck to get them out of this situation. Abruptly, she spun around and gestured an open palm out to Leroy.

"You got hurt," she said, indicating the blood on his

face. He nodded. "So they saw you." He nodded again. Still quiet. Thorn's fists clenched at her sides. "*And?* What the fuck happened?"

"I heard screaming from the Johnson's house next door and went to check it out," Leroy said. "Their little boy was dead, and the smaller guy took Mrs. Johnson away while the big one killed Mikael. I busted in, and the big guy said something about how it's been a long time and we had unfinished business. Then he took a swing at me, but I hit him first. He barely got me here with the edge of his crowbar after I pushed him through the drywall." Leroy pointed at his cheek, where Thorn could barely make out a healing line beneath the blood. "I remembered what you said, and I knew who they had to be. They're here for Samira. By the time I got her out, the farm was already surrounded."

Samira stifled a harsh cry. "I don't understand," she whispered shakily. "How did they find me?"

"They probably just saw that same fucking article we did," Thorn said. "We need to—"

But then she froze. The article. It didn't implicate Samira. It showed *Leroy.*

Something suddenly dawned on her.

Gloria. The woman who'd walked them down to the barn. She'd paused, touched her temples…

And left Thorn and Darius alone right before Leroy jammed a pitchfork into her stomach.

God, Thorn had been so *stupid* not to realize before. She turned to Leroy and ran her tongue along the bottom of her teeth behind tightly closed lips.

"How often do you use your Influence?"

Leroy froze, and Thorn felt Darius's bright, green eyes on the side of her face.

"What?" Leroy murmured.

Thorn crossed her arms and watched him. She wanted to be mad at him—god, did she want a fucking target for her rage right now—but she couldn't be. She knew this mistake. She'd *made* this mistake. Lives had been lost back then, too.

"Control people," she said. "How often do you control other people?"

His eyes widened and moved from Thorn to Darius and back to Thorn again. Samira's mouth dropped open as she stared at her husband.

"I-I don't know," he stammered. "Does it matter?"

"Yes," Thorn said. She pointed behind her, where she could feel Terrance Moore's energy in the distance. Sparkie could barely see him near the houses. More of them were on fire now. "You can feel when he does it, and *he* can feel *you*."

Leroy's face lost its luster, and he stared at Thorn like he wanted to stab her again just to shut her up. At last, he whispered, "I did this?"

Another soul smothered out. Samira choked a sob as Leroy's attention darted upward. Thorn followed his gaze. All around, she could feel dozens of cold points. Some huddled together, scared and fucking alone. Others, moving, on patrol, keeping the flock cornered until it was time for slaughter. Leroy's fingers rolled into fists, and he stomped toward the door. Darius stepped in front of him.

"Whoa, what are you doing?"

"This is my fault," Leroy said, throwing his hand up to the low ceiling. "I'm the one they're looking for!"

"If you go up there, you'll get us all killed," Darius argued. "The only reason we're still alive is because the Sins can't sense our auras, but if those Puppets see you, they'll swarm us!"

A couple of distant energies drew closer, and Sparkie spotted a man walking through nearby buildings. He paused and looked over his shoulder before he turned around. His cool energy approached them. Samira glanced up, her eyes filled with horror, as Thorn's breath caught in her throat. Neither Darius nor Leroy seemed to notice.

"I can't just sit here!" Leroy exclaimed.

Darius's nostrils flared, his jaw tightened, and he opened

it to speak again.

"So *now* you want to—"

"Shut up!" Thorn hissed. She rushed to Darius, wrapped one hand around his shoulder, and pressed the other against his mouth. He gasped, a sharp intake of cool air above Thorn's palm. She knew the moment he felt what she did because he held that gasp inside, and the four of them froze.

They all watched the ceiling. Thorn's eyes followed the cold aura as it stopped less than five feet away. She swallowed hard, released Darius, and grabbed the gun from her thigh. Sparkie leapt into the air, circling high above, watching as the Puppet's flashlight swept across the gravel path. Empty windows. A tattered brown rug against the back of a building...

He took a step toward it.

Thorn positioned herself at the bottom of the stairs, raised her pistol, and pointed it upward.

Then Sparkie dove. He tightened himself into a torpedo of scales and wings and barreled into the Puppet's temple. He was unconscious before his body hit the ground.

A handful of energies suddenly stopped moving.

Thorn's lungs felt like they were going to burst, and she exhaled a sharp swear word. Then she spun toward Darius and Leroy.

"Now is *not* the time for this," she snarled, pointing one finger at Leroy before moving it to Darius. They both had the guts not to look away, but Darius's jaw ground together, and she saw his shoulders rise and fall in a slow, measured breath. "We need to get the fuck out of here."

Samira's brown face lost its color. "W-what? You said we can't let them see us!"

"If we don't move, we're dead," Thorn said, holstering her weapon again. "Gluttony is setting the whole damned place on fire."

"What do we do?" Leroy asked.

Thorn's fists balled at her sides, and she spun away from him. Gluttony was coming back across the village, drawn to the fucking mess they'd made with the Puppet she'd disabled. More energy congregated. Near the church. From the fields. She could feel Ruiz now, too, walking up the main road. Thorn would be damned if she faced off against two Sins and thirty Puppets, cornered like a fucking rat in a cage. Sparkie quietly circled, counting heads while Thorn calculated their odds. She didn't like them.

"We run," she said suddenly. She looked to Leroy and threw her chin in Samira's direction. The Virtue still hadn't stood. Her eyes were glued to Leroy, so wide that the whites showed all the way around her dark irises. "Grab her. We've got to stay low. Move fast—"

"Wait." Leroy took Samira by the shoulders and helped her to her feet. "I'll distract them."

Thorn's eyes narrowed. "How?"

"My—my, whatever. The thing Gluttony can feel me do," Leroy said. "I'll head out to the woods and pull him to me so you can get away."

"No!" Samira blurted. She clutched the lantern against her chest and shook her head. "You can't do that. You can't let them get you. I need you!"

"They won't get me, baby," Leroy murmured. He came close, wrapped his broad hands around her face, and buried his fingers deep in her thick, black hair. Samira's eyes filled with a fresh rush of tears. "I'll get out, okay? I know these woods better than anyone. I need to do this. I need to keep you safe."

"And we need to go now," Thorn said. The energies were closer. In a few minutes, they wouldn't be able to get out of this cellar without being spotted. She turned to Darius. "Give him your gun."

Darius's eyes widened. "What?"

"Give him your gun," Thorn repeated. Darius glowered at her for a moment longer before he removed the pistol from its holster and passed it to Leroy, who swallowed hard at the weight of it in his hands. Thorn went on. "If your Influence doesn't work, this will. Get to the trees first so they can't surround you. As soon as you've got a good head start, cut the Puppets off."

Leroy frowned. "Cut them off?"

Thorn's heart sank. God, there was too much learning on the job here for her to be confident in any bullshit plan, but they had no other choice. "Yes. You can cut the line holding them to Moore. He'll notice, and he'll be pissed." Leroy's face went hollow, but he nodded. Thorn turned to Darius and Samira.

"The car is at the south gate," she said. "When Leroy pulls the Sins away, we can run on the road, but before that, we're in the woods, too." Thorn glanced over Samira. Like Leroy and the dead man in the trees, her long, white nightshirt extended past her knees, and her feet were bare beneath it. Thorn's chest constricted. Damn it, that was going to make it so much harder for them to move. She looked back up to Samira's terrified, tear-streaked face. "I'll carry you if I have to."

Thorn moved to the door and reached up to open it. Samira frantically whispered, "Where do we meet back up?"

"We don't," Leroy said. "You've got to get as far away from here as you can." Samira's eyes widened, and he turned to Thorn. "I'll make my way to Charlotte. It'll take me a couple of days, but—"

"I'll send people for you," Thorn cut in. God, she wished she had something to give him. Another card. Her phone. Anything to make contact easier. But she didn't. He was on his own. "Wait outside city hall. They'll find you there."

"City hall," Leroy confirmed. "Got it."

With a deep breath, Thorn looked from him to Darius to Samira. She didn't like this, but what the fuck else could she do? Slowly, she eased the cellar door open.

"Go."

Leroy grabbed Samira's face in one palm, told her he loved her, and kissed her deeply. As he turned away, she lowered the lantern to the ground and tried to hold him with both hands, but he pulled his fingers out of hers and vaulted up the stairs two at a time. As soon as his bare feet hit the gravel, his squirrel Familiar leapt from the rooftop and landed on his shoulder. Thorn watched as he sprinted northward and disappeared into the dark. Then she turned to Darius, and a hot, furious surge swelled in her lungs. He looked defenseless. He *was* defenseless.

"You first," she said. "Listen to your instincts. I'll be right behind you."

Darius grabbed Samira's hand and led her out. Every part of Thorn screamed at her, telling her to ignore safety, grab the Virtues, and dash through the farm's village, but it wouldn't be easy. Lust and Gluttony's Puppets were still spread out along the perimeter. Thorn's stomach twisted as she climbed out of the door and slowly closed it behind her. Darius and Samira waited beneath the kitchen window. A Puppet still stood guard by the doors while people were locked inside.

Thorn crouched low and made her way toward them, walking around the man lying unconscious on the gravel. The two Virtues, with their brown skin and dark hair, should have been hard to see in the night, but Samira's white sleep shirt stood out so much that she might as well have had a string of lights around her throat. Thorn felt exposed in the open, and she took a second to feel her way around. To the southwest, there was a break in the cold energy— where Sparkie, from his vantage point above them, could see two lines of mannequin-like men and women slowly spreading out along the tree line.

She glanced at Darius and gestured her chin in that direction. He nodded, and she started to move.

Because Samira had no shoes, and because the gravel crunched under Thorn's boots if they moved too quickly, they had to take their time. Soon, the entire eastern edge of the property was dotted by little, cold points. They had to be Lust's, Thorn thought. Too many of them, too synchronized, to belong to Terrance Moore. Sparkie flew in circles above. It was hard for him to make out details in the dark, but he could see the line. Men and women. Young and old. Armed with bats and crowbars. Gluttony had found the unconscious Puppet. His huge form looked down at him before straightening up and taking in his surroundings.

"Where are you, you little *maggot?*" he called into the night.

Thorn sped up.

They passed sheds, crouched around chicken coops, and carefully wedged under a short, wooden fence. Thorn paused as they reached the first greenhouse, kneeling beside a neatly trimmed blackberry hedge. Behind them, Puppets walked between structures. In front, a gang of them on the dirt road had almost reached the houses. More than half of them were on fire now. How many people had already died here tonight? It made Thorn's stomach broil to think about, so she didn't. Instead, she focused on the trees. Just beyond the barn, there was no energy guarding the property line. For the first time in several quiet minutes, a flicker of icy hope fluttered in Thorn's empty chest.

"You feel that?" she whispered, turning toward Darius and Samira. The two Virtues were tucked in tightly behind her. "Make your way toward—"

A sudden light flashed in their direction, and Thorn's whole body went cold. She grabbed Darius by the shoulder, hooked her arm through Samira's elbow, and tore them through the bush without giving it a second thought. It scratched at her skin, tearing her arms and face open until they fumbled onto the other side. The Puppets at the road paused before they changed direction—heading straight toward Thorn, Darius, and Samira.

"Fuck!" Thorn hissed.

The center greenhouse door was left ajar, and while she could feel two people in there, Thorn didn't see any other option. She turned to Darius. His face was marked with a handful of little cuts, cracking open shallow red slits against his skin. She pointed to the greenhouse, he nodded, and they hurried over. Thorn slipped through the gap and crouched down. Samira and Darius followed swiftly in her wake.

And Thorn froze—because another Puppet stood ten feet in front of her. He hadn't moved; his back was to them, his broad shoulders held unnaturally straight, and a crowbar dangled lazily in his right hand.

Thorn held her breath. The greenhouse smelled like the distinct, gut-churning blend of wet soil and spilled blood. Thorn glanced away from the Puppet and took in the room. There was a single aisle down the center, flanked on either side by shelves full of pots and plants, growing on high, leafy stalks or dangling down in thick, twisted vines. Halfway down the path, a body spread across damp pavers. The woman's head had been crushed, her eyes open and unseeing. Thorn tore her gaze away and looked straight across. Another woman curled up on the ground, her head tucked down, her body shaking in silent tears as her hair cascaded in dirty, matted braids around her shoulders. Gloria.

Samira stifled a quiet gasp.

Thorn held up her hand and pressed a finger against her lips, but she didn't look away from Gloria. Behind her, four cold energies approached the fence where they'd been spotted. Thorn recognized two of them, and her stomach twisted. She reached her other hand out, found Darius's forearm, and squeezed it to warn him. He grabbed her fingers back and indicated he understood.

Terrance Moore's voice floated through the open door.

"So, the son of a bitch didn't escape into the woods with the others." The deep, reverberating tones cut through the night, and Gloria glanced at the door. Her eyes found Thorn, and they shot wide open. Thorn tapped her finger against her lips again. Moore kept talking. "Bring your gnats down. I can't let this fucker get away again."

Thorn's heart sank, and Gloria gulped down hard, shallow breaths. The Puppets along the property line began to move in this direction, and those on the road joined them.

Leroy still hadn't made his move—and part of Thorn, a bitter, loathsome part, wondered if he'd abandoned them here.

"Relax," Carlos Ruiz said. "You're making this whole event so *dull.*"

"This isn't a fucking vacation!" Moore snarled. "While you're burying your dick into anything that will fight back, *I'm* working."

"You can't tell me you aren't enjoying this?" Ruiz purred. His voice was so smooth and confident that Thorn could hear the smug grin on his lips without seeing it. "It's just like the good old days!"

"I'd enjoy it a hell of a lot more if I had that maggot under my heel," Gluttony said.

"In time. We'll smoke him out soon enough. Then, we'll gather everyone in the church and force him to watch as we kill them, one by one, before we slit his throat, too. Doesn't that sound nice?"

Gluttony let out a grunt. "How do you expect they'll explain *this* one away?"

Lust laughed. "The same way they always do, I imagine. Religious zealots kill themselves in a ritual sacrifice. Who cares? We'll be long gone by the time they find the bodies, and you'll be on Hunt's good side again."

"That bitch has no room to talk," Moore scoffed.

The tone of Lust's voice shifted dangerously. "Careful…"

"Why?" Moore was louder now. "That bitch has both Alan Blaine *and* Thorn Rose running the goddamned resistance! I've got one little roach at some bullshit Jesus camp, and she loses her mind. She should take care of her *own* 'unfinished business'…"

His energy moved closer to them. Ruiz followed. Gloria's eyes darted upward and filled with tears. Thorn chanced a glance behind her, but even though she could feel the Sins on the other side of the hedges lining the road, she was too low to see them. Sparkie arced overhead and watched from above.

"Hunt has plans for Rose," Ruiz said. Thorn's breath caught in her throat, and Darius's head spun toward her. Their eyes met. His were wide, and his lips parted in quiet horror.

"Yeah," Moore growled. "Plans you two won't fucking share with the rest of us."

"Are you *trying* to get yourself killed? If she finds out—"

A gunshot went off in the distance, and at the same moment, the Puppet in front of Thorn twitched.

Gloria broke.

Thorn saw the signs. Her throat tightening. Shoulders drawing upward. She opened her mouth to scream, to cry, to beg for help and draw more attention than her human aura already had. Instinctively, Thorn reached out with her Influence. She desperately poured it into the woman, trapping the sound in her throat and keeping it there. The Puppet settled, but Thorn held onto Gloria. She found her fear, and she fed into it. She fed so much terror into her body that the woman froze where she sat. Her mouth gaped open, her eyes spilling hot tears down her cheeks. Thorn's heart hurt.

But Gloria was quiet.

"It's gotta be him," Moore said. "Come on."

Before they took three steps, Ruiz's phone rang. He pulled the device from his front pocket, looked down at the glowing screen, and said, "Speaking of Hunt... I wonder if she's done in that little shit town we passed through."

Thorn's blood ran cold, and her Influence shattered. Gloria's scream surged from her lungs. The Puppet in front of her reacted to the sound. He stepped toward her and raised his crowbar above his head, baring down, ready to swing...

Thorn leapt to her feet at the same moment as Darius. She wrapped her hands around the Puppet's face while Darius grabbed his weapon. Thorn jerked him back with a sharp twist and felt the snap in her fingertips, deep in her core, as his energy blinked out. Darius stood there with the crowbar as Thorn drew her gun and grabbed Gloria off the ground. She pointed her weapon at the back wall and pulled the trigger. The tempered glass splintered, and Darius swung the bar into it, sending a rainfall of pebble-like shards cascading to the ground. Thorn turned to Samira, who stared at them from the other side of the greenhouse.

"Run!" Thorn screamed.

Darius rushed back, lifted Samira, and carried her through. Thorn followed after. Puppets were swarming from the right. The left. Behind them. Two dozen cold energies sprinted at them wildly in the dark. Thorn shot into the masses, aiming on intuition and cold energy. They stumbled, fell over each other, but this would never be enough. Thorn stopped and spun around, firing round after round at the two Sins now running at her between the greenhouses.

She missed Moore but landed a bullet into Carlos Ruiz's gut. All at once, more than fifteen people collapsed. Thorn pointed her gun at Gluttony, pulled the trigger, and found her clip empty. He roared and came at her like a bull as Thorn holstered her weapon and dove into the trees.

Darius and Samira had already disappeared inside the woods, and Thorn felt a hopeless panic at not being able to tell where they were. Sparkie searched for them from above while Gloria clutched Thorn's neck. Thorn gripped her with one arm and pushed branches and boughs away with the other. A switch snapped against the *Peccostium* on her wrist and sent a jolt of pain down her spine. She kept running.

But she was running blind. The dense trees blocked out what little light the stars and moon provided, and she tripped and stumbled over roots, rocks, and her own damned feet. Gluttony and his Puppets were closing in behind her. Their flashlights began to break through the foliage. Then the sounds of them beating through the trees. And the cold, hard wall of their energy, coming at Thorn like a wave she knew damn well she couldn't outrun.

Suddenly, her toe caught on a hole, and she flew forward. Gloria rolled ahead of her, screaming. The Puppets moved more urgently, and Thorn clawed at the earth, trying to get back to her.

But she found herself face-first in mossy, earthen soil, hands grabbing at her clothes, her limbs, her hair. She roared and twisted around, thrashing desperately, catching a Puppet in the shins and rendering them unconscious before a crowbar swung at her and slammed into the side of her skull. Thorn's vision filled with bursting circles of pale light, and she shook her head as she stumbled to the side. Before she got her bearings back, a massive figure grabbed her left wrist and dug into her *Peccostium* as deep as it could.

Thorn screamed. Hot pain poured like a fresh vial of acid, sinking into her scars, making them pulse all the way from her palm to her elbow. The sensation flooded into her spine and made her whole body go weak. Behind her, Gloria howled one more time—a deep, primal sound—before a sickening crack echoed in the forest, and her energy cracked with it.

Thorn's vision faded in and out as Terrance Moore laughed above her.

"Gotcha."

He began to drag her back toward Reflection Farms, putting no more thought into her than he would a bag of fucking trash as Thorn's body banged against roots and rocks. Her shoulders slammed into tree trunks while her knees dug shallow trenches in the detritus on the forest floor. Thorn shook her head and tried to look around, but it was hard to see. Her eyes wouldn't focus—but what the hell could she focus on? The woods were so dark… Cold panic joined the pain as she remembered what Lust had said.

Wrath had a plan for her.

And Wrath was *here*.

Thorn groaned and tried to gather her legs beneath her—to reach her blade and fucking fight back rather than be delivered, weak and bleeding, into Autumn Hunt's hands. It hardly mattered. Thorn managed to find an exposed root and wound her foot around it. The next time Moore yanked her forward, she cried out, but she didn't budge. The four Puppets paused as Gluttony flashed his light in her face. Thorn already couldn't see, but the bright, blinding glare made her head ache, and she winced.

"You stupid *bitch*," he snarled, and he swung the light at her. Thorn held out her right hand, hoping to catch it—hoping she'd be able to grab the *Peccostium* under his left wrist, but she was too weak. The flashlight collided with Thorn's fingers, crashing them out of the way before he pulled it back and hit her on the other side of her head. Thorn flew to the right, her arm in Gluttony's hand working as an anchor to keep her from falling to the ground—and to keep her close enough to strike again. She looked up. He was a blurry mass of muscle as he raised the weapon.

A figure came at them from somewhere to Thorn's right. A flash of movement. Moore turned just in time to see something swing at him—

It struck his temple. The crunch of his skull silenced the woods. Every Puppet behind them dropped like cold curtains, slumping to the soil in a unified mass. Gluttony released Thorn's wrist, and she fell to her hands and knees as he stumbled backward, his light swinging while he covered his face with the other palm. Thorn couldn't make out details in the dark. He was fuzzy. Everything was fucking fuzzy.

Then someone stood in front of her.

Thorn pushed herself up, tilting her head back. She didn't need to see him clearly to know who it was.

Darius.

He held the crowbar like a club, ready to swing it again. The Sin didn't move, so Darius took a half-step forward. Moore stumbled back. Darius seemed to sense something Thorn didn't. The dark shape of him tensed then rushed forward, and Moore scrambled even further away. Darius swung again. The crowbar thunked against a tree as Moore's energy rolled to the ground. Then he clambered to his feet and ran in the opposite direction. His energy faded as he headed back toward the farm.

Thorn tried to climb to her feet. She reached for the bleary form of a tree in the dark and missed, slamming into it with her shoulder instead. She groaned and turned, leaning her back against the trunk.

"Fuck!"

"Are you okay?"

Darius limped up in front of her. Somehow, the closer he was, the harder he was to see. He'd rushed back to grab one of the Puppets' flashlights, and he held it upward to show their faces. His was nothing but an oval of deep, olive skin with black circles where his eyes belonged. He touched her chin with his free hand and gently moved her head to look at the wound on her left temple. She heard him wince.

"I'm fine," she lied. "Your leg—what happened to your leg?"

"It's nothing. I just tripped."

"Damn it!" A swell of anger surged through Thorn, and she groaned again. "You shouldn't have come back. Where is Samira?"

"She's safe," Darius said, "and so are you. Come on. We've got to hurry." He began to walk through the forest. Thorn hesitated before she stood up straight and went to follow him. Four steps later, she hit another trunk and stumbled again. Darius came back to her.

"You're *not* fine," he growled. Thorn shook her head. He sighed, grabbed her hand, and pulled her to her feet. Thorn linked her elbow with his, and together, they helped one another through the dark. They'd been walking for less than three minutes when another voice spoke so suddenly that it made Thorn's heart skip.

"Did you find her?" Samira asked.

"Yeah," Darius said. Another shape joined them. A blob of white. Thorn shook her head. She could just make out the terror in Samira's wide eyes as Darius's light passed over them. He gestured forward. "Let's go."

By the time they reached the main highway, Thorn's vision was functional enough to see with, and while her body still ached from Moore's assault on her *Peccostium*, she was confident on her own two feet again. When the trees broke to pavement, Thorn pulled herself away from Darius and looked around. Sparkie, who had been wandering the woods just as lost and disoriented as Thorn had been, spread his wings and took to the air. He spotted them by the road fifty feet north from where their car was hidden, and he dove down to join them. When her Familiar pressed against her chest, Thorn let out a relieved sigh.

"Let's get the fuck out of here," she said, and she started toward the vehicle. She took five steps, and suddenly, a sinking feeling in the back of her mind made her turn around.

Darius shut off the light.

"Something's wrong," Samira whispered.

"Quick," Thorn hissed. "Back to the trees!"

The three of them hurried into the safety of the forest. Thorn and Darius stood on either side of Samira, huddled tightly around her as they crouched in the dark. Thorn saw the headlights before she felt Wrath's aura—that evil, wicked coldness—flying down the highway. The Sin's anger emanated from her like a hurricane, and the storm in Thorn's heart swirled with it. Her jaw slammed together, and she took a deep breath as the car sped by...

It turned onto the farm's road so quickly that its tires spun on the dirt. A spray of rocks and soil furled into the night sky as the rear end fishtailed, crashed into the fence post, and sent it flying. Then Wrath was gone. Her energy headed toward the little community, where Thorn could feel others blinking out, disappearing forever as Gluttony and Lust killed the residents of Reflection Farms and the Puppets they'd dragged in. Deep in her throat, Samira let out a choked, desperate sob.

Thorn wrapped an arm around her shoulder and drew her to her feet. "Come on," she said, and she looked at

Darius. Now, lit by nothing but a crescent moon and the Milky Way, Thorn's vision finally stabilized enough to where she could really see him. The muscles along his jaw were tight, and a glistening of angry tears filled his eyes. She drew in a long, slow breath. "We need to go."

They got to the rental, and Thorn helped Samira into the back seat while Darius jumped behind the wheel. None of them spoke as they passed through Sandersville and got onto Highway 88. Samira curled up and cried until she couldn't stay awake anymore. Thorn looked over her shoulder. The Virtue's raw, swollen eyes were closed, and even in her sleep, silent tears streamed down her face.

"God fucking damn it," Thorn finally murmured.

Darius shook his head and let out an uneven sigh. After several seconds, he said, "Hey, Thorn?"

She glanced at him. He didn't look back. His eyes, tired and sunken, watched the black asphalt ahead of them.

"Do you believe in God?"

She was caught off guard by the question and turned to the road with a frown. "No," she said. "Not for a long time."

Darius shifted his attention to the side of her face. Thorn caught the movement in her peripheral. "But you used to?"

"I was born in the 1940s," she said with a scoff. "Everyone believed in God back then, and if you didn't, you faked it."

"When did you stop?"

Thorn cast him a glance. He watched her with morose curiosity. She took a deep breath and shook her head.

"Three years into being possessed by Wrath, when he didn't do a damned thing to help me. I decided God couldn't exist because if he did, he was a fucking asshole."

She didn't turn to look at him again, but Sparkie gazed over and saw Darius's attention—eyes narrowed, lips pursed—focus back on the dark highway, and for the rest of the drive, they were silent.

CHAPTER FIFTEEN

Darius slowly lowered himself into the chair because he knew if he weren't intentional about it, his exhausted muscles would give out beneath him. Thorn took the seat beside him, and a sigh poured from her mouth as soon as the cushion hit the back of her thighs.

"I understand how tired you both must be," Alan said as he settled behind his desk, "and I appreciate your willingness to debrief me on this situation while the details are fresh in your mind. How is Mrs. Khoury?"

What little strength Darius had left drained out, leaving him hollow as Thorn shook her head.

"Not great," she said. She closed her eyes and pressed her fingertips into the bridge of her nose. "Abraham is with her now."

Darius's mind drifted back to the last twelve hours. Samira hadn't spoken the entire drive north. Not when they stopped to clean up and heal their wounds, not when they'd rendezvoused with John and Nicholas after abandoning their old rental, and not when Thorn had insisted she wear a blindfold for the last thirty minutes of the trip. The new Virtue had endured it all stoic and quiet—a crying statue.

"She has been through a lot," Alan said. Rae sat beside

him, her ears alert, eyes bright and awake in a way that almost made Darius jealous. The wolf's tail swooped from side to side as Alan drew a breath. "The question I have is how the Sins managed to find her."

"I don't think they did," Thorn said.

"No?" Alan asked with a frown.

"No," Thorn said. "I don't think they ever realized she was there. They were after *Leroy*."

Alan's brows raised. "Let's start from the beginning."

For several minutes, Thorn laid out what they knew, referring to Darius occasionally to help her fill in the details. She covered the peril, the Puppets, the plan, every little thing, from the moment they arrived on the scene to when they overheard Terrance Moore and Carlos Ruiz outside of the greenhouse. Then, for the first time, Thorn kept something to herself.

"Hunt has plans for Rose."

Lust's voice echoed in Darius's memory, and it was enough to make the pit of his stomach drop.

But Thorn said nothing about it, jumping instead to the woods. Gloria was dead, she was captured, and Gluttony ran when Darius attacked him.

Alan's lips pressed together, and his index fingers steepled against them. Rae was less ambiguous. Her hackles raised, and the corner of her lip threatened a snarl. Darius glanced between them once before landing on Alan, who finally took a deep breath and said, "What do you make of it?"

"Obviously, Wrath found out about Leroy," Thorn said irritably. Though she didn't seem nearly as tired as Darius felt, dark circles had begun to form under her eyes. "She made it clear to Moore that he had to take care of him or she would—"

"That's not what I mean," Alan snapped. He briefly closed his eyes and exhaled in a slow stream before he continued more evenly. "About Gluttony *running*. He had an opportunity to kill a Virtue and apprehend you. Why wouldn't he take it?"

The question felt guided. Thorn shook her head, but Darius sighed. "You think it's because he didn't know my Virtue."

Alan's sharp eyes moved to him.

"That is precisely what I think," he said. "For all he knew, you could have destroyed him then and there. We have suspected this for a while, but this is the clearest example we've seen of it. It's interesting, but to be frank, I am not keen on exploring the theory further."

"I agree," Thorn said, and she threw Darius a sidelong look.

"I wasn't exploring anything," he argued.

"Of course not," Alan said. "You acted accordingly and took care of your partner. It's admirable, and you did excellent work. But I do not want this to give you a false sense of security. Do not act rashly because you think you might be safe. You are not."

Heat rose to Darius's cheeks, and he set his jaw with a nod. Alan watched him for a moment longer before he turned to Thorn. If Darius wasn't mistaken, he seemed to be giving her the same admonishing look. Thorn raised her brows, like she was challenging him to say what he was thinking, but instead, he changed the subject. "Now, let's discuss this new development: Leroy and Samira Khoury. Are we certain the Sins have no idea about Mrs. Khoury and her Virtue?"

"We're not certain about anything," Thorn responded. "But it seemed like Leroy hid her without being spotted, and they never made any indication they knew *any* of us were there until I used my Influence."

"Good," Alan said. "I had Miss Andrews do some research. Mrs. Khoury was born outside of Atlanta and moved to Sandersville when she helped establish Reflection Farms. It goes without saying that Leroy did not have any records. Even their marriage was off the books. This means we have very little to go off of in regard to finding him other than sending people down to Charlotte. Does he have a phone? Anything else we might be able to track?"

Thorn shook her head, and Alan frowned.

"He will likely resort to risky activities to move more quickly. That will draw the wrong kind of attention." Alan sighed. "Get a report together, provide as much of a physical description as you can, and we will send a Recon unit down to look for him."

"I can leave tomorrow," Thorn said.

"No," Alan said sharply, shaking his head. "No, you are needed in the Underground. As soon as your report is in, we will assign a team to Charlotte." Alan got to his feet and looked between Darius and Thorn again. "Thank you. I understand the last twenty-four hours have been extremely trying. Please, go get some sleep, and I want you both to set up an appointment to speak with Abraham in the morning."

Thorn's lip curled indignantly, but she and Darius thanked Alan and excused themselves. For the first time in months, Darius couldn't wait to go to his room and sink into bed. He moved toward the hallway, but Thorn walked across the lounge to her office. He paused.

"What are you doing?" he asked.

"Writing that report."

Darius stared at her. "*Now?*"

Her jaw tightened, and so did the fingers gripping the doorknob. "I need people looking for Leroy," she said. "I can't abandon him down there."

She watched Darius as though she expected him to argue, and he thought about doing just that, but then Leroy's face interrupted those thoughts. Darius groaned and rolled his head forward.

"Okay," he said, regretting it as soon as it came out of his mouth. "Fine. Let's make it quick."

"I've got this," Thorn said.

"What are you going to do?" Darius asked, coming beside her and grabbing the handle, too. "Make up my side of the story?"

Thorn didn't budge, and they stood there—Darius trying to pull the door open, and Thorn firmly keeping it closed. She shook her head.

"Jones—"

"Can you stop arguing for *once* in your life?" Darius asked, letting out a quiet laugh and raising his brows. Thorn frowned. He worried the joke didn't land, but after a moment, her wall cracked, and the corner of her mouth raised in a smirk.

"God, you're fucking impossible," she said as she opened the door and walked inside. Darius followed behind her. Thorn shrugged her satchel from her shoulder, hung it on the back of her chair, and gestured to the crimson sofa across the room without looking at it. "Have a seat."

He did, and while she got a notebook and pen out from her top drawer, Darius took notice of just how *comfortable* the cushions were behind his back, and he inched forward off them. Sitting here had been risky, but Thorn didn't have anywhere else for him to go. He glanced to his left, where a dark gray pillow and blanket were neatly folded on the arm of the couch. He yearned to collapse onto them.

For the first few minutes, while Thorn filled in the boring report details—time, date, involved parties, and the like—Darius looked around the room. He'd been here a handful of times, and he was always surprised at how organized Thorn's space felt. The office itself was tidy. She had neat stacks of papers at one corner of her desk, an array of maps and photographs on the other, and an empty trashcan tucked behind it. Even the table in front of Darius didn't have so much as a coffee ring staining the wood.

The walls, however, were chaos. Darius was sure Thorn understood the madness here, but he couldn't entirely make sense of what he was looking at. Two of them—the one directly behind her desk and the one across from the door— were papered in an elaborate web of intel and photographs that made the spy movies Darius had watched as a kid seem amateurish.

"Okay," Thorn said at last. She never felt like the kind of person who belonged behind a desk, and it was weird seeing her there now. Sparkie crawled out from her satchel and curled up on Thorn's shoulder as she swiped a wisp of hair behind her ear. The long strands caught on his scales. She looked up at Darius. "You ready?"

They discussed each moment, beat by beat, and Thorn would spend several minutes writing down that part of the story before moving on. They started from when they arrived on the farm and met Gloria. Thinking of her made Darius's stomach drop, and he noticed Sparkie shift uncomfortably while Thorn wrote.

For the next half hour or so, that's how it went. Slowly and meticulously. Darius's eyes were starting to glaze over by the time they reached the woods again. When Thorn spoke, he startled.

"Now," she said, and this time, she put her pen down. "When we got separated…"

Darius sighed and leaned back on the couch, running his hands down his face. "Uh, right," he murmured. "Well, we headed south. Samira's feet were pretty beaten up, so we couldn't move that quickly, but none of the Puppets were following us. I felt Gloria's aura disappear." He cleared his throat and glanced up at Thorn. Her face was impossible to read, and she watched him patiently over laced fingers. She looked so strikingly like Alan at that moment. Darius shook his head and went on. "So I told Samira to wait, and I went back. I just followed Moore's energy."

Right to him. Darius remembered catching sight of him in the dark as he whipped his flashlight around. The dull *thunk* when he hit Thorn with it and the way her screaming made the forest seem like it went on forever. Darius had been so full of rage and adrenaline that everything seemed to move in slow motion as he came crashing through the trees. The feeling of Gluttony's skull fracturing had vibrated through the crowbar, up Darius's arms, and down his spine.

"I saw an opportunity to attack him, so I did."

"And you noticed him start to run?" Thorn asked.

"Yeah. I thought he might," Darius said, and then he admitted something he had *not* mentioned when they'd spoken with Alan. "I almost went after him."

Thorn's eyes widened. "*What?*"

"If we'd been able to kill Moore, all the Programming in the NYPD would disappear—"

"Yes," Thorn cut in. "But to follow a Sin into the dark— you could've gotten yourself killed."

"I didn't, did I?" Darius snapped, and he looked hard at Thorn from across the room. She glared back, her lips a thin line of disapproval. "So it doesn't matter. We got out. We're here now. We're safe."

Even Darius could feel how bitterly that came out. Thorn looked him over for a few more quiet moments. Then she took a deep breath, held it for a beat, and exhaled it in a slow sigh.

"Yeah," she murmured. "We are."

Without another word, Thorn turned back to writing. The tension in the room hung heavy for the first few minutes, but soon it dissipated like a bad smell.

Darius's mind was too tired to hold onto the negativity, and he watched Thorn write with absent, hypnotic interest. The way her left hand glided over the paper was elegant and foreign. Her whole arm gently swooped up and down, almost on a rhythm, and Darius remembered thinking that he wanted to ask her why she didn't just type her reports, but he'd been too captivated watching her. Thorn didn't look up. Her black eyes focused on her work, and her lips pulled so subtly together Darius might have been making it up. He blinked…

When he opened his eyes again, he was in the dark.

For a few seconds, everything looked off. The hard lines and shapes of the things in front of him didn't make any sense. He took a moment to ground himself. It was quiet. Dimly lit, just enough for Darius to make out the general form and colors of the room. He could sense Martyrs below and behind him, and he felt something soft pressed against his cheek.

God, he was lying down.

Darius moved to sit up, but he was surprised to find his arms trapped beneath a warm blanket drawn nearly to his throat. The couch beneath him conformed to his body, begging him to stay nice and comfortable here. Darius was tempted to listen. With a groan, he forced his way up, the blanket slumping from his chest as he stretched and looked around. His stomach flipped as he remembered where he was.

Thorn's office.

His hands finally free, Darius rubbed the heels of his palms against his closed eyes. Damn. He'd been trying to make sure this exact thing *didn't* happen. He glanced at his watch, and his eyes went wide. It was eight in the morning.

He'd been asleep for more than *twelve* hours?

"Shit."

Darius threw the blanket off and jumped to his feet. He couldn't remember the last time he'd slept this long—or, he realized, the last time he'd woken up feeling so well-rested. As he grabbed the door handle, he turned to Thorn's office one last time, and he paused.

Her spiral notebook was closed, sitting slightly to the left of center on the desk, and a stack of torn papers sat on top of it. Attached to the corner, a bright green note stood out in the dull light. Darius frowned and came back to find his name written on it in Thorn's immaculate script.

"Darius," it read. *"Finished the report. Read it, sign it, and turn it in. - T"*

He flipped through the pages. Thorn had put more detail than Darius had remembered them discussing—a *lot* more detail. How long had he been passed out on her couch while she worked? A hot flush rose to his cheeks as he quickly turned to the last page and scanned through to the part where Thorn talked about what happened with Gluttony, his stomach in knots. She mentioned the fight, Moore running, and how they suspected he was afraid of Darius and his Virtue.

But she did *not* mention that Darius had wanted to follow him.

The knots in his stomach relaxed. Without reading the rest, he scrawled his horrendous signature beside Thorn's perfect one and snatched the report off the desk. Then he hurried into the lobby, jammed the paperwork into the intake basket pinned to the wall beside Alan's door, and rushed into the hallway.

Everything in Abraham's office fit into a handsome blue and brown color scheme. When Darius had his first mandated appointment following Eva's death, Abraham told him all about it. It was a psychological decision. Blue and brown elicited feelings of calm and stability, and Abraham wanted people to feel as comfortable as possible when they sat down on his couch—because the things they came to talk about were often violent, chilling, and painful.

"How are you holding up?"

Darius dragged his focus up from his feet. Abraham leaned back in a tall, upholstered armchair on the other side of a glass coffee table. Even the lighting in this room was different. While all the offices had bright, sterile lights installed in the ceilings, Abraham kept those off. Instead, warm lamps on end tables gave the room a more natural glow so they could pretend, for a moment, they weren't in a basement. The round lines in Abraham's long face were cast in soft shadows as he watched Darius with a calm, genuine interest, his hands clasped in his lap, one leg crossed over the other in a way that felt stereotypical for his position here. Darius thought it made him more approachable.

Probably another psychological decision.

Darius sighed and shook his head, looking back at his sneakers. They were the only pair he had—the same ones he'd been wearing five days ago—still caked in soil. He rubbed the heel of one shoe against the arch of the other and watched as flakes of dirt fell off.

"I think I'm still processing it," he admitted. "A lot happened while we were down there."

"Yeah," Abraham said. "I read the report."

Darius scoffed and rubbed his eyes with the tips of his fingers. They were so tired they stung. "Everyone's read the report."

Ever since he'd joined the Martyr leadership, Darius had never seen an incident report move throughout the lower ranks of the Underground as quickly as the one he and Thorn put together about the situation in Sandersville, Georgia. It was all anyone could talk about, and he could hardly walk through the courtyard without people asking about it.

"Is that hard for you?" Abraham asked. "Everyone reading it?"

"It's not really hard," Darius said. He sat back on the couch and ran his hand absently along the arm. The charming, tawny microsuede felt like velvet under his palm. He took a deep, centering breath. "But people want to hear more about it, and I just don't know what to tell them."

"What do they want to hear more about?"

Darius's stomach twisted. "Mostly about Samira."

"Ah." Abraham nodded. "That's not surprising."

"I guess not," Darius admitted with a frown. "It's a lot like when Gabe came in. He was all anyone could talk about for over a month."

Abraham let out a light chuckle and scratched the back of his head. "It's more than just getting new members. Gabe DuPont is a former cop. That was hard for a lot of us. He also recently passed his shooting and combat exams. I don't imagine people like the idea of him joining the team."

Darius nodded. He guessed he could see their point, but Gabe DuPont and all his history seemed like such a little thing now. Who cared about that when he had a Virtue who didn't want to destroy her Sin?

"With Samira, it's different," Abraham went on. "People are just confused. So is she. I actually had a session with her this morning."

"How's she doing?" Darius asked. Since they'd gotten back to the Underground, Samira had hardly left the room she'd been assigned, and when she did, she walked like a ghost stuck halfway between two dimensions, unsure where she really belonged.

"Well, I can't talk about her session," Abraham said, "but how would you feel if you were separated from your spouse, and they never showed up where they'd agreed to meet you? Destabilized, maybe? On top of that, a couple of neighboring farms were also found massacred…"

A tightness wrapped around Darius's chest. Yesterday morning, news broke about the "cult suicide" at three separate locations: Reflection Farms and two neighboring properties. It seemed the Sins had been angry, and that anger spilled onto even more innocent lives. Over seventy people were listed among the dead. Samira was one of them.

"Yeah," Darius said. "She's been through a lot."

"She has," Abraham agreed. "But so have you. You came face-to-face with Gluttony."

Darius let out a cold, quiet laugh and leaned back. "You know," he said, "that's the other thing people want to know about. They want to hear about the fight, but there wasn't one. I hit him once, and he ran away. I guess I should consider myself lucky."

Abraham frowned. "You don't?"

"No, I do," Darius corrected, clearing his throat as he averted his gaze. He didn't want to give Abraham any reason to think he wouldn't be fit for duty—assuming he ever passed his damned assessments. "But I was just… so ready to fight. He had already killed people, and he ended up killing more. Everyone at that farm is dead, Abraham." A silence fell, and Darius shook his head. "If he'd kept coming, maybe I could have destroyed the host."

A cold rush flooded through Darius's stomach at the thought. "Destroy the host" was just a nice way of saying, "murder the poor man trapped with a Sin in his soul."

"Or you could have been killed yourself," Abraham stated.

"That's what Thorn said," Darius scoffed. "If it were up to her, I'd never be in the same *area code* as a Sin."

Abraham chuckled. "I don't know about that. She did credit you with saving her life."

Darius's heart fluttered, and his eyes widened a bit. Abraham smiled at him, and Darius quickly shook his head. "Thorn came to her therapy appointment?"

That time, Abraham's laugh was even louder. "Of course not," he said, and he took a shallow, annoyed breath. Then he rolled up the sleeves of his patterned, button-up shirt. "No, Jacob and I joined her to register his new car with Holly. He asked about the report, too. I guess you're right. Everyone has read it." He caught Darius's eye, straightened himself again, and went on. "Anyway, Thorn talked about how lucky she was that you were there."

Darius's cheeks felt warm, and he shrugged dismissively. "We're just lucky he didn't know I'm not Temperance. If he had, he probably would've come for me."

A cold stone fell into Darius's stomach, all the warmth in his face draining through the hole it left behind.

"Hell, we're actually pretty *un*lucky," he said. "Because we did have Temperance there."

He glanced down at the table to see Abraham reflected in the glass. He sat still, collected, as he watched Darius, but he looked like a specter. "I imagine it's hard for you," Abraham acknowledged. Darius looked back up to him. "It's been hard for us, too. Most of the Martyrs have been here for years, and this battle is our life." Abraham opened his arms up with a shrug. "We were fighting it even before we had a chance at winning. Before we had Virtues. To find one who isn't willing to help is… crushing."

"I get that being a Virtue isn't easy," Darius said. "I

didn't accept mine right away, but this is different. I saw my Virtue as something that destroyed my life. Samira already Initiated hers. She saw it as 'a gift from God.'"

Darius's throat tightened, and he swallowed, trying to loosen the resentment building there.

"I can understand how she sees it that way," Abraham reasoned. That made Darius's anger more agitated. It bubbled from his chest. "She was raised in a Christian home, and we use the names for the Sins and Virtues that Christian historians adopted in their doctrine. For someone with that background, I see how Virtue power could feel holy."

"Even so," Darius growled, "how can she believe in a god that wouldn't want her to use that gift to destroy *real* evil?"

Abraham shook his head. "I'm sure she doesn't see her god that way. She did a lot of good work on that farm."

"The farm wasn't more important than the rest of the world, was it?" Darius asked, exasperated. He couldn't believe he was having this fight with Abraham, too. "How can't she see what we're doing here? How important it is?"

"How could she?" Abraham asked. "Has she ever seen a Sin first-hand?"

Darius paused, feeling the indignation in his stomach burning like bile. "No," he said. "Not until this weekend."

"Then how could she possibly understand what we're fighting against?"

"We told her," Darius defended. "We explained everything."

"And that could have made her even more resistant to it," Abraham said. "This might be the first time her faith has ever been challenged. Holding onto that life probably had more to do with preserving what she believed in than it did with anything else."

Darius frowned. "What do you mean?"

"Darius," Abraham said with a soft sigh. He leaned forward, propped his elbows on his knees, and laced his fingers in front of him. Darius leaned in, too. "Almost by necessity, most religions are not very flexible. They're a blueprint, I guess. A rulebook on what to do and what not to do, and certainty in what happens when you follow that rulebook. For some, that's heaven. Others, reincarnation. Whatever it is, it's stable, and it feels *real* to you. It makes life feel safe.

"And then," he went on, his voice low, as he looked off to the right. "Something happens that makes you question everything you thought was absolute truth, and the whole paradigm shifts. Some people find a way to blend their faith into their new reality, but others lose it entirely. And losing your faith is hard. It feels as real as losing a close friend. Your security, your comfort, your identity is just gone, and even though you can't go back to believing again, you sometimes wish you could just so the world was a little less scary."

Abraham didn't look back at him for a few long moments, and Darius found he couldn't watch the distant, empty pain on the man's face. Instead, he looked over Abraham's shoulder to the massive, oak shelf filled with volumes of books and old photographs. Darius had seen this shelf a hundred times, looked into these faces so often they were familiar to him now. An older couple Darius assumed to be Abraham's parents. Abraham and Stella, standing beneath a stunning, white canopy at their wedding. Lina, behind a podium, wearing a graduation cap and gown. A younger, healthier Jacob, with full cheeks and a military uniform, decades before the Sins had broken him. Today, Darius couldn't help but notice how much broader their smiles were, how much more life shined behind their eyes before this war sank its teeth into them.

"I'm sorry," Darius said, turning back to Abraham. Abraham turned back, too.

"Thank you," he said, smiling, but it was half-formed. "I'm not saying this because I think Samira is right. I can't say what's right or wrong for her. But she's going through more than losing her home, her family, and her husband. She's potentially losing herself, and we have no idea how she'll come out of this. It will be hard, but it's important not to get our hopes up. Samira might never choose to destroy Gluttony."

"So," Darius said, flopping against the back of the couch with a sigh, "what you're saying is I need to let go of the things I couldn't change, the things I can't control, and focus on what I can do now to move forward."

Abraham chuckled. "At the risk of sounding like a broken record, yes."

"Yeah," Darius said, not really believing it. "You're right. I just… when I Initiated, I *knew* this was where I belonged. I knew I had to play my part here, and that's never changed. Not when I thought I was going to die, and not now. Why is it *so* different for her?"

Abraham's mouth turned into a small smile. "I don't know, but maybe you could talk with her, get to know her. You might find out. She could use a friend right now."

Darius's stomach dropped, and he thought back to his first few weeks in the Underground and the Martyrs who worked hard to make him feel welcome. Abraham. William Michaels. Even Thorn, in her own way. It wasn't the purpose, or the war, or even the need for vengeance that had sold Darius on this place.

It had always been about the people.

Maybe he could be one of those people for Samira.

CHAPTER SIXTEEN

Breakfast in the courtyard was uncharacteristically busy. With most of TAC still grounded, Kenia had her work cut out. She looked a little frazzled as she set a fresh plate of bacon and eggs on the counter, and Darius thanked her earnestly as he picked it up and made his way into the dining area. Most of the tables were taken by individuals, and Darius spotted Mackenzie at the edge. She was already halfway through her meal, reading something on a tablet. He put down his plate, and she glanced up at him.

"Good morning, sunshine," she said with a grin.

"Morning." Darius looked over the device in her hands, where he saw a firearm manual. He chuckled and pointed at it with his fork. "Trying to pass your exams the Lina way?"

Mackenzie ran her hands down her face and exhaled a dramatic groan. "Fuck—*yes*, I *am*. This shouldn't be so goddamned hard. DuPont passed his shooting test after three fuckin' lessons!"

The corners of her mouth curled into a subtle sneer.

"He was a cop before he came to the Underground," Darius said. "What did you expect?"

Mackenzie scoffed as she looked down at her plate. "I didn't expect him to *stay* in the Underground."

Darius's brows drew together. Gabe was doing well here, and once he passed his Influence Resistance test, he was set to join TAC officially. Darius, for one, was grateful. It felt like only he and Chris were. Mackenzie and Conrad complained about the decision loudly whenever anyone would listen.

"So." Mackenzie cleared her throat and turned off the tablet. "What's on your agenda for the day? Still harassing that new Virtue?"

Now it was Darius's turn to groan, and Mackenzie cast him a sly smile.

"I've gone by her room every morning for a week," he said. "I've offered to show her around, asked her to join me for dinner, invited her on a walk above ground… Nothing's working."

"Did Abraham have any bright ideas?" Mackenzie asked.

"He says I should 'give her time.'"

"Sounds like an Abraham solution."

"I just don't know what else to try," Darius muttered.

"Bring her up to R&D," Mackenzie suggested with a shrug before shoving a bite of egg into her mouth.

Darius frowned. "She has no interest in joining the Underground at all. I don't want her to feel like I'm pressuring her."

Because he knew pressuring her wouldn't solve a damn thing. He was hoping more to *endear* her—make her feel as at home here as he did so maybe she wouldn't want to leave.

Mackenzie shook her head and wiped her mouth with the back of her hand. A rainbow assortment of band bracelets hung from her wrist, making her short, vibrant orange hair somehow not the most colorful thing about her.

"You're looking at it wrong," she said. "She doesn't give a fuck about this place, but you know what she *does* give a fuck about? Her husband."

Darius covered his mouth with his fingertips as his jaw fell open.

"Leroy—oh, man, Mackenzie. You're right."

"I know."

"R&D is looking for him," Darius thought aloud.

Mackenzie took another bite. "I know," she said again, this time with a mouth full of food. She quickly got that down, too, and leaned across the table. "I'd put ten bucks down that she jumps at the chance to see what we're doing to find him. She seems like the type who's too shy to ask herself."

Darius nodded, but his eyes were focused behind Mackenzie's head, where Samira's Virtue tugged at him from the western block of rooms. He got to his feet.

"Thanks a ton," Darius said as he grabbed Mackenzie's shoulder with one hand and squeezed it gratefully.

"Oy," she said, turning to watch him as he walked away. "What about breakfast?"

"Not hungry," Darius called back to her.

Samira had been assigned quarters close to the court-yard—just like Darius and Eva had been when they'd first arrived—to ensure she didn't get lost in the labyrinth of the Underground.

His stomach turned in on itself as he passed their old room. In the last seven days, Darius had walked by it more often than he had in months. He could almost feel the ghost of Eva's aura walking around, and he forced the memories away as he turned the next corner and stopped outside Samira's door.

He didn't even need to knock. Before he raised his hand, Samira's voice rang out. "Thank you, Darius, but I would rather be alone."

Darius leaned his head against the door and spoke into the crease where it met the frame. "I thought you might want to see what we're doing to find Leroy."

Through the wood, he felt Samira's whole body freeze, and a moment later, her Virtuous aura leapt up. Darius smirked as she pulled the door open, just enough for him to see one of her beautiful, brown eyes in the crack.

"What do you mean?" she asked.

"It's been over ten days since we left Georgia," Darius said. "Our Research and Discovery Department is starting a wider search for Leroy." He paused and raised his hands at his sides in a half-shrug. "I figured you might want to see what that looks like. Maybe you can help. You know him better than anyone."

Samira's eyes filled with quiet tears, but they didn't fall. Instead, she opened the door a little wider, poked her head out, and said, "I would like that very much. I need a few minutes to get dressed. Is that okay?"

Darius's smile stretched wider. "No problem. I'll be waiting in the courtyard."

He made his way back with a kick in his step that hadn't been there in a long time. Mackenzie's fiery orange hair was still sitting at the same table, and a few more Martyrs had filled in the space around her. As he approached, Mackenzie's weak, fuzzy aura came to life.

"That worked," he said as he came up beside her. Mackenzie looked up sheepishly, and he glanced down to see she'd grabbed the plate of food he hadn't touched. He raised a brow, chuckled, and went on. "Samira's getting dressed now. You were right."

"Of course I was," Mackenzie said with a grin, and she put her fork down before she threw her hands behind her head. Darius noticed a half-dozen or so tiny, white scars spidering down from the inside of her left elbow. "Happens a lot. Now, can you tell Lina that? Thorn, too. Actually, just tell the whole damn Underground. I deserve some recognition." She winked, and Darius laughed.

"You got it," he said. Then the lure from Samira's soul stepped into the courtyard. It was the most powerful sensation in the Underground now, and it immediately drew Darius's attention. He still hadn't gotten used to having another Virtue around again.

When she reached the courtyard, she hesitated. Darius knew she'd never left her room with the Underground this busy. Typically, he felt her moving early in the morning, showering, gathering food, and doing whatever else she needed to do well before the rest of the Martyrs were up and active. That felt familiar, too. He waved to catch her attention, and she smiled nervously as she continued his way.

While Darius noticed Samira right away, it took the rest of the Martyrs a little longer. Mackenzie was first, following Darius's cue and glancing over her shoulder, followed by Seth Graves and Alexis Claytor. They sat at the table to Darius's right, and Alexis elbowed Seth and gestured with her chin to where Samira was walking toward them. Then Stevie, who was eating alone, turned up, too. Her dark eyes were unreadable, and she quietly chewed her food while Samira approached. Even Kenia paused, holding a plate of fresh bacon above the serving counter as the new Virtue stopped at Darius's side. Samira looked up, and the rest of the Martyrs quickly busied themselves with their food again. Mackenzie got to her feet.

"Samira!" she said. "It's nice to finally meet you."

Mackenzie's voice worked like a valve, releasing the pressure in the room and making it easier to breathe again. The Irishwoman held out a hand. For a moment, Samira just stared at her, taking in all of Mackenzie's details—from the distressed shoes on her feet, her hole-ridden skinny jeans, and the bright paint on her nails. When she finally looked at Mackenzie's face again, it was plastered with a wide smile.

"Name's Mackenzie. I'm the director of the 'Discovery' half of the Research and Discovery Department."

Samira took her hand, shaking it awkwardly. "*You* are the one leading the search for my husband?"

"Eh, kinda," Mackenzie said. "My guys follow up on our leads. The research team is behind most of the really hard work. Lina Brooks runs that side of things, and not to brag, but she's the smartest person I have ever met. You're in good hands."

She grinned wider, and Samira's mouth turned up in a

tight, nervous smile. Darius glanced at Mackenzie, raising his brows, which she did in return. "We're headed up there now," he said. "You coming?"

Mackenzie shook her head and thrust a thumb back at the table. "I'll hustle up once I finish my breakfast—I'm sorry, *your* breakfast."

Darius laughed. "Sounds good. We'll catch you in a bit."

After Mackenzie said her goodbyes and sat back down, Darius led Samira away from the crowd—and the staring. All kinds of Martyrs from all walks of the Underground followed them with their eyes. At one of the last tables, sitting with Skylar, was Nicholas. He and Darius exchanged a look. The hollow spots beneath Nicholas's cheekbones looked deeper than Darius was used to as he watched the side of Samira's face. She met his eye and quickly focused on the path in front of her again. When the elevator doors closed behind him, Darius exhaled a breath and hit the button for the first floor. They slowly began to rise.

After a few seconds, Samira said, "Who is he?"

Darius turned to her. "Hmm?"

"That man, Nicholas? Was that his name?" she asked. Darius nodded, and Samira went on. "He was one of the men who picked us up. At first, I thought he might be another lost—sorry, Forgotten Sin—like Leroy, but he looks different."

"What do you mean 'different?'" Darius asked.

"More broken," Samira said quietly. "Like the pain is fresher."

Darius's body suddenly felt cold. "Yeah," he murmured. "That's because it is. Nicholas isn't a Forgotten Sin. He was Diligence. Eight months ago, he gave up his soul to destroy Sloth."

Samira's jaw dropped, and Darius looked back at the doors, wishing they would open.

While the TAC unit was trudging along at limited capacity until they could acquire a new fleet of vehicles, R&D was working like mad. Their load had been divided for a while, with half the department trying to verify that the Sins had returned to New York. Now, though, since Caleb Claytor spotted Ruiz in his usual haunts, Thorn felt Hunt's Influence bobbing around the city again, and Holly had been able to track Gluttony's phone to Manhattan, each and every person in this room was set to look for Leroy Khoury.

Darius opened the R&D door to a wave of hot, human energy and a disjointed chorus of typing, clicking, and murmuring. Researchers dug through the previous day's news articles, social posts, and police calls for any sign of the Forgotten Sin. Samira paused in the doorway.

"Ideally," Darius said, "this department is focused on tracking down more Virtues, but we get pulled in different directions a lot. Last year, we were trying to find a Sin who was on the run, and—" his throat suddenly cinched around the words as he thought about Saul, Juniper, and Lindsay, and he let out a little cough "—a few other missing people. Right now, they're all looking for your husband."

When Darius closed the door, it shut with a click, and Parker Boseman looked up from the nearest computer. Her eager face broke into a smile as she saw him, and that smile faded a bit as she took in Samira. She waved, and Darius raised a hand back.

"C'mon," he murmured to Samira. "Lina can give you the full breakdown… maybe a bit more than you need, to be honest."

He chuckled, but Samira just gave an uncomfortable smile, and they walked to the back of the room. Lina, as usual, was so absorbed in her reading that she didn't notice them until Darius gently touched her arm. She startled a bit and spun around. Then her mouth opened in a soft, kind smile.

"Darius!" She got to her feet and grabbed his forearm. "I'm sorry! I didn't realize you were coming in today!"

"It's fine," Darius said with a chuckle. "I just wanted to show Samira what we're working on up here. Lina, this is Samira. Samira, Lina."

Then he gestured to where the new Virtue stood timidly behind him. Like Mackenzie, Lina gladly held out a hand. Her thin, graceful fingers wrapped around Samira's palm.

"It's a pleasure to finally meet you, Samira," Lina said, her eyes crinkling happily at the corners. "That's such a beautiful name. Arabic, right?"

Samira blinked, and her forced smile softened as her shoulders finally relaxed. "Yes, it is. My great-grandparents immigrated from Lebanon."

"Oh," Lina said longingly. "Lebanon is *such* a fascinating country. Have you ever been?"

"I wish I could say I have," Samira said. "We were supposed to go the year I graduated high school, but the Israeli Civil War broke out that summer, and my parents felt it was too dangerous."

Lina gave a conceding nod. "Ah, yes, that would do it. Well, you have an incredible heritage. Many of the leading theories on the Sins argue that their modern rise to power was centered in what is now Lebanon, Jordan, and Syria."

Darius frowned. "Their *modern* rise to power? Did they have a fall in power?"

An eager glint lit up Lina's eyes. "They absolutely did. Looking at our ancient history, especially in the earlier eras when there were more than just the seven Sins we know today, we can see clear signs of their power waxing and waning. They appear to have been strongest when they came together and centralized their efforts and weaker when they divided. But, more importantly, I've found some evidence that the *Virtues* have cycles like this, too! Come look at this."

She moved back to her desk, closed the book she'd been buried in, and tapped the cover: *The Many Rises And Falls Of Mankind,* by Teresa E. Solomon. Darius's eyes went wide.

"Wait," he said, leaning over further, his eyes narrow. "Is that *our* Teresa?"

Lina nodded enthusiastically. "Yes! This is a first edition that we grabbed from her study. I read this book when I was getting my doctorate!"

Samira's eyes widened. "You're a doctor?"

"I suppose, technically," Lina said absently as she opened Teresa's book again. "I have a Ph.D. in history with a dual focus on world history and religious studies."

"And you read *Teresa's* book?" Darius repeated.

"It was a staple for one of my classes," Lina said. "I've been following in Dr. Solomon's footsteps all these years, learning about Sins and Virtues from a woman studying them herself, and I never even knew."

Darius's chest filled with a bittersweet warmth. "That's amazing," he began, but Lina raised her hand.

"It is," she agreed, "and it gets even better."

She opened the book again and began to flip through it. Hundreds of handwritten notes in Teresa's neat, familiar print lined the margins. Darius had spent months looking at that writing. It felt like seeing an old friend again.

"According to Dr. Solomon's notes," Lina said, wetting her thumb against her lower lip as she continued turning pages, "she believed Virtues appeared in boom-and-bust cycles. Human civilizations around the world have gone through huge bursts of cultural development followed by devastating crashes. The most familiar for those of us raised with Western Doctrine is the shift from the Classical Era into the Dark Ages, but it also happened with the collapse of the Indigenous populations in South America as well as the fall of the Bronze Age."

Darius's eyes widened. "You think we're in a boom?"

"It certainly seems like it, don't you think?" Lina asked. "The theory is that Virtues would Initiate and come together all at once, or in a short period of time, and their combined Influence brought out the best in people, generating revolution. Of course, this would be followed by Sin retaliation. Virtues would be killed, wars would break out. Dr. Solomon even suggested that the destruction of Sins *by*

Virtues could cause cultural collapse, too. Destroying the Sins would ruin a lot of centuries-old infrastructure and control, which might create chaos."

Darius's stomach dropped, and he shook his head. "So, what, destroying the Sins made things *worse* for society?"

Lina shrugged. "Maybe! Maybe not. Probably a little bit of both." She ran her hand over the book affectionately. "Mackenzie and I actually discussed this same boom-and-bust theory when we went to Egypt."

"When did you and Mackenzie go to *Egypt?*" Darius asked.

"Oh, fifteen, sixteen years ago," Lina said with a childlike exuberance. "Shortly after she joined the Martyrs. It was for my thesis, and Mackenzie had just been cleared to leave the Underground, so I asked Alan if she could come with me."

Samira's mouth turned down in a frown. "Why couldn't she leave the Underground?"

Lina paused, her bright eyes wide and lips parted as though she realized she'd accidentally said something she wasn't meant to. She looked between Darius and Samira awkwardly before she simply said, "Mackenzie had a lot of healing to do when she got here. Anyway." Lina cleared her throat as her right hand drifted to the pendant around her neck. "I'm sorry, you weren't here for a history lesson, were you?"

"No," Darius said. "We actually wanted to see if Samira can do anything to help find Leroy."

"Hmm." Lina's forehead furrowed thoughtfully, and she looked around the room. "Well, Daniel is in charge of organizing the search. Daniel?" A round-faced man looked up from his station. "Can you show Samira what you're doing in your search for Leroy Khoury? She's understandably very anxious about her husband, and she might be able to help."

"Uh, yeah, no problem," Daniel said.

He rolled his seat over, and Darius thanked Lina as he grabbed a couple of extra folding chairs from the table in the middle of the room. Samira lowered into the one beside

Daniel and looked over his desk. Her eyes lingered on the clutter of paper notes, dusty toys, and a screen full of so many tabs that even Darius had a hard time figuring out what was important and what wasn't. When her attention landed on an old photograph of a woman with a beautiful, full figure and dirty-blonde hair laughing against a backdrop of leafy trees in the fall, she paused.

"Is this your wife?" Samira asked. "She's very pretty."

Daniel's expression fell, and what little color he had in his face drained from it with a sigh. A guilty swell made Darius's gut feel heavy.

"Thanks," Daniel said. "We lost her less than a year ago."

Samira's lips opened in a quiet gasp, and she pressed her fingers against them. Darius stared at the photograph, numb and cold. Sara had been with him on different trip to find a Virtue—another disaster situation where the Sins somehow showed up, too. He hadn't even been able to bring her body home.

"I'm so sorry," Samira said, but Daniel shrugged.

"It's fine. Anyway," he started, forcing through the painful subject change by clearing his throat. His voice was tighter now. Samira stared at the side of his face with glistening, sad eyes. "Leroy. Uh. We're basically looking for any sign that he's in Charlotte. We've got live feeds for anything we can find in the city. Emergency responders, newspapers, social media…"

"What kind of signs do you expect to see?" she asked.

"Well, it depends," Daniel said. "Some would be really obvious—police reports, hospital check-ins—but it's way more likely it will be quieter than that. If your husband is *really* good, we might not see signs at all."

"What can I do to help?"

"Any info on him would be useful," Daniel said. He leaned back in his chair and scratched his patchy stubble as his face scrunched up. "If you know where he's more likely to go or what he likes to do… We're flying a little blind, so anything is better than nothing."

Samira let out a short scoff and looked down at her feet.

"Honestly," she said quietly, and the blush rose to her cheeks again, making her soft, tanned complexion a richer, warmer color. Her eyes began to fill with a new brush of tears. "Leroy and I didn't talk much about his past. He didn't remember much, and what he did was painful. We focused on building our future, and that future was always at Reflection Farms. I don't know where he would go without it."

Daniel cast a glance at Darius. Before either of them had a chance to say anything, the door to the room opened. Mackenzie arrived like a loud, colorful storm. She looked around, and when her bright eyes landed on Darius and Samira, she broke into a wide grin and made right for them.

"How's it going?" she asked as she grabbed one of the nearby chairs, pulled it up, and sat on it backward next to Darius. "Any luck on the husband hunt?"

Samira's eyes flashed with muted anger, but Daniel shook his head. "Not really. We were just talking about what kind of thing we're looking for and what information Samira could help us with."

"I'm afraid it's not much," Samira said. "We didn't talk about anything other than work."

Mackenzie ran her tongue piercing against the back of her teeth thoughtfully. "There's got to be something valuable in there," she said. "Did he have any special skills or anything?"

"Special skills?" Samira asked with a frown. "Like what?"

"Well," Mackenzie continued, scratching the back of her head. "Could he, I dunno… pick locks? Hack into any of your vehicles to start them without the key? Were there weapons he knew how to use or preferred to use?"

Samira's lips parted, her expression dark and indignant. "What are you implying?"

"I'm not implying anything," Mackenzie said. "I'm just

trying to get an idea of what he might resort to as he travels north. Anything illegal or dangerous will draw attention."

"My husband isn't a criminal," Samira went on, louder this time. Her voice silenced the cacophony of clicking as the nearest researchers paused to watch her. Parker, whose station was on Daniel's far side, threw Darius a quick, confused look.

For a moment, Mackenzie gawked, her blue eyes wide, her eyebrows so high on her head that her piercing hid behind her hair. "Uh, I didn't say he was," she said at last, "but he's got no money, right?" Samira didn't answer, but her lips tightened, which gave Mackenzie an answer anyway. "No car. No *network*. It's a long walk to Charlotte from Sandersville."

"That doesn't mean he's going to do anything bad," Samira defended. "He could hitchhike. Or work for bus fare. Or—"

"I didn't say *bad*," Mackenzie argued, and she cast a glance at Darius, who nodded in support. "I said *illegal*. I don't expect him to kill anyone, but if he's gonna get around without using Influence or Gluttony tracking him down, chances are he'll have to steal a car, cash, *something*, and that could get him caught."

"He won't," Samira asserted. Her voice was rising a little more, drawing attention from other researchers until no one was working anymore. Lina shifted at her desk. Darius felt her stand and move toward them as Samira kept talking. "Leroy's a good man. He has worked hard to be a good man. Just because *you're* willing to abandon your morals doesn't mean he is." She paused and took Mackenzie in again. Her face pinched together, affronted, like she'd been personally attacked. "He'll make it here without straying from His path as you have. You'll see."

All eyes locked on Mackenzie. Her entire body had gone rigid, and her arms crossed around her chest so hard that she might have been trying to crush the air from her lungs.

"Really?" Mackenzie's voice was low, almost shaky.

Every word came out louder than the one before it. "He hasn't 'strayed?' We're just going to pretend he didn't use his Influence to get people to do what he wanted, then? And *lied* to you about it?" She shook her head. Dug her fingers into her bicep. Darius glanced at Lina, looking for an idea of what to do, but Lina's attention held to Mackenzie like a lifeline. "Not to mention the fact that he fucking *stabbed somebody.*"

"That's not his fault," Samira said. She sat with her back straight and her hands clasped desperately in her lap. "*He* has something inside of him that he didn't understand, that he can't fully control without me—without the Lord. Whatever horrible thing happened to *your* soul… *you* did to *yourself.*"

Then Samira gestured at Mackenzie's heart, and the Irishwoman's teeth gnashed together. She got to her feet, and Darius followed, ready to step in, but Mackenzie held a hand up to stop him.

"You're right," Mackenzie hissed, tight with emotion. "I did. I wasn't always a good person. I got hooked on heroin and worked with my dealer—with *Sloth*—to get my fix. I sold myself, I sold *other people,* and it fucked me up. It fucked up a lot of other girls who didn't deserve it. All I've done since then is work my ass off to be better. You don't get to tell me that I'm not."

Samira shook her head. "A few good deeds can't erase a lifetime of sins. Only accepting Jesus into your heart can do that. 'No one comes to the Father except through Me…'"

Mackenzie raised a fist, and Lina jumped forward. Samira gasped as Lina wrapped her hand around Mackenzie's wrist and spun her around. While Darius told everyone the show was over and they needed to get back to work, he caught Lina whispering against Mackenzie's forehead. Mackenzie shook her head, her cheeks a fuming shade of pink, her eyes full and gleaming. Then Lina pulled her from the room. Everyone else turned back to their screens—staring at them without doing anything else that could be mistaken for something productive—except Samira. Her eyes followed the two women through the door and tracked their movement along the wall until they turned down another hallway and shut themselves inside Mackenzie's office.

When they were gone, Darius came up to Samira's side. "Come with me."

She glanced at him, surprised—maybe even intimidated—but she stood all the same and followed him out. Darius took them to the conference room one door over. He opened it, turned on the light, and ushered Samira in. When he closed them inside, his hand shook on the doorknob.

Then he turned around. "What the *hell* was that?"

"She was trying—"

"She was trying to find your husband," Darius interjected, his voice rising, and he pointed a finger behind them, where he could feel Mackenzie and Lina huddled together several yards back. "And you attacked her!"

Samira's lips slammed shut, and she wound her arms around the standard-issue Martyr t-shirt she'd been provided. It dwarfed her, making her seem even smaller than she was trying to make herself.

"You have no idea what Mackenzie's life has been like," Darius went on. "But you just treated her like a villain—no, worse, like she's going to *hell*, and for what? Doesn't your God teach you better than this? Aren't you supposed to love your neighbor? Was that love?"

Samira looked down at her feet.

"It wasn't," Darius said. "It was judgment. And I'm pretty sure your God tells you not to do that, too."

Now, Samira's whole face was a deep, purple-red, and her eyes filled with tears. She shoved her way past Darius, out the door, and ran down the hallway. Darius stood in the middle of the room and tried to center himself until he felt that Virtuous pull lock away in Samira's quarters again.

Then he walked to Mackenzie's office, but she wouldn't open the door.

CHAPTER SEVENTEEN

The gymnasium hummed with quiet, warm energy. Darius stood at the center of the recruits who had shown up for their Influence Resistance assessment. People from all of his different classes were here. John stood by the door. Ever since he'd been used in Darius's demonstration last month, he tended to keep further away, where he would draw less attention. Lucas Olsen, the first of the recruits Chris's new protocols had brought in, sat on the mat by the mirror behind him. Alexis Claytor. Daniel Park. Gabe DuPont. He walked in last, ducking down as he squeezed past John to stand on the wall beside him. John's face went cold, and his jaw clenched. Darius took a long, slow breath.

This was getting old.

In the days since his outburst at Samira, all Darius wanted was a break from the drama, but no matter where he looked, it followed him. When it wasn't people gossiping about what had happened in R&D that afternoon, it was about Gabe. Abraham wasn't wrong: between their newest recruit and their newest Virtue, the Martyrs had plenty to talk about, and Darius was so sick of the talking. The only relief he seemed to get was when he and Thorn trained or meditated. She hated the rumors more than he did.

"All right," Darius said, clearing his throat as he clapped his hands together. It echoed on the hard walls back at him. "You're all here to test for Influence Resistance. This will look a little different from what you did in our classes. As you can imagine, it's a lot easier to hold Influence off when you're in a controlled environment, so we're going to make it *less* controlled."

He held a hand out beside him, where Holly was situated at a table in the middle of the room. She had her laptop, a tall stool, and one of the Tactical VR headsets and gun devices. Her thick-rimmed glasses reflected her computer screen as she poured over it, making it impossible for Darius to see her eyes. She rustled her boyish, brown hair with her fingertips as she sorted through a few more things, completely unaware of—or, more likely, totally indifferent to—the students eyeing her nervously.

"You all know Holly Andrews," he went on. "On top of being our security lead, she's also a software genius. She's put together a program—"

"Purchased a program," Holly interrupted.

"*Purchased* a program that will put you right in the middle of a combat situation, similar to what you might see with the Sins," Darius said. "The idea is to get your emotions running high and see whether or not I can Influence your decisions. It's like the virtual shooting practice, but I'll be trying to mess you up."

"We're doing this *here?*" Alexis asked, her icy eyes wide. "In front of everyone?"

Darius nodded as he indicated a pop-up screen across the room. Alexis and the others turned toward it. "We're all here to observe each other," he confirmed. "Think of it as another layer of stress. The more stress you're under, the harder it will be to fight me off. The Sins won't wait to Influence you until you're alone in a comfortable room. They're going to take advantage of your environment and the way that environment affects you."

Alexis nodded, her pale face going even whiter. Daniel

Park raised his hand and said, "What do we have to… do? Exactly?"

"There are three possible scenarios: a crowded subway terminal, a barricaded bridge, and an industrial basement. Your goal is to get out of the situation," Darius said. He grabbed the VR handgun from the table and held it up. "Shooting the guys in red and trying to avoid everyone else." Daniel nodded, and Darius put the VR weapon back down, welcoming more questions. When none came, he took a deep breath and propped his hands on his hips. "So," he said on the exhale, "any volunteers to start us off?"

It was like someone pressed a button and paused the room. No one moved. No one spoke. Darius raised his brows and looked around, searching for someone brave enough to catch his eye. Anyone other than Gabe, who locked onto Darius, his shoulders square and hands clasped behind his back. With the contention surrounding Gabe, Darius didn't want him to go first. He was about to make an executive decision—put John on the spot again—when Gabe stepped off the wall.

"I'll go," he said.

Darius's jaw ground together. In the weeks since joining the Underground, Gabe's low fade haircut had grown out, but he'd styled it back in a way that still looked clean-cut and professional. His amber eyes were just as sharp, and they watched Darius with an intensity he was only used to seeing in Thorn. The silence in the room shattered as people shifted uncomfortably or whispered to their neighbors. Darius raised a hand to hush them.

"All right," he said with a nod. "Come on up."

Gabe walked around the people sitting on the edge of the mat. Alexis scooted over, holding her knees close, and shot him a cold glare when his back was to her. John crossed his arms and glowered across the room. None of it broke Gabe's poise. He took the stool with the same unwavering steadiness. When Holly handed him the headset, he put it on without a hitch and popped the wireless headphones into his ears. Darius put the fake pistol into Gabe's hands and stood behind him, where he could see the screen on the opposite wall. He wrapped his palm around the back of Gabe's neck. The man's skin was warm, his strong aura gripping Darius in a way that matched his attitude. Constant. Reliable.

"I'm going to maintain contact with you," Darius said, as much to the rest of the students as to Gabe directly. He looked around at them, and a few heads nodded. "That way, you won't know when it's coming. Are you ready?"

"Let's do it," Gabe said.

Holly sat back down, hit a button on her computer, and the program came to life.

Gabe started on the bridge. Immediately, a bright blast of gunfire sounded to the left. It poured from speakers at the corners of the room, and the entire group gasped and jumped as Gabe ducked down to cover his head. He slipped out of Darius's grip, and Darius swore quietly as he leaned forward to grab him again.

"Take a second to get used to the controls," Darius said. He blocked the rest of the students out as he focused on the screen and got into a better position to mirror Gabe's movements more quickly. Gabe nodded, and he took a deep breath as he centered himself.

The VR weapon also functioned as a controller, and Gabe used the joystick to direct his avatar to the right and hide behind a car. He spent a few moments there, playing with his view, testing the sights, and checking his surroundings. Then he turned, looked over the smoking hood of the abandoned vehicle, and down the bridge. Traffic in both directions ground to a halt, and though the sounds from the speakers were more muted, Darius knew the headphones in Gabe's ears were full of screaming, sirens, and shooting.

After another few seconds, Darius was tempted to push his Influence in just to get Gabe moving again, but as the thought crossed his mind, Gabe's avatar got up and started running.

Even in-game, Gabe was competent. He held the firearm ahead of him in perfect form, the virtual weapon aimed straight up the street while the physical one was directed at John's stomach. He watched Gabe, his glower fading, and his frown becoming more serious as Gabe spun in his stool. Gabe let out a small sigh as a mother hurried by with her children tucked under her arm as they sprinted away. More movement in the corner of his eye made him twist around again.

And Darius reached in. He felt Gabe's tension in the muscles along his neck, and Darius fed into that tension. A gun, he told him. There was a gun pointed right at Gabe's face. He should pull the trigger. It's either him or them.

But Gabe didn't respond. His energy molded into Darius's for a moment before Darius felt himself being pushed against. When Gabe's sights landed on the motion, it was another innocent. A man this time. Gabe rolled his shoulders and moved again.

It went like that for the next ten yards. Gabe ducked beneath deserted sedans and SUVs, shot at men in red shirts wielding weapons, and every time Darius tried to get him to pull the trigger on a civilian, Gabe told him no. He ducked again, swore and almost dove from the stool when an explosion blasted off to his left. Darius told him to run. Gabe didn't run. The rest of the room watched the screen, all animosity replaced by a rapt commitment. Not a single face wasn't focused on Gabe, and they all leaned forward. When he jumped, they jumped. When he swore, they would wring their hands. Cross their arms. Bite at their cuticles.

Gabe dove behind another car. He was almost to the end of the run now. Darius watched the screen, his hand still held tight against the back of Gabe's neck, as he peered over the hood, shot another enemy, and ducked again before he leapt up and made a run for it.

And another man screamed. Gabe turned to him. Saw the red shirt. The weapon. Went to pull the trigger.

But Darius pushed in. One last time. One last shot.

Because what if, what *if*, Gabe was wrong? What if it wasn't an armed adversary? What if it was another kid trying to escape?

Gabe hesitated. His energy mingled with Darius's again, considering the thought, and the uncertainty pulled Darius in further. Gabe took a breath, his finger hovering over the trigger…

And the man shot.

Gabe startled and swore, pulling the trigger as his avatar's health plummeted to near zero. The distraction allowed more enemies to close in, and suddenly, shots came in on two more sides. His character screamed, and the screen went red. Gabe groaned and tilted his head back, letting his hands go limp on his lap as he shook his head at the ceiling.

"Fuck!" he exclaimed, disappointment biting at the word.

But Darius wasn't disappointed. He grabbed the headset and model weapon from Gabe's hands and glanced at Holly. She was normally inscrutable, but even her eyes were wide, and her mouth turned down in an impressed frown as she nodded and reset the program. They'd run this system on a dozen people so far.

No one had come this close.

"Not bad," Darius said, trying to keep his tone even as he held out a hand and helped Gabe to his feet. "How do you feel?"

"Like I'll do better next time," Gabe stated.

Darius raised his brows. He couldn't imagine *anyone* doing better.

"You did fine," he said as he put a firm hand on Gabe's shoulder. Gabe's lips pressed together, and his eyes darted between Darius's. "Have a seat. Who's next?"

After Gabe's thrilling display, the rest of the sessions went by more predictably. Daniel Park hardly made it twenty feet before Darius was able to tap into his stress and make him accidentally shoot a civilian. John got halfway through the course, and while Darius was able to Influence him to run into the line of fire once or twice, John's nerves got the best of him. He was killed by his jumpiness, fumbling with the trigger when under fire. Darius made a note to tell Abraham about that and have it written up in John's psychological profile.

Besides Gabe, Alexis performed the best. She moved quickly, reacted well, and though Darius could feel her anxiety in the way her muscles hardened under his fingertips and the cold sweat broken out against her shoulders, she only let him in a couple of times. In every instance, she realized what she was doing before any real damage was done. Her biggest mistake was getting turned around, moving backward, and ending up shot in the back. Darius wondered if she could have gotten as close to the end as Gabe had.

"Good job," he said, helping Alexis to her feet, too. Her hands were a little shaky, but a smile played on her lips as she fixed up her short hair that the headset left ruffled. She was the last one to test, and Darius looked around the room. Somehow, the people here felt more connected than when they walked in. They'd hedged closer to the center, shoulders brushing, knees touching, as they exchanged nervous smiles and glances with one another—including Gabe.

Not that Gabe was paying attention to them. He watched Darius with a sharp, calculating look in his eyes.

Darius cleared his throat.

"That's it," he said. The room felt hot and muggy now, and Darius realized he was coated in a fine layer of sweat. Thorn once told him that Influence took a lot out of a Sin. He supposed that had to be true for Virtues, too. "I'll be looking over these in the next couple of days and letting you know how you did next time we have class. Good job. Now get out of here and get some rest. Maybe meditate."

He chuckled, and a round of edgy laughter echoed back at him. People began to file out as Darius turned to Holly. She had already snapped her computer shut and was jamming it into an old backpack with the VR headset and gun.

"How soon do you want these videos back?" she asked

as she hoisted the bag over her shoulder.

"How soon can you get them done?"

She shrugged. "Three days. We're finally ordering new cars, and I've gotta make sure it's done in a good and sneaky way."

"You figured out the registration problem?" Darius asked.

Holly scoffed. "I figured out a registration *solution* that solves about six problems all at once," she said. "If the Sins can still find us after this, I'll eat my keyboard." Darius laughed, and Holly cast a glance over his shoulder. "Anyway, I'll leave you to it. Looks like you're not done yet…"

Then she ducked out. Gabe was standing by the door, and she passed him a nod, which he returned. As soon as the doors swung shut behind her, he turned to Darius.

"Hey, man," Darius said. "You good?"

"I'm good." Gabe took a step further into the room. Those sharp eyes zeroed in on Darius's. "Did I pass the test?"

"I told you—"

"I got through the shooting assessment," Gabe cut in. "And the combat one. This is all I need to go out on the field. I gotta know if I passed it and, if not, what I need to do better."

For a moment, Darius just watched him. He let out a soft, surprised breath. "You're really determined to get out there, aren't you?"

"Yes." Gabe's expression went dark, his gaze distant. "As an officer, I swore an oath to protect innocent people, and Gluttony made me break that oath. I'd be lying to you if I said this wasn't personal."

Darius nodded. "It's personal for all of us," he said. "The Sins killed my whole family."

"I know," Gabe said. "I—"

"Read the reports?" Darius asked. Gabe nodded, and Darius chuckled. "You know, I don't understand your drive, but I appreciate it."

Gabe's brows drew together. "What do you mean?"

"This hasn't been an easy transition for you," Darius said. He opened his arms, gesturing toward the door behind Gabe's back. Gabe didn't turn to look. His focus never strayed from Darius's face. "There are a lot of people here who don't like you, who don't *want* you on Tactical, but that doesn't seem to bother you."

"Why should it?" Gabe asked. He shook his head, breaking eye contact for the first time as he looked at his reflection in the mirror over Darius's shoulder. He sighed. "Look, I've worked in two precincts—one in New York and one back home in Pittsburg—and you don't always get along with the guys you're stuck with. Hell, you might flat-out hate some of them. But I didn't become a cop because I wanted people to *like* me. I did it to serve the public, and that's what I'm gonna do here. Maybe, the Martyrs will eventually see that, and even if they don't like me, they can trust me."

Darius nodded slowly. He couldn't help but admire the man standing in front of him.

"It's possible they won't work with you," he said. "I don't want you to get your hopes up."

"The only way to find out is to try," Gabe countered. "So. Did I pass the Influence test?"

A smirk crept onto Darius's face before he could stop it, and Gabe's eyes lit up. He raised his brows, his mouth parting in a charming, uneven smile. "I did, didn't I?"

"Yeah," Darius said, nodding. "You did."

Gabe's smile widened to a grin, and he punched the air in front of him. Darius laughed. It was a nice change of pace to have someone this passionate about the war they were waging.

―――――――――

Caleb Claytor took a blow right to the chin. His head snapped back as he sprawled to the mat, a lump of gangly limbs and pale skin, and Seth Graves stood over him. Thorn winced and shook her head as Chris came up between the two men, speaking to them, but her voice didn't come through the muted speakers.

"Can you rewind that?" Thorn asked, glancing to her right, where the real Chris sat at the conference table beside her. "And show camera two."

"Sure," Chris said. She tapped a button on her laptop, and the screen on the far wall jumped to the start of the fight. There were three individual feeds, and she highlighted the second one to take up the majority of the display. Thorn leaned backward, her feet propped on the table, and she frowned as she focused on Claytor's form. Within thirty seconds, he dropped his guard, and Graves squeezed a punch through a gap on Claytor's left to land him flat on his ass.

Thorn swore as she looked down at her tablet and marked "fail" under the defense category. "He didn't even have the chance to score for offense, footwork, and balance," she said. She placed the device back on the table and sighed. "At this rate, no one is going to pass these fucking qualifications."

Chris didn't answer, but the way she shook her head told Thorn she was just as frustrated. Where Thorn was giving simple, pass or fail marks for each of the four categories they were grading, Chris took detailed notes, and she was quietly typing away with a frown across her lips.

"Okay," she said after a moment, pulling Claytor's test down and loading another. "Next up: Charlotte Davis."

"Our youngest recruit." Thorn turned back to the screen. Davis's footage took over three individual windows. "Let's see how she does."

Davis was an impressive woman. Taller than Thorn, she had long, black hair put together into neat locs, which she'd pulled into a tight bundle at the back of her head. A stunning network of intricate, black tattoos covered every inch of her dark brown skin, starting at her arms, curling onto her chest, and dripping down her back. As Davis stretched, she turned toward the mat and faced her instructor. This time, Chris stood across the mat. Davis had several inches on her, but Thorn shook her head.

"This is hardly a fair fight," she said, casting Chris a look.

"None of them are," Chris responded with a shrug.

Davis lasted one minute. Besides Thorn herself, Chris had the best technique in hand-to-hand combat, and she disabled Davis with a swift combination of disorienting jabs and a swipe under her legs. Thorn swore and marked her sheet.

"Is her brother any better?" she asked.

"No," Chris admitted with a sigh. "Charlotte is the only new recruit I'll even let take the test. Andre is close, but Lucas has a long way to go. What do you expect? None of them were trained for anything like this before we picked them up…"

Chris's brows drew together, and she tucked her chin back in, jotting more notes. Thorn glanced at her, but Chris just cleared her throat and said, "Okay. Moving onto… Mackenzie McKay."

Thorn's jaw tightened as Chris changed the file over. She pulled her feet off the table and leaned over it instead. Sparkie, clinging to her back behind her hair, wiggled upward to watch the screen from over her shoulder.

As the Irishwoman walked onto the mat, Chris took a slow breath. "Did you hear about what happened in R&D last week?" she murmured.

Thorn kept her lips firmly shut and ran her tongue along the bottom of her top teeth. All she did was nod.

She'd heard, all right. Everyone had fucking heard. That was one of many reasons Thorn hated spending so much time in the Underground. Collect enough people in a small space like this, and gossiping was unavoidable. The story of Mackenzie and Samira's fight had become so overblown that Thorn wasn't sure what to believe and what was bullshit sensationalism. She had a feeling most of it was true. Mackenzie was usually the culprit behind the hyperbole, and she seemed to be one of the only Martyrs *not* talking about it.

On the screen, she and Graves began to square off, slowly circling, their hands raised, legs spread in a wide, defensive stance. Mackenzie was the second-shortest person in the Underground, standing at five feet, two inches, but her heart-shaped face was set in fierce determination. Graves looked down at her, waited a moment, and charged.

And Mackenzie returned like a wildcat. For the first several seconds of the match, Graves couldn't land a hit on her. She ducked down, twisted around, and played the defensive game well enough that Graves struggled to keep an eye on where she was and what she was doing. She managed to land a couple of light hits on him before he spun and clocked her on the chin. She stumbled backward, recovered quickly, and got right back into position.

Thorn's eyebrows shot up.

"She's been doing really well," Chris said as she pulled a loose strand of yellow hair behind her ear. "Even in the shooting classes. Ever since DuPont joined her group."

Fueled by rage, Thorn thought. She recognized it in Mackenzie's eyes. It was like looking into a fucking mirror. She had no doubt the incident with Samira had just added more gasoline, making the fire an inferno. Thorn supposed she should be grateful; maybe now that she was taking things more seriously, Mackenzie would stop being late to meetings or cracking inappropriate jokes in hard conversations, but that was part of the problem. Even though those things could be annoying, Thorn was afraid of losing them. She glanced at Chris, her empty chest aching. Chris's green eyes were hard, her shoulders unyielding as she watched the Martyrs beat themselves up on the screen.

The Underground needed *more* of Mackenzie and less of Thorn.

She shook her head. "DuPont's still in her class?" Thorn asked. "I thought he already passed the assessment."

"He did," Chris confirmed. "*And* his combat test. He cleaned the floor with Conrad. Yesterday he went down to Holly's to get his new paperwork set up, and as of this morning, he's officially in TAC field training."

Thorn frowned. "He's cleared for Influence Resistance, too?"

Chris nodded. "Darius says he's 'naturally gifted.'"

Thorn nodded absently, and she turned back to the screen, where Mackenzie took another hit like a fucking stone wall and kept on coming, but her mind was on DuPont. The man *was* impressive. He'd fought off Wrath's Influence. Not many people could do that. Not outside the Martyrs.

"Speaking of Darius," Chris said. "The one-on-one training has helped a lot. He wants to test soon."

Thorn's stomach dropped. Sparkie pulled himself behind her hair and out of sight again. "Good," she said, but the thought tightened her fists. She stretched her fingers to relax them.

"How close is he to testing for combat?" Chris pressed. Thorn focused on the fight without really seeing it—watching Mackenzie move and duck and hit without fully comprehending what she was doing. "When we go after Moore, it would be good to have a Virtue on site."

Thorn's face went cold, and she thought back to the forest—to Darius breaking Moore's skull with a crowbar and wanting to chase after him in the dark. She could just imagine what kind of stupid shit he would do on a mission like this.

"He's not ready," Thorn said.

"Damn," Chris murmured, and Thorn was saved from having to explain more by a flurry of movement on the screen. Mackenzie managed to get Graves's legs out from underneath him, using his height and weight to her advantage. He stumbled, and she threw her shoulder into the back of his knees. They both sprawled onto the mat, a tangled mess of long legs, strong arms, and a sunburst of bright orange hair. Chris raised her brows and let out a low whistle of appreciation as she jotted some notes. Thorn passed Mackenzie in all categories.

Then, the movement of cold energy behind them drew Thorn's attention, and an annoyed blip lit up in her chest. She glanced at the door as that energy moved down the hallway, stopped outside the conference room, and knocked. Chris frowned and glanced at Thorn.

"John," she said. Chris's eyes widened a bit, her shoulders rising and falling in a soft sigh. Thorn turned back to the door. "Come in."

He opened it and passed Thorn a curt but polite nod before his eyes landed on Chris. His face broke into a grin as he slipped into the room.

"Good morning," John said. He carried a disposable cup, and he handed it to Chris as he leaned forward to kiss her forehead. "I figured you might need this since we were too busy to grab some this morning." He raised his brows, and Chris's cheeks went pink.

"Thank you," she said, smiling as she looked down at the light, milky coffee in her hand. Her smile tightened. John didn't seem to notice.

"Absolutely," he said. "We still on for lunch?"

"Yeah, of course," Chris said.

"Awesome," he said. Then an awkward quiet fell, and John glanced from Chris to Thorn and back again. Thorn sat back and watched him, her arms crossed, her lips pressed together. After a moment, he cleared his throat. "Anyway, I'll let you get back to it. See you in a bit."

He leaned in for another kiss, lingered a little longer than usual, and excused himself from the room without saying a word to Thorn. She followed his movement until he shut the door, and then she turned to Chris. The TAC director pushed the coffee away, focused on the screen, and pulled up another video.

"He leaves tomorrow?" Thorn asked.

"Yes," Chris said without looking at her. "He and Nicholas are headed back to Charlotte. Lina's team found a report of a man matching Leroy Khoury's description—supposedly a violent offender hitchhiking his way north. Every cop between Georgia and Jersey is on the lookout for him, so Mackenzie wanted to send more people down."

"How do you feel about that?" Thorn pressed.

"I don't feel any way about it," Chris said shortly. She looked back down at her tablet. "Next up: Skylar Fulton."

Thorn's brows drew together. Before she could speak, her phone buzzed on the table. Chris glanced at her, and Thorn met her eyes, looking for any sign that Chris wanted to talk about this, but she was all business again. Thorn took a deep breath and answered her phone at last.

"Claytor," she said.

"Hey, we have a situation developing." Alexis's voice crackled through the earpiece. She was whispering, like she didn't want to be overheard. Thorn suspected she'd stepped away from work and was trying not to draw attention. Her spine straightened, and she felt Sparkie's body stiffen as Alexis continued. "We've been getting calls about a crowd gathering at city hall. Looks like a protest."

"A protest?" Thorn got to her feet; Chris followed without question. "What for?"

"I'm not sure," Alexis murmured. Thorn was already walking out of the conference room and headed toward tactical, Chris's faint, cold energy on her heels. "I think it's about the recent incidents with police. There were six more this last week. Jacob drove by the scene. He says people are ready to riot."

Thorn swore. She heard Chris's voice behind her as she called Graves and told him to come suit up. "How many people are there?" Thorn asked.

"Fifty, at least," Alexis said, "and Moore's on his way." Thorn's heart plummeted, falling into the cavern in her chest and lighting a fire there. "According to the program Holly's using to track his phone, he's heading south on Broadway. I'm sure he's going to investigate. Could just be a show to save face as the commissioner…"

"I'm not taking chances," Thorn said. She hurried to her locker and pressed her thumb against the knob on the door.

It clicked open, and she grabbed her vest. "I'll be there soon. Keep me updated."

"Will do."

Thorn hung up and spun to see Chris already fully dressed, clipping a munitions belt around her waist. She slammed her handgun into place as Thorn asked, "Who's on patrol?"

"Fourth and Fifth. Everyone else is grounded, and we only have rental cars for two more units on hand right now."

"Fourth?" Thorn asked. The door swung open, and Seth hurried in. While he started getting ready, Thorn frowned. "Isn't that Chan's unit? I thought she didn't have a partner since we lost Nichols?"

"She doesn't," Chris said. Seth paused and looked over at her. "She's training DuPont to replace him. They're in New York now. Should I call them back?"

Thorn groaned as she considered Chris, noting the hard, ready expression settled into her delicate features. It hadn't been long ago when her serious brow was softer, her cheeks fuller, and her eyes filled with more hope than duty. Graves finished putting his gear together, and Thorn took a deep breath as she moved toward the door.

"No," she said. "Looks like we're going to get to test our newest recruit."

CHAPTER EIGHTEEN

Lower Manhattan was a madhouse.

What started out as a small march outside of the court-house at Broadway and Park Row was now a roaring stampede of sweaty, screaming people rallying at Foley Square. Thorn, Chris, and Seth Graves walked through the crowds, wearing large sweatshirts over their bulletproof vests while they toted their weapons and helmets in black duffle bags across their backs.

Thorn paused at the bottom edge of the square, frowning as she overlooked the fountain monument. The Triumph of the Human Spirit. It stabbed into the sky, an angry, black sword looking down on hundreds of furious souls— a sea of ice-cold energy full of people carrying the same signs they always carried: Who Polices The Police? No Justice, No Peace. Silence is Compliance.

The pattern continued. Every generation left their kids and their grandkids to fight this same fucking fight. Thorn had been to hundreds of protests just like this over the years. Each of them felt as futile as the last.

Chris stepped up beside Thorn. Her aura was almost impossible to distinguish, even this close, thanks to the overwhelming presence of so many others pushing in on all sides.

"This isn't looking good," Chris shouted above the commotion. She threw her arms behind her head and wrapped her long, blonde hair in a tight ponytail at the base of her skull. Her green eyes searched the crowd, serious and unafraid. "I'm already wishing Darius was here."

Thorn's teeth clenched, and her fingers tightened around her bag's strap as she turned around again.

"Any sign of the Sins?" she said into the headset inside her ear.

Holly Andrews's voice cut through the chanting, clear as the morning sun shining down on them between the skyscrapers.

"Lust and Greed aren't on scene," she said. "Mulligan's got Claytor in midtown, and Ruiz is at *The Times'* broadcasting headquarters. They're probably pulling some strings behind the scenes. You know how the Sins are. They'll be working to pit people against each other and make this worse. Anyways, Moore is…" She paused, and Thorn's ears filled with a rapid, sharp clicking. "At Criminal, just up the street. My system says he's headed south."

Thorn's attention moved a block up Centre Street, where she could barely see the corner of the Manhattan Criminal Court building over the crowd. "And Hunt?"

"Not on the cams," Holly said. "If she's there, like you think she is, we haven't found her yet."

She was there. An hour ago, shortly after Thorn, Chris, and Graves had jumped into the car and headed to the city, Thorn felt Wrath's Influence pull at her, and it kept pulling for twenty minutes before it disappeared. Since then, it was radio silence. Thorn had no doubt that Wrath expected a Martyr presence here. The Sins liked to sow discontent. The Martyrs tried to stop it from happening.

Or at least keep the body count as low as possible when the riots officially broke out.

Thorn's brows drew in, and Sparkie circled overhead, searching the crowd—shit, there had to be hundreds of people here—for the one person who could make this situation a goddamned disaster. Thorn shook her head and cleared her throat.

"Carter, Chan," she said. "Positions?"

"Liz and I got Worth and Lafayette," Conrad Carter reported, his voice a rumble of gravel in Thorn's ear. She could practically hear the wad of chew he had perpetually pinched behind his lip. "There's a shit ton of fuckin' people up here…"

"There's a shit ton of people everywhere," Amelia Chan said. "We're on the steps to the Supreme Court. The whole damn park is full."

Thorn glanced to her left. The tall, white pillars of the courthouse towered over the crowd, and while most people were on the sidewalk below, the stairs were a hive of activity. Thorn spotted Chan and DuPont near the top. Like her, both of them wore oversized clothing to obscure their protective gear and had massive, black bags full of weaponry and even more fucking armor slung across their backs.

"DuPont," Thorn stated, "how are you feeling about your first mission?"

"I'm ready, ma'am," he said. Thorn heard someone grumble on the line. She would've taken one of Mackenzie's ten-buck-bets that it was Carter. She thought about calling him out on it, but she didn't want to add more animosity to an already contentious situation. It could wait.

"Good," she said instead. "Here's the plan. Chan, you and DuPont stay where you're at. Keep watch from a higher position. Silver and Graves—" Thorn spun around, where the First Response team was standing behind her "—are going to stay here and cover the southern point. I want all eyes on this damn crowd. If this starts looking dangerous, we need to get people out of here."

"What are you going to do?" Graves asked, his voice louder in Thorn's earpiece. Even though he was only standing feet from her, his mouth didn't sync up with the words.

"I'm looking for Moore," Thorn responded.

Chris's eyes flashed. "You think we can take him out?" she asked. "Here? There are a *lot* of people here."

"If an opportunity presents itself, we have to try," Thorn said.

Because right now, Moore's Programming was making the whole damned city more dangerous. This protest was proof of that. People were sick and fucking tired of getting shot at, and Thorn couldn't blame them.

"But that only matters when we find him," she went on. "*If* we find him. Until then, you know the drill. Prevent damage. Stop Puppets. Keep people from fucking dying. If shit goes south, the monument is our meeting point."

"Roger that," Chan said while Carter grumbled in agreement. Chris's eyes were still locked onto Thorn's, and she nodded. Thorn was hesitant to leave her. The image of Chris lying on that bed, soaked in so much blood that her pale skin was sticky and white, jolted into Thorn's brain. Suddenly, part of her *did* wish Darius was here. She wanted to reach out and grab Chris by the shoulders, to tell her to watch herself—but Chris already knew that.

And Thorn knew there wasn't anything she could do to stop her from working. From getting hurt. From giving her all for a fight she believed in.

So, her stomach a furious tangle of knots, Thorn turned away and headed up the street. Sparkie took one long, swooping arc around the protest to find their team. Carter, by the Abandoned Worth Street Station, back-to-back with Liz Wright while they both watched the northwestern edge of the crowd. Chan, shielding her eyes with her palm as she looked out over the rest of the protest. DuPont stood beside her, a pillar of professional stature, his eyes hidden behind reflective sunglasses so it was impossible to see exactly where he was looking. Chris and Graves pushed south against the grain of more people pouring into the rally. They stopped on the edge of the street where Centre, Duane, and Federal Plaza came together. Content, or at least begrudgingly satisfied, that everyone was in the safest position they could be—close enough to the mob to spot any riots without being so close that they'd get sucked into the violence—Thorn's Familiar spread his wings, caught a draft, and lurched higher into the sky. He made his way toward the Criminal Court building. Thorn hurried after him.

If New York City was known for one thing, it was large crowds with strong opinions. Civil dissent seemed to run in the very blood of the people who lived here. Protests, riots, and marches flooded through, full of rallying cries for change that rarely seemed to *spur* change. People felt empowered, like they'd done something that mattered, but it just wasn't good enough. Passion didn't stop the Sins.

Thorn knew because she'd been one.

While Thorn had lived in New York as a Martyr for ninety years, she had memories of this place beyond that—memories of events like this one, where she'd walked through the cold and angry crowd, just making it colder and angrier, pouring her loathing into the souls around her until they hated each other just as much as she hated them. It didn't always need to get violent, though Wrath had always been goddamned giddy when the blood began to spill. The goal for these kinds of events was never *truly* violence. It was division.

Thorn stood up straight, her head held high, as she searched for any sign of conflict. God, there was so much potential—so much *anger* for the Sins to tap into. It swirled around her, settling in her gut. Gun "enthusiasts" moved through the crowd, open-carrying ridiculously oversized firearms just to make a point that they could. A local church congregation gathered by the monument, preaching scripture through megaphones while holding bloody signage of aborted fetuses and crucified men. At the western edge, a line of anti-protestors framed the sidewalk, and a banner stretched between them with the faces of Gabe DuPont's fallen SWAT team plastered upon it. "Who protects our protectors?" they screamed. Thorn's stomach twisted, hoping DuPont couldn't see them, as she kept walking.

The Sins didn't create these divides, but they fed them, pouring their power into people already looking for any excuse to act out on their worst impulses. Thorn remembered doing it herself—watching like she was trapped in a dark movie theater with her eyes glued open. She had Influenced a middle-aged woman to spit in a trans kid's face at a Pride event. A teen boy to break windows and loot the business during an immigration march. A cop to aim his gun at a Black man's back as he walked away from a fight. Thorn remembered how Wrath had compelled him to pull the fucking trigger and watched as their victim landed face-first on the pavement, dead before he hit the ground.

Her lip curled up as hot contempt and shame bubbled into her mouth, and she wanted to scream. Leroy was lucky. Alan and Cain were fucking *lucky* they didn't remember all the things the Sins had turned them into. All the things they'd made them do.

Thorn swallowed the bitterness down like poison as she made her way toward the courthouse. All around the edges of the protest, little pods of police stalked the crowd like wolves hunting for the sick and the weak among the herd. Thorn eyed a pair of officers at the base of the steps. Full body armor, tinted helmets, and heavy black batons showed everyone here they knew how to use deadly force, and they weren't afraid to fucking do it.

She ducked her head, hiding her face. Sparkie swooped ahead of her, high above the rooftop, and watched as more people walked through the barricades in the intersections to join the throng building there. Thorn kept following Centre Street north, pushing through a wall of cold energy emanating from the horde of bodies streaming into the square as she hunted for Moore's massive, towering form. Another set of officers leaned against a barricade, and Thorn made to disappear into the crowd again.

But one of the men paused, his head locked in her direction. He reached his hand into his pocket and drew out a phone. The world around Thorn slowed on a rush of cold adrenaline.

"I think I've been made," she murmured as she took a sharp left and forced her way into a line of people. "Worth and Centre. Get me eyes on Worth and Centre."

Thorn pushed deeper into the hive of protesters. Their auras pressed around her like the icy depths of the East River, chilling her to the bone, making the hairs along the nape of her neck stand on end.

Chan's voice chirped in her ear.

"I see two cops," she said. "Moving toward the crowd."

Thorn cast a glance over her shoulder, and Sparkie came in a little lower to get a better view. Two tanks of black kevlar and heavy shields rushed at the place she'd disappeared. Thorn could barely see their faces behind the shaded visors. She'd seen the look before—at the hospital ward, in Gabe DuPont's cognac eyes. Terror. Panic.

It flooded through these men, too. They slammed into the protestors like a battering ram. Where the crowd had accepted Thorn, allowing her to slip between bodies and merge into its energy like she belonged there, it met the cops like a wall. Men and women jammed themselves together and pushed back against heavy riot shields, shouting and raging and swinging their picket signs like children wielding plastic bats against an army.

Suddenly, the crowd stopped pushing forward. Thorn spun on her heels as she heard a new chorus of shouting. It was different now. Not the chanting, constant hum of peaceful dissent. A shrill, blood-chilling scream of someone in pain. The fire in Thorn's chest flared.

"Moore's at the park," Holly said, but now that Thorn was surrounded in chaos, tight on all sides, she could barely hear her over the shouting. Another scream, louder now, rocked Thorn's core.

"I think I got him," she said. The crowd turned around as people rushed toward the same thing she was rushing toward. At the far end of Thomas Paine Park, a woman shrieked into her hands. Her face was beet red and burning as a cop shouted at her.

"Get on the ground!" he ordered. He held a canister of pepper spray in her direction. "Do you hear me? Get on the ground!"

The woman desperately rubbed at her eyes. They opened in weeping slivers through the swelling. A man rushed toward her, and the cop turned on him and pushed the button. He roared as a hard mist of orange spray slammed into his face. The crowd surged forward, shouting and spitting and swearing. Thorn searched above it, trying to find Terrance Moore hovering over them all.

Wrath's Influence filled the square.

Thorn's breath caught in her throat, and her heart ground to a deafening stop. Wrath's power surged out, egging the protestors on, telling them to attack. To charge. Thorn backed up, her eyes wide, now looking lower into the throng of moving bodies. She pulled her bag of weaponry back until she found a spot to squat down, open it, and reach inside—

A rush of cold energy came at her. Thorn dove to the side just in time to avoid being tackled from behind. When she spun back to her feet, Autumn Hunt stood five yards away. Through a sea of people, she watched Thorn, her mouth sliced open in a grin, her dark hair draped around her face in a tangled mess. She laughed. Thorn couldn't hear it, but she felt it in her stomach. In her chest. Wrath's joyous hatred pulsed through Thorn in a way that felt horrifyingly familiar, like returning to an abusive childhood memory her brain had been trying to lock away.

All at once, Wrath's Influence grew, and Thorn screamed, "Backup! I need backup!"

Three dozen people surrounding Thorn stopped moving. They reeked of Wrath's cold, frenzied power, connected to her center on a network of fragile strands. Thorn's body went numb, and she stood frozen to the spot as those three dozen people turned around slowly.

And looked right at her.

But she didn't look at them. Thorn's eyes never left Wrath's face. The Sin cackled and held up her right hand. She gripped a phone.

"A little piggy told me you were here," Wrath said, and her smile broadened on her tawny face, wrinkling the bridge of her nose. Thorn's mouth went dry. Hunt slipped the phone back into her front pocket and took a step forward. Thorn's instinct was to step back, but she stood her ground. "Did'ja bring your little Virtue out to play? The Jones boy? I *miss* him."

Thorn barked a short, cold laugh. "I figured we could use some one-on-one time…"

They'd get plenty of that. She could feel more than Wrath's strings wrapped around the Puppets surrounding them, an eerie eye in the middle of a human hurricane. Her Influence also spread beyond them, into the masses of people swirling outside their little circle. Thorn couldn't see past the wall of Puppets, but she knew no one outside of it was watching them.

She was trapped.

Wrath's eyes narrowed, but her smile didn't fade. She stepped to the left, and Thorn mirrored her. They walked in a semi-circle inside the break. It felt oddly quiet here. Thorn was aware of the screaming and protesting churning outside, but the noise didn't seem to reach her.

"You're lying," Hunt said at last. She stopped walking. Thorn stopped, too. "Your Virtue is here. Somewhere. To heal your people. The Martyrs' fucking *messiah*." Her smile faltered, and a manic hunger filled her steely eyes. Thorn wanted to turn around—to use her own Influence to cut Wrath off from her Puppets and make a mad dash for it— but she couldn't disable them all at once. Not on her own.

Sparkie flew in tight, nervous circles above. He spotted a black figure moving through the crowd. Chris's voice shouted in Thorn's earpiece. "I'm closing in! Hold on!"

"D'you think he'll come for *you?*" Wrath cooed. She took another step closer. Thorn moved back this time. A wall of cold energy pressed up against her spine. Wrath kept coming. "Like he did back at that cute, little farm?"

She was close enough to touch, and Thorn threw a punch, but the Sin caught her fist. Puppets pulled in. The circle grew tighter. Thorn pushed against Wrath, the bones in her hand grinding together.

"Let him try," Wrath murmured, her breath whispering against Thorn's cheek. "I'm not afraid of a little… *Kindness.*"

Thorn's eyes went wide, and her heart stopped beating. Wrath's whole face split in a laugh, her wide mouth open in a vengeful joy that sucked the breath from Thorn's lungs.

"That's right," Hunt said. "That *impotent* little Virtue of yours can't hurt me, can he? He can't hurt any of us. So much for your *secret weapon.*"

Thorn twisted away, breaking Wrath's grip, and spun around with her elbow. The hard point of it slammed into Wrath's jaw, throwing her head to the side. Three Puppets fell, and Wrath came back roaring.

Then a small, cylindrical item sailed over the crowd. It landed on the ground behind Hunt. Sparkie dove from the sky, and as Thorn covered her ears with her hands, he wrapped his leathery wings around her head.

The explosive went off. Thorn and Wrath were thrown back, and half of the Puppets dropped around them. Thorn scrambled to her feet, rolling over unconscious men and women as Sparkie released her head and clung to her clothing. She didn't look back as she sprinted toward the monument.

The square erupted in chaos.

The explosion broke whatever fragile control these people still had. Gunshots blasted through the air. Screaming. Squealing tires and a grating crash as a vehicle slammed into the metal barricades on the street corner and tore through the rally. Reports poured into Thorn's headset.

"People are charging officers over here," Wright shouted.

"And the cops are fuckin' *pissed,*" Carter growled.

Sparkie vaulted from Thorn's shoulder and watched as a wall of protestors turned around and barreled toward a line of armored cops. They fell, one by one, by baton, pepper spray, or rubber bullets shot deep into the mob. It was hard to feel in the tangled mess, hundreds of lives jammed so tightly together that Thorn couldn't tell where one energy ended and another began, but she knew people were dying. Her chest flared, but she kept running. Over her shoulder, Wrath stood, searched for Thorn, and screamed.

Her Influence cast out like a web.

Thorn felt it all around the square. Pinpoints of rage held together on frail strings. The closest one was just feet away from where Thorn stood at the base of the Triumph of the Human Spirit. A protester lifted her sign and swung it wildly at a wounded medic sitting on the statue wall. The wood caught against the side of his skull, tearing his scalp open. He stumbled as blood pooled down the back of his neck. Thorn reached into the Puppet's mind, found her connection to Wrath, and severed it.

The woman went down, and Wrath's Influenced barreled toward her.

"Hunt's Puppetting the crowd!" Thorn shouted. She dove into the shallow water and pressed her back against the monument to sort herself out. She had no weapon. No helmet. Nothing but a kevlar vest and a goddamned earpiece connecting her to her team. "Civilians. Fuck! We've got to get her. Put them all down at once. Come in. Andrews, get me an evac—someone to pull us the fuck out of here. Where the hell is everyone? We need to surround Hunt!"

They sounded off in her ear. Chan and DuPont were closest. Thorn could see two helmets peering over a parked vehicle near the Supreme Court building. Carter and Wright, on the other edge of the square, slowly made their way down Federal Plaza. Chris and Graves were fighting south through Thomas Paine Park, trying to avoid being obvious in a crowd of people running in the exact opposite direction. Sparkie circled overhead.

"What's the plan?" Chris said.

"Just come in shooting?" Carter offered.

"No," DuPont cut in. "We'll hit innocent people."

"Sometimes innocent people get hurt," Carter growled. "You should know. You used to hurt 'em!"

"Shut up, Carter," Thorn said. "DuPont's right. No shooting. Not yet. Let me get her closer. I'll take some Puppets out first." She could feel Wrath now, and Sparkie spotted her from overhead. While the protesters ran and screamed, either charging at police or away from them, Wrath slowly walked through the square, an entourage of Puppets surrounding her. Her Influence poured out like a wave. Not only did she have more than thirty-five people linked to her, but she was pushing out a general command of rage and passion that sank deep into Thorn's core. That wave was almost more dangerous than the Puppets. It incensed the rest of the crowd and gave the police the excuse they needed to respond with deadly force.

At the base of the monument, right in front of Thorn, another Puppet rushed at a cop. He held up a weapon and launched a rubber bullet into the woman's face. Her head snapped back, and she collapsed onto the ground. He turned to Thorn, spotted her in the water, and leveled his gun at her, too. She ducked, and the projectile bounced off the statue at her back. Thorn thrust her Influence forward and made the officer pause. He looked at her, confused, his weapon still pointed between her eyes...

And Wrath sprinted toward her.

Thorn's teeth gritted together as she held onto the officer, but his resistance was strong, and he began to break through. His finger tightened on the trigger...

Autumn Hunt and her Puppets rounded the fountain. He glanced over and brought his weapon with him.

Thorn told him to shoot.

The rubber bullet landed in Wrath's stomach, and she toppled backward. Puppets dropped around her, and Thorn reached into the ones that hadn't. She severed a woman, watching her collapse over the retaining wall and into the pool of water at Thorn's feet. A man next. He folded where he stood. Now Wrath just had two guards—two lives—and when Thorn reached in, she couldn't cut them off.

She screamed, "NOW!"

TAC rushed in. Chan and DuPont got there first. Thorn ducked down as bullets flew overhead, landing in the stone monument, and a rainfall of dust showered over her. One hit a Puppet. His life blinked out, and he fell to the ground. Blood poured from his chest and onto the concrete steps, flowing down them like the Nile sick with plague.

Then Wrath roared. Carter and Wright arrived on scene. Hunt's Influence spread again, capturing more people as the cops closed in. Some of them were under Wrath's control, but more were not. Suddenly, the Martyrs were bombarded by weapon fire. Cold energy swarmed around them, followed by a barrage of rubber bullets. Graves was hit in the back of the head, knocking his helmet off as he flew forward. Chris dove to the ground and covered him with her body, then cried out as a live round dug between the seams in the armor at her back. A projectile slammed into DuPont's chest and sent him tumbling into the fountain. Chan screamed and went down—Thorn didn't even see what the fuck happened to her.

And Wrath—Wrath was running. She sprinted toward the subway entrance on Duane Street as weapon fire flew in her direction, too. Her Puppets covered her, filling in the space between them as officers kept shooting. Carter took one to the leg and collapsed while Wright grabbed her gun and ducked behind the half-wall lining the steps. Thorn leapt from the fountain and joined her. Wright glanced up, and Thorn gestured her head over the black stone.

"I'll slow them down," she said. "Just shoot."

"Yes, ma'am," Wright said with a nod.

They rose up. Thorn drove her Influence into the link she felt between one of the last three Puppets and Wrath, and though it wasn't enough to cut the man off, it slowed him down. He shot; a bullet clattered into the rock, chipping shards up. They dug into Thorn's cheek, but she kept fucking pushing.

Wright pulled the trigger over and over again.

She missed. Missed again. Then one hit Hunt in the thigh. The back. The Sin stumbled. All her Puppets collapsed, weapons stopping, but she'd made it to the subway entrance. As Thorn leapt over the wall, Wrath ran down the stairs and underground. Thorn sprinted after her.

Another round of shots rang out, and suddenly, Thorn was flying forward. The force of a bullet against her back, digging deep into her kevlar vest, disoriented her for a moment.

Then Carter was screaming.

"Liz? *Liz!*"

Thorn rolled to the ground and spun to her feet. A new line of cops came at them from the other side of the square. Three of them. Fully armored. Shields up. The one in the center hid behind them, propping a pistol at Thorn.

"Everybody down!" he screamed.

But Thorn hardly heard him because less than twenty feet away, she saw Liz Wright's body lying half-exposed behind the black, stone wall. Her helmet was still in place, her brown hair flowing from its base soaked in dark, crimson blood. Carter crawled toward her, his injured leg too weak to hold his bulky weight. The officer pointed a gun at him.

"I said get *down!*"

"Jesus, man, he's unarmed!" DuPont screamed. He was standing, soaking wet in the water underneath the huge, black monument. The Triumph of the Human Spirit cast a dark shadow over him. He took a half step forward, raised his hands with his finger off the trigger, and said, "Let's talk about this."

"Get fucking *down!*"

DuPont nodded. He lowered his weapon and began to take a knee, but a chill rushed down Thorn's back as the cop's hand tightened.

He was going to shoot anyway.

Thorn pushed out her Influence, coating the square in a blind blanket of fear as she sprinted forward. The officer went to pull the trigger, but the moment he did, he spun to her instead. The bullet slammed into her shoulder, but it didn't stop her from plowing into him. She leapt up, took another bullet to the vest on her abdomen, and clambered over the riot shields.

Her Influence created a wave—the rest of the protestors and officers at the edge began to run in other directions. Thorn deftly disabled the shooter, snatching his gun, and she slammed its butt into the man's throat exposed beneath his visor. He choked, and Thorn thrust him backward. Then she spun to the officers holding the shields. One swung at her. She ducked beneath it and turned the gun on him, hitting him in the chest plate at point-blank range. He gasped and stumbled away, fighting for breath.

When the third man tried to grab her from behind, Thorn twisted around and shot again. He was shorter than she anticipated. Her bullet cut through his armor above his collar, and he collapsed. For a couple of devastating seconds, he gurgled on his blood before his energy extinguished.

Then Thorn stood in the middle of an empty bubble as a frantic mob sped away from her. Chris was up and moving, blood drizzling through the lines in her armor as she tried to get a dazed Seth Graves to his feet. Chan lay unconscious at the base of the monument steps, and Carter had finally made it to Liz Wright. He cradled her dead body, talking to her like she was still there. Like she could hear him. Like she was going to be fucking okay. Gabe DuPont knelt in the water, watching Thorn, awestruck.

And Wrath was gone. Blocks away by now. Thorn tapped into her headset as she looked at the chaos around her.

"Andrews," she screamed. "Where the *fuck* is my evac?"

CHAPTER NINETEEN

Darius's ears were still ringing from the sound of the emergency alarm as he knocked on Samira's door. She didn't answer, didn't even bother to tell him to go away this time, but Darius knew she was inside. Her Virtue tugged at him, betraying her silence. He knocked again. His hands shook so badly that he had a difficult time hitting the door hard enough to get his urgency across.

Still nothing.

He groaned and pounded harder, leaning his weight into it. "Samira," he yelled through the wood. "I need your help. People are hurt."

She moved at last. The pull shifted, stood, and rushed to the door. Samira threw it open. She looked older than Darius remembered. Dark shadows framed her eyes, and even though the baggy, unisex Martyrs clothing made it hard for him to tell, Darius felt like she was thinner than she'd been when he met her a few weeks ago. Her brows drew together in concern.

"Who?" she asked. "How?"

"Some of our TAC team," he said, his heart a lump in his throat that his words struggled to work past. "They ran into the Sins in town. I don't know all the details. I just know people are hurt, and I might not be able to save all of them by myself."

For a moment, she just watched him in stunned silence, and all he could see was the hospital ward two months ago. The alarm sounding. Conrad climbing out of the car, his face a slick of deep, red blood. Chris, lying with her eyes open and unseeing as she bled out on the table. Jason Nichols dead under a sheet.

"Samira," Darius said, his voice tight. "Please."

She nodded and rushed back into her room. Darius held the door open as she pulled on a pair of sneakers the Martyrs had provided and jumped back to her feet. "Where are they?"

Darius's throat opened, and he drew a deep, grateful breath. They sped down the hallway, side by side.

"On their way back," he said. "All I know is that Thorn and six TAC members were dealing with a situation in Manhattan that got out of control."

"Are they all injured?" Samira asked.

"Probably." Darius felt the blood draining from his face. They reached the courtyard, and the few souls sitting there felt heavy and stagnant. Parker Boseman and her father, Marcus, looked up as Darius and Samira went by. Darius couldn't even pretend to smile.

They took the elevator, and for the first time, Darius understood why Thorn never did in times like this. While the lift slowly drew upward, he tapped his foot impatiently, willing the number glowing above the door forward, wishing he could Influence the machine to move faster.

When it dinged, he all but leapt off and led Samira down the hall into the waiting room. John was sitting there with a couple of other worried Martyrs—family and friends of the people on duty today. Lina and Alan were talking quietly as Darius walked into the room. They turned to him, and his heart sank.

"What's going on?" Darius asked. "Have we heard anything?"

Lina nodded. "Alan just got off the phone with Thorn," she said. "For those who need healing, nothing seems to be life-threatening. Thank goodness."

But there was a tightness to Lina's voice that made Darius's heart fall further.

"Who didn't make it?" he asked.

Samira's focus snapped to him, and her jaw dropped open. Lina's eyes glistened.

"Elizabeth Wright," Alan said. A woman let out a hard sob behind him, and Darius glanced over Alan's shoulder. Lina quietly excused herself and went to speak to her. Darius swore.

"How many other people are hurt?" he asked.

"Everyone," Alan said, and his brows knitted as he turned to Samira. He bowed his head in her direction, his curtain of black hair dipping down around his head. "Mrs. Khoury. Thank you for assisting us today."

"Of course," she said weakly. "I just hope it's enough. God willing."

"It will be," Darius said. He broke away from the rest and made his way through the waiting room, Samira following on his tail like a bright shadow. The hospital ward was empty except for two nurses waiting at the station by the door. Darius threw them a quick wave as he turned toward triage.

"Mr. Jones," Elijah said as Darius walked through the door. His voice carried the numb exhaustion of a man who's had to do this too many times to count. Raquel stood beside him. She'd already put on her mask and cap, so all Darius could see were her eyes. They seemed numb, too. Elijah snapped gloves over his hands and glanced to Darius then did a double take when he saw Samira beside him. "We have a guest today? Good. We could use the help."

"That's what we're here for," Darius said. He strode past the hospital staff toward the double doors on the other side of the room, and he stood right up against them, his arms crossed, fingertips tapping on his bicep as he peered through the glass windows into the garage. Samira didn't follow him this time. He felt her by the other entrance, frozen in place.

A speaker in the corner of the room sounded out a loud, three-tone alert. Samira's energy startled.

"What does that mean?" she asked.

"They've arrived," Elijah said. Colette came up behind him and placed a medical cap over his graying hair. Darius felt them now. He looked toward the ceiling, where a warm ball of human life slowly spiraled downward. From the corner of his eye, he saw Samira look up, too. Elijah spoke again. "Everyone, in position."

Minutes later, a blue SUV Darius didn't recognize pulled up outside the triage doors. The passenger seat was empty, and Jacob Locke sat behind the wheel. An orange ball cap was pulled so low over his eyes that Darius couldn't see them, but his hand darted to the shifter so quickly that, when he threw the car into park, it rocked back and forth. As soon as it stopped, Darius pushed the doors open, and the back of the SUV flew up.

Thorn jumped out.

"Get me a stretcher," she shouted, her voice echoing through the concrete garage like thunder. She pointed to Raquel. Her fingers, exposed around her black gloves, were covered in blood. "Now!"

Darius stepped to the side and held the door ajar as Raquel and Colette rolled two emergency stretchers into the lot. Elijah and another couple of nurses followed after them. Samira stayed back in the room, her tan face hollow and washed out. Darius held out his hand to her, and she glanced at his open palm. She wrapped her fingers around his, and they went into the garage together.

Thorn was still shouting.

"Chan's been unconscious for over an hour," she said, effortlessly lifting Amelia out of the back of the SUV. As she laid her out on one of the cots, she turned back to Elijah. "I have no fucking clue what happened to her, but her vitals are stable. Chris and Carter got shot. Graves has a concussion. DuPont's a little bruised. Jones, get on—"

Thorn turned to look at him and stopped when she saw Samira. Her brows remained low and hard over her eyes, but her mouth opened in surprise. She shook it off. "You and Khoury, get on it."

"Samira," Darius said, releasing her hand so he could help Thorn ease Seth onto the second stretcher. "Go with them. Take it slow, okay?" She nodded, and as Raquel began to push Seth back into the hospital, Samira hurried after her. Darius came around the side of the SUV. Gabe had been the only passenger in the second row of seats, and he stepped out unassisted. He moved gingerly, but he *could* move, and as he and Darius crossed paths, they shared a look. Darius wondered if being out on the field was all he'd expected.

"I'll be right in to heal you up," Darius murmured, putting a hand on Gabe's shoulder. The other man nodded before walking back to the hospital. Jacob, who had gotten out of the car and was wildly pacing in front of it, glared after him, murmuring under his breath. Thorn cast him an exasperated look before she turned back to Darius.

"How's Chris?" he asked.

"She'll survive," Thorn said. Chris was getting out of the SUV now, armor off, shirt torn open, and a bandage wrapped around her lower back. She sucked in a gasp as she gingerly got to her feet. Thorn reached out to help her, and Chris swore.

As soon as they hit the concrete, the door to the waiting room flew open, and John rushed out. His face was long and colorless.

"Chris!" he exclaimed, grabbing her head in his hands. Her blonde ponytail carried red streaks of dried blood, and she winced as Raquel wheeled a chair behind her. As she sank into it, John bowed down with her. "Are you okay?"

"I'm fine," Chris said, and she tried to smile through the pain. "But I think I'll be late for lunch."

John forced out a desperate laugh as Raquel began to push Chris into the triage room. He stood to follow them, but Thorn grabbed him by the back of the arm. When he turned to her, looking ready to fight, Darius said, "It's going to be busy in there." He put a hand on John's shoulder. "Don't worry, okay? I've got her."

John looked past him, watched until Chris disappeared inside triage, and then turned to Darius again. His dark, ocean eyes were deep with anguish, but he nodded. He walked back to the waiting room like a zombie as Colette returned with another stretcher. Thorn and Darius moved back to the SUV. Conrad was the only man left.

But when Conrad came out of the vehicle, he didn't come alone. Colette spoke to him quietly, asking him to lie down, but he propped his hip on the back bumper to avoid putting weight onto his injured leg and draped Liz's body onto the cot instead. Her helmet had been removed, and a dried slick of blood coated her throat and the side of her dusky face. Conrad pushed her hair away from her forehead, gently tilted her jaw closed with the side of his hand, and looked at Darius. His brown eyes were bloodshot and swollen.

"Fix her," he said. Darius's mouth dropped open. Conrad's teeth set, and he swallowed hard as he grabbed Liz's cold, pale hand in his thick fingers. "I need you to fix her, all right? Just. Just make her better."

A cold silence fell. Colette's lips parted in a silent gasp, and she glanced at Darius. For a few awkward moments, Darius stared at Conrad, and Conrad stared back. At last, Darius shook his head. "I can't."

"You have to," Conrad said. "You have to *fix her*. She's just a kid. Just a *fucking kid*."

Thorn stood behind Conrad, one hand on the raised hatchback door; her mouth thinned into a furious line. Darius looked at her, and she held his gaze. Firm, steady, but not surprised. Darius knew she must have told Conrad that Liz was gone—must have told him her soul had faded—but

Conrad didn't seem to care. Hadn't listened, or hadn't heard. His grip tightened around Liz's fingers, and his lower lip began to quiver.

"Conrad," Darius murmured. He put his hand over Conrad's. Colette quietly excused herself, wiping her eyes as she headed back toward the hospital ward. Darius felt Samira's Virtue draw closer, but she stopped at the door behind his back. He ignored them all as he spoke to the man right in front of him. "I can't fix this."

Conrad broke. The dam fractured at first, sending torrents of quakes through Conrad's shoulders as he dipped his head into his other hand. Then, it burst entirely. Hard, echoing sobs poured from his mouth. Thorn's focus pierced the back of Conrad's head, her black eyes full of cold sympathy.

"I promised I'd protect her," Conrad finally got out, and big, fat tears fell from the corner of his eyes. They leaked around his palm and left wet trails against his ruddy cheeks. "She was so fuckin' *excited* to join TAC, and I told her I'd watch out for her. I let her down. I fucking let her down."

"You didn't let her down," Darius said. Conrad gazed at him from over his fingers. "You were always there for her. She knew it. She felt it."

A new wave of sobbing rocked through Conrad, and the vehicle shook beneath his weight. "I've seen a lot of people die here," he howled. "I've lost a lot of friends. Why the hell is this one *so* hard?"

Darius's chest felt hollowed out, and hot tears pooled behind his lashes, too. He didn't wipe them away. Didn't hide them. He just grabbed Conrad's shoulder with his other hand and held it firmly. "I don't know," Darius said honestly, "and it doesn't matter. It doesn't need a reason to be hard. It just is. It's hard, and it sucks, and it *hurts*. But just because Liz is gone doesn't mean she didn't matter, okay? She mattered. They all mattered. We'll keep fighting for her. For everyone. We'll get through this."

Whatever walls Conrad had left to hold him together

crumbled. First, he nodded. Quickly. Erratically. Then he finally let go of Liz's hand and instead grabbed Darius's. Instinctively, Darius came in, keeping their fists between them like a buffer, and put his arm around Conrad's shoulders. As soon as he did, Conrad broke down. His grief poured out of him like a wave, and Darius was swept away in it. Tears fell down his own cheeks, and he caught Thorn's eye. She took a slow, deep breath. Her fingers held so tightly to the door that they were pressed white.

Moments later, Colette returned with a wheelchair, and together she and Darius helped Conrad into it. While Colette brought Liz's body back to the hospital, Darius pushed Conrad. Samira watched them from the triage doors, her eyes wide, her face coated in fresh tears.

Chris was lying on her stomach, her arms crossed under the pillow beneath her face. Her bloodied turtleneck had been cut off, and the hospital gown opened to expose her entire back. Like every time he healed her, Darius marveled that she wasn't dead. Not just from this new injury—which had hit close enough to the spine that it was a damned miracle she wasn't paralyzed—but from the old ones. Chris's body was marred by dozens of healed wounds. Gunshots here. Cuts there. A deep, ragged scar dragged all the way from her left shoulder to her right hip. His stomach turned.

"Everything okay?" Chris asked. She twisted her neck around to look at him.

"Yeah." He pressed his fingers to her open wound. She winced, and he murmured a quick apology as warm, healing energy flooded to his fingertips and poured into her flesh.

The five injured TAC members had been moved to the main ward. Seth and Conrad had been healed already, and Gabe, the best off of them, was waiting on a cot down the hall. Samira was working with Amelia on the bed beside Chris. Darius glanced at her. Her brows were drawn together in concern. "How's it going?" he asked.

"I think I'm done," she murmured. She had one hand on Amelia's forehead and the other pressed against her own, just below her hairline. "But she won't wake up."

Samira released Amelia and turned around just as the bullet lodged in Chris's body forced its way through her closing skin. Darius grabbed it and dropped it onto a tray beside the hospital bed.

"She just needs rest," he said. Samira nodded, but her eyes had gone to the bloody bullet and didn't move away. "We saw this last year. Healing can fix the damage but won't necessarily make people conscious again. Good work." He glanced at her, providing a smile that felt heavy on his tired face. Samira's mouth twitched toward one. "How are you feeling?"

"Okay," Samira said with a sigh. She raised her hand. It was shaking. "This is the most I've ever had to heal."

Darius grabbed a juice box off of Chris's bedside table and tossed it onto the sheets next to Amelia. Samira picked it up and looked at him with a frown.

"Trust me," Darius said as the energy in his fingertips slowed to a stop. "It'll help." Then he turned to Chris. "Good as new."

Chris rolled over on the cot, holding the loose gown against her chest. Even her collar and arms were marred by scars, which stood out rigid and white against her skin. She went to speak, but a sudden sound outside of the hospital ward caught her attention. The rumble of angry voices. She and Darius glanced at the door, then at each other, and exchanged a frown.

"Is that Thorn?" Chris asked.

Darius didn't answer as he got to his feet and strode through the hall. He felt Chris leap up behind him and heard Elijah call after her angrily as they rushed into the waiting room. Thorn was storming toward the exit, cigarette in one hand, lighter in the other, and Sparkie flared up on her shoulder like a bright red warning sign. Alan followed, a statue of black and crimson against the white.

"We do not have enough information," he called after her. "We should avoid jumping to conclusions."

"Somebody did this," Thorn argued, pulling the door open and pointing at Alan with two fingers, her cigarette clutched between them. When she noticed Darius, her black eyes darted from Alan to him and back again. Her lips pressed together. "Find out who it was!"

With that, she spun around and vanished into the garage. Alan took a slow, measured breath, exhaled it in a sigh, and shook his head.

"What happened?" Darius asked.

Alan looked at him, his black eyes cold.

"The Sins know you're Kindness," he said.

Darius's heart dropped to his stomach.

"How the hell did the Sins figure out which Virtue you are?" Skylar asked.

She and Raquel sat across from Darius at a little card table in the middle of the break room while Chris was on his left. Like every other TAC member involved in the protest, she'd been pulled from duty for the next two weeks, but she'd still been busy. In the three days since the incident, they'd been stuck in meetings, running extra training classes, and trying to get to the bottom of the very question Skylar had just asked.

"We don't know," Darius said.

Chris brought a cup of black coffee to her lips and shook her head as she took a sip. "Alan thinks it was an accidental leak," she said, moving her mug back to the table. Her nose wrinkled up, and she clicked her tongue against the roof of her mouth. "Most likely, one of our guys on patrol talked about it around someone they didn't realize was associated with the Sins, but no one knows or will admit to anything."

Skylar frowned as she sat back in her chair, crossed her

arms, and looked around. The break room was packed to-day. Conrad, Alexis, and Caleb were at the pool table, play-ing their monthly game, while Julien and Remy Harris, Eli-jah and Colette's two teenaged sons, hovered over some hand-held video game at a table on the far wall. A couple of other off-duty nurses sat a few feet away, laughing over a deck of cards. Skylar turned back to Chris. "You think that's possible?"

Chris shrugged, and Darius's chest opened in a deep breath. "Well, either that or Envy repossessed," he said through a sigh. His heart fluttered uncomfortably at the thought.

"Envy?" Raquel asked. "What does Envy have to do with it?"

"I was there when its last host was killed," Darius said, and he glanced at Chris. Her eyes went distant and cold, much like they had been the evening she'd killed Cassandra Smith and sent Envy's spirit into the void to possess again. She looked past Raquel's shoulder, staring, unseeing, into the distance.

"Ah," Skylar said. Her long, hoop earrings dangled around her cheeks as she nodded. She considered Chris, too, a flash of concern in her brown eyes before she spoke to Darius again. "As Kindness, you'd trap it in the body, right?"

"Yeah," Darius said. "We saw it with Sloth. When the Virtue that can destroy the Sin is around, it can't abandon the host. I'm sure Envy tried to escape, but it would have been stuck. Either way, Alan doesn't think it has possessed this quickly, and Cain promised he'd tell us if he felt Envy use its Influence again."

Darius wasn't sure he believed that promise, but he'd have to trust it for now.

"So, what happens next?" Raquel asked. "If the Sins know your Virtue, does that mean you won't be able to join TAC as a medic?"

"He just has to be more careful," Chris said. Then she

threw Darius a look that spoke of a worry she rarely said out loud.

Raquel's eyebrows raised, and she and Skylar glanced at one another. "Alan's okay with that?" Raquel ventured.

"He has his concerns," Chris said. "We all do, but we're not changing our original plan. As soon as Darius passes his assessments for shooting and combat, he'll be cleared to go out on TAC missions."

"Forget Alan," Skylar said, waving a hand. "I'm surprised *Thorn* is on board."

A hot flush rose to Darius's cheeks.

The truth was, they hadn't spoken to Thorn about this yet. After she'd stormed from the waiting room, Darius hadn't seen her. As far as he knew, she was back in the city, working through her problems however she usually did, well away from the Underground. But Darius didn't need to talk to her to know how she'd feel about this whole damned situation. He was positive Thorn would want him grounded indefinitely.

But Chris didn't comment on Thorn. "We knew this was going to happen eventually," she said. "Just because we assumed it would take longer for the Sins to figure it out doesn't mean we need to keep Darius locked up."

Chris took another sip, and a surge of gratitude suddenly moved through Darius's chest. He nudged her elbow as a thank you. She cast him a look out of the corner of her eye and shrugged as she turned back to Raquel.

"Plus, having a Virtue in the field will cut down on our casualties," she went on.

Raquel nodded. "Well, having one in the hospital has certainly helped a lot. Did I tell you Samira came and talked to Dr. Harris this morning?"

Darius's brows rose. "No. What about?"

"She asked if she could get alerts when people come in hurt," Raquel said. Darius's eyes widened more. "Holly is getting her set up with a phone today."

For a few moments, Darius didn't know what to say. He

was shocked, and part of him hated that he was shocked—
that he had so little faith in Samira that he never would have
imagined her making a request like this. At last, he scoffed,
shook his head, and leaned forward on the table. "That's…
amazing."

"Maybe she finally realized that dumb religion of hers
isn't all she's cracked it up to be," Skylar said.

"Dumb religion?" Raquel repeated, frowning as she
threw Skylar an affronted look. "That's a pretty mean thing
to say."

Skylar's brown eyes closed slowly as she shook her head.
"You're right." She reached for Raquel's hand on the table's
vinyl surface and squeezed her fingers. "That was shitty of
me. Thanks for calling me out."

She smiled, and Raquel rolled her eyes, but her lips softened into a smirk. "Well, who *else* is going to do it?" she
asked. "I'll be sure to add that to my vows. *'I promise to love
you, and cherish you, and always tell you when you're being a jerk.'*"

The rest of the table laughed, and Darius smiled, happy
for the subject change. He wasn't in the mood to talk about
Samira and whether or not she was changing her mind on
the Martyrs, on her Virtue, and on destroying Gluttony. He
didn't want to get his hopes up too far. Dealing with the
disappointment once had been bad enough.

"When is the wedding, anyway?" he asked.

"February," Raquel said. "We always wanted a winter
wedding."

"Are you doing it here?"

"No," Skylar said. "At Cain's."

Darius's nose wrinkled. "*Cain's?* You aren't worried it's
going to be…"

"Depressing?" Chris offered like she'd been sitting on
that opinion for a while. Darius held his hand out to her,
and Skylar chuckled.

"You could think about it that way," she said. "*Or* you
could not be such a downer and instead think about how
you're celebrating with whole generations of Martyrs

around you. John seemed to love the idea of a wedding at Cain's. Maybe you should ask him about it when he gets back from Georgia…"

Skylar bit her lower lip and grinned in Chris's direction. Chris's face fell, and she busied herself with her coffee again. Darius glanced at her, but before he could say anything, a robust, warm energy neared the door, and Gabe walked through it.

His entrance changed the atmosphere of the whole space.

The regular chorus of droning voices hushed as Gabe paused in the doorway. He looked around, his bright, amber eyes moving from the nurses on the far wall to Darius and the others before finally landing on the Martyrs playing pool in the back of the room. Conrad glared at him, his bulky body as hard as a rock, as Gabe nodded in his direction. Conrad did not nod back, and Alexis and her brother exchanged a tense look behind him.

Then Gabe made his way to the couch, sat down, and turned on the television. The local New York news blared to life, creating a new round of background noise. Footage from the protests immediately filled the screen.

Activists charging officers in riot gear. Paramedics trying to force their way through police blockades. Injured journalists, reportedly attacked by people holding signs calling for an end to violence. Damaged and destroyed storefronts, the sidewalks littered with broken glass and debris. Missing people who hadn't been found in the aftermath.

"Yeah, Steve," the female newscaster said from her position in front of a desecrated City Hall. "It's pretty clear from where I'm standing that the protesters turned violent, and the NYPD had no choice but to respond with deadly force."

Chris's jaw clenched, and her fist tightened around her coffee cup. "What a load of bullshit…"

"Reports are claiming that at least twenty rioters were killed," the newscaster went on, "and dozens of others have been brought to the hospital under protected custody. Those numbers are still coming in…"

Darius swore, his stomach sick, as Raquel let out a sigh.

"I'm surprised it wasn't worse, actually," she said. "With two Sins on site—"

"There weren't two," Alexis chimed in, and Darius glanced at her. He hadn't realized she'd been listening. Her eyes were glued to the screen across the room as she chalked the tip of her pool stick. "Hunt had Moore's phone. He wasn't there. We're starting to think he's not even in the city."

Skylar's expression darkened. "What?"

"We've been tracking him based on that phone," Alexis replied, "but there haven't been any sightings of him *personally* since Georgia. Even now. Look." She gestured her stick toward the television, and they spun to see one of Moore's undersheriffs, a man named Cassius LaFleur, handling the press conference. Over Alexis's shoulder, Conrad was glaring at the screen, too, his eyes dark and glassy.

"Then where is he?" Chris asked.

Alexis shrugged. "We don't know. Thorn has been searching for him for the last few days without any luck. I'm starting to think he's still looking for that Forgotten Sin we lost. If Moore's still fucking around down south, it explains why Leroy Khoury popped up on police radar all of a sudden."

"Couldn't he do that kind of thing from here, though?" Skylar asked. "Why stay?"

Alexis tilted her head at Darius. "Ask *him*. The report he and Thorn put together implied Wrath was pretty fucking mad that Moore let the guy live. He might not be allowed back until he handles it."

Raquel gasped, and she spun to Chris. "When do John and Nicholas get back?"

Chris shook her head, and her mouth jammed hard together. "Not for another ten days."

"Let's hope they don't run into him," Alexis murmured.

She and Darius exchanged a look.

"Maybe we need to pull them out," he said with a groan. He looked back at the screen where they were now showing clips of a distant explosion in the crowd. People ran by screaming. He thought he saw TAC members, dressed in black and beige, pushing through a wave of protestors. His mind went back to Samira helping out in the hospital. Would she leave if they abandoned their search for Leroy?

Darius shook his head bitterly. There was that hope.

"I don't know," Alexis said. "But it's gonna be a lot fucking harder to kill Gluttony if he's not here."

By now, everyone in the room was watching the television. More chaos. More violence. Every single carefully-curated shot showed civilians—screaming at cops, smashing windows, and sticking their middle fingers in the lenses of news cameras. Not a single clip of the police shooting innocent people. If Darius didn't know any better, it would have been easy to believe they'd magically controlled the crowd with kind words and gentle scolding. Gabe leaned over the edge of the couch so far that it was a miracle he hadn't lost balance and fallen to the floor. The screen shifted, showing the aftermath now. Discarded picket signs. Broken glass. Bodies—strewn out like trash. It made Darius's stomach twist, not knowing if they were alive or dead.

"Turn it off."

Conrad's voice boomed so loudly over the room that nearly everyone startled in their seats. Everyone but Gabe. He glanced over his shoulder, catching Conrad's eye, before turning back to the program.

"No. I want to see what they're saying."

Conrad walked around the side of the pool table, slamming his cue onto it, and made his way toward Gabe. Chris put her coffee down and got to her feet, tracking Conrad as he moved across the room. He reached the arm of the couch and glowered down at the side of Gabe's head. His massive hands balled into fists at his sides.

"I said turn it *off*."

Heavy anticipation made the room feel numb. Chris stepped away from their table, pulling her blonde hair into a low ponytail. Gabe slowly turned to take Conrad in again, but he didn't stand.

"We need to know what they're saying," he said.

"Bullshit," Conrad growled. "We already know what fuckin' story they're spinning. You're just making sure none of your *pig friends* got what they deserved."

"Conrad," Chris cautioned, "back off."

But neither man looked at her. Gabe's spine stiffened, and he sat up straighter. Darius couldn't see his face, but the muscles along Gabe's back tightened. He got up and faced Conrad, his hands loose by his hips. "Gluttony corrupted those officers. They're victims, too."

"Victims?" Conrad said with a scoff. "Nice try, pretty boy, but Gluttony ain't there twenty-four seven. How do you explain all the people they hurt when he's not around? The poor folks? Black and brown kids? People who love or look different?" Conrad didn't take his eyes off Gabe as he threw a hand out toward Darius, Raquel, and Skylar. Gabe cast them a dark look. Conrad's voice just got louder as he kept talking. "You can blame that Sin all you want, but we all know what you are. Fuckin' bullies."

"Carter," Chris warned again, more loudly this time, as she hedged nearer, "DuPont! Knock it off!"

Gabe glanced at her but quickly looked back as Conrad moved toward him. He was shorter by a couple of inches but almost doubled Gabe in bulk. The two men stood nearly nose to nose. Conrad's mouth curled into a sneer as Gabe's nostrils flared.

"Turn it the fuck off," Conrad growled.

Gabe scoffed. "Who's the bully now, Carter?"

Conrad swung first. The room erupted as he hurled a huge fist at Gabe's head, and Gabe ducked beneath it. Darius leapt up as the nurses on the far wall tucked to the side. Chris rushed in, avoiding one of Gabe's punches as she tried to push herself between the two and force them apart, but they brawled like she wasn't there.

"I said knock it *off!*"

She grabbed Gabe around the wrist as he threw his elbow back. It slammed into her nose. She swore and stumbled back; blood poured down her face. Darius hurried over and got her to her feet.

Then someone came sprinting through the door like a rabid animal.

Jacob Locke jumped onto Gabe's back with a silent fury that left Darius speechless. His brown eyes were wide and wild, his hollow face contorted as he wrapped his arm around Gabe's throat. Gabe gasped, choked, spun around, but Jacob's grip was too tight. Conrad, his lip swollen, stepped back and stared as Gabe's face went a dangerous shade of red.

Darius let go of Chris and came up behind Jacob. He tried to loosen his hold, but Jacob was surprisingly strong. The hard sinews and muscles in his scrawny arms were taut and ropy, and Darius couldn't jam his fingertips between Jacob's elbow and Gabe's throat. Cold panic shot down his spine.

Jacob was going to kill him.

"STOP," Chris shouted.

Her eyes hard, her lips curled into a snarl, she shoved Darius away and threw the heel of her palm into the side of Jacob's jaw. He immediately stumbled, his hold loosening, and Chris dug her fingers deep into his tricep. He cried out, and Gabe pulled himself free. Chris wrapped Jacob's arm behind his back, forced him down, and pressed his face into the ground. Droplets of blood fell from her nose onto his faded, orange ball cap.

"He *hurt* him!" Jacob screamed. His voice was rough and garbled against the carpet. "I told you! Fuck! He's going to hurt *more* of us!"

Chris ignored him. With one knee pressed firmly between Jacob's shoulders, she pointed a finger at Conrad. "Carter," she yelled over Jacob's continued protests. "What the hell is wrong with you?"

He blanched. "What's wrong with—?"

"Go to my office," Chris snarled. "Now."

Conrad stared at her blankly, his eyes wide, mouth agape, and Chris just pointed a finger out the door and glared at him. He stomped off, his energy pushing through the crowd growing outside the rec room door. Chris turned and spotted Seth in the throng. She indicated for him to help her. He took Jacob, and they all got back to their feet.

"Take him to Dr. Harris," Chris said, wincing as she wiped the blood from her upper lip with the side of her hand. Seth nodded and dragged a hissing, spitting Jacob out of the room with his hands pinned behind his back. He glowered at Gabe, eyes full of venom. The Martyrs in the doorway parted to let them through, and Chris said, "Everyone, get *out*."

They all moved to leave, but as Gabe tried to pass her, Chris held a hand out and stopped him where he stood. Darius waited by the door, ushering everyone else into the courtyard as Chris started talking again.

"Where do you stand?" she asked.

Gabe stared at her, rubbing one hand against his throat. "What?"

"Because I can't help you if you're not all-in," she went on, her voice raised. "You can't have allegiance to the police force and the Martyrs. You can't see them as people we need to save. That's not why we're here."

"But Gluttony—"

"Gluttony isn't the problem!" Chris shouted. "The problem is people like *you*."

Gabe's mouth dropped open.

"You don't want to see what's really happening here," Chris went on. "You want to defend the system, but you need to understand that these cops have been Programmed to see people like us as a threat. To kill us, and they have killed *so many* of us."

"But if we get rid of Moore," Gabe tried to defend, but

Chris lifted her hand to silence him.

"It won't fix anything," she said. "The Sins have had the police force, the prosecutors, the entire *judicial system* under their thumb for *centuries*. They've used that power to pit people against each other, to target anyone who tries to stand up against them, to make us all *hate* each other, and it's worked! The corruption goes so deep it will take more than destroying Gluttony to clean it out. It will take years of hard work, and it's not our job!"

Silence fell. Chris's whole body was rigid. All but her hands. They shook, in fists, at her sides. Gabe just stared at her, his piercing eyes wide.

"If you want to help us," Chris said, more quietly this time, and Darius could hear a quaver in her voice, "then you need to stand *with* us. You can't play both sides. They won't protect you the way you're trying to protect them. Stop defending a system that has killed so many of our friends, our families, and people we love—a system that would kill you without a second thought now that you're not a part of it. You need to pick a side, or you need to get out."

Then Chris turned around and saw Darius by the door. Her nose was swollen and raw, and while the blood had stopped pouring, it smeared underneath her nostrils in a bright, crimson stroke. "Fix him up," she murmured as she brushed past him through the doorway. Darius spun to follow her.

"What about you?"

"I'll find you in a bit," she said. "First, I'm going to go scream at Conrad. I want to fucking scare him."

Then she strode across the courtyard, drawing attention from everyone who had stepped back to watch the situation from afar. Raquel's eyes widened, and she looked at Darius. He took a deep breath and shook his head before he turned back to the abandoned rec room. Gabe hadn't moved. He just watched the spot where Chris had disappeared, his eyes cold and distant.

CHAPTER TWENTY

Thorn leaned against the door to Alan's office, her arms crossed and jaw clenched. When she'd gotten the call about the incident with DuPont, Carter, and Jacob, she couldn't say she was surprised, but fuck, it still made her blood boil. The Martyrs had enough to deal with; the last thing they needed was to send each other to the infirmary with broken noses and bruised egos.

"I understand that tensions around Mr. DuPont and the events at the courthouse are high," Alan said. He looked at the people gathered in his office from over the rims of his reading glasses. "But brawling in the Underground is not an acceptable way for our people to handle those tensions."

Chris nodded. She stood between the two chairs by Alan's desk while Lina sat in one of them. Abraham hovered behind the other and gripped its back with rigid fingers.

"I agree, sir," Chris said.

Alan put down the report and removed his glasses. Rae laid to his right, her head resting calmly upon folded paws. "How are the involved parties being reprimanded?" he asked.

"DuPont and Carter have been suspended from duty for two weeks," Chris stated. She stood with her feet planted firmly shoulder-width apart and her hands clasped behind her back. Her voice carried the same professional stature. "They are required to complete sixty hours with Stevie's crew and are confined to their quarters outside of meals and their maintenance shifts. I have also mandated individual therapy with Abraham, and at the end of the week, DuPont and Carter will have a session with me."

Alan frowned, got to his feet, and walked around his desk. He sat on top of it, wrapping his arms around his chest as he turned to Thorn. "And Mr. Locke?"

Abraham hung his head with a sigh as Thorn said, "He has also been assigned work with maintenance, opposite shifts from DuPont to guarantee there isn't any more conflict."

"That's all?" Alan asked. "He is not also confined to his quarters?"

"Confining him would just make his condition worse," Lina said quietly. Her hand toyed with the pendant around her neck. Abraham stood up straight and put his hands on his hips.

"Quite frankly, we should have seen this coming," he grumbled.

"You may be right," Alan said, "but this behavior is unacceptable."

"I completely agree," Abraham said.

"Jacob's body is flooded with more adrenaline than it knows what to do with," Lina reasoned. "We *know* spending too much time in the Underground is a trigger for him."

"Yes," Alan said, his mouth twitching into a frown. "But if he is going to start attacking other people—"

"Carter instigated the fight," Thorn interrupted, stepping away from the door and coming to Chris's side. "Jacob was trying to—"

"He asked for Programming to prevent this exact kind of scenario," Alan snapped. "Programming to prevent him from harming Martyrs."

"It's clear he doesn't see DuPont as a Martyr," Abraham

said, shaking his head. "And he's not the only one. Conrad, Mackenzie, and a handful of others can't see anything other than an ex-cop who hurt people they cared about."

Alan paused, furrowing his brow and stroking a hand over his goatee. "That is a fair point," he said. "We might want to consider adjusting his Programming."

"We can't just fix every problem we have with Jacob through Programming," Lina argued. She scooted to the edge of her chair and wrapped her hands in her lap. "He's just been stuck here helping TAC move in and out of the city for too long."

"He's hurting people, Lina," Abraham tried to reason.

"Give him a fucking break," Thorn cut in, throwing her hands up. Chris stepped to the right to get out of her way, and Sparkie's wings rustled impatiently. Abraham's face went red. "His anxiety has got to be through the goddamned roof."

"We haven't had any issues with Jacob for sixteen years," Lina said. "Let him get back to *his* normal before we mess with his head any more than we already have."

For a few moments, Alan considered Lina. At last, he turned to Thorn and said, "Miss Andrews tells me our vehicles will be ready in less than a week. Once Mr. Locke's maintenance duty has been fulfilled, get him back into his Gray Unit role."

Thorn nodded, and the tightness across her hollow chest loosened. Good. She needed Locke back out there. He was her best agent, and she wanted him tracking Moore. If Gluttony was really after Leroy Khoury, like Claytor suspected, they had to know as soon as fucking possible.

"Thank you, Alan," Lina said. Abraham's head bobbed in a stiff nod.

"Of course," Alan said with a smile. "You two are free to go. I need to speak with Miss Silver a moment longer."

Lina and Abraham made a graceful exit, Abraham avoiding Thorn's eye as they moved past her. When the door was closed and their energies moved through the lounge, Alan turned his attention to Chris.

"Miss Silver," he said. "I want TAC back at full capacity as soon as our vehicles are secured. As for this situation with Mr. Carter and Mr. DuPont…" Alan paused, and his expression darkened. "You have had many tests since your promotion to TAC director, and you have passed them all with flying colors. All except this one." Thorn's breath caught in her throat, and her mouth pulled into a frown. Chris's face paled. She nodded as Alan continued. "If your team does not trust one another, they will not defend one another. One weak link can destroy the entire chain. Identify those links and either strengthen them or eliminate them. Do not ignore them."

"Yes, sir," Chris said. Alan bowed his head once and gestured to the exit. Chris strode from the room; Thorn thought she saw a flash of tears behind her lashes. Her chest filled with a new plume of fire, and as soon as the door closed, she turned on Alan.

"What the fuck was *that* about?"

"If Christine wants to be a leader," Alan said reasonably, "she must be willing to accept all that comes with it."

"People are going to fight," Thorn argued, walking to the front of Alan's desk as he sat behind it again. She placed her palms down on the surface and leaned forward. Her dark hair poured over her shoulders. "You can't expect her to force everyone to sit in a fucking circle and sing songs until they're best friends. This isn't her fault."

"No," Alan said, "but it is her responsibility. She is taking on an impressive mission. She doesn't want to simply command the Tactical Department. She wants to *grow* it. To do that, she must embrace her authority over her people. When they fall, she falls even further. Christine must become unshakable, and I think she will do a phenomenal job."

Thorn stared at him, the flame in her empty chest slowly dying to a dull roar as she stood straight again. "Then why did you tear her down like that? She's working her ass off!"

"Of course she is," Alan said, "but just because she is working hard does not mean we should not bring attention to what she can improve. It does not serve us *or* her to treat her like a child. She isn't one, and she has not been for a long time."

Thorn's mouth fell open. "You think that's what I'm doing?"

"I think," Alan said slowly, and he considered Thorn with a calculating, thoughtful gaze, "that you are prepared to fiercely defend the people under your charge, both on and off the battlefield. But I am not trying to wound Christine. I am trying to help her grow. We do not grow when our lives are easy; we grow when we are challenged. That's what I did today. I showed her an area she could grow in and challenged her to do so. If I know Christine, she will exceed all my expectations, and TAC will be a stronger team because of her."

For a moment, Thorn watched Alan, her eyes hard, her mouth harder, and took a slow breath. Sparkie's wings quivered under her hair and sent a cold chill down her spine.

"I do want her to grow," she said, "but she's burning at both ends, Alan. She can't do it all forever."

Alan nodded, lifted another report, and put his glasses back on. "You're right," he agreed. "That's another valuable lesson for her, and one that can only be learned through experience. I hope she does so quickly."

Then Alan looked down at the paper in his hands, and Thorn stared at the top of his head. Rae lifted hers and peered at Thorn, her bright, intelligent eyes searching her face with a primal curiosity. Thorn bit back the snarl on her lips and left the room. Sparkie peeked over her shoulder, and he caught Alan glancing up just before the door clicked shut.

Terrance Moore. He imagined the paper target standing

in front of him was Terrance Moore. Not a blank silhouette. Not an innocent Puppet. Gluttony, looming through the trees. Holding up a weapon. Getting ready to drive it down onto Thorn's head again.

Darius took a deep breath and drew his gun upward. He lined the sights up with the target. Don't curl your wrist, he told himself. Chris was always reminding him not to curl his wrist. Straight line. From shoulder to fingertip.

He released his breath—a long, slow stream—and pulled the trigger.

A hole ripped through the target's neck. Darius swore, rolled his shoulders, and repositioned. Down and to the right. He pulled the trigger again. This time, the shot hit the chest, neatly grouped with fourteen others. Darius let out a relieved sigh.

"Good work," Chris's voice rang out in his ear.

Darius threw a smile over his shoulder. She stood by the back wall, her arms crossed over a black v-neck shirt. A tablet sat on the pop-up table to her side, and she looked down at it, her mouth pursed and brows drawn together. In the stark light of the shooting range, her eyelids looked puffy. Darius set the gun down and turned to her. "Hey, are you okay?"

Chris glanced at him, raised her brows, and shook her head. "I'm fine," she said, looking back at the tablet. A pink tint raised to the apples of her cheeks. "You're about a third of the way through. Next up: seven yards."

She tapped a few icons, and the mechanized target stand began to rumble backward. As it did, the paper rolled up, pulling the figure he'd just hit into the top of the machine to expose a fresh silhouette. Darius's attention lingered on Chris for a moment, but she didn't look at him again, so he turned around, picked up his weapon, and swapped the spent clip for a new one as he stared down the firing lane.

"You have thirty seconds to fire all seventeen rounds," Chris continued, repeating the same mantra she did for every shooting test with a comfortable monotony, "and you need an accuracy over seventy percent to pass. Ready?"

Darius nodded, stretched his head from side to side, and raised his weapon. A tone chimed in his ear.

And he pulled the trigger.

For the next few minutes, they worked in silence. Darius spent a clip at seven yards. At ten. Fifteen. He counted his shots and did the math in his head. Seventy percent meant at least twelve had to land. He was confident with the first five distance tests. When Chris moved the target back to twenty, twenty-five, and thirty, his nerves began to get the better of him. He switched to a new clip and found his hands were shaking.

"Last one," Chris said. Her eyes moved from the tablet to Darius. "Get ready."

Darius held up his handgun and leveled the sights down the range. The next half-second felt like an hour. His breath sounded loud in his headphones as he inhaled long and slow…

The tone beeped.

Darius shot. Paused. Corrected his wrist. Straight line. Shoulder to fingertip.

And he emptied the clip.

As soon as the last bullet left the barrel, Darius removed the clip, put the handgun on the stand in front of him, and pulled his protective glasses off as he squinted down the firing lane. His heart was beating hard in his throat, and his tongue darted out to wet his dry lips as he counted. The target began to move, rolling up into the mechanism as it slowly drew closer.

"Thirteen," Chris said behind him.

Darius spun toward her, and she lifted the tablet.

"What?"

Chris's lips pulled into a smile, and she turned the screen toward him. It was a still image, showing a close-up shot of a black silhouette against white paper. Darius's mouth dropped open, and he looked back to Chris. Her smile widened. "You got thirteen."

"I passed?" Darius asked.

"You passed."

"Hah!" Darius pumped his fists at his sides, ran back to Chris, and grabbed her in a hug. Her laugh echoed down the range, bouncing back at them from the concrete walls and ceiling, surrounding Darius as fully as Chris's warm aura did. The anxious hole in his gut filled up and poured over, and he lifted her feet from the ground.

"One step closer," she said, laughing again, as Darius lowered her back down. Up close, he could really see the heaviness in her eyes. She smiled through it. "Great job. You'll be joining me on Tactical assignments before you know it."

"Thanks," he said, and he studied her face. "You sure you're okay?"

"Yes." The muscles along her jaw tightened, and she turned to gather her things. "Just tired. Our new cars should be here in three days, and coordinating all that has been taking a lot of my time."

She didn't look at him as she walked back to his shooting lane. He followed her, collecting clips while she grabbed the gun. Chris made a point not to look at him, and he leaned around her shoulder so it would be impossible for her not to.

"I can tell you're lying," he said. Her green eyes darted to his. He raised his brows, pinched one corner of his mouth in, and shrugged. She shook her head.

"It's just been a long week," she said with a sigh as she headed back up the stairs to the control booth. "And I'm kind of sick of talking about it. I've had to talk with Abraham. With Alan. With John." She reached the door, cleared her throat, and shook her head as she grabbed the handle. Before she opened it, she turned to Darius. "So, can *we* not?"

And she watched him with a weary, defeated look that felt like staring into a goddamned mirror.

"Whatever you need," he said. She smiled and opened

the door to the control booth. As the two of them walked into the room, Darius went on. "If you want to get your mind off things, you should join Thorn and me tonight for combat training. I'm sure she wouldn't mind."

And maybe, Darius thought, having Chris there would force Thorn into letting him take *that* test, too.

But Chris shook her head again. "Thanks, but I have more shooting assessments to run." She unlocked the weapons case on the wall, put the firearm into it, and pulled out a different gun. Darius recognized it as the one Mackenzie was training on. "Alexis is coming in later, and Mackenzie should be here any minute. Did you know this is her *fifth* time taking this test?" She turned around at last, her eyebrows high, and Darius laughed. Chris smiled, too, but the smile faded. "Then I promised John I'd call him tonight. I'm all booked up."

"When does he get back?" Darius asked as he put his protective headphones and glasses on the square table in the center of the room.

Chris shrugged. "I have no idea."

Darius frowned, but energy moving through the basement caught his attention. He glanced at the door, and his eyes narrowed. "Isn't Gabe supposed to be in his room?"

Chris's body stiffened. Her arms drew up around her chest, a splattering of white scars highlighted on her pale skin in the overhead light. "Yes," she said, her voice hard. "Why?"

"Because he's here," Darius said.

They both turned to the door as Mackenzie pushed it open. She stomped over the threshold, her tongue piercing clacking against her teeth as she walked toward the gear locker. She opened it and started to grab out protective equipment.

Gabe came in behind her.

"You're confined to your quarters," Chris stated. Gabe had several inches on her, but Chris's tone made Darius feel like a child caught stealing apples off a cart. He busied himself with putting his things away. When he stepped up to the locker beside Mackenzie, he found she'd stopped moving. Her hands were out, resting on a headset, while her chin tilted inward and her eyes focused on the ground beneath her feet.

"I needed to talk to you," Gabe said. Darius cast a glance over his shoulder to see him standing at attention. His feet together, his hands locked in at his sides. He didn't look Chris in the eye but just over her head. "I asked Mackenzie if she could escort me here to see you."

"More like he waited like a lost puppy in the fucking stairwell till someone came by to let him in," Mackenzie muttered. Chris threw them a harsh look over her shoulder, and she and Darius both quickly turned back to the gear locker.

"Whatever it is," Chris said, "it can wait. Return to your quarters."

"Yes, ma'am," Gabe began, but his voice was less professional now. The pitch raised, the tempo quickened, and he cleared his throat. "I understand. I just wanted to tell you I thought about what you said. You're right, and I'm all in."

Silence. Darius and Mackenzie exchanged a look, her thin brows drawn in, and she mouthed something that looked like, "What the fuck?" Darius shrugged.

"You are?" Chris asked at last.

"Yes, ma'am."

"Don't call me 'ma'am,'" Chris snapped. A shorter stretch of silence. "How can I trust that? How can I trust you?"

"You can't," Gabe said. Darius chanced another look back at them. Gabe wasn't focusing over Chris's shoulder anymore. His bright, intense eyes were locked onto hers. "Not yet. But I'll do whatever it takes to prove it to you. Just tell me what I need to do."

Chris stared at him, took a deep breath, and said, "For starters, you could get back to your quarters."

Gabe nodded, his mouth pushing out as he ran his

tongue against his teeth behind it. "Yes, ma'a—" He caught himself, cleared his throat, and nodded again. "Yes. Of course." Then he went to bow and to salute at the same time, stumbling a little over both and doing neither well. He glanced up, caught Darius's eye, and spun around. When the door closed behind him, Mackenzie and Darius turned at last.

"What the hell was *that* all about?" Mackenzie asked.

"He's trying to fix his mistakes," Chris said as she headed back to the weapons locker.

Mackenzie scoffed and put a pair of headphones around her neck. "Fat lotta good that will do him, huh?"

Chris paused, looked over her shoulder, and frowned. "What does that mean?"

"I mean, he thinks he can win us over just like that?" Mackenzie went on. "After everything that's happened? It's not gonna work."

"What's happened?" Chris pressed. Her hands landed on her hips as she turned around. "You mean him being a cop?"

Mackenzie's mouth twisted up incredulously. "I mean him *killing* Elena."

"We can't verify who killed Elena," Chris said. "And either way, it doesn't matter."

"Doesn't matter?" Mackenzie growled. "A Martyr *died*, and you say it doesn't matter?"

"Look, I'm not here to argue with you," Chris said, "so I won't. I've lived in the Underground for thirty years. I've seen a lot of people come into this place, and a *lot* of them have been involved with the Sins before we found them." She paused and considered Mackenzie a little more critically, her brows together, lips pulled between her teeth. After a moment, Chris shook her head. "If we didn't give people like that a chance, the Martyrs would have died. We wouldn't have you. Jacob. Even Thorn and Alan. You don't have to like it, but Gabe is part of the team."

"Oh," Mackenzie said bitterly, "it's *Gabe* now?"

"He's trying to earn his place on TAC," Chris went on, "and he deserves a chance. If you can't work with him, then you don't need to worry about taking the shooting test. I don't want you on the field if you won't defend your team. Your *whole* team."

For a few seconds, Chris and Mackenzie stared at one another, and Darius stood off to the side in stunned silence. His eyes shifted between Chris, whose face was stern and unyielding, to Mackenzie, who seemed to be holding back a rush of furious tears. Her jaw clenched, her nose wrinkled up, and for a moment, Darius thought she was going to rip her headphones off her neck and storm out of the room.

But instead, she jammed them over her ears and went down into the shooting range. Chris followed her movement until the door shut behind her. Then she and Darius looked out the window, where Mackenzie was getting situated in one of the firing lanes. Darius exhaled a heavy breath and turned to Chris.

She didn't look at him as she put her headset on, grabbed Mackenzie's gun, and followed her down the stairs. Darius stuck around to watch the first half of Mackenzie's test. She hardly missed a single shot.

Thorn wiped her mouth, smearing blood against the back of her hand from a cut on her lip that had healed almost as soon as it opened. Darius smiled, and through his heavy breathing, he let out a low, proud laugh. He glanced at Sparkie, who had perked up, surprised, on the weight rack on the back wall.

It felt weird to celebrate landing a hit on Thorn—on making her bleed—but it was the first time he'd gotten that far, and he couldn't help it. It felt like another win. Another step in the right direction. Everything was finally starting to come together.

"Hands up," Darius said, imitating her as he drew his

fists over his face. He grinned. "You live *here*."

She looked at him from beneath thick, black lashes, her eyes moving from his face to his hands. The corner of her thin lips drew into a smile as she pulled her ponytail tighter and returned to a fighting stance. Her shoulders raised in a deep inhale. She released the breath, and she rushed toward him.

Darius rushed back.

That lucky blow was the only one he managed to land. For the next several minutes, he was on the defensive. Dodging. Ducking. Deflecting. Thorn's finesse seemed sharper—like slipping up and getting hit did nothing more than make her more determined not to let it happen again.

But Thorn wasn't the only one with something to prove today.

Darius took his time and focused less on fighting and more on observing. Thorn was on the offensive, coming in over and over again with unrelenting power, and Darius just made sure to avoid taking a hit that landed him flat on his back. Sweat blossomed across his shoulders and trickled in a fine line down his spine as he threw his hands up, blocked one of Thorn's strikes, and rolled away to avoid the one that followed. After the last few months, Darius hadn't just gotten stronger and faster.

He was starting to recognize Thorn's patterns.

"Not bad," she said as Darius feinted to the side, and her punch glanced off his forearms. He smirked.

While he grew more breathless with every passing moment, Thorn moved as seamlessly as though she'd just walked out of the locker room. He wiped the sweat from his brow, and Thorn tried to sneak in while he was distracted, but he avoided her and spun around. She squared up with him, and they began to circle. Their bare feet slid silently on the padded floor. Every muscle in Thorn's body was wound up, like they were ready to explode, but her expression was steady.

In the calm before more chaos, Darius said, "Have you

talked to Chris?"

"Not for a few days," she said. She threw herself forward, and Darius countered, keeping safely out of her path. Thorn's eyes glittered dangerously as she went on. "But I did hear you passed your shooting test. Congratulations."

Her tone mismatched the words. Darius's brows came together, and his stomach twisted uncomfortably. When Thorn punched at him again, he barely managed to move to the side in time.

"Well," he breathed, clearing his throat of the dry film that had gathered there, "I want to schedule my combat test, too."

"You're not ready."

Thorn's answer came as quickly as her open palm curled toward his gut. Darius hunched over himself, catching the heel of her hand on his elbows and taking a couple of awkward steps back as she came at him again. He barely managed to block that one, too, before he twisted away and recovered his stance.

"I am."

"No."

"Thorn—"

Her strike came from below, an uppercut that broke his guard and hit him square on the jaw. Darius's head knocked backward, and suddenly his legs were kicked from underneath him. Thorn's face disappeared, replaced instead with bright, fluorescent lights in the ceiling overhead. He groaned, reaching up to touch his lip, which had been crunched between his teeth, and he winced.

Thorn stood over him.

"I told you. You're not ready."

She held out her left hand. Darius looked at it for a moment, following the thick acid scars extending beyond her *Peccostium*, before he met her eye. Her mouth was set, but her brows drew together in subtle penitence. He ignored her offer and rolled over to stand up on his own.

"That's not fair," he said.

Thorn pulled her hand back and propped it with the other on her hips.

"It's never going to *be* fair," she said. "Fairness is human. The Sins aren't going to hold back. They're not going to be nice. They'll come at you like a pack of wolves and tear you to fucking pieces. If you can't beat me, what makes you think you're ready for them?"

"I'm not trying to beat them!" Darius exclaimed, accidentally biting the swollen spot on his lip. He swore, pressed his fingers against it, and shook his head. "That's not even the point of combat training. We just need to hold our own until we can escape or backup arrives. If it were about beating the Sins, no one would pass except you!"

Thorn's fingertips tightened on her hips until the beds of her nails were white. Somehow, her body seemed tenser than it had when they were actively sparring. Her shoulders were rigid, her flat stomach a hard-lined canvas of pale agitation. Sparkie paced the weight rack, his wings flared up behind him. Darius took a deep breath, ran his tongue over his injury, and sighed.

"Look, I *know* I'm better than other people who have passed this damned test," he said.

"Other people aren't *Virtues*," Thorn responded.

"Why the hell does that matter?"

"Because it *does*," Thorn said. "As far as the Sins are concerned, everyone else is a nameless, faceless helmet. They're ants. Fucking irrelevant. But you? You're *so much more* than that, and now they *know* you can't hurt them." Her voice dropped a little, and the pull on her eyebrows became softer. More repentant. "The Sins will throw everything they've got at you, and I need to make sure you have the best shot of getting out of it alive."

"Okay," Darius said, "then tell me what I need to do! What criteria do I need to meet?"

Thorn paused, her mouth parted in quiet surprise, and Darius knew then that she didn't have an answer for him. His stomach twisted as she said, "I'll let you know when you're ready."

Darius watched her for a moment, sighed, and raised his hands dejectedly at his sides. "I don't think I can do this anymore, Thorn."

She blinked, and her arms crossed around her chest, like somehow they could erect a shield for her to hide behind. "What the hell do you mean?"

"I mean, I'm done with this training," Darius said. The light, airy confidence he'd felt since his shooting test dissolved, and he was left hollow and numb. His teeth clenched together as he looked down at the guards wrapped around his wrists. He began to take them off as he turned away from her. "If the goalposts keep moving, what's the goddamned point?"

"Darius," Thorn said, but he reached the men's room and disappeared inside without letting her finish. The door swung shut behind him, and he walked back toward his locker like a ghost. He opened the door, drew his phone from his bag, and frowned.

He had six missed calls from John and a text that said, "Call me ASAP."

John answered on the first ring.

"Darius! We found survivors."

"Survivors?" Darius froze to the spot. "Survivors from what?"

"The farm," John said. "It's a long story, but Nicholas and I were waiting at the rendezvous point today, and a woman came up to us. She's from Reflection Farms. She survived the massacre. There are two more."

For a moment, Darius could hardly think. His mouth gaped open, and he shook his head. "Reflection Farm—? Wait, is Leroy there?"

"No. He left Charlotte, but we know where he's going."

Darius ran a hand down his face. "Holy *shit*."

"I know," John said.

"Get them back here," Darius said. "As soon as you can."

"You got it."

Darius hung up, anticipation catching in his throat. His injured lip screamed at him, but he pushed through it and rushed into the gym. Thorn had left, but Sparkie sat on the weight rack by the wall. His beady eyes followed Darius as he ran into the courtyard, and he heard the sound of wings beating the air over his head as he hurried toward the elevators.

CHAPTER TWENTY-ONE

High above, just inside the Underground, John's aura came to life. Darius glanced at the waiting room ceiling, his hands clasped between his knees. Samira looked up, too. She frowned, the tip of her nose dipping down as she did so, and her dark eyes narrowed as she focused on the energy slowly spiraling into the earth.

"It's Reverend Weston," she said, letting out a quiet, desperate breath. Tears glistened behind her lashes. "And Carmen and Kayce. They're really here. They're really alive. Oh, praise God."

She closed her eyes, laced her fingers, and pressed her lips against tense, shaking knuckles. Darius glanced at her. So did Abraham. He was waiting by the doors, ready to bring the Reflection Farms survivors to Alan as soon as they arrived. His gaze shifted to Darius, his expression dark. Darius sighed.

"Listen," he began, "a lot has happened in the last month…"

Samira shook her head. "Darius," she said. She didn't open her eyes as she spoke, but her face scrunched in, and the bridge of her nose wrinkled. "I understand that Mr. Blaine wants to speak to them before I do, but they are not the only ones who have been through a lot. I need this. Please."

He watched her profile, his empty stomach knotted. Outside the doors, a rental car pulled up to the loading area.

"Okay," Darius said as he got to his feet. He held his hand out to Samira and helped her up. "But you can't answer any questions."

"Fine," Samira responded. Her voice broke over the word, creaking like old wood, and she let go of Darius to smooth the lines out of her shirt. Abraham opened the doors.

Alongside John and Nicholas, three tired, hollow-looking people stepped into the garage. Nearest to them, an older woman tenderly got to her feet, removing the black blindfold from her throat as she gazed up at the cavern around them. She wrung her hands together as her attention slowly drifted downward, landing on Abraham, then Darius, and finally, over Darius's shoulder.

The minute her eyes found Samira, she yelped a sob.

"Oh!" she said. *"Mi 'manita!"*

The woman shuffled awkwardly past Nicholas, wincing with every other step, and held her palms out wide.

"Carmen," Samira managed to get out. She wrapped her arms around Carmen's center, nestling her head beside her cheek. Her lips opened up in a ragged, choking laugh that made Darius's eyes sting. He cleared his throat. "Thank the Lord," Samira went on. "I thought you were gone."

"We thought the same of you," Carmen said. Gray streaks highlighted her curly, brown hair, and tears poured down her cheeks, following the smile lines etched into her face like freshwater rivers at the base of brown canyons.

"How are you?" Samira asked. She wiped the corners of her eyes with her shirt sleeves as she looked at Carmen's left leg. "Are you hurt? What about Kayce and Weston?"

Samira looked back up. John had pulled the car away to park, and Nicholas stood with two other survivors. One, a younger woman with wide, buggy eyes, spoke quietly to

Abraham as she untied the blindfold around her neck. The other, though, watched Samira with a deep frown contorting his face into an ugly, gargoyle-like expression. Samira blinked a couple of times when their eyes met, and Darius frowned.

"We're fine," Carmen insisted. "Now, at least. These weeks have been hard."

"Yes, I know," Samira said. "What happened to your leg?"

"It was broken," Carmen said, the joy on her face muting, and her eyes went distant. She shook her head, like she was resetting herself. "But Mr. Leroy, he helped fix it up. God bless him."

"He'll need more than God's blessing!" A sharp, twangy voice cut through the garage. It echoed back at them, and everyone went silent as the other man stepped forward. Darius drew nearer to Samira. The man was shorter than him by a couple of inches and wiry underneath his second-hand button-up. His wide mouth turned down, and his bushy, yellow brows drew so close over his eyes that they almost merged into one. Carmen's cheeks darkened in a hard blush, and she ducked down as Samira shook her head.

"I'm sorry," Samira murmured, "I'm not sure I understand what you mean, Reverend Weston?"

The reverend's teeth gnashed together. He was slender, but his hands were thick with callouses, and they wrapped into fists at his sides.

"Look at the Hell you brought down on us," he said in a pointed Southern drawl. He glowered at Samira and shoved a finger in her face. "You yoked yourself to the Devil. You allowed him into your home. Into your *bed*. May God have mercy on your soul, Samira Khoury, and all of ours for believing in you."

Samira gasped, and Darius stepped around her and Carmen to stand between them and the reverend. "Whoa," he said, holding up a hand. "What's wrong with you?"

Weston's bright, blue eyes snapped to Darius's face, and

his nostrils flared dangerously. Darius felt Samira behind him, frozen in place. Over Weston's shoulder, Abraham and the other survivor gaped at him. John, walking back from the other side of the garage, frowned and started to come in at a jog. Nicholas, however, grew dark. His jaw slammed shut, and the corner of his lip curled up in a snarl.

"I'll tell you what's wrong, young man," Weston growled, and he pointed at Samira again. Tears filled her eyes. "Lying about the abomination living in our parish and dishonoring the name of God for her own personal gain. This false prophet—" he thrust his chin forward "—brought God's wrath down upon us all."

Hot anger bubbled up Darius's windpipe. "You need to stop."

"She damned us all!" Weston spat. "Claiming to have God's Grace while she was in Satan's pocket. Did'ja sell your soul to that demon you're fucking to get your power, huh? You little *whore*."

Weston tried to move around him, but Darius pushed him away. Weston's eyes widened, and he looked down at his chest like he couldn't believe Darius had the audacity to touch him.

"I said *stop*," Darius growled. Weston's lip curled, he pulled his shoulders back, and he came forward a second time. Darius grounded himself, raised his arms, and as Weston went to shove him, he knocked both his hands away. Weston's mouth dropped open, but before he had the chance to do anything else, Nicholas grabbed him by the shoulder, forced him around, and punched him square in the jaw.

Weston spun to the ground and landed in a crumpled lump of gangly limbs and blonde stubble. Nicholas shook the sting from his fingers as Weston lifted his head and gingerly touched the side of his face.

"Welcome to the Martyrs, asshole," Nicholas said. "Now shut the *fuck* up."

Then Nicholas looked to Darius, brushed his hands

together, and walked into the Underground. Samira and the others stared after him, eyes wide, as John rushed to Weston's side and helped him to his feet. The reverend seemed dazed, and John kept a firm grip on the back of his arm. "Right, uh…" John started awkwardly. "Welcome. Abraham, we're headed to Alan, yeah?"

"Uh, yeah," Abraham stammered. He ran a hand through his short, curly hair and took a deep breath. It filled his cheeks in a huff. "Yes. This way…"

Together, he and John led Weston, Carmen, and Kayce through the double glass doors. Samira stared after them, tears silently streaming down her cheeks. For a moment, they stood in silence. Then Darius wrapped an arm around her shoulders. Without hesitation, she leaned into him and cried.

———

The door to the conference room opened, and Mackenzie hurried through, her orange hair a frazzled mess as she bowed into the meeting six minutes late.

"Sorry," she said with a grimace. She scurried around Darius, Chris, and Thorn, behind Alan's back at the head of the table, to sit beside Abraham and Lina on the far side. Darius met her eye, and she sent him a sheepish smile and wave before she looked at Alan. "What'd I miss?"

Alan's face was an impassive stone that barely registered his annoyance except in the slight twitch at the corner of his mouth. "Leroy Khoury is no longer in Charlotte."

Mackenzie's eyes widened. "Really? Then where the hell is he?"

"We were just getting to that," Abraham said.

"God, I'm gonna need to pull my people out," Mackenzie murmured.

Alan cleared his throat and raised a hand to regain control of the room. "I spoke with the survivors Mr. Wolfe and Mr. Waters found when they arrived this morning," he said.

"It seems that, after too many close calls with Gluttony and his Puppets in Charlotte, Mr. Khoury decided to draw the Sin away. His goal was to give the others a chance to meet our men at the rendezvous point. They last saw him five days ago when he hopped on a freight train to Nashville."

"That's a long way from New York," Lina said.

"It is," Alan agreed. "But according to Mrs. Cervantes, Mr. Khoury intends to train-hop the rest of the way here. Now that he is not responsible for human civilians, he should be able to move much more freely."

"Yeah, but *trains?*" Mackenzie asked, wrinkling her nose up as she shook her head. "I dunno, it seems complicated. Why not hitchhike? Or, like, steal a car?"

"He refuses to do anything harmful, or, I should say, 'commit any sins,' on his journey north." Alan's voice carried a hint of annoyance, and Mackenzie's face fell. "And, from what I gathered, they did try hitchhiking from Sandersville to Charlotte, but Gluttony had too many people out searching for him. In the end, for safety's sake, they resorted to walking through rural Georgia."

Darius's brows raised. "They *walked?*"

Alan nodded. "That's what I was told."

Chris let out a soft scoff. "No wonder he missed the rendezvous."

"Yes," Alan said. "By the time they arrived in Charlotte, Gluttony had already begun his campaign targeting Mr. Khoury. He was recognized almost immediately. After a few close calls, he decided to use the trains."

Thorn took a deep breath, crossed her arms, and said, "Well, it's a start. We can put people on all the freight lines coming into the city. There aren't any in Manhattan, but we can start in the Bronx and Brooklyn. Still, it's a long shot. Those rail yards are huge."

"A long shot is better than no shot at all," Alan said. "Start right away. There is no telling how soon Mr. Khoury might arrive."

Thorn nodded, her dark eyes hard.

"Now," Alan went on, his tone shift heralding a new topic, and he clasped his hands on the table. "On top of adjusting our search for Mr. Khoury, we now have two new additions to the Underground to prepare for."

Abraham frowned. "Two?"

Alan cast him a sullen look. "Mr. Weston Cunningham informed me that the only reason he came as far as he did was to protect the others from Mr. Khoury's evil influence. He said, under no uncertain terms, that he wants nothing to do with our little... what did he call it?" Alan's lips pressed together, and he briefly closed his eyes. "Ah, yes—'devil-worshipping satanic cult.'"

"Hah!" Mackenzie barked a loud laugh into the room. "I mean. Oh, no. What a shame..."

Alan nodded in her direction. "I told him I could not let him leave without first clearing his memory of any details on this place, our people, and the Sins. He was... less than enthusiastic about the idea. I reminded him it was *not* up for debate. Tomorrow morning, I will be taking him to Scranton and performing the Programming—*with* a guard," he added, looking at Thorn, and she watched him back with a piercing gaze.

"In the meantime," Alan continued, "we must set up long-term quarters for Mrs. Cervantes and Mrs. Farrow. Abraham, please ask Miss Arias to have her team clean and prepare their rooms."

"Yes, sir," Abraham said.

"And Miss McKay." Alan considered her seriously. "Even though the good Reverend Cunningham is blessing us by leaving, we must reprimand Mr. Wolfe for his involvement in the situation. I do not care," he went on, holding up a hand as Mackenzie opened her mouth to argue, "how much the man deserved what he got. We must be better. When we value hate over reason, we mark men like him as our equals. Mr. Cunningham and his kind should *never* be our equals."

Mackenzie's jaw snapped shut, and Darius heard her

tongue piercing clicking against the back of her teeth. Thorn's eyes slowly shifted, and she watched Alan from beneath thick, dark lashes. When he dismissed them moments later, she was the first one up. She didn't look back, and her black hair whipped through the door as it snapped shut behind her.

Chairs scraped along the tile as the rest of them began to leave, too. They quietly filed into the hallway, going in different directions. Chris, Darius, and Mackenzie headed to the waiting room. For the first time since Darius had met her, Mackenzie didn't immediately break the tense quiet. She walked on Chris's other side, and they both stared intently ahead.

"So," Mackenzie said at last, clearing her throat. Chris and Darius turned to look at her. "How long should Wolfe's punishment be, you think? On the one hand, he punched a guy, but on the other hand, that guy was a twatwaffle."

Darius's eyes widened, and he laughed so hard it echoed around the waiting room. Chris's professionalism broke in a grin, and Mackenzie raised her hands unapologetically. "I'm just saying! John told me 'the reverend' was lucky *he* didn't punch him, too."

Chris's smile faded. "When did you talk to John?"

"Right before the meeting," Mackenzie said. "Ran into him outside the elevator."

Darius chuckled. "Is that why you were late?"

Mackenzie held a finger in front of his mouth and shushed him. "Doesn't matter. He was asking how much trouble Nicholas was gonna be in, and he seemed to think he… shouldn't be."

"But he should," Chris argued, her green eyes flashing as she crossed her arms over her black turtleneck.

"I *agree*," Mackenzie said. "Can't have Martyrs going off and popping people in the mouth. Except Thorn. Actually, she's probably gotta quit, too. I wonder how Alan reprimands her… *Anyway*." Mackenzie scrunched her face and pressed her fingertips against her temples as she took a deep breath. Her long, electric blue nails disappeared inside her fiery hair. "My point is, I want something that says, 'I get why you did the thing, but next time, don't do the thing.' Any thoughts?"

She looked between them. Darius was about to shrug when Chris said, "Three days on maintenance. With a short assignment, he'll think it's just a formality but talk to Stevie. She has some *hard* jobs that will make him hate himself by the end of the third day."

"Excellent," Mackenzie said with a smile. "Thanks a ton." Then she held out a hand. Chris's shoulders relaxed, the hard lines on her throat softening as she grabbed Mackenzie's palm in her own.

"No problem," she said. "We're a team."

She held onto Mackenzie a little longer, watched her a little more intently, and Mackenzie's smile widened. She reached forward and firmly thumped Chris's other shoulder with her free hand. Then they started walking back toward the elevator again, Darius following behind them. All the tension in the hallway melted like snow in the sun.

———

"Hey, Darius, have you seen Samira?"

Darius glanced up from his laptop as Abraham grabbed a chair at the table. This late in the afternoon, the R&D headquarters was full of researchers clicking away at their stations, so Darius had taken his work to the courtyard. It was a lot quieter down here. A few people filtered around them while Kenia started prepping for dinner in the kitchen, and the quiet let Darius dig through Virtue leads in relative peace.

"No," he said with a frown. He looked at the vaulted ceiling, where he could feel Samira's Virtue pulling at him from above. Now that he was focusing on it, he realized something felt off—like it was more distant than the other energies congregated up there. "I figured she was in her session with you…"

Abraham sighed and shook his head. "She didn't show up."

"She didn't?" Darius asked.

"No," Abraham said. "I think this whole thing with the survivors from Reflection Farms rattled her." Then he paused like he had more to say. Darius watched him patiently, and at last, Abraham sighed again. "Honestly, she's been less and less receptive the longer she's been here, and I'm not sure talking to me will help…"

His voice drifted off, and Darius leaned back in his chair, wrapping his hands in his lap. "You think it's a Virtue thing?" he asked.

"I worry it might be," Abraham admitted. "I know your relationship with her isn't always smooth, but you are the only person who really understands what she's going through."

Darius's chest tightened uncomfortably. "Nicholas would," he said.

Abraham shook his head. "Nicholas isn't in the place to help anyone right now."

With a sigh, Darius's focus drifted upward again. "I'll go check in on her."

A flood of relief washed over Abraham's expression, and the lines on his forehead relaxed. "Thanks, Darius."

He had been right. After dropping off his laptop, Darius followed Samira's Virtue through the main doors and into the parking garage, where he could still feel her sitting above him. The spot for Thorn's motorcycle was empty, and his heart plunged at the thought of her, bitterness resurfacing as he shook his head and kept walking.

His shoes echoed along the concrete drive as he passed rows of brand-new Martyr vehicles. Chris's new fleet had finally been delivered—a colorful array of deep navy, metallic red, and forest green in various makes and models to make it harder for the Sins to pinpoint and Program them. Every vehicle was equipped with the most impressive array of amenities Darius had ever heard of. The latest electric engines. Thin, bulletproof glass in all the windows. Secret compartments for weapons, armor, and first aid supplies in each unit, from the big SUVs to the small, two-door coupes.

It took several minutes for Darius to reach Samira, and he found her sitting on the ground at the top of the drive, her knees pulled into her chest. Her dark eyes locked onto his as soon as he turned the corner, and once he was close enough to be heard without shouting, he said, "What are you doing up here?"

Darius smiled, but Samira didn't return it. Her shoulders lifted in a listless shrug, and she glanced at the closed ramp behind her back.

"I just wanted some fresh air," she murmured. "Carmen and Kayce are out with Mr. Blaine right now, getting Programmed, and I'm feeling very… anxious with them gone again…"

Her voice faded to nothing, and Darius said, "That's not surprising. You've all been through a lot."

Samira nodded, a quick dip that made it feel like she was barely holding herself together. Up close, Darius could see that her eyes pooled with water, and her fingers held tight against her arms. He slowly lowered himself beside her and propped his elbows on his knees.

"Well," he went on. "The exit here only opens with a key card, and the door to the convenience store is locked unless you have your thumbprint registered in the system. I could take you out that way. We could go on a walk—"

"No," Samira cut in. She shook her head and got to her feet, brushing her hands against her thighs. The whole time, she avoided Darius's eye. "Thank you. I'm fine, really. The whole thing is just… silly."

She started walking away as Darius stood up, too. He followed after her. "It's not silly," he said.

"*I* feel silly," Samira responded. Her voice cracked, and she cleared her throat. A brush of tears glittered in her eyelashes, and Darius knew he couldn't let her go to her room, or she'd just spend the next few hours crying. He gently touched a hand to her shoulder, and she looked at him at last.

"When was the last time you had something to eat?" he asked.

"I, uh…" Samira paused, biting her lower lip. "I don't know. Yesterday, I think."

"Yeah, I thought so," he said with a smile. "When I'm anxious, I forget to eat, too. Let's grab some dinner, okay?"

Samira's shoulders finally relaxed, and so much relief poured from her that Darius could feel it washing against him.

"I would like that," she murmured. "Thank you."

They made their way to the cafeteria, finding it busy and loud. Kenia was in the full swing of dinner prep now, and a few dozen Martyrs were lining up for bowls of spaghetti, hunks of garlic bread, and juicy meatballs. Samira and Darius stepped in with Caleb Claytor, and before long, more people pressed behind them.

For the first few minutes, they didn't speak. They stood awkwardly, side by side, as the line slowly shuffled them forward. Then, they began small talk. About food. The Underground. Its people. By the time they reached the counter, they were chatting more openly about what it was like to heal the wounded and how hard it was to adjust to feeling people's energy during the burnout period after they'd first initiated their Virtues.

When they reached the table ten minutes later, Samira was talking about the farm, Leroy, and the night it all fell apart.

"That's why it took Leroy so long to draw the Sins away from us," she was saying as she stabbed her fork into her noodles. She twisted it without looking down at her plate. Instead, she leaned forward and watched Darius with an intensity he hadn't expected from her—a desperate need, like she wanted someone to connect to.

And who else had been there other than Darius?

"Because he found Carmen?" Darius clarified. Samira nodded.

"Yes! She was hurt. It seems that the Puppets were Programmed to attack anyone who made too much noise, and Carmen screamed. Her shin was broken. Leroy found her and shot the Puppet to save her. Then, when he reached the woods, he found Weston, Kayce, and a few others. He couldn't leave them behind, either."

"How did he explain what happened?" Darius asked.

Samira took a deep breath and shook her head. "He told them everything. They hid out at one of our neighbor's houses to get Carmen some medical care, and while they were there, he explained what I am, what he is, his connection to Gluttony…" Her voice drifted off, and she cleared her throat. "Anyway, the police raided them a few days later, and when they were refused access to the property, they…"

Her voice tightened, and Darius's teeth clenched together. "They destroyed it, too?"

Samira nodded. "Leroy only managed to get Carmen, Weston, and Kayce out. They tried to hitchhike, but they were recognized on the side of the road, probably by people Gluttony Programmed, and Leroy decided to take a slower way through. Since Carmen was still hurt, he had to carry her. It took them quite a while…"

"He's a good man," Darius said. "It would have been easier for him to go alone. Faster, too." He smiled, and Samira mirrored him. Her rich, brown eyes glistened with tears.

"That's Leroy," she said. "He's always been scared. Paranoid, even. He didn't understand what happened to him, and most of his memories from his lost years—I guess, the years he was a Sin—a lot of them were very violent… He was afraid people from his past would find him and hurt him. I think he felt like he *deserved* that hurt… But even through that, he wanted to help people. That's what drew him to my farm in the first place. He wanted to be part of something."

A tear escaped the corner of Samira's eye, fought through her thick lashes, and drew a wet line down her face. She sniffed, rubbed it away with the back of her hand, and looked down at her plate again. Darius leaned forward.

"What's wrong?"

She shook her head and looked around the room nervously, stopping suddenly as she caught sight of something. Darius glanced over his shoulder to see Nicholas walking out from the stairwell. His pale, freckled face was smudged in black dirt, and as the door shut behind him, he caught Darius's eye. Samira took a shaky breath, and Darius turned back to her.

"It's Reverend Weston," she murmured. "I know you all feel he was out of line, but these last few weeks, I have been wondering about exactly the things he said… I know my husband. I know Leroy wants to do good. But what if his sins are too heavy? What if the evil he did in this world was so great that it really *did* bring God's wrath down upon us? What if—" she choked back a sob "—what if my family is dead because of *me*? Because I wanted to save someone who simply cannot be saved?"

Darius's stomach seized so suddenly that he felt sick. For a moment, he just stared at Samira. At the pain pooling in her eyes and threatening to flood down her cheeks in thick, wet rivers. And as he stared at her, he saw himself there. For the first time since meeting her, Darius recognized something familiar.

He reached across the table and grabbed her hand. She squeezed his fingers desperately.

"I don't know your god," Darius said. "But I don't believe any being worth worshipping would slaughter innocent people because *one man* sinned and *one woman* forgave him. Do you?"

"No, but Reverend Weston—"

Someone groaned above them. "That guy again?"

Darius spun to see Nicholas standing behind his shoulder. Samira pulled her hand out of Darius's and wiped her eyes with her sleeves. Nicholas shook his head bitterly. "I thought Alan kicked him the fuck out?"

"He left a couple of days ago," Darius said. His eyes moved from the grime coating Nicholas's nose and cheeks to the dark streaks down his forearms, covering his fingers in a fine, dusty layer. "What does Stevie have you doing?"

Nicholas's hard brows raised high enough for Darius to see slivers of clean, pale skin in the creases above his eyelids. "I just finished cleaning out air vents with Jacob. The guy's a fucking nutcase. Thank god he's out of here tomorrow." Then he turned to Samira again, and for the first time in months, Darius saw the Nicholas he remembered—the Nicholas with Diligence on board. He zeroed in on the other Virtue, his blue, half-empty eyes driven, and he said, "Thank god Weston's gone, too. Don't let that dick get to you."

Samira's eyes filled with a new rush of emotion. "He was my family—"

"He wasn't," Nicholas interrupted, crossing his arms over his shirt and discoloring it with more inky, black marks. "He never cared about you. None of them did. They used you because you were better than they could ever hope to be, and they thought you could take them there, too."

A hole opened up in Darius's gut. "Maybe *Weston* was like that, but not everyone," he argued.

Nicholas's lip curled up in a sneer. "Yes, they were," he growled. "She wasn't a person to them. She was a bridge to the Big Guy upstairs. Even her husband! She filled the void in his chest?" Nicholas pressed his palm against his sternum. "No wonder he wanted to marry her. If someone could fill this fucking hole inside me, I'd do anything for them. That's not love. That's obsession."

Samira's mouth dropped open, and Darius got to his feet. "Man, cool it. It's not like that."

"No?" Nicholas challenged. "You can tell me that's not true for every fucking Virtue out there? I call bullshit. Our power draws people in because people are drawn *to* power.

Even the good ones. They needed what we gave them. Security. Passion. A weapon." His brows pinched hard together, and his lips tightened against his teeth. "Maybe they don't mean it, but that's all we've ever been to anyone, and when it's gone, we don't matter anymore."

"Nicholas!"

Darius stepped forward, but the former Virtue, the forgotten Diligence, shoved past him and came up to Samira. She stared at him with wide, tearful eyes. "Fuck Weston, okay?" he said. "You're better than him. They never deserved you."

Then he threw Darius a look and stormed toward the western block of rooms. Darius groaned as he pressed his fingertips against his eyes. Samira got to her feet.

"I'm not feeling very hungry," she murmured, and as Darius dropped his hands, he saw water pouring down her cheeks. She wiped it away, turned around, and headed across the courtyard, too.

CHAPTER TWENTY-TWO

New York City was the center point of all mankind's vices. Tourists flocked here by the millions, bringing with them an excess of money to pour into an industry designed around consumerism for consumerism's sake, and they took home suitcases full of shit they didn't need and souls tainted by the Sins' corruption. That kind of fast-paced, eat-or-be-eaten attitude made the city a hub for commerce of all kinds. Sixteen freight yards surrounded the place, from Long to Staten Island, Queens to Brooklyn, and even up here in the Bronx.

Thorn walked down the street, a cigarette smoldering between her lips while she looked down at her phone with a frown. In the six days since the Reflection Farms survivors had come to the Underground, she had visited over half of these yards, hoping to find some sign of Leroy Khoury, but she wasn't sure what the fuck she was even looking for.

A sigh escaped from the corner of her mouth, sending whirling ribbons of smoke into the air. Dawn reflected in the windows around her, announcing a morning busied with hurried New Yorkers trying to catch buses and trains. The map on her device highlighted all the freight yards, indicating those she'd already checked with green markers while the rest were bright orange. Today, she'd head south to see if she had any luck across the East River.

With a few quick taps, Thorn selected a handful of target locations, and the application automatically generated the fastest route to get through them. Before she went, though, Thorn had one more stop to make. She turned up East 138th Street. A block away, an open sign glowed in the half-light of daybreak. Grind House Coffee.

Even as her stomach rolled in hungry waves and Sparkie spun in a circle within the satchel cinched to her hip, Thorn drew a quiet, slow breath. She sucked the last dregs of her cigarette to ashes and crushed the butt on the sidewalk with her heel.

Why was this still so damned hard? After nine decades, Thorn thought she'd be used to it by now. She shook her head, and she reached for the door.

A familiar face looked up as it opened. The second he saw her, that face fell.

"The usual?" her barista asked.

Thorn nodded, and he busied himself with the coffee machine. Another customer skirted past her as she made her way to the counter; the man behind it filled a large, paper cup to the brim without glancing up.

"Thanks," she said, passing money over the laminate. A dense silence followed it, full of unhealed injuries and the lies that held them open.

"No problem," the man said as he shoved the to-go cup in front of her. He scooped up the cash and began counting her change. Still, he didn't look at her.

A twinge of loss ached between Thorn's lungs. Eight months ago, he'd have been excited to see her—impossible to shut up as he rattled on about the latest happenings and conspiracies circulating through the city. She'd been his favorite customer, so he used to say. He hadn't in a long time.

She recognized the signs: the aging regulars, the damaged rapport, the bitterness. She knew she had to move on—she'd known it for a while now—but knowing didn't make it easier. As the man slid her change back, careful to stay out of Thorn's reach, her jaw tightened.

"Did I tell you I'm moving?" she stated abruptly.

The barista finally looked at her properly, his eyes a little wide. He shuffled behind the counter and wrapped his arms around his soft middle. "Yeah?"

"Yeah," Thorn said. She hated the way his shoulders relaxed at the word. "I just wanted to say thanks for keeping me awake these last couple of years." She grabbed her cup off the counter and lifted it in his direction. He relaxed further, and Thorn saw a smile hinting at his lips for the first time in months.

"Where you headed?" he asked.

"Brooklyn," Thorn lied smoothly, like she'd lied hundreds of times before to hundreds of different people.

"Good for you," he said. "And good luck."

"You, too," Thorn said. Then she cleared her throat and turned away, leaving a pile of bills behind on the counter that more than tripled what she'd paid. The barista didn't say anything else as she walked through the door, but Thorn felt his energy frozen there, watching her back until she strode past the window and out of sight. The early, summer air felt colder this morning, and Thorn shook it off as she headed south.

It was a little thing, she knew. Just a coffee shop. Just a man. She could find another cafe to fill the void this one would leave behind—another barista to pour caffeinated sludge she couldn't feel straight into that pit she called a heart.

She could, but she didn't want to. Thorn was growing weary of saying goodbye, even to the little things.

Especially to the little things.

Hours later, Thorn sat on the bed of an empty flat car at the western edge of the 65th Street Rail Yard, where the lines ended at the ocean. She frowned into the afternoon sun, looked across the upper bay, and opened her satchel. Sparkie circled overhead. Every so often, his shadow skittered past on the gravel by Thorn's feet so quickly that he might as well have been a ghost. She grabbed her cigarette box and flipped open the lid. Only one left. She pulled it out and lit the tip, drawing the hot, bitter air into her lungs before she exhaled in a slow stream.

Nothing. This was the twelfth yard she'd searched, and she'd come up with nothing again. If Khoury was here, he was damn good at laying low.

She sighed and took another long drag on her cigarette. The heat from the sun above poured over her shoulders. This isolated little area of Brooklyn was one of the few places in the city where Thorn wasn't so thoroughly surrounded by human beings that their icy corruption was all she could fucking feel. She closed her eyes and tilted her head backward, mindlessly flicking her ashes over the edge of the train car before bringing the cigarette back to her lips.

This wasn't working. There had to be a better way.

Approaching cold energy disrupted the warmth. Thorn's eyes snapped open, and she pinched the burning tip of her cigarette out with her thumb and forefinger. As two people changed direction and made their way down the aisle between this train and the one beside it, Thorn slipped through a couple of boxcars on the other side of the tracks. As they neared, she heard voices.

"What do you think he's doing here?" one man murmured. Thorn tilted toward the gap, where the loudest sounds filtered through. Their shoes crackled on the rough gravel underfoot, nearly behind Thorn now. She could feel them on the other side of the car.

"You got me," another man said. "Seems weird, though, don't it? Commissioner Moore's gotta have better shit to do on a Sunday than visit the 65th? Nothing ever fucking happens here…"

Thorn froze. High above, Sparkie took a hard turn and

barreled toward the ground. He unfurled his wings just above the train car at Thorn's back, catching air like a parachute, and landed silently on the steel. He slithered closer to the edge as the first man chuckled nervously.

"Think he knows 'bout the grit we're getting in?" he asked. "No one's reported anything…"

"Shh!"

Sparkie peered down at them. Both men wore bright yellow vests and had safety glasses pushed up on their heads. As the shusher roughly elbowed his companion, his glasses fell off and clattered to the ground at their feet.

"Hey, watch it, *pendejo!*"

The first man squatted down, and the other hissed, "What the hell's wrong with you? Keep your fucking mouth shut. Craig's listening outside the foreman's office. We'll ask him about it later…"

"Yeah, you're right," he grumbled. He put his glasses back on, reached into his breast pocket, and pulled out a small, glass pipe. The bulb at the end was caked with black, smoky residue. The two of them continued toward the transfer bridges and slowly disappeared. First, their voices became a whisper. The grinding of their shoes faded. Their piercing, cold energy grew fainter and fainter until Thorn could hardly feel it. She was surrounded by comfortable, late spring warmth again, and the pit in her chest filled with a buzzing, furious fire.

Thorn tied her hair back, zipped her bike jacket up to her throat, and secured her satchel around her torso. She reached into the bag, drew out a pistol, and checked that the clip was full and the safety off. Then she headed toward the rail yard's main office where, apparently, Terrance Moore was paying a visit.

The offices were over four hundred meters from where Thorn started. She rushed between the tracks, moving as quickly as she could with her weapon drawn and pointed downward, trying to minimize the slamming of her boots against the ground. But Thorn was only halfway across the rail yard when a new point of cold energy appeared, and she stopped running so suddenly that she nearly stumbled. Her heart lodged itself in her throat. For a moment, she couldn't breathe.

Autumn Hunt.

The primal part of Thorn's brain froze, trapped somewhere between wanting to rip Wrath to shreds and get the fuck out of there as fast as she could. Her breath came in short, shallow gulps while every muscle along her body seized, ready to jump into action—whatever action that meant.

And her brain tried to wrap around what was happening… This was all too convenient.

Moore talking with the foreman was one thing, and it made sense. Leroy was traveling by train. But Hunt walking the grounds? For a moment, Thorn wondered if a Puppet had spotted her. Brooklyn was Wrath's favorite territory, but if she were here for Thorn, she would've come with an army. There weren't enough people around for her to build one.

Thorn took a deep breath to center herself while Sparkie got his bearings and circled overhead a few more times. Soon, he found the only living soul still moving on the tracks, and he quietly approached her. Dark brown hair. Smooth, tanned skin. Her mouth was curled into a hard sneer. Thorn's stomach churned.

Hunt was coming this direction, one track over, at the edge of the yard. She moved slowly, without the manic haste Thorn saw when she was actively stalking her prey, but instead, something more calculating. Her piercing eyes swooped from the right to the left as she took in the train cars and the trees at the property line. For a moment, the instinct of revenge began to win—the desire to kill Wrath's host for the first time in ninety years. To make it *pay* for all the ways it had hurt Thorn.

Here she was. Alone. Thorn could corner her. Surprise her. Shoot her in the fucking head without her ever knowing what happened…

Thorn started forward again, more slowly this time, taking extra care to walk silently on the gravel underfoot. She was almost thirty feet away from Autumn Hunt's piercing, evil energy when a new sensation came up the tracks. Four auras she didn't know and one she did. Her stomach dropped. Thorn's gaze darted up the aisle. The ground here was too flat—Gluttony would spot her the minute he walked into the open, even from one hundred yards away. Swearing under her breath, she quickly climbed between two massive boxcars, leapt onto the coupler linking them together, and pressed her back against the metal. Moments later, Moore and his men walked by, and she held her breath.

When they crossed onto the other side, Hunt cut through the thick, weighty silence first.

"So," she mused. "Did you take care of that pesky *problem* of yours? I'm assuming not, considering what you've been up to the last couple of days…"

"He's still out there, if that's what you're asking," Moore said. His deep, baritone voice rolled through the yard like the pre-shocks leading to an eruption. While Thorn could hear the Sins perfectly well from where she was standing, Sparkie had positioned himself in a tree just outside the rail yard, and he tracked their movements. Gluttony was wearing his NYPD blues, armed with a pistol on one hip and a baton hanging from the other. His Puppets looked to be the foreman and a few guys from the crew. They stood in front of Moore—a neon and denim wall of receding hairlines and thick midsections.

Hunt's sharp face split in a cackle, and she propped her hands on her hips. In her right, she palmed a massive, folded pocket knife.

"You really were stupid enough to come back without him."

"He got away—"

"*Clearly he got away!*" Wrath screamed. The trees behind

her exploded with feathers and screeching as two dozen birds took flight. Sparkie was momentarily disoriented by the noise and the movement, and Thorn closed her eyes. Hunt kept screaming. "I want to know how the *fuck* you let this happen!"

"He jumped on a fucking *train*," Moore snarled, throwing his left hand up. His right hovered by the firearm, softly open, ready to grab it. "What did you expect me to do?"

Wrath's mouth twisted into a snarl. "I expected you to kill the fucker when he got away from you seven decades ago," she roared, "but you couldn't manage that! Do you know where he's headed?"

Moore glared at her from over the heads of his pathetic Puppet barricade. He stood several inches taller than all of them. "He tried to make me think he was going west," Gluttony growled, "but we know he talked to Rose. He has to be coming up here—"

"*Of course he is!*" Wrath screamed again. Her hands raised on either side of her head, her arms so tight every muscle, every sinew, stood out against her flesh. Stiff, angry fingers still clutched the unopened knife. "Do you know how bad it would be for the Martyrs to get *another* Forgotten Sin on their team? Do you remember how fucked we were when there were six of them?"

"And now there are only two!" Gluttony roared back. His Puppets shifted, pulling tighter in front of him.

"Thanks to my hard work!"

"Both of them *are yours*," Moore spat, "and you have the audacity—"

Wrath moved so quickly that Thorn let out a gasp. The knife opened with a sharp *click!* She plunged it into the foreman's neck, tore it out, twisted devound, and just as Gluttony raised his gun, she slashed his hand with the tip of her blade. He howled, and the sound strangled deep in his chest as Wrath wrapped her fingers around his windpipe. Her nails dug into his flesh, and she drew her knife underneath his chin. The skin cut open, dribbled blood down his throat, and sealed back up again. The three surviving Puppets stood just as still and shocked as Moore was.

And Thorn's nerves lit up like New York City at night. She let out a shallow breath.

"If he makes it here," Hunt whispered beneath Moore's full, shaking lips, and she jerked him downward. He landed hard on his knees in front of her. "If he finds Rose and her Martyrs, you will *wish* all I did was kill you. Do you understand me?"

"Yes," he choked out.

"So," Wrath pressed. "Where is he?"

"I don't know," Gluttony said. His voice was tight as he forced the air past Wrath's grip. "I alerted every major station and rail yard between Georgia and New York to be on the lookout for a stowaway in their freight cars, and I have Sentries at over a dozen of them. Last I heard, he had to turn around in Ohio!"

Wrath's nose curled up, drawing her upper lip into a contemptuous sneer.

"What about your little friend? Your Martyrs *rat?*" she asked bitterly. "Have they let you know if Rose and her sheep have any leads on him?"

Thorn's eyes widened, and her jaw plummeted toward the ground. Her heart pounded so hard it rocked the empty pit in her chest, magnifying it like a war drum. She turned her head to hear more clearly, but suddenly her ears felt like they were full of water, and she barely caught Gluttony's next words.

"I told you," he spat through a cough. "I don't have a friend in the Martyrs! I don't have any control over what kind of information we get or when we get it. Since learning Jones is Kindness, they haven't dropped anything valuable!"

Wrath swore and thrust him backward. He stumbled a few steps but caught himself before he slipped and drew back to his full, impressive height. Wrath turned her back on him and began to walk away. For a moment, he looked like he was going to send his Puppets after her. Beads of sweat speckled his dark forehead, and he clenched his hands hard at his sides. One of the men stepped forward, and Wrath turned back around. She looked from the Puppet to Moore with little concern.

"Take care of this," she commanded.

Then Wrath stormed up the side of the rail yard until her energy disappeared. Moore stared after her, swore, and made his Puppets lift the foreman's body. They came toward Thorn, and she shuffled around the side of the train car, putting it between them as they dragged the dead man toward the bay. When she was confident they were too far to hear her, she turned north, and she sprinted.

The Sins had found a Martyr. They'd found a link. Someone they were mining for information on the Underground, and no one else spent as much time exposed to them as her people did.

Thorn had to get the entire Gray Unit out of the city. Immediately.

When she hit 64th Avenue and found her motorcycle, she hopped on, slammed her helmet over her head, and hit her first speed dial. The phone trilled in her ears.

Alan answered on the second ring.

"We have a fucking problem," Thorn started.

Darius reached the top of the stairs and threw the door open, breathing hard as he walked into the foyer and down the hall. The tactical room was empty, but beyond it, the R&D headquarters buzzed with researchers looking for incidents involving Leroy Khoury at train stations across the North East. As Darius reached the waiting area outside of the hospital, he felt warm movement in the garage, and he glanced over his shoulder to see Alexis walking through the double doors. Gabe DuPont and Amelia Chan came in behind her. Darius met Gabe's eyes, and they exchanged an awkward nod before Darius turned down the other hallway.

Every room in the Martyr leadership alcove was empty, but Darius could feel Chris's strong, robust energy further back. He strode into the lounge between Thorn and Alan's offices and opened Alan's door. Chris sat in one of the chairs in front of his desk, and she looked over her shoulder as Alan's attention darted up from the computer. Rae sat next to him, her bushy, black tail curled around her haunches and her bright blue eyes sharp and dangerous.

"Mr. Jones," Alan said as he turned back to his screen. The light reflected in his reading glasses, obscuring his eyes behind white ovals. "Take a seat."

"Did everyone make it out of New York okay?" Darius asked as he sat on Chris's right.

"They did." Alan tilted his head in the slightest nod Darius had ever seen. A ball of tension dissolved between his lungs. Suddenly, he felt heavier, and he sank deeper into the chair as Alan went on. "Miss Claytor just arrived."

"Yeah, I saw her," Darius said.

"Mr. Claytor is en route as we speak, and moments ago, Thorn let me know that Mr. Mulligan has successfully been evacuated from his apartment," Alan said. "He just got outside the city limits, and Miss Andrews is monitoring his activity as he takes precautionary routes to confuse and lose any potential tails."

"With a guard?" Darius asked.

"Yes," Chris said. "Every TAC unit on patrol has been reassigned to provide security for the Gray Unit as they make arrangements and evacuate."

Darius nodded. "What about Jacob?"

"Thorn spoke with him," Alan said. "As his position in the city includes providing transportation in his personal vehicle, he was already on the move and easily able to get out of New York without detection. He should be here any minute now if he is not already."

"And Thorn?" Darius's chest tightened anxiously. "When will she be back?"

Alan's chin tucked in just enough for the shadows over

his eyes to grow darker. "She is not returning for a few days."

Chris and Darius exchanged a look, and Chris said, "She's too angry?"

Alan sighed and pulled the reading glasses from his face with a sharp snap. "She is searching for the Sentries who have endangered her team. It is a much more productive use of her energy than sitting here would be."

The tightness in Darius's chest grew. He leaned back and ran his hands down his face. "I can't believe the Sins found one of our people…"

"That is our suspicion," Alan confirmed, and Rae's ears twitched. The long line of her lips began to curl up, briefly exposing long, sharp canine teeth, before they settled again. Alan went on. "The problem now is determining *who* they have found…"

"Which, I'm assuming, is why you asked to talk to us," Chris said. While Darius had reclined back in his chair, Chris still sat with pin-straight professionalism. Even her hair was pulled back into an immaculate, low ponytail, which draped down her black turtleneck in a perfect, yellow line, not a strand out of place.

"Yes," Alan said. "We *must* get to the bottom of this immediately to protect the individual who has been compromised while getting the others back on duty. I want to interview everyone in the Gray Unit privately. We are looking for any sign that they have been Programmed or indications that someone in their circle is associated with the Sins. I want both of your help in making this process go as quickly as possible."

Darius frowned and leaned forward, propping his elbows on his knees. "Of course. What can we do?"

"We will be using the private rooms you have set up in the hospital ward to conduct these interviews," Alan went on, looking at Chris. She nodded. "I would like you in the control center, recording and monitoring for anything noteworthy that may come up while Abraham and I speak to them. Mr. Jones, I want you in the room with us. Your ability to read people is unprecedented."

Darius let out a short, awkward chuckle. "Thank Kindness for that."

The corner of Alan's mouth played with a smile, but he snuffed it out as he nodded. "Yes, that brings me to my next question. Mrs. Khoury." Darius's face suddenly felt numb, and Alan continued. "It may be beneficial to have *two* Virtues watching these interviews to get a read on the room. In that case, we may even be able to divide the work and expedite the process. Do you think she would be willing to help us?"

Alan watched Darius with a cold intensity, sitting rigidly behind his desk with his long fingers laced on top of it. Darius bit the inside of his cheek.

"I'm not sure she's the right person for the job," Darius said after a moment. Chris turned to watch him, too. He felt her gaze on the side of his face.

Alan frowned. "Why not?"

"She means well," Darius started, and he chose his next words carefully. "But I think she has… biases… that might get in the way here."

A tickling sensation moved from the tightness in his chest and up Darius's spine.

"Biases?" Alan went on, but his voice sounded distant. Darius sat up straighter, and Alan's brows drew together. "Similar to the biases we experienced with Miss McKay?"

Darius frowned. The tickling grew stronger. More intense. Until it prodded at the hairs at the base of his neck and made them stand on end. A strange, chemical smell twitched at his nose—so subtle he thought he imagined it.

"Mr. Jones?"

"Something's not right…"

Darius slowly looked around the room. He didn't mean to be slow, but the world seemed to drag behind him. At first, he didn't notice anything wrong. Not until he made it to the open closet door to the side of Alan's desk…

And found a reflection of himself looking back.

He startled at the image—a smaller, scrawnier, dirtier version of him, hiding behind the coats like he had almost two years ago. He blinked. The apparition blinked, too.

"Alan," Darius said. "Do you see that?"

He gestured into the closet. Alan turned, and when he frowned, the expression looked dramatic on his face. A caricature of a frown.

"See what?" he asked.

Icy dread filled Darius's whole body.

This wasn't real.

"I'm hallucinating," Darius realized.

Chris gasped beside him. "So am I," she whispered, thick and heavy, like she was speaking through water. Darius turned around, and when the room caught up, she seemed far away. The wall behind her melted into a muddy slick of beige and maroon. She met his eyes, or he thought she did, but her face was distant, too. Her jaw dropped—and kept dropping until it was so wide open Darius could have shoved his whole arm down her throat. "God, Darius, your face!"

He touched his nose, and as Alan jumped to his feet, Darius looked at him. He darted around his desk. A trail oozed behind him—dark and bleeding—as he and Rae rushed to the door. "Stay here," he hissed. "I am going to investigate. Do *not* leave this room."

Then the door opened and slammed shut with a clap of thunder. Darius covered his ears and dipped his head between his legs. Even with his eyes closed, he felt unmoored, like his mind was no longer connected to his body. His ears were full of a rushing sound—a faded blend of screaming and laughter. He heard Eva whisper his name. Felt her hand lingering on his back and tracing the arch of his spine. A chill rushed into his stomach.

"What is happening?" Chris murmured beside him. *"How is this happening?"*

"I don't know," he said, but the words felt stuck in his

mouth, like his teeth were growing to keep them trapped there. Who else was affected? He tried to feel around him, but it wasn't just his physical senses that were screwed up. The warm Martyr energy flickered like dying lightbulbs, writhing around in indistinct shapes that Darius couldn't make sense of. He didn't recognize them. He couldn't distinguish them.

He had no idea if they were okay.

"We need help," Chris echoed.

Thorn's face suddenly filled Darius's mind.

It was a reprieve—an oasis in the chaos outside his brain. He still heard the screaming of dead children, Autumn Hunt's laughter piercing into his ears, Eva sobbing—but the image of Thorn didn't contort with reality. It was reliable and unshakable.

Just like the real thing.

He opened his eyes at last and found the shelves around him dripping with sticky, red liquid. It wasn't real, he reminded himself. None of it was. Not the blood. Not the scared Darius peering out of the closet. Not Chris—Jesus, Chris—who now watched him with dead eyes and gray skin. He shook his head. Covered his face with his palms.

Thorn. He had to talk to Thorn.

So he pried his hands back and reached into his pocket. The denim felt like glass against the back of his hand as he drew his phone out and turned on the screen. Mackenzie's face on his background warped. Her tongue lengthened, and her eyes looked just as dead and empty as Chris's. Darius unlocked the device and navigated to his contacts. He *tried* to, but the icons on the screen kept moving, avoiding his finger like squirming maggots on a rotten body.

At last, he hit it. Thorn wasn't in his speed dial menu. He scrolled past the people he called often. Lina. Chris. Eva. His stomach lurched, and he kept scrolling through lines of Martyr names, Martyr faces, which all looked dead and empty to him now, until he got to the Ts.

Thorn's picture. The only thing in this room that felt

alive.

He slammed his thumb onto it, covered his eyes with one hand, and held the device to his ear.

While he did, he felt a warm snake slithering up the hallway. The sense of danger at the back of his neck growled.

Thorn answered on the first ring. Her voice snapped like static.

"Jones?"

"I need you," he blurted out.

"What?"

"Back here. I—*fuck*." Darius dipped his head back between his legs. The ground at his feet was slick and red. Everything was red. "Thorn, something's wrong."

The snake glittered behind Darius now. His senses blared at him. Screamed. Pulled at his hair and tightened around his throat. The door began to open. Chris stood and turned toward it.

"I'm on my way," Thorn's voice crackled. "Darius, what—"

Suddenly his mind filled with visions of blood. Thad and Sophie. William Michaels. Teresa. Saul, Juniper, and Lindsay. Eva.

Eva.

Darius jumped to his feet and turned around as the door swung open. A round of gunshots went off. Darius was thrown backward by a blow to the shoulder, and he slammed into Alan's desk. A black-faced monster with the head of a housefly and a swirling miasma of distorted, hot energy stood on the threshold. As Darius collapsed, it turned and ran from the room.

Something gurgled on the ground by Darius's knees. He looked down. Chris gasped at the ceiling, a corpse clawing at an open wound on the side of her neck.

No. Not a corpse. Darius felt her heat—fragmented, unlike her own—but he *felt* it. He crawled forward, through a pool of crimson tar, and grabbed Chris in his hands, wincing at the pain shooting through his shoulder as he did it. He wasn't sure what parts of her were real and which were illusions, but by the way healing energy surged from his palms and into her flesh, he knew she was hurt, and she was hurt *badly*.

So badly that before Darius knew it, his vision faded, and he collapsed backward. His head landed beside his phone, dropped onto Alan's crimson carpet, where Thorn was screaming his name.

———

Light filtered through the stained-glass windows at the front of The Cross, sending a beautifully broken mosaic of stunning colors across the dark, wood flooring and brick walls. Thorn leaned back, her spine aligned with the doorframe of a women's restroom she'd spent an hour wiping blood out of less than a year ago, playing with the brand-new box of cigarettes she'd purchased on her walk over here. The cellophane crinkled in her fingers, and her aching chest burned with a fury she just fucking needed to release.

She felt Jay's cold energy walk out from behind the bar, distancing itself from the congregation of regular patrons who came here nightly to pay tribute to the gods of bottom-shelf liquor and bad decisions. It was only 6:00 p.m., and more than a dozen people sat around the room, gathered by the tattered pool tables or sitting along pews that had been repurposed into booth benches, where a whole different kind of praying happened. Thorn slipped her cigarettes into the satchel hanging at her hip.

As soon as Jay turned the corner, she grabbed him by the collar, pressed him against the wall, and kissed him.

She'd come here for an escape—a quick fuck in the back storage room followed by a couple glasses of scotch just to make the monster inside more manageable before she got back out into the city and looked for answers. Jay's mouth opened up to her, accepting the beast, sucking the life from it as his lips drank her in. The tension in Thorn's chest began to relax, and she reached for the button at his waistband.

Then he gently pushed her backward.

"Wait," he said, holding his hands up between them. "I can't do this right now. I have *work*, Tea."

Thorn gawked at him, her mouth gently open, her eyes more so, and she shook her head.

Jay had never said no to her before.

"We've done this while you've been at work," she challenged, propping her hands on her hips.

"Yeah, well," Jay responded, "we're not tonight."

The way he watched her felt different. His eyes focused on hers, refusing to see the rest of her, like he knew he wouldn't be able to resist if she was standing naked before him. She hated that he resisted now. The swirling mass of fire in her core flared.

"Why the fuck not?" she asked.

"Because that's all this is with you anymore," Jay said.

Thorn crossed her arms, digging her fingernails so deeply into the bare skin on her bicep that even she was aware of how painful it was, and her nose wrinkled into a snarl. "This is all it's *ever* been with me. You *agreed* to this! It's always been about sex—"

"I'm not talking about that," Jay cut in. His eyes were full of a rage Thorn knew she'd planted there. Toxic seeds poisoning the garden. "We didn't have sex like *this*."

He gestured to her, and her stomach twisted.

"What the fuck do you mean?"

"We used to have fun," Jay said, throwing his hands up, "but now you're just… damn it, Teagan, you're so angry all the time, and it seems like all you want to do is fuck me when you're pissed off and then disappear again."

A hot flush rose to Thorn's face, and her fists clenched at her sides. Sparkie spun in her satchel, aching to scream, but he didn't. "That's not true."

"The last *seven* times we hooked up, it was," Jay said. "You punched a fucking *hole* in my wall, for Christ's sake!"

"I paid to have it fixed!"

"You think that makes it better?" Jay asked. "You can't just slap some paint over the damage and pretend it never happened! All you do is hide behind shit like this!"

The rage in Thorn's chest spiraled. "I'm *not* hiding."

"Then that's worse!" Jay challenged, his voice rising. The cold energy on the other side of the wall hesitated. Thorn felt people shifting, approaching the hallway to listen in like eavesdroppers outside a confessional booth. Jay kept yelling. "It's so much fucking worse if this is the *real* you."

Thorn's breath caught in her throat, and while she was aware of the inferno in her chest feeding off her anger, growing with it, threatening to burn her to the ground, she felt far away from it. Like she was seeing it from a distance. Watching it happen to somebody else. She stepped back, sucked air between her teeth, and shook her head.

But she didn't say anything. She didn't know what to say.

"I need to get back to work," Jay went on, tearing her back to reality, where her anger was so hot that Thorn felt like she was melting from the inside out. "I'll call you later, but I can't talk to you right now. Not when you're like this."

Then he walked away without so much as a glance over his shoulder, and he left her alone in the dim corridor.

Alone with her thoughts and the roaring beast inside.

Thorn's fingers tightened on the strap to her satchel. Her teeth ground together. She thought about going into the main room, picking at Jay until he screamed again, maybe finding the biggest fucking guy in there and starting a fight just to have someone to take this out on, but instead, she spun on her heels and stormed out the back exit and into the alley. As the door swung shut behind her, Thorn roared and threw her satchel to the ground. Sparkie screamed inside of it, and the jolt of pain made Thorn drop to her knees.

"Fuck!"

She grabbed her bag again and opened it. Sparkie nipped at her fingers when she reached for him—something she fucking deserved—but then pressed the top of his head against her palm. She closed her eyes, clenched her jaw, and went for the new pack of cigarettes.

If she couldn't fuck the fury away, she'd smoke it out.

Her phone rang.

Thorn paused and picked it up instead. A new web of cracks disrupted the glass, cutting Darius's face into pieces as it stared at her from the screen. She frowned and answered.

"Jones?"

His voice came through harshly, filling the receiver with a desperation Thorn could feel from fifty miles away.

"I need you!"

Her stomach lurched.

"What?"

"Back here," Darius went on, and Thorn leapt to her feet. He sounded off, like he'd been drinking. The words all slurred together. "I—*fuck*. Thorn, something's wrong."

Thorn's eyes widened. She turned away from The Cross, sprinted onto the street, and pushed through pedestrians on the sidewalk.

"I'm on my way," Thorn said as she ran. "Darius, what—"

But she choked on the words as gunshots blasted through the speaker.

And the phone went quiet.

A cold rush doused Thorn's whole body, and she couldn't breathe. "Darius?" she said. He didn't respond. Panic grew. Even in the hot summer sun, Thorn's fingers and face felt numb as she turned the corner and spotted her motorcycle up the street. She heard shuffling. A thud.

Then nothing.

"Darius!"

Thorn leapt onto the bike, slammed on her helmet, and tore away from the curb so quickly she burned her tires on the asphalt. Disconnecting the call felt like tearing out her lungs, and when she hit Alan's speed dial icon, he didn't answer.

CHAPTER TWENTY-THREE

The city zoomed past Thorn in the dark, somewhere outside the tunnel of focus she had on the road in front of her. On the bridges she crossed, the cars she darted around, the people she avoided. Her ears filled with a rushing, white noise—the sounds of her heartbeat and shallow breath the only things keeping her company as she made her way back to the Underground. She called Alan again. Twice. Three times. On the fourth, it didn't even go through. Straight to voicemail.

Terrified nausea wrapped around her stomach.

When she reached the gas station, sitting hundreds of feet above the entire Underground complex, Thorn didn't bother with the carwash entrance. She didn't have the time—the patience—to wait for it. Instead, she screeched to a stop on the sidewalk so suddenly that the bike lurched forward. She leapt off before it had fully settled and ran to the glass doors, slamming into them, finding them locked.

Thorn's hands fumbled with her satchel as she drew out her wallet, where she kept the mag key for the building. Sparkie climbed from her bag and clung to her shoulder, his wings quivering as she swiped the key by the lock and pushed again. Nothing.

Sparkie screeched, and Thorn's heart pounded painfully in the empty pit between her lungs. She stepped back, planted her feet, and kicked the joist between the double doors. They rattled. The metal between them groaned and bent, cracking along the lock. Thorn kicked again.

Suddenly, a point of cold energy rushed out from the back of the store, and someone appeared on the other side of the glass.

Stefan Brandt, dressed in his Tactical uniform, waved his hands frantically. He punched in a complicated code only the TAC agents assigned to the storefront knew, and the lock clicked. Thorn pulled at the doors, but they stuck together, the bent metal grinding painfully against itself as she pried them open.

When she spoke, she screamed.

"What the *fuck* is going on!?"

"We're on lockdown," Brandt said.

"What happened?"

"I don't know," he said as he struggled to pull the doors back together and set the lock again. Thorn tore her helmet off. She rushed through aisles of goods toward the storage room at the back of the building. Brandt ran to follow her. "About forty-five minutes ago, the emergency protocols took over. All external communications shut down, entrances closed, but Mr. Blaine says it's under control."

Every muscle along Thorn's body ached with tension as she opened the storage room and headed to the hidden entrance. Brandt's voice sounded distant now—irrelevant. Thorn typed in her override access codes, and the door to the Underground opened. She sped through it to the stairs, her feet producing an echoing drumbeat all the way down the deep, concrete shaft. The cold energy of Martyrs below her grew with every step, calling to her, letting her know that, fuck, they were okay. Moving. Breathing. But Thorn knew what she heard. Gunshots.

Gunshots in the Underground.

Her gut broiled as she reached the main floor and threw

the door open.

Cold, human life pulled at her. A huge group in the hospital. Thorn hadn't felt this many people in the hospital in years. Not since they found Darius.

Darius.

Thorn's chest felt hollow as she rushed down the hallway. Through the waiting area. Almost as soon as she entered the room, Alan grabbed her, like he'd been expecting her to burst in at any moment. His fingers dug deep into Thorn's arms, even through her protective jacket, and stopped her in her tracks.

"Where's Darius?" Thorn asked. She tried to push past him, but Alan was just as strong as she was, and he braced himself on the tile floor to hold her in place. "He called. I heard gunshots. Alan, *where the fuck is Darius?*"

"He's fine," Alan said. "Christine, too."

Thorn exploded backward, pulling out of her uncle's grasp, and Sparkie roared on her shoulder. "*Chris?*" she screamed. "Chris was hurt, too?"

"Yes, but—"

"What happened?" Thorn pushed on. "*What the fuck is going on here?*"

"Someone flooded our ventilation system with a hallucinogenic drug," Alan said as he stepped up to her, raising his hands between them.

"Who?" she demanded, and she looked over Alan's shoulder. Abraham and Conrad were standing in the middle of the room, staring at her. Beyond them, the doors to the hospital opened, and Darius stepped out. His black shirt was torn. A bullet hole through the shoulder. Behind it, Thorn could see the deep pink of wounded flesh. His green eyes met hers, and he watched her with a soft, anxious frown. Her stomach dropped.

"Alan," Thorn snarled, turning to him again. Her fingers were so tight around her helmet that they ached. "Who the *fuck* did this?"

"That is under investigation—"

"*Who* is under investigation?" Thorn interrupted. "I want names!"

"Thorn. Please." Alan stepped toward her again. She moved further back. "I have this situation under control."

"The hell you do!"

"You are not helping," Alan pressed. "Not like this. You *must* collect yourself."

Thorn's resolve shattered, and the hot swell of fury seeped through the cracks, eating her up, making her stomach, her lungs, her throat burn with a fire she couldn't hold back anymore. Her eyes darted from Alan to Darius and back again.

Like this. Why was she always fucking *like this?*

Alan reached for her, but Thorn pushed around him. Down the hallway. Past the offices. Into the waiting area between hers and his. Alan's door was wide open, and Thorn glanced through it. The crimson carpet in front of his desk was stained in a heavy, dark pool.

Chris's blood. *Darius's* blood.

Her body rocked with warning shocks as she rushed into her office and slammed the door behind her. A high-pitched ringing filled her ears. She launched her helmet to the ground as Sparkie threw himself into the walls, tearing paper and maps down as he writhed and growled. Thorn tried to breathe, but it came in hard, ragged gasps. She felt like she was drowning. Underwater. Crushed and confined. She grabbed her satchel from her shoulder; it caught on her jacket, and she frantically pulled them both off in a tangled mess of straps and kevlar. When she was finally free, she reached in, drew out a lighter and her new pack of cigarettes, and threw the rest to the floor.

Then she pulled at the cellophane. Tore at it. Pinched it between shaking fingers and nails that were too damn short to be any good. The squeaking plastic taunted her. Laughed at her.

Her door gently opened.

"Thorn?" Darius asked. "Are you okay?"

She broke.

"No!" Thorn spun around and hurled the unopened cigarettes and lighter across the room, where they crashed into the wall beside the door. "Someone in the Underground—*in the fucking Underground*—shot you! They shot *Chris!* And I wasn't here! I couldn't do *anything!*"

Thorn's vision began to go gray. Black dots slowly spiraled around it, obscuring the room, obscuring everything but Darius. He stared at her with wide eyes, and the muscles along his strong throat shifted as he swallowed. A loathing, venomous wave of guilt made Thorn twist away from him. She swiped her arm across her desk, knocking off papers. Maps. A flurry of office supplies. It all fluttered to the ground behind it. She wanted to hide. Where the *fuck* could she hide?

"Get out!" Thorn screamed.

Then she slammed her hands against the top of her desk, dipping her head so her hair closed like a curtain around her. Sparkie collapsed where he was and tumbled into a pile of paper beneath her chair. The door clicked shut again, and Thorn roared in the silence.

She couldn't stand that Darius had seen her here. *Like this.* Again! The monster inside howled, egging Thorn on, tempting her to tear the room to shreds—to flip the furniture and throw it into the walls until all that remained was a pile of splintered wood. Her legs tensed, ready to listen to it.

When she heard the soft, quiet crackle of cellophane.

Thorn spun so quickly that she smashed her hip into her desk and moved the whole thing back three inches. Darius crouched down, grabbed her cigarettes and lighter from the floor, and as he stood up, he pulled the plastic packaging off. Thorn's heart lodged in her throat as Darius opened the little red box and searched for one she hadn't crushed. He pulled it out, held it between his lips, and lit the tip. Smoke poured into his mouth, and he coughed it out in a gray puff.

Then he met her eye, stepped forward, and extended the

smoldering cigarette toward her.

Thorn stared at him.

"Here," he said.

"What are you doing?"

"This is what you wanted, right?" Darius held the cigarette out further. Thorn's brows drew together, and she looked from Darius's face to the cigarette between his thumb and forefinger. The lines around his nails were caked in ruddy, red grime. Her eyes traveled up his arm until she reached his shoulder, where just below his collarbone, she found the tear in his shirt and the partially-healed bullet wound behind it.

"Take the damn thing," Darius said, and Thorn's attention snapped to his face again. His eyebrows raised, so she reached out. Her fingers brushed against his as she grabbed the cigarette. Darius turned to take in the room. Thorn's cheeks warmed at the shame of it.

"So," he went on, placing the lighter and cigarette box on the desk. "What's next?"

Darius looked back to Thorn. She shook her head.

"What?"

"What else do we need to do?" Darius asked, and he gestured around them. "Rip up the maps? Punch the wall?"

Thorn felt her whole face flush hot, furious pink. "This isn't fucking funny," she yelled.

"I'm not joking," Darius yelled back. "I can't just sit outside and let you go through this on your own." Thorn continued to watch him, her brows tight together, and he put his hands on his hips. "I'm here with you, whatever you want to do—"

"Want?" Thorn exclaimed, throwing her arms out. A column of ash from the cigarette she hadn't smoked tumbled onto the carpet. "I don't *want* to do this!"

"Then why do you?"

"Because it's all I have!" Thorn spun away from Darius again and looked at the mess she'd made. Reports and papers flung everywhere, the wall demolished to the point where she'd have to redo everything from scratch. Sparkie detangled himself from the debris and leapt up to her shoulder. Thorn shook her head, but the anger in her stomach faded a bit, making room for disgrace instead. "It's the only thing I know *how* to do—the only way I know how to be."

"For now."

Darius's voice was quiet and level. Thorn snapped around to glare at him.

"For forever. This *is me*, Darius! Wrath—"

"Doesn't define you," Darius interrupted. He grabbed Thorn by the arm, spun her to face him, and caught the other in his open hand. His fingers held her securely, warm on the bare skin just above her elbows. Her breath caught in her throat as he came closer and spoke again, louder than Thorn. Almost shouting. "Stop letting Wrath define you! It never has, and it never will. *You* get to decide who you are. So, do *you* want to do this?"

He let go of her and gestured around the room again. Thorn shook her head.

"No."

Darius's eyes moved between hers slowly, in a way that made Thorn feel exposed. She crossed her arms as he nodded, just once, with resolution. "Then we'll find something else. You're the one who taught me how to meditate, I've been trying out grounding exercises, plus I've got my Influence lessons… We'll figure this out, and we'll do it together, but until then, *this* works for you, so we'll do this."

He faced the desk, squatted down, and put the heels of his hands underneath the top lip. He grunted as he pushed it up and away from him, and it landed on its side with an anticlimactic thump. He stood and scratched the back of his head. "Man, you make that look a lot easier than it is."

Darius smiled at her, but Thorn didn't smile back. She couldn't. Her forehead knitted together, and her mouth pulled into a tight frown as she took in his face.

This wasn't the man she'd found in that orphanage. Though the determination was the same, there was pain in the way his strong jaw clenched together, and he showed the signs of cold, familiar experience. He'd seen a lot. Survived a lot.

Yet somehow, through that, through the darkness Thorn knew was slowly devouring her, Darius's bright, green eyes glittered with hope.

How had she never noticed how striking they were before now?

"Why are you doing this?" she asked at last.

Darius's smile faded. "Because you're not alone here, Thorn, and I'm not afraid of getting my hands a little dirty if it helps you see that."

Whatever remained of Thorn's anger drowned in a sudden rush, and the corners of her eyes began to sting. She gritted her teeth, and Darius leaned toward her. "You okay?" His deep voice vibrated through the empty chamber in her chest. She cleared her throat and took a small step back.

"Yes," she said. Then she let out a hard, forced laugh. "Fuck, I should be asking if *you're* okay."

She tilted her head toward his injured shoulder. He glanced at it and nodded. "I'm fine."

"And Chris?" Thorn said, surprised to find her voice tight around the name.

Darius nodded again. "Recovering. So is everyone else. Samira and I can't heal them all, but it doesn't look like whatever we were dosed with is lethal, so most people are just waiting out the effects in the hospital."

A knot formed in Thorn's chest. "I should've been here."

"Thorn, none of us could have seen this coming," Darius reasoned, but then he sighed and shook his head. "Except maybe Mackenzie."

The knot tightened. Thorn closed her eyes and groaned. "*DuPont.*"

"That's what we think," Darius said. "I haven't heard the whole story, but he's locked in one of the private rooms in the hospital right now. Alan wants to talk with all of us as soon as Holly's feeling better."

A flicker of anger lit up again. "When will that be?"

"Any time," Darius said. "Samira was working on her when you got here."

"You should probably get back," Thorn said.

Darius paused and looked around the room again. "You sure you're okay? I can help clean up."

"No," Thorn snapped. Then she closed her eyes, took a deep breath, and went on more evenly. "I've got it."

"Okay." Darius turned to leave, but he paused on the far side of the room, considering Thorn for a moment before he gestured to her left hand. "Better hurry. It's almost gone."

He smiled, opened the door, and disappeared behind it. Thorn looked down at the cigarette still held delicately between her fingers. It was little more than a pillar of white ash. She ran her thumb along the base, where Darius's lips had gently held it, and pulled hers through her teeth.

Then Thorn crushed it. The stinging fire slapped her back to reality, and she tilted her head backward. Sparkie groaned on her shoulder.

"*Fuck.*"

———

Samira pressed her fingertips into Darius's injured shoulder, and he winced.

"Sorry," she said. The bridge of her nose wrinkled in a grimace. They sat behind the nursing station, facing one another in two swivel chairs as Samira finished healing him. She'd removed the bullet and stopped the bleeding a while ago, but since then, both of them had been busy tending to other sick and wounded Martyrs.

"Is everyone else okay?" Darius asked. He let out a relieved sigh as her warm healing power poured into him. The tingling sensation of his flesh being knit back together sent a pleasant chill down his back.

"Yes," Samira said. "I've taken care of all the emergency cases, and Dr. Harris is getting IV fluids set up for the people who are still feeling the effects of the drug."

She looked around the room, and Darius followed her gaze. Every bed was full. He'd never seen it like this. Curtains pulled closed all down the hall, and people groaned or murmured from behind layers of white cloth.

"Thanks for all your help," he said.

Samira's lips turned into a small smile, and she shook her head. "I just wish I could do more," she murmured. Darius's injury was fully healed now, and she removed her hand to fold it with the other in her lap. "I don't have any formal medical training, so outside of my gifts, I'm afraid I'm not very helpful."

Darius rolled his shoulder. Good as new.

"Your gifts are more than enough," he said, and his heart ached. After saving Chris, Darius's abilities had been stretched thin, and even once Samira had mended him and pushed the drug from his system, he could hardly see straight. Without her, this ward wouldn't be full of healing Martyrs. It'd be full of hurting ones.

"Well, thank you," Samira said. "Now that most of Dr. Harris's staff is feeling better, they can handle the rest."

An awkward quiet fell, and Samira wrung her hands in her lap. She wore a simple, golden band on her left ring finger, and she toyed with it absently. It shone brightly in the fluorescent lights overhead. Darius cleared his throat.

"You know," he started slowly, raising his shoulders in a low shrug. "We can always use more nurses here. Alan might pay for school…"

His voice drifted off, and Samira's cheeks reddened. She looked down at her hands, and Darius sensed he may have overstepped. Cursing himself, he quickly spoke before she could reject the idea outright.

"No strings attached," he said. She glanced up to him again, her brows pulled together skeptically, and he sighed.

"Look, when I first found out I was a Virtue, I didn't want *anything* to do with it, but Alan made sure I knew that I still had a home. That stands for you and Leroy, too."

She didn't respond. Instead, Samira simply watched him, mouth tight, her rich, brown eyes glistening. The silence extended, and Darius felt like he had to say something just to fill the space.

Then his phone trilled, and he gratefully snatched it off the desk. Alan was calling them all together. Darius cleared his throat and got to his feet.

"So," he said, scratching the back of his neck. "Just think about it. Okay?"

Samira nodded, and Darius excused himself with all the grace of a clumsy teenager. He strode around the desk and started to make his way to the door. A harsh voice drew him back.

"Darius!" Chris called. She was sitting in a bed halfway down the ward, Dr. Harris at her side. "Tell him I'm fine!"

Darius frowned and walked over. "I have already spoken with Alan," Elijah stated with forced nonchalance, clearly using all of his self-control to avoid raising his voice, "and let him know that my *patient* is in no state to attend this—"

"Darius healed me," Chris interjected, pulling the blanket off her lap. "I'm good to go."

Though the drug had long since worn off, she still looked enough like a corpse that it made Darius's stomach twist. Her white skin was gray, dark circles shadowed her eyes, and her lips were tinted blue. As she spoke, her teeth chattered, and her whole body shook with cold.

"Your injuries may have been healed, but you are anything *but* good to go," Elijah said, concern seeping into his words. "You took a bullet to the *throat,* and even with Darius's healing, you lost so much blood it's a goddamned miracle you're alive. Unless he has some otherwise unheard-of ability to fill you *back up* with blood, you need a transfusion, and you aren't going anywhere until you get it."

Chris sighed and looked up to Darius. Her lips were dry

and chapped, and her complexion had an almost waxy quality. "Please, Darius." She reached out for him. Her nails
were dark and dusky. "Tell him I'm good to go."

Darius grabbed her hand and shook his head.

"You've gotta stay here," he said, and Chris's expression
fell. "I *just* told Thorn you're fine, and if you walk into that
room looking like this, she'll kill me—*and* you, probably."

He tried to smile, but Chris's bright eyes, about the only
part of her face that still had any color at all, glistened with
tears. "Come back and tell me everything as soon as it's
done, okay?"

"Of course," Darius said. Then he leaned in and hugged
Chris tightly, closing his eyes as he pressed his mouth
against the top of her head. Her skin felt unnaturally cold
beneath his hands, and his heart panged at how close they'd
come to losing her. Again. "I'll be back in a flash."

He stepped away. Dr. Harris shook his head and returned to Chris's bedside, where he began preparing her for
an IV. As Darius walked across the ward, he passed by
Samira at the nurses' station. She didn't look up to him, instead sipping at a grape juice box with feigned focus. He
took a deep breath and glanced behind her. Gabe DuPont's
energy sat alone in one of the private rooms, as strong and
powerful as ever. Darius's stomach clenched uncomfortably.

He left the hospital ward and headed to the conference
room, where he felt most of the Martyr directors gathered.
From the hallway, Darius heard a woman screaming on the
other side, and he sighed. He'd been hoping Thorn would
be calmer now, but he should have known it would take
more than one conversation. He took a deep breath, readied
himself, and opened the door.

Holly's voice barreled toward him.

"That Neanderthal destroyed my entire computer system," she screamed. The security lead was so worked up
that she was standing behind the chairs on the far side of
the room. Her open-backed hospital gown was cinched

tight at her waist and hung long over her jeans. An IV bag dangled from a pole to her right, and as she jerked her hands up to pull her fingers through her hair, it swayed dangerously. Mackenzie leaned back and steadied it before it crashed to the floor. Holly kept going, completely unaware. "Absolutely destroyed it! It will take me weeks to get everything running smoothly again!"

Darius paused in the doorway and looked around the room. Alan was at the head of the table, sitting calmly while he watched Holly speak. Abraham and Lina were to either side of him, Mackenzie and Stevie beside them. Darius frowned and turned to close the door.

His heart jumped to his throat to find Thorn leaning against the wall behind it, a statue of fragile, tightly-wound composure. She glanced up, caught Darius's eye, and he chanced a small smile. She didn't return it, but her jaw did relax before she focused on Holly again. Darius turned to face the room, too.

"Don't you have backups?" Abraham was asking as Darius moved to the table and sat beside Stevie. Holly turned to him indignantly, her eyes wide behind her glasses. The thick lenses made them seem even larger and angrier.

"Of course I have backups!" she yelled again. "And backups of my backups! But getting the whole interface together again isn't as easy as just plugging shit back in! My entire hard drive is *fried!*"

"Miss Andrews," Alan cut in with a polite but decisive nod. "We will spare no expense in getting our security systems up and running as soon as possible. At the moment, though, I am trying to determine what exactly happened here today. Do your backups include video footage from the cameras around the Underground?"

Holly turned to him, her round face hard, her nostrils flared, and she shook her head. "No." She spat the word like dirt from her mouth. "The internal cameras are saved to a local drive that recycles every seven days. Thanks to *fuckhead* over there—" she gestured vaguely in the direction of the hospital ward "—we don't have any footage of the attack."

Alan's frown deepened. "That hardly seems a coincidence."

"No shit," Mackenzie murmured, shaking her head. She was extra pale right now but alert, and her eyes narrowed. "He started in the basement, right? How the hell'd he even get down there? The door's locked for a goddamned reason."

"He shot through it," Alan responded. He leaned onto the table and laced his fingers on top of it. "We believe the security headquarters was his first stop. We found a canister of military-grade, aerosolized hallucinogenics beside the door."

Alan looked to Holly, and Darius followed suit. His stomach dropped. He remembered very little after healing Chris. The chaos and noise of Alan coming back into the room. Being dragged to the hospital. Waking up on a cot surrounded by other Martyrs going through a bad trip. Holly had been a couple of beds over, seizing and unresponsive. Most of the tech department had been in that state. He remembered Raquel sobbing beside the bed while Samira healed Skylar, forcing the drug out of her system until she stopped convulsing.

"What kind of hallucinogenics?" Mackenzie asked.

"It seemed to have been a blend of several," Alan answered.

"Maybe LSD or PCP," Mackenzie said, almost thoughtfully. "How'd he get everyone all at once?"

"Through the air ducts," Stevie said. She cleared her throat and pressed her fingertips against her eyes. Her warm, golden skin looked ashy. "We found another canister jammed behind one of the grates, and I have a maintenance team out looking for more. It spread through the whole Underground in a matter of minutes. People in closed rooms, like offices or bedrooms, got hit the hardest. It was more concentrated there than it was in the garage or courtyard.

When Mr. Blaine and I realized what had happened, we vented the system. Should be fine now."

"Still," Lina said quietly, glancing back at Holly. "A lot of people got hurt. We're lucky Samira was eating dinner in the courtyard when it hit. She didn't suffer the same effects."

"Yes." Alan nodded, and he cast Thorn a look. "We are fortunate. However, we still have a very large problem on our hands. This attack was carried out inside our own walls, and we must get to the bottom of it immediately."

Mackenzie snorted and crossed her arms. "The fuck do you mean? We *caught* the guy who did it! DuPont was wearing the mask, wasn't he?"

"*What?*" Thorn's voice shook, and she pushed herself away from the wall to approach the table. "What mask?"

"A gas mask," Mackenzie said, turning to Abraham for confirmation. "Didn't Conrad say DuPont had it on?"

Abraham sighed and pinched the bridge of his nose. "Yeah. When Conrad got back from escorting Caleb to the Underground, he found Jacob and DuPont fighting in the waiting room. Well, it wasn't really a fight. Jacob was smashing DuPont's head into the floor when Conrad broke them up. We're lucky Jacob didn't kill him."

"And that Mr. Carter arrived when he did," Alan said. "Mr. Locke was experiencing severe hallucinations by the time I got upstairs, and he tried to attack me as soon as I walked into the room. They are now both confined to private suites in the hospital: Mr. Locke for his own protection and Mr. DuPont for ours."

"So," Mackenzie said. Darius heard her tongue piercing clacking against her teeth from across the table. "What else do we need to get to the bottom *of?* He's clearly guilty."

"Is he?" Alan asked calmly. He brought his laced fingers to his face and pressed them against his chin. "I have spoken to Mr. DuPont. He has no memory of this attack and maintains his innocence."

"He shot Darius," Thorn snapped, throwing an arm out

in Darius's direction.

"He is not arguing against that," Alan said.

Thorn's eyes narrowed. "Then what the fuck *is* he arguing?"

"He is worried that we have not successfully broken all of Gluttony's Programming," Alan stated. "Mr. Wolfe and Miss Fulton did warn us about this possibility. Terrance Moore's Programming system is far more sophisticated than they anticipated. It is possible that Mr. DuPont was always designed to be a Programmed spy in the Underground, feeding the Sins information without even knowing about it."

A tense, heavy quiet filled the room around them.

"You think the attack on Elena's apartment was *designed* to plant someone in the Underground?" Thorn asked, her lip curling into a snarl. Alan nodded, but Lina shook her head.

"Then why would he do this?" she asked. "It would expose his position."

"Unless the Program stipulated this kind of thing in case he was discovered," Alan said. "Mr. DuPont was part of the Tactical Team chaperoning our Gray Units back into the Underground. He was well aware that we suspected the Sins were getting information from the inside. That could have triggered this unbroken Programming and pushed him into this part of the plan."

"What *plan?*" Thorn challenged.

"My best guess would be to destroy Darius," Alan stated. "It is entirely possible that Mr. DuPont's Programming was triggered because he was likely to be caught, and before he went, he was supposed to destroy the biggest threat to the Sins… Our Virtue."

Then Thorn looked toward Darius. Her dark eyes considered his face, lingering a little longer than Darius was used to, and a flash of fear filled them. His heart skipped into his throat. By now, he should have been used to being a target, but he never imagined that threat would follow him *here.*

"If that's true," Abraham said, "then it's some *seriously* complex Programming. Is that even possible?"

"Assuming we know all there is to know about the Sins' Programming is an act of hubris we cannot afford to make," Alan said. "We should err on the side of caution and assume it to be possible until proven otherwise, or we may very well find ourselves with our necks in the noose."

The room stilled, and Alan let them steep in it for a moment before he turned to Holly and Stevie. "Miss Andrews, Miss Arias," he said. "Go get some rest. We have a busy week ahead of us."

The two women nodded and left. Stevie got to the door first and held it open while Holly dragged her IV pole out behind her. When they were alone, Alan turned to the rest of the room.

"Now," he said. "What do we do with Mr. DuPont?"

"Get rid of him," Mackenzie said immediately, with the same unreserved hostility she'd had when she voiced this same opinion two months ago. "Programming or not, he's clearly a fucking threat."

"Getting rid of him will not be so easy now," Alan reasoned, his tone grim. "Programming him to forget the time he has spent here will leave gaps in his memory, and he will very likely return to the most familiar locations he knows—locations the Sins will undoubtedly track him to. I fear he will end up dead within a week if we let him go in that condition."

"Can we somehow make him stay away from New York?" Abraham asked. "Cover more memories or implant new ones?"

Alan nodded. "It is possible, but the more we mold his mind, the more likely it is for Mr. DuPont to suffer long-term complications from Programming."

"What other options do we have?" Lina asked.

"We could allow him to stay," Alan said, and the room went quiet. "We could either attempt to uncover and remove this Programming, or we could keep him under observation until Gluttony's host has been destroyed."

"That could be years," Thorn said.

Alan looked at her. "Yes. You see, then, my dilemma. Do we condemn a man guilty of nothing more than being Programmed by the Sins to death, insanity, or imprisonment?"

A cold heaviness fell over the room. Darius glanced around, but no one rose to meet his eyes. No one but Thorn. She was watching the side of his face, and when he turned to her, the muscles in her jaw went tight.

"Let's take it to a vote," Alan said after a moment. "All in favor of sending Mr. DuPont back into the world Programmed?"

He raised his hand. So did Mackenzie and Thorn. The entire time, Thorn didn't look away from Darius's eyes, and her chest lifted in a shallow, slow breath. Alan looked around them all and put his hand down. Thorn and Mackenzie followed.

"For keeping Mr. DuPont here in our custody?"

Darius's hand went up, followed by Lina's and Abraham's. Alan considered the room again and nodded.

"I suppose," he said at last, "the decision lies with Christine."

Finally, Thorn looked away from Darius. She turned to her uncle, her brows tight and her mouth tighter. Darius heaved a sigh and glanced back toward the hospital room, where two of the strongest auras in the Underground rested fewer than fifty feet apart.

Gabe DuPont, locked in a private room, and Chris Silver, recovering from the bullet he'd shot into her throat.

CHAPTER TWENTY-FOUR

"You sure this is a good idea?"

Conrad considered Chris, his heavy brows low over his eyes, as she and Darius stood outside the medical suite. Gabe DuPont's powerful, warm energy emanated from the other side of the door.

"I didn't ask for your opinion," Chris said. "I gave you a direct order. Stand aside."

In the three days since the attack on the Underground, the entire organization had come to a halt. Holly's systems were still in shambles, so every unit was grounded again. No one, not even Thorn, was permitted to leave the complex or communicate with the outside world until the tech team got themselves and their equipment back in order. The R&D department was helping track down and order new parts for Holly's computer, and TAC was working with Stevie and her maintenance staff to search the entire building for more security threats. Above all that, Chris had a decision to make that Darius didn't envy at all.

Conrad's jaw clenched, highlighting the wad of chew jammed between his cheek and gums. Though she had physically recovered, it was clear she wasn't altogether well. Her eyes looked tired, and her lips were dry and chapped.

Elijah cleared her the morning after the incident, but Darius was still worried about her. Clearly, he wasn't the only one. Conrad's forehead knitted in concern before he nodded and stepped aside. "I'll be out here if you need anything, all right?" Even his gruff voice was softer than usual. "Just holler."

Chris nodded, and he plodded off toward the nurses' station. Raquel stood behind the desk, her mouth tight with worry. When Conrad was out of earshot, Darius leaned toward Chris.

"You good?" he asked.

She took a deep breath. "Let me know if you sense *anything*, okay? And… thank you. For doing this with me."

She grabbed his shoulder gratefully. He smiled.

"I've got you," he said. Chris tried to smile back, but the sentiment was strained on her face. Then she turned to Gabe's room, opened the door, and walked in.

Gabe sat on a metal chair bolted to the far wall. He didn't stand. His dark gray sweatpants and white shirt made him look like a prisoner here. Or maybe it was the cuffs linking his hands together. They dipped between his knees, the chain dangling low. Chris took a step toward him while Darius stood back by the door. Gabe's piercing, somber eyes didn't leave Chris's face.

"I'm going to cuff you to your chair," Chris said. Gabe nodded, so she came even closer, and he lifted his hands so she could more easily access his restraints. Chris unlocked the ring from one of his wrists and quickly fastened it around the arm of his seat instead. The whole time, Gabe kept still, not speaking until Chris stepped back out of reach.

"Thank you for coming to see me," he said. He cleared his throat. The muscles along his shoulders tensed up. "I'm sorry."

"We're not here for an apology," Chris said as she pulled up another chair and sat across from him. Her voice was firm, but her hands shook. "We're here to talk about what happens next."

Gabe's eyes widened as Darius grabbed another chair to sit beside her. Gabe desperately looked at him before focusing on Chris again. "What do you mean?"

"You attacked your fellow Martyrs," Chris said. "You drugged the Underground. You tried to kill Darius."

"And you," Darius murmured. Chris nodded, and Gabe swallowed hard.

"And me."

"I don't remember any of it," Gabe said, speaking more quickly now. A little more desperately. For the first time since he'd come to the Underground, Gabe seemed frayed. Dark lines made his eyes look deeper in his face, and three days of stubble coated his chin. "I was in the tactical room putting my gear away, and the next thing I know, I'm in here, chained to the bed, with that new Virtue healing me. I had no idea what happened until Mr. Blaine talked to me. I know that doesn't excuse anything, but I think I was—"

Chris raised her hand, and Gabe's words died on his tongue. "Programmed," she said. "I know. I've talked with Alan, too. In the last couple of days, I've talked with everyone you've ever worked with here. The only person I have left to talk to is you."

Gabe's mouth slammed shut. Chris went on.

"I'm willing to believe this was all the Sins," she said. "Our experts say it's possible… That's the only reason you're still here. Otherwise, we'd have wiped your memory and put you back into the city by now. We still might do that. Alan left it up to me." The color drained from Gabe's face, leaving his cheeks ashy. Chris considered him for a hard, quiet moment before she shook her head. "Before I tell you what I've decided, I want to know… what would you do if you were in my position?"

Gabe didn't speak right away. He leaned forward, his dark brows drawn in, before he said, "I'd make sure I never had another opportunity to hurt anyone else, no matter what."

Chris's mouth tightened. Gabe kept talking.

"Look, I know I don't deserve any more chances," he said, straightening up. His hands wrapped into fists on his knees. The chain to his cuffs rattled against the chair's metal arm. "But Moore will kill me if you erase my memory and send me back to New York."

"I know," Chris said.

Gabe nodded slowly—so slowly Darius wasn't sure he was aware he was doing it at all—and he looked down at his feet. Chris took a deep breath and said, "And I can't have that on my conscience."

Darius glanced at Chris as Gabe's head snapped back up. Chris crossed her arms, her fingers pale against her black sleeves. "I have three options: I let you stay and risk you hurting more of my people, I send you back out there where I *know* the Sins will find and kill you, or I tell Alan to mess with your mind so much that you'd never dream of coming to New York again and risk damaging it beyond repair. None of them are good." She paused, and Gabe watched her, completely still. "But I hurt enough innocent people in this job, and I can't knowingly hurt you, too."

"You think I'm innocent?" Gabe's breath caught in his throat as he sat up taller.

Chris didn't respond right away. Her bright eyes were fierce as she considered him carefully.

"I think," she said at last, "that I can't take the chance that you are. But you're not joining the Martyrs again," she clarified as Gabe's face began to lighten. "You're restricted to house arrest. Your door will be locked between 8:00 p.m. to 8:00 a.m., and you will be accompanied by an armed guard everywhere you go. Probably Conrad, and he's biting for a chance to hit you again, so don't give it to him."

Gabe nodded. Darius was surprised to see nothing but a firm, dedicated resolution in his eyes. "I understand," he said, and he genuinely seemed to. "For how long?"

"Until we've managed to kill Terrance Moore," Chris said, getting to her feet. Darius stood up beside her. "Or you fuck up again. Whichever comes first. Either way, we'll know where you really stand then, won't we?"

She cast Gabe one final look as she walked away. Darius waited a moment, and Gabe met his eye for the first time in several minutes. He sighed, squaring his broad shoulders, and his mouth set. Darius nodded in his direction. Gabe tilted his chin back.

Then Darius followed Chris out the door. Conrad leapt away from it as it swung open—like he'd been standing with his ear pressed against the seams.

"Get his cuffs back in order," Chris said. Conrad nodded and headed into the room as Chris passed the nursing station. Raquel offered her a soft smile, which Chris returned wearily before she glanced at Darius.

"I hope I didn't make the wrong call," she said. Her worries leaked through with a shaking voice.

"Leading with your conscience is never the wrong call," Darius said with a smile, grabbing her shoulder. Chris chuckled, the sound strangled and tense, as she reached up and squeezed his hand.

They reached the doors to the waiting room, Darius opened one for her, and John stood up on the other side. Chris's shoulders tensed under Darius's touch, and he stepped back as John rushed in.

"Hey," he said, wrapping his arms around her. "Are you okay?"

"Yeah," Chris said. She pulled away so she could look up into John's face. His was a canvas of concern, while the smile on her mouth was half-formed. "It wasn't a big deal."

"Not a big deal?" John scoffed, and he held Chris's shoulders as he looked at her, like he couldn't believe what he was seeing. "He *shot* you, Chris!"

"Under the influence of Programming," she corrected sharply, and she stepped further back, shrugging John's hands off her. He frowned as Chris walked around him and headed toward the elevator. He followed, and Darius came behind them.

"That doesn't mean it wasn't traumatic," John argued. "I

imagine it was hard to see him after that. How'd he take the news?"

"Fine," Chris said. She didn't meet John's gaze.

A strained silence pulled them apart as they reached the elevator and paused. John's eyes narrowed. "Wait," he said, shaking his head. "Are you letting him *stay?*"

Chris reached across him and hit the call button. "Yes."

Darius glanced down at his feet. He had half a mind to take the stairs instead, but a warm sensation moving up them made him think twice about it. Jacob Locke was headed this way from the courtyard. Darius wasn't sure which situation would be more awkward—talking to Jacob alone in a dark stairwell or sharing an elevator with Chris and John while they argued again.

"*What?*" John said. "This is *insane!* How the hell can you expect the Tactical Department to work with him after this?"

"Are you trying to tell me how to do my job?" Chris asked, and her eyes flashed with a hot anger that reminded Darius chillingly of Thorn.

"No!" John exclaimed, running one hand through his black hair, pulling it out of place. "But damn it, Chris, this promotion has been killing you, and you're going to let this... this guy who *actually tried* to kill you stay? It's like you're asking for it! Darius." John turned toward him and opened a palm at his chest. "Do *you* think this is a good idea?"

Darius blanched while Chris's jaw tightened, and he glanced at the stairs again. Jacob was starting to look better by the second. He cleared his throat. "I—"

"Don't drag Darius into this," Chris cut in. "This was *my* call."

John scoffed. "Jeremiah would never—"

"Jeremiah is *dead!*" Chris's voice rang out loud in the foyer. Darius stared at her, and Jacob's warm energy paused on the other side of the door, where it fidgeted anxiously. "And I'm doing my best to step in and live up to the standards he set for me, but I can't do it if I'm fighting you on everything! I just… Fuck, John, this isn't *working* anymore."

She threw her arms out in his direction, and John stared blindly back. The door to the stairwell cracked open, and Jacob's wide, frazzled eye stared through it. The elevator dinged at the top, and the doors slid apart, but no one stepped toward it. They closed again, and John said, "Wait, are you seriously mad at me because I want DuPont out of here?"

"Gabe has nothing to do with this."

John's eyebrows raised. *"Gabe?"*

"John, this job is important to me," Chris said, her voice deep with frustration.

"I get that," John shouted. "It just seems like it's more important than anything else—than *me.*"

"It is," Chris said. John's mouth fell open. "I told you that when you decided to join the Martyrs for me. I don't want to get married. I don't want to have kids. I don't want *any* of the things you keep asking from me! I just want this."

John gawked at her while Chris sighed and glanced at Darius like she just remembered he was there. Her cheeks went pink. "Let's talk about this later, okay?"

She moved to hit the elevator button again, but John put a hand over it.

"No," he said. Suddenly, his voice was quieter. His jaw clenched, and he swallowed hard. "I want to talk about it now."

Chris shook her head. "John, you deserve someone who wants the same things you do," she said. "And I can't be that person."

His shoulders tensed, and when he spoke, his voice constricted around the words. "Can't… or won't?"

"Does it matter?" Chris asked with a sigh. "I'll get my things tonight."

She turned away from the elevator and opened the door to the stairwell. Jacob stumbled back, frantically adjusting his orange ball cap as Chris walked past him without so much as a cursory glance in his direction. John ran one hand down his face as he moved to follow her, but then he caught Darius's eye. Instead, he swore and turned around, pushing the doors to the garage open. As soon as he walked through them, he roared into the cavern. His voice howled back at him.

Darius hardly had the chance to groan before the stairwell opened again, and Jacob darted out from it. He grabbed Darius by the shoulder, and his stomach gave an uncomfortable flip as Jacob turned him around so they were standing face to face.

"Is it true?" he asked. "Is he *staying?*" Jacob's voice became more aggressive, and his fingers dug in painfully. "That... that *murderer* is *staying?*"

He flung one arm toward the hospital, where Darius felt Gabe's strong, warm energy tucked into his room.

"Yeah," he said. "Chris decided to keep him around until Gluttony's host is killed."

"That won't *help!*" Jacob yelled, shaking his head desperately, clinging even more to Darius. "He's been tainted! The Sins have their fingers in his brain! He *hurt* people! He'll hurt *more* people!"

Then his wild eyes darted from Darius's face to his shoulder, where the bullet had ripped into him. Darius forced Jacob's hands away and took a step back. Jacob stumbled a few paces. He ripped his hat off his head and wrapped his fingers up in his thinning, curly hair while he walked in circles around the room, muttering under his breath.

"Hey," Darius said, his voice low and calm. Jacob spun to look at him again. "I get what you're worried about, okay? We're taking it seriously. He's going to have a guard, be locked up—"

"I almost got rid of him," Jacob went on, like he wasn't hearing Darius anymore. "No one else is fucking brave enough to get rid of him! Not Alan. Not Thorn. I thought

Chris would see it, but she's just as bad as they are! You all are!"

Before Darius had the chance to speak, Jacob shoved past him and stormed down the hallway. For a terrifying moment, Darius thought he was going back to the hospital to try to kill DuPont again. He turned to chase after him, but Jacob stomped back toward the offices. He threw open the door to Lina's, and Darius breathed a sigh of relief.

The Underground was in lockdown, and no one was permitted to leave until Holly's systems were back in place. Not Thorn.

And not Jacob Locke.

And Jacob did not do well behind closed doors.

The maps tacked across the wall behind Thorn's desk were a Frankenstein disaster. Shredded pieces clung together on frail lines of tape, hung up like she hadn't ripped them apart less than a week ago. With Holly and her team still focused on getting essential systems up and running, the printers were not high on the list—but this monstrosity functioned enough to let Thorn see what she needed for this damned assignment.

And this assignment was a good distraction from her discomfort in knowing that DuPont was still in the Underground.

Ever since he'd been moved back to his room, Thorn's senses were on edge—constantly tracking him, searching for him, no matter where she was in the building. Even now, she felt him beneath her feet, sitting in his quarters with Conrad Carter standing outside the door. His weak, cold energy tugged at a guilty string in her hollow chest, reminding her that he wasn't as bad as he should have been for someone who drugged the Martyrs and tried to kill two people. Rather than try to reconcile the conflict in her brain, she distracted herself with her maps again.

Orange pins and ochre thread traced along the major freight lines leading in and out of New York City, and large, white tacks marked the stations and rail yards along the way. Thorn followed the paths with her eyes.

At last, she took a deep breath, holding it for a beat, before she turned around and propped her hands on her hips. Three people crammed together on the couch along the opposite wall. Samira was in the middle, fingers clasped, while the survivors from Reflection Farms sat on either side.

"I need to know everything you can tell me about Leroy," Thorn said.

Carmen Cervantes wrung her hands in her lap, her sun-weathered face furrowed. "I'm sorry, miss," she said politely. "Leroy didn't tell us where he was going when he left. Just that he was using the trains."

"I'm not looking for specifics," Thorn said, though, damnit, she'd give anything for specifics right about now. She turned back to the map. Sparkie, who had hidden inside a desk drawer to avoid intimidating people still uncomfortable with the idea of Forgotten Sins and broken souls, fidgeted her frustration. "There are dozens of rail lines and hundreds of potential stops for Leroy to jump off. Gluttony is Programming people at all the major transit points in New York to try to find him as soon as he enters the city. I want to do the same, but I have limitations Gluttony doesn't have."

"Limitations?" Kayce Farrow asked. She pulled her wispy, brown hair behind one ear. "What's that mean?"

Thorn looked down at her. "You know how Leroy would use his Influence and draw Gluttony right to him?" she asked, and Kayce nodded. "The same thing happens to me. In my case, it's Wrath. She'll feel me while I place these Programs, so I have to do it quickly, and I can't stay in one place for long. Every one has to count, so I need to narrow down where Leroy is most likely to go."

She crossed her arms and watched the three women. When they still didn't speak, an annoyed flicker sparked in her chest, and she ran her tongue against the bottom of her teeth.

"What does he like?" she went on, snapping more than she intended, and she walked around to the front of her desk. "What *doesn't* he like? What are his habits? Where has he been before? Anything that can give me *something* to go off of."

Samira sighed. "Well, he liked being out in the country…" She paused, and Thorn gestured an open palm out for her to continue. "That's one reason he was drawn to the farm. People felt cold to him, and he didn't like to be surrounded by it."

Thorn could fucking relate to that.

"He did that while we were traveling, too," Kayce said. "Kept us to rural roads. Part of it was because we kept getting spotted, but he was always more comfortable away from other people."

"And walking," Carmen added. "He preferred to walk. He said he had more control that way?"

"Yes," Samira said, almost sadly. "He even hated driving the truck to the markets around Augusta. Leroy was terrified someone from his old life was going to find him. Wherever we went, he was always looking for a quick escape. Cars were too confining. Too obvious. He liked to stay under the radar."

Thorn nodded thoughtfully and spun back around, grabbing a box of pushpins from the desk as she approached her maps again.

"That makes me think," she murmured as she traced one of the rail lines *out* of New York, "he's not actually going to make it into the city at all."

Someone shifted on the couch behind her, and Samira approached from the other side of the room. Thorn's finger drew past several white tacks until it hit one just outside the city's border. She pulled it out and replaced it with a bright green pin instead.

"He's going to stop short," she said, looking at Samira.

The Virtue pressed her fingertips against her lips as she nodded. Thorn started tracing another line. "He'll jump off on one of the less busy stations or rail yards so he's not trapped in a train car, surrounded by people." Thorn found another and swapped the white for green again. For the first time in weeks, she felt a glimmer of hope. "Good. This is good. Now." She spun around and looked from Samira to the other women. "What else have you got?"

For the next several minutes, Thorn moved pins around while Samira and Carmen went back and forth with stories and anecdotes from their time with Leroy. Kayce, who had only been at Reflection Farms for six months before the Sins had come in and killed her husband and daughter, had little to say, so Thorn pulled out a laptop she rarely used and set her up at the desk to research any stops that sounded promising.

Soon, Thorn's office was alight with chatter. More than once, while discussing old friends tragically lost in the slaughter, emotions ran high and tears were shed. All the same, laughter sprinkled in occasionally when Carmen and Samira discussed more lighthearted memories. Thorn found herself swept up in it. She paused at the map, her brows drawn neatly together as Samira told a story about the first farmers market Leroy attended.

"I didn't know what he was yet," she said, her dark eyes little half-circles as her cheeks pressed up in a smile. "Or what *I* was, so I had no idea he could feel every human soul but mine. While he was setting up our display, I walked up behind him and touched his shoulder. He jumped so hard he knocked the entire thing over."

She and Carmen dissolved into laughter, and Kayce's lips pulled up in a smile.

"Ah, it all makes so much more sense now," Carmen said wistfully as she limped back to the couch. The leg she'd broken during the attack never healed right, and it had been too late for Samira or Darius to fix it when she arrived. She sat down tenderly and went on. "Leroy, I mean. He was always so private… I suppose he had to be."

The laughter in Samira's eyes faded, and she watched Carmen sadly. "I'm so sorry we never told you about us," she said. "Reverend Weston wanted to keep my power a secret, and Leroy… He was so scared people would hate him if they knew what he was."

"Seems to me that Weston proved him right," Kayce said. Thorn glanced down at her and then up to Samira, but the Virtue just nodded at her feet.

"Some people need something to hate," Thorn said, speaking for the first time since they started, and the three women turned to her. "And it's easy to hate things you don't understand—things that scare you."

A pensive silence fell. While Carmen and Kayce drifted off, their gazes fading into memories instead of reality, Samira's eyes locked with Thorn's, and they held there for a long time. Thorn watched her back until, finally, Samira looked at the ground again. Then Thorn cleared her throat.

"Okay," she said. "What else is there?"

By the time they were done, an hour had passed. The four of them narrowed the list of potential rail yards and stations from over one hundred to just under twenty, all far enough outside of city limits that Thorn was confident she could instill Programming at them all within a matter of days. Her next challenge was figuring out how to do it without drawing too much attention from Wrath and the other Sins—and making sure they hadn't gotten there first.

As they wrapped up, Thorn snapped the tin of tacks shut and opened her desk drawer. Sparkie slithered out, grabbed her glove, and climbed behind her hair as she said, "If you think of anything else that might help, let me know as soon as possible."

The women nodded, and Kayce pulled the door to the lobby open. As Carmen hobbled toward it, Samira turned to Thorn. She drew her hands in front of her chest, lacing her fingers almost as though in prayer. "Excuse me, uhm," she began, glancing over her shoulder, where Carmen and

Kayce paused in the doorway. "I actually wanted to speak with you alone. Do you have time?"

Thorn's brows pinched together curiously, and she nodded once. Samira moved to her friends again, told them she'd catch up downstairs, and hugged them. When the door shut, she stepped back a few paces but didn't look at Thorn again until Carmen and Kayce's auras reached the hallway. Then Samira turned around, and Thorn was surprised to see her brown cheeks filled with a soft blush.

"Is everything all right?" she asked as she walked around the front of her desk and sat up against it. She crossed her arms as Samira pattered back into the room, her long hair pulled over one shoulder. She anxiously ran her fingers through its silky strands.

Then she plopped down on the couch and met Thorn's gaze with an earnest, urgent intensity.

"I want to know more about Forgotten Sins."

Thorn's heart skipped a beat, and the facade she tried to hide her emotions behind began to fracture. Her eyes widened, and her lips parted gently—just enough for Thorn to feel the cool air suck in against her tongue. She pressed them back together and said, "What do you want to know?"

Samira took a slow, measured breath. "Well, first, how do the Sins choose the people they possess? Is it people who feel... weaker? People with bad souls already?"

The corner of Thorn's mouth curled indignantly. "You mean like Mackenzie's?"

Samira's blush went deeper. "Well, I—yes. I guess I do."

"Let's get something straight, right now," Thorn said, holding herself a little taller and consciously working to relax the tight, angry muscles in her shoulders. "People fuck up. We make mistakes. Some of those mistakes leave a permanent mark. Like a scar." She paused, her left hand flexing against her bicep, the gnarled flesh on her forearm taut and rigid inside her glove. "Mackenzie wasn't born with scars on her soul. They were carved into her—by parents who neglected her, men who used her, and a Sin who gave her a way to stop the pain. If all you can see is the scars and not the woman who has risen above them, that's on you. Not her."

Samira's jaw clenched together, and she looked down at her knees.

"But," Thorn went on, and Samira glanced up again, "to answer your question, no. Not necessarily. The Sins possess for different reasons. Pride, Greed, and Lust choose hosts with power, assets, or influence. It makes it easier for them to get what they want. Wrath and Envy possess for more personal reasons. Me, for example. Wrath took me to punish Alan. Gluttony and Sloth, more than the others, look for targets that are easier to control—targets already aligned with those Sins."

Samira's brows furrowed. "So Leroy was aligned with Gluttony?"

Thorn paused and looked her over, a light frown across her face. "Most likely," she said. "Leroy doesn't remember much about his time as the Sin, which tells me he and Gluttony were more intimately linked. When a host is harmonious with the Sin, they lose more of their memory if they ever manage to get out."

That wasn't what Samira wanted to hear. Her expression fell, and a brush of tears built up behind her lashes as she slowly nodded. "So, uhm," she murmured, gently spinning a simple, gold band around her left ring finger. "Not having your soul, feeling that emptiness… How bad is it? Really?"

The air in the room grew heavy, and Thorn hung in it for a moment. Her arms, still crossed around her chest—around a ribcage that worked as a tomb for the pit in her soul—hardened. She took a deep breath, filling her lungs, pushing them against that emptiness, feeling the way it collapsed in on itself like a dying star. Alight with fury and sadness and a deep, aching longing.

Like loss. She always thought it felt like loss—like a heartbreak that never fucking ended. What had Leroy said about it? Ah, yes…

"It's hell," Thorn murmured at last.

"And if something made it go away," Samira went on, more quickly now, the words tumbling from her lips. "You'd do anything to keep it?"

Thorn's eyes narrowed, and her stomach twisted uncomfortably. "Why are you asking about this?"

"I need to know," Samira said, and while her brown eyes glittered with tears, they didn't fall. She took a deep breath. "I *need* to know if that's all I ever was to my husband. I loved him. I wanted to help him. But… what if he only ever cared about my Virtue? What if that's all that mattered?"

Thorn's mouth slipped open as a desperate silence fell around them. The dam began to break, and slow streams of water poured down Samira's brown cheeks. At first, all Thorn could do was watch her—watch this fraying Virtue cling to the threads to keep herself together. After a few moments, Thorn let out a slow sigh, pushed away from her desk, and walked to the couch. She didn't sit beside Samira, but instead, on the coffee table in front of her, and she leaned forward.

"Look," Thorn began slowly. "I don't know much about you or Leroy or your marriage… And god knows I don't know much about love, either." She paused, her heart flipping in the cavern in her chest as Samira looked down at her hands. She was still fingering the ring, spinning it in circles. Thorn saw herself reflected in the gold—a black smudge in the simplistic beauty. She took a deep breath. "But I do know your Virtue is *not* the only thing that mattered to him."

"How can you know that, though?" Samira asked, her voice deeper, more strained. "I completed him. He told me I completed him, and I thought that was a good thing. I thought that was love. I feel so *stupid*."

Tears poured more urgently now, and Samira dipped her face into her hands and cried. Thorn didn't know what to do, and she awkwardly watched the top of Samira's head while it shook with sobbing. Tentatively, she lifted her hand, reached forward, and placed her palm on Samira's forearm.

The Virtue peeked between her fingers. Thorn leaned in closer.

"Leroy didn't want you to destroy Gluttony. Do you know what that meant for him?"

Samira shook her head, and Thorn gave a single, slow nod.

"It meant," she said, "that he's willing to suffer an eternity in hell so that you don't have to live a single lifetime with this horrible fucking hole in your chest." Thorn pressed her palm flat between her lungs, and Samira's crying slowed. "He had a choice between *his* soul and yours, and he chose yours. If that's not love, I don't know what the fuck is."

Something inside Samira settled. Her shoulders relaxed, and she took a shaky breath. Thorn's brows drew compassionately together as the Virtue sat back on the couch and dabbed at the corners of her eyes. "Are you okay?" Thorn asked.

"Yes, thank you," Samira said through a sniffle. "We've got to find him. Before Gluttony does."

Thorn smirked as she got to her feet and held out a hand to help Samira do the same. "With this new plan," Thorn said, gesturing to the map behind her, "we stand a pretty good chance."

Together, they walked to the door. Thorn pulled it open as Samira thanked her again. She stepped into the lobby, and Thorn stood in the doorway until Samira disappeared. A cold stone formed in Thorn's stomach as she walked back into her office. When she was alone, she pressed her palm against her chest again. Sparkie wound himself around her neck and held on tight.

CHAPTER TWENTY-FIVE

Darius woke up feeling like something was *off.* He sat up in bed and checked his watch. Six in the morning—early enough that the Underground's overhead lights would still be set to night mode, and most people would be in bed. But they weren't. Darius took in the sensation of warm Martyr energy.

It felt oddly empty.

For the last ten days, this place had been full. While Holly and her tech team got their critical systems back up and running, the men and women who lived here hadn't been allowed to leave. Stuck indoors, the Martyrs filled their time with training and classes. Several people, including Mackenzie, even finished the rest of their assessments and got cleared for TAC duty. The Martyrs were ready to go out in full force.

And yesterday, the clearance had come. For the first morning in nearly two weeks, Darius woke up to find people missing. Thorn and the Gray Unit were all back on duty. She was hard at work setting up Programs to find Leroy Khoury at rail yards and train stations while her people went back to life as usual in New York City. Every recon team was out searching for Virtues in the greater Tristate area. As for TAC, a quarter of the force would have left for the day shift a half hour or so ago.

The Underground was officially back up and running. That meant more Martyrs in the line of fire of Programmed cops, Puppetted civilians, and pissed-off Sins who wanted to see the whole organization yanked from the ground by its roots. Darius's chest constricted as the illusion of safety cracked.

He still wasn't allowed to go out there and help.

His anger made him feel sick, and he took a deep breath to ease the tightness between his lungs. He sensed Mackenzie nearby, out cold, her fragmented energy completely still. Lina, too. He never stopped to realize how many people were *alone* in this place before. It was hard to build a family here. Hard to find a connection. Harder to keep it.

Maybe Chris had the right idea. It was better this way. Fewer attachments meant less pain.

But that thought was somehow worse. Darius felt for her, too. Her new room, now just a hallway off of his, was empty, and for a second, he panicked. She should have returned from her first graveyard shift in the city by now. His brows came together, and he searched until he found her in the gymnasium. Her strong, warm energy bounced with a stable, rhythmic beat.

In the days since she and John had split up, Chris had kept busy helping Thorn plan an attack on Terrance Moore, organizing her team in new training routines, and running classes. She never *stopped* moving. Darius knew he should try to get more sleep, but instead, he threw off his blanket and pulled out his running gear.

Bright light poured from the gym door windows, stretching across the concrete tile in stark, white rectangles. Darius squinted, his eyes adjusting as he walked in.

The room hummed with a droning treadmill and the steady, consistent pounding of Chris's sneakers on the track. The machines were off to the left, the wall in front of them one of the only ones without massive mirrors. Chris didn't turn around. She was focused, her body a hard knot of tension as she ran. Her high-waisted leggings and sports bra covered much of her back, making it hard for Darius to see the thick scar cutting across it. She reached behind her head and tightened her ponytail. A pair of headphones stuck out of her ears, which meant she hadn't heard him enter.

Darius grabbed his own headphones, set his bag by the door, and put them on as he came to the machine beside Chris. Finally, movement made her glance over her shoulder. Darius gave a short wave, a shorter smile, and turned his treadmill on. Chris watched for a moment as he got up to speed, and when their eyes met, he saw hers were red and tired.

But she smiled gratefully, and though she didn't say anything as she faced forward again, his tight chest began to relax.

Connections *were* harder here, he thought, as heavy music blared in his ears, and he matched Chris's pace. They were harder because they were more fragile. Because caring came with a cost. Because every single soul in the Underground was one bad day away from losing everything, and the waves of heartbreak washed over this place like the tide.

But they could ride those waves together. Otherwise, they drowned alone.

For the next hour, Darius and Chris ran side by side in silence. When she finally headed off to sleep, he went to the men's room and showered. Then he spent the next part of his morning meditating by the pool. By the time Darius left the gym, feeling tired but spread less thin, the morning rush for breakfast had petered out. He opened the doors to the courtyard.

The first thing he focused on was Gabe.

His aura, still just as strong as Chris's, sat at the same table he used every morning. It was part of his daily routine. Breakfast first thing after his door unlocked, followed by a quick workout, quicker shower, and lunch before he returned to his room and stared at his ceiling until dinner time.

All monitored. Gabe didn't get a minute of freedom.

But as far as Darius knew, he'd been an exemplary detainee. No matter who was fighting against him, Gabe still wanted to be here. He never complained. Not once. He just gritted his teeth and took on the punishment with dignity.

And he did it all alone—unless you counted Conrad. He hovered over Gabe's shoulder while he quietly devoured his breakfast. Darius's chest twinged with sympathy. This morning, when he grabbed a lukewarm plate of French toast off the counter and called a grateful thank you to Kenia, he turned back around and came to Gabe's table. Gabe spotted him, and he froze, mid-chew, as Darius pulled up a chair and sat down. Conrad's thick brows drew together.

"Good morning," Darius said.

Gabe watched him blankly for a moment before clearing his throat. "Good morning."

They both turned to their food, and for the first few minutes, they ate quietly. A few lingering Martyrs came in for late breakfast, and Darius felt their energy hesitate as soon as they noticed him and Gabe together, but no one said anything. At one point, Samira and the other women from Reflection Farms walked in, too, and they took a nearby table. Darius glanced up at them, met Samira's eye, and gave her a friendly nod.

Then he cleared his throat and looked back to Gabe.

"So," he said, "how are you doing with all this?"

He used the blunt end of his fork to gesture vaguely around them. As he popped a bite into his mouth, Gabe gave an awkward but kind smile.

"It's fine," he said. "Better than the alternative. I can't trust my own mind, man. That's weird as fuck. I'm just glad I'm not a threat right now."

Darius's jaw went tight, and he found his food suddenly hard to swallow. Gabe's bright, amber eyes were no less driven than the first day he walked into the Underground. Finally, Darius managed to get the bite down, and he shook his head. "I'm sorry. That's rough."

Gabe nodded, but his expression hardened. "How's the strike on Moore going?"

Darius paused. "It's slow. His routine has been all messed up since Georgia. Alexis is working with R&D to figure out if they can corner him."

"Is there anything I can do to help?" Gabe asked. "I didn't work with Moore, but I know how the NYPD functions—"

Suddenly, Conrad let out a gruff scoff. Gabe's whole body went rigid as his guard glowered down at them. The muscles on Conrad's face were so tense that the wad of chew behind his lip looked like a marble pressed up against his gums.

Darius raised a brow. "Do you have something to say?"

Conrad's eyes snapped to him and narrowed. "I just don't think it's a great idea to talk to this traitor about internal Martyr business, that's all."

A deep, angry red filled Gabe's face. Darius glanced down at him and then back to Conrad. He crossed his arms.

"I appreciate it, but I've got this handled. You need to take a step back," Darius said. Gabe's head shot up to look at him as Conrad's eyes went wide.

"What?" he said.

"Step back," Darius repeated. "You can stand guard from over there." He gestured to the left, where a lone table sat ten feet away. Conrad's jaw dropped, and he started to argue, but Darius cut him off. "Or I can have you reassigned. Your choice."

For a few long seconds, Conrad didn't move. He watched Darius, struck dumb, and Darius stared back without getting to his feet. At last, Conrad's teeth slammed shut again, his face red and rigid, and he stomped away. He pulled a chair out so forcefully that it scraped against the tile. The noise ground through the courtyard, silencing the few people still eating there. All the energy froze as eyes turned to Darius, but he just took a deep breath. Then someone approached him, and Darius turned to see Lina walking up from the kitchen with a warm cup of coffee.

"What's going on?" she asked, her voice full of concern as she glanced from Conrad to Gabe and finally back to Darius. "Are you okay?"

"We're fine," Darius said. He got up to help Lina pull out a chair. She thanked him, and they both lowered back to the table. "You're eating late."

Lina let out a soft laugh and pulled a strand of hair behind her ear. She wasn't wearing her traditional braid, and she looked younger with her caramel waves flowing around her shoulders. "Yes, I spent my morning on the phone with Jacob. He's back in the city helping Alexis track Gluttony, but he's struggling to adjust."

Darius frowned. "What's bothering him?"

Lina raised her cup to her lips and took a sip. "The same things," she said, and her bright, gray eyes darted to Gabe before coming back to Darius. "He's afraid to be out of the Underground. He thinks it isn't safe here."

"Because of me?" Gabe asked. His voice was thick with guilt.

Lina sighed. "Don't take it personally. Jacob has some problems with paranoia, and it's always worse when he's trapped in closed quarters. He'll feel better once he's had the chance to move around a little."

"Plus," Darius said, "the Underground is as safe as it's ever been. Holly got all the critical security protocols back in place. The internal cameras and some other nonessential things are still down, but everything we need to protect the Martyrs is good to go."

"Including having me locked up," Gabe said. Lina opened her mouth to speak, but he raised a hand to stop her. "I get it. I caused a lot of fucking problems here that you're all still cleaning up. Just… keep me updated on Gluttony, all right? And if I can help, I want to." He turned to Darius, his dark brows drawn hard over fierce eyes. "That son of a bitch ruined my life. I'd like a chance to return the favor."

"You got it," Darius said.

Gabe nodded as a device attached to his wrist chirped an alarm. He glanced down at it and sighed as Conrad got to his feet. "Mealtime's over. Thanks for coming to talk to me."

He stood up and held out a hand to Darius, which Darius shook. Gabe's grip was as strong as the rest of him, and as Conrad approached, he grabbed his plate and took it back to the kitchen before walking toward the gym. Lina and Darius watched after him. When he was out of earshot, Lina said, "I can't imagine how hard this has been for him."

"Me, neither," Darius said, shaking his head. "We've *got* to get rid of that damned Sin."

"I agree," Lina said, "but these plans can take a long time. The last successful strike against a host was eight years ago."

"Which Sin was it?" Darius asked.

"Pride," Lina said. "Isla Diamandis. I don't know if you remember her… she was a famous actress and the host who made Jacob kill his family. Diamandis is, well… the reason Abraham, Jacob, and I are here in the first place." She looked into her coffee and cleared her throat. "When Jacob was assigned to the Gray Unit, she was his target. It took *six years* before we had enough on her to kill the host without hurting a lot of other people…"

Darius swore. "We can't wait that long."

"You're right," Lina said. "This solution works for now, but keeping someone on house arrest for years isn't sustainable. I guess we'll cross that bridge when we come to it." Then she got to her feet and stifled a yawn with the back of her hand. "Anyway, I need to go get ready. I have a lot to do before Abraham and I go to Cain's this afternoon."

"Visiting Stella?" Darius asked, and he stood, too. The two of them walked to the kitchen together.

"Yes," she said, grabbing the coffee pot and topping off her mug. "Her birthday was four days ago. We usually go lay flowers on her grave, but with the lockdown, we had to put it off. Would you like to join us?"

Darius's cheeks went warm, and he shook his head. "Thanks, but I'm good. I've got too much to do." His brain quickly made a list of all the stuff on his plate, looking for something he could bring up if Lina challenged him on it.

But she didn't. Instead, she nodded with a compassionate smile. "I completely understand," Lina said in a way that made Darius think she really did. She touched his forearm reassuringly. "I'll lay flowers for your family, too. Take care, Darius."

Then she headed back to her room. Darius watched her for a moment, a shock of guilt biting at his mind, telling him to take the day off, go with her, and lay flowers for them himself. Maybe it was what he needed.

With a sigh, he put his plate away and headed to the R&D department. There, he buried himself in the search for Terrance Moore, trying not to think about Lina visiting Eva and the others while he hid behind this bullshit.

Thorn hid behind a huge tractor-trailer as a woman in a bright yellow safety vest walked back toward the main office at the South Kearny Yard, rubbing her temples. The minute her cold energy tucked into the building, Thorn released her breath in a long, slow sigh.

The last Sentry, the last location. Finally, she was done, and it had only taken thirty-six hours.

Jesus, Thorn had been awake for thirty-six hours. Her eyes stung in the afternoon sun, and she pressed her fingers hard against them. For the first time in years, she found herself grateful to return to the Underground—to go back to that lonely little room and sleep for a couple of hours.

After that, all they had to do was wait for one of the hundreds of rail workers Thorn had spent the last two days Programming to spot Leroy Khoury and text her a location stamp... or for him to show up in one of the few camera feeds Holly had been able to find and tap into… or for the Sins to catch him first. Thorn hated waiting. She preferred *doing*, but she'd done all she could for the time being.

She strode along an old, neglected sidewalk, careful to avoid catching her toes on the upheaved cracks jutting up from the concrete as she hurried back to her ride. She didn't have time to pause here—or anywhere, really. That was one reason she hadn't slept. Autumn Hunt's Influence had spiked yesterday, drawn in this direction by Thorn's activity, and though she'd never gotten close enough for Thorn to worry, Wrath had been dormant for a few hours now. That made Thorn nervous—meant that, maybe, the Sin was closing in. Sparkie spiraled overhead, keeping an eye out, but he didn't see anything suspicious.

Thorn's motorcycle stuck out like a diamond on a bed of coal—polished and clean in a way that clashed with everything else in this little, nothing town. She tightened her satchel around her torso and grabbed her cigarettes from the side pocket. For a moment, she gently turned the red box around in her fingertips before she decided against it and shoved them away. Then she threw a leg over her bike, pulled back her hair, and put on her helmet. Sparkie swooped inside her jacket before she zipped it to her throat. As she turned on the ignition, ready to get the hell out of there, her phone rang. Jacob Locke's name scrolled along the top of her visor display.

"What's up?" she said as she answered.

"He fucking told them," Jacob snarled. His voice came through so loudly that her headset garbled the higher tones.

Thorn frowned. "What?"

"That *fucker*, DuPont," Jacob said. "I was just by the precinct. Moore is on his way to Princeton, New Jersey!"

Thorn's stomach dropped, and her mouth fell open. "Princeton?"

"That's by where that other Forgotten Sin is, isn't it?" Jacob asked. "That *son of a bitch*—"

"Calm down," Thorn snapped, peeling out of the lot and

rushing toward I-90. Air whipped around her body. "You're absolutely *sure*—"

"Yes, I'm fucking sure!" Jacob shouted. "I had one of his secretaries in my car! She said he had business in Princeton. What would the New York City Police Commissioner have to do in *Jersey?*"

Nothing. Thorn knew there was nothing. It all made sense now. Hunt giving up on the chase, her Influence going radio silent while Thorn worked on the train stations. She couldn't risk being detected as she went well outside New York.

Thorn's stomach filled with a horrified, cold fire. "Fuck. They found Cain."

"What are you gonna do?" Jacob asked, but Thorn hardly heard him—instead talking right over him as she snarled something about how she had to go before she hung up and immediately called Alan. Almost like God had a sense of humor, Autumn Hunt's Influence drove into Thorn's brain like an ice pick.

And Thorn's heart seized. Wrath was to the southwest, in the same direction as the Martyrs Memorial Garden.

Alan answered, and Thorn immediately yelled, "They found Cain. The Sins have found Cain!"

Silence. Briefly. Then Alan's voice, deep and dark. "You are certain?"

"You feel her," Thorn snapped. "I know you do. She's headed there now!"

More silence. A heavy silence. Until Alan said, "Lina and Abraham are with Cain."

It was as though all the air had been sucked from Thorn's lungs, and she couldn't breathe. Her fingers tightened on her bike's handles. "Jesus, Alan! I'm an hour away! *Fuck.*"

"I'm linking Christine," Alan said, and Thorn heard a tone sound out as another device connected to the call. It took all of six seconds for him to fill Chris in. Immediately, the young TAC director was ready for action.

"I'll get all available units out there now," she said. Thorn heard her shuffling in the background—undoubtedly throwing clothes on. "We can be there in forty minutes."

Forty minutes. It wasn't fast enough.

"I must attempt to reach Cain," Alan said. "Though I am certain the Sins will have cut off his communication. Is there anything else you need from me?"

"Darius," Chris said before Alan could hang up, and Thorn's stomach lurched. "Should we bring Darius? He can mitigate casualties—"

"No," Thorn cut in. "He hasn't passed his combat assessment yet."

"But Thorn—"

"The answer is *no*," Thorn snarled. "Why the fuck do we have protocols in place if we're not going to use them?"

No one spoke on the other end of the line for a few long seconds, and Thorn shook her head, willing her furious heart to slow its barrage against her ribcage. At last, Chris said, "All right. I'm going to get our people out there. I'll see you soon."

Then she hung up, Alan did the same, and Thorn tore down I-90. For the first two-thirds of the ride, she was alone, kept company by nothing more than her own hot fury and the ice-cold beacon of Autumn Hunt's Influence pulling her toward the Martyrs Memorial Garden.

The first horrifying thing to happen was that Influence disappearing. Thorn was less than twenty minutes away when Wrath's sharp, cold draw snapped like a brittle rubber band. The second was the smoke. Thorn pulled off the main highway and headed down the rural roads leading to Cain's property, and it furled above her. Massive, rolling clouds of thick, black smog filled the blue, summer sky with a miasma that blotted out the sun. Soon, she was shrouded in poisonous shadows, and ash floated onto her shoulders like dusky snow.

The third was the screaming.

Thorn skidded to a stop at the bottom of Cain's gravel

driveway. Chris stormed across the front lawn, shouting commands. The entire house was engulfed in mountainous flames, and heat poured toward Thorn in a tsunami of panic. She sprinted up to Chris while Sparkie climbed from her jacket and shot into the air. All he could see was a black, smoky haze.

"Go around the side!" Chris roared, pointing at a couple of black-clad Martyrs in emergency fire gear running up the yard, their guns and rifles replaced with arms full of fire-fighting devices. "Break through the fence! We've got to get in there!"

Thorn tapped into the headset radios to be heard over the fire. "Where are the Sins?"

Chris spun toward her. Even from twenty feet back, the heat was so intense that the exposed skin on Chris's face was already tinted pink. Sweat rolled down the bridge of her nose and wet her lips.

"Gone," she said, turning away, yelling more orders as she rushed around the edge of the house. Martyrs swarmed back and forth from the vehicles parked on the road to grab more equipment. "They left as soon as we got here."

"What about Cain?" Thorn asked. "Lina? Abraham?"

"I don't know," Chris called back, and Thorn's gut churned. The terrified fury in her chest roared to match the fire behind her, and she turned around. At least thirty people—their cold energy a startling contrast with the intense heat—dotted the property. Frantic Martyrs and uncon-scious Puppets at the perimeter. But a smaller point, a tight, frigid signal of life, called to Thorn from *inside* the blaze. She took in a sharp gasp, and the smoke burned her throat.

"They're alive," she murmured. Then, more loudly, "I found them! Follow me."

"We need to get the fire out."

"We just need to carve a path through it!" Thorn shouted as she headed to the front of the house. The closer she got, the more sharply those energies came into focus. Two of them. Thank god, there were two of them. The fence by the garage was still standing—a black, charred wall of fragile wood—and Thorn kicked through it. She coughed and covered her mouth as black ash unfurled around her. On the other side, the yard was smoking, embers glowing at her feet. The Martyrs filed into a line behind her.

"Right here!" Thorn screamed, tucking her ponytail into the back of her jacket. Through the blaze, she could feel Abraham and Lina's energy. She pointed into the chaos. "We need to get through this. Make sure the fire doesn't close in behind us!"

The TAC team began to launch fire-smothering devices over Thorn's head. She grabbed a wearable extinguisher off Seth Grave's back, threw it over her shoulders, and watched as round after round of projectiles exploded, dousing the flames in red, chemical bursts. Thorn walked into the path, the heat squeezing around her as she pushed forward and poured a stream of white foam in a wide arc. Just as she hit the back corner of Cain's house, part of the roof caved in. She ducked as a flume of orange fire poured out a broken bedroom window. The Martyrs behind her backed up.

"Come on!" Thorn screamed. "Keep going!"

Slowly, Thorn drove toward the inferno. They passed the house and back deck, which lay in smoldering ruins at the edge of the garden. Just ahead of her, a solitary grave-stone, the granite charred, jutted up from the black earth. As the extinguishing clouds slammed into it, the stone fractured and flaked. She looked at its face; Donovan's name was cleaved into pieces. Unreadable. Her heart ached, the fury in her core a monstrous, swirling beast, as she stopped at the edge of the house.

A massive wall of fire stretched out before her. Trees lit up like match sticks, their skeletal branches reaching high into a dancing spread of red, orange, and yellow flames twenty feet from where she stood. The smoke was too thick for Sparkie to see, so he dove into the black clouds and landed on Thorn's shoulder. She held her hand up against the harsh, bright light. A bough in the distance cracked and crashed to the ground, sending up a spray of hot, dangerous sparks.

Lina and Abraham's energy was closer now. Thorn took a deep breath. The hot air scorched her throat all the way down. She had to find them.

Thorn's teeth gritted together, and her fingers tightened around the extinguisher hose as Sparkie shuddered on her shoulder. All at once, he launched himself into the garden.

Thorn let out a low, repressed gasp as the flames licked at Sparkie's wings and tail—as the pain shot through her flesh like she herself was darting through the fire—and she faltered. Chris came up to her side, and Thorn grabbed her shoulder to keep herself standing as Sparkie followed the footpath, twisting and turning and screaming as he whipped around burning shrubs and flower beds. Fallen trees obscured the walkway, sending blazing leaves into the air. Projectiles continued to fly overhead and exploded into steamy clouds of red mist.

At last, Sparkie found a reprieve. A tight circle around the pond where the flames hadn't reached. He collapsed from the sky, Thorn nearly collapsing with him, and he landed hard on the scalding ground.

Wet, bleeding hands scooped him up.

Disoriented, stinging, Sparkie looked around. Cain laid him out on top of a warm body. Lina. Lying back, her eyes wide open, tears streaming down her face. Half of her was covered in dark soil, and her head rested in Abraham's lap. He choked out a harsh, desperate sound as he saw Sparkie, and he looked into the fire like he was searching for Thorn through the flames. Crescendo leapt from the pond, his fur sogging and wet, and briefly touched nose-to-nose with Sparkie before he shook himself off, spraying Lina with a shower of water before he dove back in again.

Cain, meanwhile, worked on the blaze. He dug trenches with his heels, kicking away the detritus at his feet to rob the flames of more fuel to burn. His hands were a canvas of dark, bleeding lesions. Half of his face was blistered, and his salt and pepper hair had been singed nearly to his scalp.

Thorn gasped as Chris steadied her on her feet.

"Did you find them?" Chris yelled over the sound of the crackling flames. Another tree branch snapped, swinging wildly down and fanning a dangerous arc of burning debris.

Thorn nodded. "We have to hurry."

The pond was less than fifty feet away, but those fifty feet were hell. She led the pack, following the path through the garden as the Martyrs around her pushed back the heat on either side. Every inch they moved felt like a mile, and by the time Thorn could see Cain over the body of a burning maple, her skin felt parched and painful. Another fire-smothering projectile exploded ahead of her and cleared just narrow enough of a path for Thorn to leap through. The fire lapped at her hands and legs, but Thorn roared to the other side on a gust of chemical foam and fury.

"Thank *god*," Cain breathed. He fell roughly to one knee as Thorn grabbed his shoulders. His whole body shook, and the smell of burned hair and charred flesh made her stomach clench. "I tried to get them out," he gasped, "but we were surrounded by Puppets. Where are the Sins?"

"Gone," Thorn said as Sparkie leapt to her shoulder. Cain looked back up at her. His left eye was cloudy and sightless, but the other shone bright. "We've got to go, too."

"Lina's hurt!" Abraham called. Harsh, black marks streaked across his face, and his brown eyes were wide with terror and full of hot tears. "She can't walk!"

"I've got her. Cain, help him."

Cain nodded as he heaved himself back to his feet. His shoes were charred nearly to nothing, and he walked gingerly on the coals underfoot as he and Thorn ran to the pond. Cain pulled Abraham up, wincing as he grabbed the other man by the hand. They headed back to where the Martyrs held the path through the fire, Crescendo plowing ahead. Abraham cast a horrified look over his shoulder as Thorn knelt by Lina's side and began to scrape the dirt off her torso.

She gasped.

Lina's whole right side was burned to the point that Thorn could not see where her skin ended and her clothing began. Her leg, her side, her arm—it all oozed black and red, cracking open at the surface and exposing bright pink flesh beneath. Her silver, pendant necklace stuck to her throat—branded against her. Thorn hesitated, looking from the burns to Lina's face. Her eyes were open and disconnected, tears pouring through the gray ash on her cheeks.

"Thorn!" Chris screamed through the fire, snapping her back. "Hurry!"

Her gut a twisted knot of pain and horror, Thorn shook her head. "Okay, Lina," she said, her voice tight. "This is going to hurt. Just… Fuck, stay with me."

She dug her hands into the earth beneath Lina's body and lifted her from the ground. Lina screamed. Hard, primal sobs poured from her throat as Thorn's fingers pressed against the injured skin. It was hot, and it shifted, peeling away from the muscle beneath. Blood and melted fat coated Thorn's fingertips, making them slick, making the feeling of Lina's body falling to pieces inside them more gruesome, and for a moment, Thorn's stomach buckled. She felt like she was going to be sick.

But she swallowed it down and ran through the fire. Lina's screaming faded, her eyes rolling back. Sparkie flew ahead, and Chris was waiting on the other side. She took one look at Lina, and her jaw dropped.

"Oh my god," she murmured.

"I need a med kit. Sedative. Painkillers. Whatever the fuck we have," Thorn said as she rushed through Cain's property. Past the trees. The deck. Donovan's grave. She didn't stop. Didn't look. Didn't focus on anything but the feeling of Lina's cold energy and hot skin pressed against her chest. Chris barked orders into her helmet, and the TAC unit moved seamlessly, retreating to the cars, putting Abraham and Cain into the back of one while Thorn hurried to another and climbed in with Lina. Someone pushed a med kit beside her as she laid the other woman down against the upholstery. When she pulled her hands away, parts of Lina's arm stuck to her gloves and the sleeves of her jacket. Thorn ripped them off, throwing the extinguisher and her helmet to the side, too. Her fingers shook.

"Get us to the Underground," Thorn screamed as Chris jumped into the driver's seat. They tore away so quickly that gravel flew up behind them. Lina's eyes were still open, but the tears had stopped. She had no water left to lose. Her dry lips opened and let out a harsh, pained moan as her body began to convulse from shock. Thorn opened the kit and pulled out a tube of burn cream. She stared at it blindly. Helplessly.

This wasn't enough. Fuck, it wouldn't be enough. Thorn had to get her to Darius.

Desperate, not knowing what the fuck else to do, Thorn grabbed a sedative and tilted Lina's head back. She poured the liquid into her mouth, and Lina choked on it, coughing, spraying Thorn's face with the medication she couldn't get down. Seconds later, though, her gray eyes fluttered closed, and her shaking body went still. Thorn turned back to the kit, pulled out a thin emergency blanket, and threw it over Lina's body. It clung to her seeping wounds like plastic wrap. The back of the car reeked so heavily of burned human flesh that Thorn was sure it would cake inside her nostrils—that she'd never smell anything else as long as she fucking lived. She gently grabbed Lina by the face, turned her head so she could look at her, and brushed a thumb against her cheek to wipe away the ashes there. Her skin was gray beneath them.

"Oh, fuck," Thorn murmured, her heart pounding in her throat. "You got this, Lina. You hear me? You can do this." She grabbed Lina's unburned hand and wrapped her fingers tightly around it. "You're going to be okay."

They flew down the highway and made it back to the Underground in under thirty minutes. Thirty long, horrifying minutes of Lina's limp, unconscious body rocking back and forth with every turn. Thirty minutes of her blood soaking into the brand-new upholstery in the back of this forest green SUV. Thirty minutes of her fragile skin slipping, peeling backward, exposing muscle and sinew and charred fat tissue. Thorn's stomach twisted, and she had to close her eyes and cover them with her spare hand while the other clutched Lina's cold fingers.

"We're here," Chris said at last. Thorn looked in the mirror. Chris's helmet was gone, and the bottom half of her face was bright pink, like a bad sunburn. Her filthy, soot-stained fingers quaked as she rolled down the window and inserted her card in the lock. The carwash doors opened, she pulled them inside, and seconds later, they were on their way into the ground.

Thorn felt the medical staff, Mackenzie, and a handful of others gathered outside the doors. They pattered nervously as Chris drove downward so quickly that the tires squealed on every turn. Thorn looked out as the light from the loading area came in the tinted window, and she searched the Martyrs gathered there for one person. One face.

Darius.

He was in the front, his deep, olive complexion washed out as he ran to the car. He didn't wait for it to stop—just reached for the latch at the back. Thorn's chest expanded and sucked in a relieved breath. She wanted to laugh—

Lina's energy disappeared as the door swung open.

Thorn froze. She stared at Lina, and a numbing wave shuddered through every bone, every muscle, in her body. For a few long seconds, all Thorn could do was hold on—hold tightly to the hand in hers—in disbelief. She didn't realize her eyes had filled with water until Darius said her name. The word floated through her head. When she looked up at him, a tear dropped from her lashes and trailed a hot line down her cheek. Darius's brows drew together. "Thorn, she's gone."

"We made it," Thorn murmured. Her voice sounded

foreign, like it didn't belong to her. She shook her head, and this time, she shouted. "We fucking *made it!*"

She dropped Lina's hand. It landed on the upholstery, dull and heavy. Elijah rushed up beside Darius. Thorn hardly heard him as he called his team to get Lina out of the back of the car. Hardly felt his cold energy as she pulled herself past him and walked around the vehicle. Darius said something to her and laid a hand on her shoulder. The warmth of his skin broke the dam.

Thorn's numbness washed away, flooded by hot fire and cold pain. She spun away from Darius and roared as she slammed her fists on the side of the SUV. Colette walked back to the group gathered at the entrance to the Underground. Muttered something.

Then Mackenzie screamed. The sound pierced through the garage, through the car, through Thorn, and landed in her brain like a bullet.

CHAPTER TWENTY-SIX

A dozen Martyrs sat in cots along the hospital ward, hands covered in roiling blisters and eyes wide and tired. The typical chatter among the nurses and the wounded was muted, reduced to nothing more than quiet murmurings of "did that hurt?" and "not that much longer now" as they applied numbing salves and waited for Samira and Darius to make their rounds. Chris stood by the door, her burns already healed. She pressed her fingertips against her lips as she looked over her team. The whites of her eyes were bloodshot, and she blinked twice as often to keep the storm of tears pressed up behind her lashes from falling. Raquel came up to her, spoke to her, and hugged her, and Chris dipped her head into the crook of Raquel's shoulder.

Darius watched them, and he took a deep breath—or he began to, but the smell of burned hair and melted polyester coated his nose and made him queasy. He cleared his throat and looked back down at the patient beside him.

Abraham stared at the ceiling. He didn't say anything as Darius's palms pressed against his bare chest, pouring healing power into his body to mend the burns on his legs and clear the smoke from his lungs. In fact, Abraham hadn't spoken since he'd gotten to the Underground at all. The

SUV carrying him and Cain arrived shortly after Thorn and Lina. He had stepped out to see a body under a white sheet whipping through the triage doors.

No one had to tell him what happened. And he didn't ask.

"How is that feeling?" Darius asked after a few quiet moments. His bedside training kicked in slowly, detached, like it didn't matter anymore. Talk to them, Elijah had said. Ask them questions.

Abraham didn't respond. His jaw clenched together, and his brown eyes pooled. The muscles in his face were tight, pulling his long nose up, and for a moment, Darius was sure he was going to break down. But he didn't. Somehow, he didn't. He brought his hands up—his fingers still layered in soot, soil, and dried blood—and covered his face. Darius's throat constricted. The healing flow slowed as Abraham's body demanded fewer resources, and Darius pulled his palms away. Abraham seemed to be breathing better, and the burned skin on his calves and feet was an aggressive shade of pink rather than the gnarled, blistered mess it had been.

"I'll be back," Darius murmured. "I've got to go help other people while—"

He stopped abruptly. There was no point. Abraham knew the protocol, and he clearly didn't care to hear it. Darius pressed his lips together, took a shallow breath, and excused himself. As he pulled the curtain shut around Abraham's bed, Samira's Virtuous energy approached from behind.

"Dr. Harris said we're expecting more casualties," she said, anxiously twisting her hands together. Her complexion was washed out.

"Yeah," Darius said through a rough sigh. He slammed his eyes shut and rubbed the closed lids with the fingers and thumb of one hand. "Half of our TAC team is still up there, trying to get the fire out, and Thorn took the Cleaning Crew to help. We need to be ready for more burns, so take it slow."

Samira's lips parted in surprise. "What about the authorities?" she asked. "Can't they handle the fire?"

"This is where the Martyrs' dead are buried," Darius said, and his voice caught on the words. He coughed in the back of his throat. "We need to make sure we don't leave anything behind that might point to us."

Samira's eyes softened, and she gave a sympathetic frown. Darius thought she was going to comment on the garden, but instead she said, "Let's focus on pain relief. Heal them just enough not to hurt quite as badly?"

The knot in Darius's chest loosened, and he nodded, grateful for a plan. Elijah's voice echoed in his head.

"Keep them busy."

That meant the Virtues, too.

"Sounds good," Darius said. "I'll take these six; you get the others?" Samira agreed, and they split up. Dividing the work made it move quickly, and fifteen minutes later, the two of them were sucking down juice boxes side by side at the nurses' station. Chris had slipped out a few minutes ago, and with Dr. Harris's team prepping the beds at the far end of the room and every other patient safely tucked behind white curtains, Darius and Samira were left alone. He felt the toll of healing on his body—his mind tired, his muscles a little weaker than they had been this morning. He took a deep breath and closed his eyes, rubbing his knuckles against them.

"Did you know her well?" Samira asked. "Lina, I mean. You worked with her, didn't you?"

A hard lump formed in Darius's throat, and when he tried to swallow, it hurt all the way up his neck. He pulled his hands away from his face and let out a soft sigh.

"Yeah," he said. "I did."

The door to one of the private rooms behind them opened, and Elijah emerged. He looked just as tired, just as emotionally drained, as Darius felt. As he walked by, pulling bloodstained gloves from his hands and depositing them in a biohazard receptacle by the door, he glanced up at Darius. The two shared a solemn look before the doctor made his way to his office, and the door snapped shut behind him.

"What was she like?" Samira went on.

Darius turned to her again. She pulled her knees up to her chest, and the office chair she was sitting in slowly swiveled toward him. For a moment, she reminded him of the children at the orphanage. Oversized, ill-fitted clothes. Intense focus. Even a genuine, heartfelt curiosity. It made his heart ache even more, and his lungs pressed in around the pain.

"She was one in a million," a quiet voice said behind them.

Both Darius and Samira startled as they twisted around. The door Elijah had come from was open again, and standing just inside the frame, dressed in nothing but an open-backed hospital gown, was Cain Guttuso. Samira barely managed to stifle a gasp. Harsh, angry lesions covered his arms, and the gooey salve that had been applied to them made Cain look like a melted wax figure. His legs were in better shape except for his gnarled, bare feet.

But it was his *face* that made Darius's breath catch.

The whole left side was mangled. The charred, black parts had been cleaned and tended to, leaving behind a wet mix of red and pink. Burns extended up to his scalp, where his hair had been singed away, leaving nothing but a messy quilt of ashen, patchwork swatches above his ear and at the base of his head. His right eye was as bright and eager as ever, but the left was clouded in a hazy cataract.

It was easy to forget how much Forgotten Sins could endure until it was staring you in the face.

Cain didn't seem perturbed by Samira's shock or Darius's silence. He winced as he crossed his arms and leaned his shoulder against the frame. Crescendo, completely untouched by the fire, peered out of the door by Cain's ankles. His orange, lamp-like eyes looked Darius over.

"Lina brightened every room she walked into," Cain

went on. "She was infinitely kind, beautifully intelligent, with a thirst to learn and to grow. If I could say one bad thing about her, it's that she never once flaunted her worth. It was a worth that deserved to be flaunted."

The tightness around Darius's chest twisted until it hurt, and as Cain met his eyes, all he could do was nod. Samira hadn't quit staring, open-mouthed. Darius cleared his throat.

"Samira, this is Cain," he said, gesturing a palm toward him, and finally, her eyes pulled away from Cain's damaged face to look at Darius again. "He's a Forgotten Sin, and he built the Memorial Garden. Cain, meet Samira. She's—"

"Temperance," Cain cut in with an almost dreamlike quality to his voice. Dreamlike, except for the bite of pain sharpening the syllables. "I gathered. Lina and Abraham told me so much about you. I'd shake your hand, but, well…"

Cain drew one away from his chest and held it out. His swollen fingers looked like overcooked sausages. Darius's stomach swirled, and Samira's complexion lost its color.

"How are you feeling?" Darius asked.

Cain gingerly returned his arm to its place around his chest. "I feel as good as I look, I'm afraid. Though, the good doctor was kind enough to give me such an overabundance of painkillers that anyone else would undoubtedly be comatose by now."

Darius nodded. "I'm sorry about your garden."

Briefly, Cain's head dipped down. "Thank you," he said, "but gardens can be regrown. Homes, rebuilt. Lives can never be replaced."

The air around them went quiet, and the ache in Darius's heart started to feel heavy. After a moment, Samira spoke. The rhythm of the words sounded recited. "We have to trust in God's plan for us," she said. "Even if we don't understand it. Everything happens for a reason."

Cain's one good eyebrow twitched inward, furrowing lightly over his bright eye. "With all due respect, my dear, there is no plan. There has never *been* a plan. There has only been chaos. Beautiful, awe-inspiring, and terrible chaos."

Samira's eyes widened, and her dry lips parted. She shook her head. "I'm so sorry you feel that way. It's sad... to think that life and death are so meaningless."

The corner of Cain's mouth turned up in a half-smirk. "Why in the world would you think there has to be a higher plan for life to have meaning?" he asked. "The very fact that you and I are in the same room, right now, is the product of thousands of years of choices and happenstance and coincidence. One tiny change, one decision, could have derailed everything we know, everything we *are*. Predestination makes us a cog in a machine, with no control over our life or our death. But chaos? In chaos, it's a miracle we were ever born, and *everything* we do matters. Every action makes a difference. I don't find that sad. I find it *inspiring*."

Samira stared at Cain, and her eyebrows drew together. "If you don't believe in a Divine plan, how can you possibly explain Sins and Virtues?" she asked. "Aren't we destined to destroy one another?"

"You chose to reject that 'destiny,' didn't you?" Cain pressed. The apples of Samira's cheeks turned a dark maroon, and Cain shrugged. The motion made him wince. "If you can walk away from what you were meant to do—and, dear girl, I want it to be very clear that you *can* walk away— then it goes to show there is no plan except for the one we create, and our choices will have an impact well after we're gone."

Samira's face flushed even deeper, and she murmured some generic excuse about checking on the Martyrs as she stood up and walked around the nurses' station. Darius watched her until she disappeared behind one of the many white curtains around the ward. Then he turned back to Cain.

"Trying to change her mind?" he asked. "About destroying Gluttony?"

"Oh, no," Cain said dismissively with a quick shake of

his head. "But she must *own* that decision and the consequences of it. Too many wars have been fought on the backs of gods by those who never had to face what violence they started *or* ignored."

Darius leaned back in his chair, crossing his arms, and considered Cain. The old Forgotten Sin's one good eye twinkled, and the cat trilled at his feet. A warm energy from above began to spiral into the Underground. Darius and Cain both glanced at it, and Darius's stomach dropped.

"What's wrong?" Cain asked, and Darius looked back at him. Cain was watching the side of his face with a keen, attentive focus. "Who is it?"

"Jacob Locke," Darius murmured, and Cain's eyes widened. "I wonder if he knows…"

By the way his aura flew around corners, Darius had no doubt he did. The warmth slammed to a stop just outside the loading area, and Darius got to his feet as it sped into the Underground.

The hospital doors flung inward.

"Is it true?" Jacob exclaimed. Nearly every point of human energy in the ward jumped at the sudden outburst, and Dr. Harris's office opened. Jacob glanced around, his head moving with quick, sharp motions as he looked at Elijah, Darius, and Cain. He flinched at the last one, nearly falling back through the double doors behind him, before he ran a hand down his scruffy face and focused on Darius. He rushed forward and leaned so far over the nursing counter that Darius could feel Jacob's breath on his face as he screamed, "*Is Lina dead?*"

Darius didn't have the chance to answer. Jacob stepped back and tore his orange ball cap off his head. He ran his fingers through his hair so hard that Darius thought he'd rip it out. His brown eyes were swollen and bloodshot, the dark circles beneath them full of a puffy redness that made him look exhausted through the mania.

"Jacob," the doctor said, his voice a low drone of practiced calm, and he held his hands up gently. Jacob's focus snapped to him like a whip. Elijah approached slowly. "Let's talk in my office."

"NO," Jacob yelled, shaking his head as he took a few paces back. Now, white curtains shifted, and faces peered through them. Jacob didn't seem to notice any of them. "No! Where is she? *Where is Lina?*"

Warm movement in the back of the ward caught Darius's attention. Abraham had come out from his bed, and he walked toward his older brother. Every step was labored, his legs still dry and tight from the burns Darius hadn't finished healing, but he focused on Jacob's face and didn't look away.

"Abraham," Jacob managed to spit out. "Abe." He crossed the space between them, clutching desperately to Abraham's shoulders as he leaned up and into his face. Abraham stumbled but managed to stay on his feet as Jacob said, "Tell me she's fine. *Tell me Lina is fine!*"

"Jacob," Abraham choked, his eyes full of tears, but his jaw hardened as he grabbed his brother by the face and held him still, forcing him to stop moving, to look into his eyes. "I need you, okay? I need you to hear me. She… she didn't make it. Lina's gone."

Jacob froze. Every muscle in his body seized, like he was malfunctioning. He stared at Abraham with his mouth wide open and eyes full of deep, broken anguish. By now, every patient and nurse in the ward was watching, and Elijah pressed a fist to his mouth. Jacob finally gasped out one word.

"No."

Abraham nodded. Jacob pulled away, nearly knocking his brother over, and threw his cap onto the ground at his feet.

"No! What—why? How? What was she *doing* there?"

"Jacob," Abraham began. He took a step forward, but Jacob floundered back.

"This isn't supposed to happen. She's *safe* here! The Sins can't get her *here!*"

"Please—"

But Jacob turned around, threw the doors open, and almost fell through them. His energy, frenetic, desperate, sprinted down the hallway to Lina's office, where it collapsed onto the carpet and didn't move again. Darius took a breath—his lungs hungry for air—and he turned to Abraham.

To find the man crying silently into his hands in the middle of the hospital ward. For a few seconds, the room just watched him. Then Raquel came up from the far end of the hall. She walked at first, but soon she was running, and she threw her arms around Abraham without saying a word. White curtains fluttered as wounded Martyrs came off their cots, as nurses stopped prepping beds, and before Darius could even come around the counter, Abraham was encircled in a tight, huddled ring of green scrubs and black shirts. They wrapped around him, linking their arms over one another's shoulders in silence.

And Abraham sobbed.

***

The conference room had never felt this empty.

Darius sat beside Chris and stared without really seeing as Thorn and Cain took their seats across from him. Alan lowered himself into a chair at the head of the table with a somber, defeated mood that Darius had never seen him display so openly.

"What we need to address today is going to be challenging," Alan said, his deep voice a rumble of remorse. "Neither Mackenzie nor Abraham are in any state to discuss this, so they will not be attending."

Darius nodded, and Chris shifted beside him. She was the only person here with an aura he could detect, and her warmth anchored him. He cast her a grateful glance, but she focused on Alan with a forced calm and did not look back.

"I do not need to describe the gravity of what we have

lost," Alan went on. "Lina Brooks was more than simply another Martyr. To many of us, she was a friend, a sister… She was family."

He cleared his throat and looked down at his hands folded on the table. Darius took a shallow breath. Thorn's jaw was set so hard it looked painful, and her black eyes glistened with hot, angry tears that refused to fall. Beside her, Cain sat still, fingers laced in his lap. He had healed almost entirely by now. If not for the pink tint on his arms and his freshly-buzzed head, there was no sign that he'd been in the fire at all.

"Before we go into the details of what happened at the garden three days ago," Alan said, gazing around at all of them again, "I wanted to announce that we will be holding a celebration of life for Lina this weekend. All Recon units have been recalled, and most arrived back at the Underground yesterday morning. Mackenzie asked to organize it, but she will need assistance."

"I can help," Cain said. Alan turned to him, and their eyes met. Alan's spine stiffened as Cain continued. "This is a subject I know all too well."

"Your insight will be much appreciated," Alan said. "When this is all done, we will find you a new home and property where you can resume your work."

"Actually," Cain said, the corner of his mouth twitching upward, "I think it's time I return to the Underground. Given the current circumstances, I believe I might be useful." Then he cast a quick glance in Darius's direction before putting all his attention on Alan again. He raised his brows dramatically. "That is, if *you* are comfortable with it."

The muscles along Alan's jaw tightened, but he bowed his head in a curt nod. "Of course."

Thorn cleared her throat, her sharp eyes flashing dangerously between the men on either side of her. Alan sat back in his chair again, and Cain's smirk faded.

"Now," Alan went on. "Thorn, can you detail how our coverup operation went?"

She took a deep breath, her arms rising and falling from their position wrapped around her chest. "As well as we could have asked for," she said. "By the time I got back, the local fire department was putting out the flames. I distracted them with Influence while Marcus and his team worked on cleaning out any evidence that could point back to us. There wasn't much. The fire burned hot and fast, and nearly everything was destroyed. Even the grave markers crumbled to pieces."

Alan's brows drew in a solemn furrow. "How did the fire start?"

"The marshal found incendiary devices around the perimeter designed to explode with some kind of gel-based fuel," Thorn said.

"They started at the back of the property," Cain added. "By the time I noticed the smoke and went to get Abraham and Lina inside, Puppets had surrounded us. Those devices began to explode before we even made it back to the house. Lina was caught in one of them."

"And you could not get her off the grounds?" Alan asked with a frown.

"No," Cain said defensively. "As I said, we were *surrounded*, outnumbered, and wounded. The best I could do was hold out by the pond and pray help arrived." Cain gestured an open palm in Chris's direction. "Without you, none of us would have survived. Thank you."

Chris's teeth clenched together. "We're just lucky the Sins left when we got there."

"I don't think they had any choice," Thorn growled, her voice singed at the edges, like it had caught fire, too, and the embers still smoldered. "Almost every single Puppet left behind had died by the time we got back."

"What?" Darius asked. "How?"

"It looked like they got too close to the flames," Thorn said. "The pain cut them off from the Sins' control, and they left them behind to burn."

Darius's stomach twisted as Alan sighed. "Without

Puppets, they would not risk an altercation," he agreed. "All of our wounded have been fully healed?"

"Yes," Darius said. "Other than Abraham and Cain, the burns weren't that serious. Second-degree, at worst. Everyone is back to one hundred percent."

"Good," Alan said, nodding before he took in the table again. "My primary concern now is how exactly the Sins discovered the garden in the first place. We know they have been getting information from Mr. DuPont, but he has been under surveillance for the last two weeks. Mr. Carter insists he has not been left alone outside of the hours he spends in his room at night, so it is incredibly unlikely he gained access to any device that could communicate with the Sins. As far as I can tell, Mr. DuPont did *not* contact anyone with this information since he has been detained."

"He could have done it beforehand," Chris said. She sighed and closed her eyes as she pressed her fingertips into the sides of her nose. "Though I don't know why they would have waited so long to attack."

"If I'm not mistaken," Cain observed quietly, looking from Chris to Darius and finally landing on Alan. "This man has never been to the garden before. How would he have known where to send the Sins in the first place?"

"He did read a ton of our reports when we first brought him in," Darius said.

Chris dropped her hands back to the table, crossed her arms, and leaned against them. "That's true," she said. "Since all of the specific details in our non-restricted documentation have been redacted, he wouldn't have an address or exact location. It's possible they've been searching the area for months."

Cain offered a nod, and Darius glanced at Thorn. Her dark eyes disconnected from the conversation, distant and narrow, and her mouth slowly opened to expose a sliver of pink lips and white teeth. Darius frowned as Alan stood.

"We will look into it," he said, and down the table, chairs scraped backward. Thorn jumped to her feet and walked around Alan's back before he even finished speaking. "In the meantime, the next few days will be hard for us all. Please, check in with your teams and with each other. Abraham will not be available to discuss this situation, so we must do what we can to help one another."

Alan turned toward Thorn as he said this, but she'd already opened the door and rushed into the hallway. It slammed shut behind her.

CHAPTER TWENTY-SEVEN

Thorn's chest tightened, her mind alight with curious, terrifying possibilities that prodded at the monster in her gut until they tempted it awake.

The top floor of the Underground was mostly empty. Thorn felt Martyrs moving beneath her feet, swarming the courtyard for the lunch rush as she strode down the hallway, around the corner, and past the alcove of director offices until she reached the lobby between hers and Alan's. She unlocked her door, pushed it open, stepped inside…

And the uneasy feeling twisting in her stomach churned.

Sparkie was already pacing in agitated circles on her desk as Thorn came to sit behind it, his tail a twitch of frenetic movement. She pulled her laptop out. The screen took forever to load, and Thorn tapped her fingernails impatiently against the plastic casing while she waited. All the while, she chewed on the thought.

It didn't make fucking *sense.*

Thorn logged into her account—one of only three in the whole Underground with maximum security clearance—and headed to the user logs. Images of the fire roared at her. Intense heat, followed by an even more intense hatred that the Sins had tracked down this sacred place. Burned it to the ground. Desecrated Donovan's grave and ended Lina's life. Thorn's heart clenched painfully, but what Cain said got her thinking.

DuPont had never been to the Martyrs Memorial Garden.

She scrolled through the list of names until she found DuPont, Gabriel. His face looked back at her. The headshot had been taken shortly after his Programming was unwritten—or they'd *thought* it was unwritten. She looked into those cognac eyes for a moment. Her own narrowed, and she took a deep breath.

He had never felt like a killer. Not at the beginning, and certainly not now.

Frustrated, Thorn clicked on his profile, and his records filled her screen. Everything the Martyrs did was tracked here. Every call made. Every text sent. Every file opened. The last log made was on June tenth, when Thorn had sent DuPont the coordinates to Alexis Claytor's Midtown apartment so he and Chan could escort her safely back to the Underground. Before that, nothing out of the ordinary. When he'd contacted the Sins—*if* he'd contacted the Sins— he hadn't done it on his Martyr-issued device.

That should have raised red flags, and Thorn was kicking herself that it hadn't.

She moved onto the accounts from his first few weeks— before he'd passed his assessments and joined TAC on the field. Hundreds of internal Martyr reports, going back a couple of years at least, intermixed with the occasional texts to Chris, thanking her for the opportunity to be a part of her team, or to Darius, asking for advice on fighting off In- fluence. Thorn disregarded these, and she began to open the files, filling her screen with two at a time. Sparkie crawled onto her shoulder, and while she scanned one, he looked over another, searching for any indication that DuPont had read about the garden somewhere. Anywhere.

But an hour passed, the articles all searched through, and Thorn came back empty-handed. The unease grew to worry, and she got to her feet, pacing the wall behind her desk while she pressed her fingertips to her lips.

She had to have missed something.

Thorn slammed back into the chair and read the reports again, this time taking care to examine them, to make sure every detail, every moment, was analyzed. The most recent file was on DuPont's own Deprogramming. It outlined the Sins showing up on scene. The car chase. The moment Thorn worried he might turn the gun on her, and instead, he threw it out the window.

She kept reading. Kept remembering. Kept reliving moments where the Sins had been one step ahead of them and lives had been lost. Eva, gasping on the concrete while Nicholas healed Darius instead. Spokane, when Wrath's Puppet shot wildly into the gala crowd and landed a bullet in Sara Park's back, murdering her right there in the middle of the dance floor. Even Cyrus Murphy, the poor kid from the orphanage who had bled out in Thorn's arms with Envy's knife pierced through his throat. She'd promised him that she would find Darius before the Sins did. Another lie. Another person she'd let down.

Thorn revisited years upon years of Martyr trauma and heartbreak. Failed missions and successful ones. Deaths and injuries and emergencies. DuPont had read back to November 2083, nearly nine years ago, when Thorn and Jeremiah successfully raided Isla Diamandis's apartment and destroyed that iteration of Pride for good. They'd lost one Martyr and six civilians that day. Thorn remembered it being one of the cleanest victories they'd had in a while. She remembered the celebration, bittersweet like they always were.

Thorn shut her computer, running her tongue against the bottom of her teeth.

Nine years of history. Nine years of reports.

And in all that time, there had never been an incident at the garden to write about.

A frantic knocking startled Thorn. Sparkie's wings flared out behind him, his tiny spine arching away from her shoulder as he hissed and dove down the back of her shirt. Thorn walked to the door, pulled it open, and found Nicholas Wolfe standing on the other side. She frowned.

"What—"

"It doesn't make any sense," Nicholas said before she could finish her thought. He pushed his way inside and spun in the middle of the room. His arms crossed around his chest—he was thinner than Thorn remembered—and he watched her with a suspicious, almost manic expression. "DuPont and the garden. He couldn't have done it."

Thorn's heart leapt to her throat, and she quickly shut the door.

"Go on," she said.

Nicholas blanched. His eyes widened, then narrowed, and he leaned toward her.

"You knew?"

"I just started suspecting it," Thorn said. She propped her hands on her hips as she walked back behind her desk. The maps and markers of train stations and rail yards looked down at her, and she considered them absently while her mind chewed on this fresh problem.

"There's no way he's contacted the Sins since he's been locked up," Nicholas said as he came around to stand by her. She felt his attention on the side of her face. "I tried to talk to John about it when we were driving back. He's convinced DuPont told them beforehand, but we would have noticed them searching for it."

"He couldn't have told them at all," Thorn said quietly. "He's never been to the garden. Never read about it… As far as I can tell, he didn't even know it existed."

She turned back to Nicholas. His face was pale underneath the splattering of freckles across his nose and cheeks. He blinked a couple of times before throwing his hands out in front of him. "You know what this means, don't you?"

Thorn pulled her lower lip between her teeth, afraid to voice her fears out loud. "Someone else had to have given them that information."

Nicholas's hands fell back to his sides with a hard, defeated swing. "Maybe *all* the information. Do you really think there are two leaks in the Underground? I don't."

Thorn strode past him, drawing her fingers through her hair. The silky strands flowed back down in soft, black sheets. "But who the fuck else could it be?" she went on. The monster in her stomach swirled again. "And why?"

"I don't know," Nicholas said, speaking slowly. The change in tempo made Thorn turn to him. His jaw tightened, and he squared his shoulders. "But it *is* pretty convenient that Jacob just happened to overhear the information about the garden right as the Sins got there."

The monster choked as Thorn's eyes sharpened.

"You think *Jacob* told them?"

"*I don't know*," Nicholas repeated, holding his hands up. "But based on what we *do* know, it couldn't have been DuPont, and Jacob is the only link we have—"

"But he couldn't," Thorn pressed, shaking her head and crossing her arms. Her fingers tightened around her bicep, and Sparkie's wings shivered under her shirt. "The Martyrs are his life. All he cares about is keeping this place safe, and he has Programming installed to prevent him from hurting anybody."

Nicholas shrugged. "Programming that didn't stop him from attacking DuPont in the break room…"

Thorn stared at him, her jaw clenched so hard together it ached, and Nicholas stared back. His bright eyes glistened with a drive she hadn't seen in him since his soul had been ripped in two, and the determination there was enough to make her wonder. She took a deep breath.

An alert on her phone cracked the tension. Thorn grabbed it to see a message from an unknown number with nothing but a location marker for one of the rail yards. Thorn's heart dipped.

A lead on Leroy Khoury. Fuck. She couldn't deal with all of it right now.

"Have you talked to anyone else about this?" she asked.

Nicholas shook his head. "No."

"Don't," she said. "Where is Jacob now?"

"In his quarters, I think," Nicholas said.

Thorn nodded. "Find Waters, and the two of you keep an eye on him while I'm gone. I don't want to accuse *anyone* of anything until you and I look into it. You understand?"

Nicholas's lips pressed together, but he nodded.

"Good," Thorn said, and she ushered him out the door. "We'll make a plan when I get back." Then she sped down the hallway and called Holly. When the tech lead answered, Thorn said, "I'm sending you coordinates. Check if there's a camera there, and see if you can spot Khoury on any of the footage. I think we got him."

Darius found Chris getting ready in Tactical. Martyrs swarmed around him, their hot energy a bustle of movement as he walked around the corner, past rows of tall, gray lockers, and hurried to her side.

"Did I hear right?" he asked. Chris glanced at him as she grabbed a semi-automatic rifle from her gear locker. "We found Leroy?"

"In South Kearny," she said, checking the safety and putting the weapon in a case at her feet. "One of Thorn's Sentries sent an alert, and Holly found him on a camera hopping off the back of a grain car."

Chris reached back into her locker for her armor. While she cinched it around her chest, Darius felt the room. There were six TAC officers in here. Three units. His throat tightened, and he swallowed through it.

"Did the Sins find him, too?"

"No clue." Chris threw her helmet into a black bag at her feet. The team around her was doing the same—gathering their things, getting ready for combat. "But we're not taking chances. Thorn sent Sparkie ahead to try to find him, and I have two patrolling units on the way."

Chris leaned down, grabbed her equipment, and headed toward another locker bay, where most of the other TAC teams were suiting up. Darius followed on her heels.

"I want to come," he said.

Chris sighed. "I do, too, but it's not up to me."

"Hey, Chris?" Seth Graves called from the furthest alcove, and he leaned around the edge. He already had a helmet slammed over his buzzed head. "We grabbing stuff for that other Virtue? A vest, at least?"

Darius's stomach twisted as Chris's cheeks turned bright pink. She confirmed, and as Seth dipped away again, Darius said, "Wait—*Samira's* going?"

At last, Chris looked at him properly. "I don't like it, either, but I'm just following my orders."

She pulled away from him; he kept close behind her. "But—"

"Darius!" Chris reeled around and threw her hand in the air. Then she closed her eyes, sucked a quick breath between her teeth, and grabbed him by the shoulders. "I hear you," she said, quieter now, as she leaned in, "and I agree with you, but I can't help you. I have a job to do, and you're in my way, so please, *go.*"

Her fingers squeezed around him, tight and affectionate, before she turned and began barking orders to the Martyrs tucked back in the locker bays. Darius's heart pounded furiously against his ribs, and his fists clenched into hard knots. He rushed out of the room. Once he hit the hallway, he took an immediate left and strode through the waiting area. He could feel Samira's Virtue in the garage, and he knew who he'd find with her.

Thorn stood by the back of a maroon SUV outside the loading area, three spots down from a navy vehicle that seemed misplaced with the rest. Darius heard her voice as soon as he opened the door.

"We assume the range for Leroy sensing you is the same as our range for human energy," she was saying, her back turned to the Underground. Her long hair was already pulled into a ponytail at the base of her skull, and it fell between the hard lines of her shoulder blades. She was tossing duffle bags into the vehicle, totally unaware of Darius coming up behind her, but Samira noticed him immediately. Her face, wide-eyed and terrified, turned to him as he walked over. Thorn kept talking. "It could be anywhere from two to three hundred yards. My hope is that he'll quit running when he feels you. If he gets into New York, we're—"

"Thorn," Darius called across the garage. She turned to face him, hard eyes and tight lips making it clear that she had been anticipating a fight and was ready to have it. "I should come!"

"No," she said the second the last syllable left his lips. She propped her hands onto her hips and squared off with him. He stopped three feet from her. "You're not cleared for field duty."

"Neither is Samira," Darius argued, throwing an open palm in the other Virtue's direction. "She hasn't had *any* training!"

"She's not coming for field duty," Thorn snarled. "Her Virtue masks the emptiness in Leroy's soul. We need her to help us *find him.*"

Darius shook his head. "What if people get hurt?"

"Then I guess it's a good thing we'll have a Virtue," Thorn snapped back.

Darius groaned and ran a hand through his hair, taking another step toward her. Thorn didn't back away.

"This is *insane,*" he exclaimed. "You *know* I'm qualified to be out there, but you won't let me take the stupid test! Maybe if you had, then Lina—"

Darius stopped. His mouth opened but stalled out because the words he was about to say were the kind of words he couldn't take back. Words that carved lesions and caused scars. No matter how mad he was at Thorn, he didn't want to leave her with more.

But Thorn's dark eyes widened. She moved toward him. They were so close he could almost feel her breath as she murmured, "Then what? Then Lina would still be alive?" A sudden, sharp sting of pain pooled in her eyes, and finally, Darius stepped back. She swallowed hard. "*You're right.* Lina's death is on my hands, and I'm going to have to live with that for the rest of my life. But the fact is, you're *not* ready, and it has nothing to do with combat training. You're not *thinking* straight."

Darius's lungs constricted, forcing the air from them in a soft sigh. He stepped back again. "Has Abraham been talking—"

"No," Thorn cut in, and her brows drew downward in concern. She held a hand out to him, gesturing to his chest—to the pain nestled there. A void, waiting dormant but inevitable. He crossed his arms as Thorn went on. "I don't need to talk to Abraham to see how fucking hard you're pushing yourself—how you're willing to put yourself in danger, no matter what the cost, and damn it, Darius, losing *you* is a cost I *can't* live with."

Her voice cracked over his name, and the muscles in her throat tightened. Samira stood behind her, gaping at them like she was watching a street fight and had no idea who to call for help. Thorn shook her head. "I can't send you out there until I know you're not going to do something stupid. You need to take care of yourself *just* as much as you take care of everyone else, or you'll get yourself fucking killed."

For several long, aching seconds, Darius stared at her, and Thorn stared back. Unsinkable. A rush of energy came at him from behind, and Darius tore his eyes away at last, shaking his head as Chris and the TAC units poured out of the Underground. Chris shouted to Thorn over the sound of boots slamming against concrete.

"Ready?" she asked, tossing Thorn an extra ballistics vest as she headed to a separate SUV. Thorn caught it casually, and Darius glanced back to her one last time to see her still watching him. Then she threw the vest into the back of her car, shut the door, and looked at Chris.

"Yeah. Let's go."

Four vehicles, six Martyr energies, and Samira's Virtuous pull spiraled upward until they disappeared. An anxious, horrifying seed of dread nestled inside Darius's stomach as he ambled into the waiting room—the only feeling he had outside of the numb disappointment of being left behind *again*. He grabbed the back of a white, plastic chair against the wall. His fingers tightened around it, and he slammed his eyes shut.

"God *damn it!*" he yelled. The words echoed through the waiting area. A few distant points of energy in the hospital and R&D department paused. Another, though, moved toward him. From the elevator doors, someone scurried around the corner and down the hallway. Darius groaned and ran his hands over his face as a nervous tickle ran up his spine. The hairs on the back of his neck stood up on end. The aura stopped just shy of the waiting room.

"What's wrong? What happened?" Jacob Locke asked.

Darius looked up to him. Jacob seemed more frayed than usual. His ball cap was gone, exposing a receding hairline of thin, curly hair, and he shoved his hands deep into the pockets of pants so wrinkled Darius was sure he was living in his car now. The chilling sensation that something wasn't right made Darius's stomach sick, and he looked back into the garage.

"They're going out there again," Darius said, indicating the doors. "And it's going to be bad."

"Why didn't you go?" Jacob hedged into the room.

Darius's teeth clenched. "Thorn won't let me."

Jacob let out a harsh scoff, and Darius turned to him. "She thinks she knows what's best for everyone, but she doesn't. She's wrong. She's going to get people hurt."

Darius took a deep breath and looked back out the doors. Jacob shifted closer to him and cleared his throat.

"I'll take you," he said, drawing closer still until he was in Darius's peripheral vision.

For a moment, Darius thought about Thorn and what she'd said. That he wasn't *thinking* straight. But the sense of danger told him otherwise—it told him that something big was going to happen, and he couldn't help them if he were trapped down here.

Jacob was right. More people were going to die.

"Okay," Darius said, and Jacob's tongue darted out to wet his dry, chapped smile. "Let's go."

They rushed out of the Underground. Jacob headed straight for the navy SUV, and Darius realized why he hadn't thought it fit before. It wasn't one of the new cars Chris had ordered, equipped with the finest Martyr protective and tracking capabilities. It was Jacob's personal vehicle. He moved around the side, but as he did, the rear hatch flew open. Darius jumped back.

And Nicholas stepped down.

"Well," he said, loud and victorious. Jacob stood stone-still, like a child caught stealing. Something heavy and black dangled from Nicholas's hand. He held it up in Jacob's direction. "Look at what I—"

Jacob lunged forward with such blind ferocity that Darius hardly had the time to process what happened as he grabbed Nicholas by the face and slammed his head into the back corner of his car. The glass around the rear light shattered, cutting into Nicholas's scalp, drenching the shoulders of his blue button-up in a gush of deep red blood. Jacob threw him to the side, and Darius's jaw dropped.

Then Jacob was upon him, too. He yanked Darius into him, wrapping his strong arms around his throat in a reverse chokehold. Darius gasped, pulling uselessly at Jacob's wrists to loosen his grip. "I thought," he spat out, "you couldn't hurt Martyrs?"

As his vision faded, as Darius gagged for a breath he couldn't take in, he looked down at Nicholas. At the item in his hands...

A gas mask.

The last thing he heard before he lost consciousness was Jacob growling in his ear.

"There are *no* Martyrs."

CHAPTER TWENTY-EIGHT

The clock on the dashboard read 7:00 p.m., but the sun was still high in the sky and showed no signs of falling soon. South Kearny was a speck on the map—an industrial district outside of a nothing town, vastly overshadowed by larger cities on all sides. Smokestacks from abandoned coal refineries jutted into the air, casting long, fat fingers of shade to the east. Thorn opened the door and stepped out, her boots grinding on the gravel lot as she looked around. By now, most people who worked in this area had gone home, leaving it oddly devoid of human sensation. She couldn't feel anyone.

"How do we know Leroy's still here?" Samira asked, getting out of the car and coming to Thorn's side.

"We don't," Thorn admitted, taking a low, slow breath. "I Programmed my Sentries to tell him to wait for you before they message me. I hoped that would keep him from running, but who knows if they had the chance to do it. Holly's camera showed him headed toward Pennsylvania Avenue. I couldn't tell you where the hell he went afterward."

"Can we check other cameras?"

"There aren't other cameras," Thorn said, looking up at

the South Kearny Yard main office. The old, brick building had been painted beige to make it look less dilapidated than it actually was. A tiny lens dangling off the back corner pointed at a tall, locked fence, behind which was the train car Leroy had been caught climbing out of.

Samira's shoulders heaved up in a massive sigh. "I wish I could feel him," she said. Then she glanced up at Thorn. Thorn had never really considered how much shorter Samira was until this moment. The desperate, hopeful glint in her brown eyes made her seem younger, more childlike than before. "He'll be drawn to me, though, right? Like Virtues are drawn together?"

Thorn looked back down the abandoned road and shook her head. "No," she said. "Virtues pull on each other, which is why you get a sense of direction. This is different. Leroy doesn't feel *you*. He feels the effect of your Virtue on his soul. Think about it like a wireless signal. When you're close enough, your phone connects to it, and the closer you are to the source, the stronger it feels, but you have no idea what way you've got to go to find it. At least, that's how Alan explained it to me."

The empty pit in Thorn's chest constricted, and Samira frowned. "You've never felt the Virtue against Wrath?"

Thorn's teeth pressed together. "No," she said bitterly. "Come on, let's go."

They locked the car and began to walk away from the South Kearny Yard, heading into the sun. Thorn squinted and covered her eyes with a flat palm while she looked at her phone. A map shined back at her, showing five blinking green points driving in a perimeter around the whole town: Chris and her TAC teams, securing the area to prevent the Sins from getting in and Leroy from getting out. If he hadn't already.

They walked for a quarter of a mile, never finding themselves any closer to another human being than they had when they parked. Their left was dominated by a sprawling power plant, its older, unused amenities still on-site even though solar and nuclear energy had largely replaced fossil fuels decades ago. The sun reflected off an impressive array of panels while powerlines crisscrossed above, and every so often, Thorn would feel a fleeting point of cold human aura appear and disappear as workers checked on units deep in the field.

To the right, the road pushed up against a rainbow ocean of enclosed trailers. Boxy, beaten-up cargo containers as far as the eye could see. Sparkie flew in graceful figure-eights above, on the lookout for someone moving between or hiding inside of them. He focused further back, at the edge of where Thorn assumed Leroy would start to feel Samira's Virtue. She peered through the gaps, hoping to spot something…

But there was nothing. For all she knew, Leroy was already in New York—already with the Sins.

Several minutes passed in silence. They hit a fork in the road, turned left, and found more of the same. Warehouses. Storage cubes. Big trucks. There were more people in this direction. Thorn felt a cluster of cold auras approach as they wandered along the curb—there weren't even sidewalks out here—and she gazed up at a sign in the distance. The security office. Thorn doubted Leroy would have come anywhere close to a building with the word "security" slapped onto it. Her jaw clenched, and she glanced down at Samira.

If she was feeling disheartened, she didn't show it. Samira's face set into a determined look Thorn wasn't used to seeing on her. She decided to follow her lead—to go until Samira felt like it was time to call it quits.

It was her husband they were chasing, after all. Thorn knew how hard it was to search for the people you loved when the Sins could have them. She understood that desperate hope and how it was the only thing that kept you going sometimes.

"So," Thorn said, checking her device again. Chris had sent a round of updates, all boring and uneventful. No sign of Leroy. No sign of the Sins. For some reason, that wasn't encouraging. She pocketed the phone and focused on Samira to ignore the unsettled feeling in her gut. "What do you plan to do once we find Leroy?"

Samira turned to Thorn for the first time since they'd begun to walk, a frown pulling at her lips. "I don't really have one," she murmured thoughtfully. "All I want is to get him back. I'll worry about the rest after."

Thorn nodded just as Sparkie caught something in the distance. He veered hard to the left while Thorn looked at the horizon—not at the ground, but at something dangling above it.

An animal, perched at the top of a massive transmission tower, peered down at them from one hundred and fifty feet in the air. Thorn's heart skipped a beat.

"Look," she said, pointing into the sky, and she started to jog toward it. The animal vaulted downward, expertly making its way to the ground as Sparkie dove closer. The nearer he came, the harder it was to ignore, and the faster Thorn ran. A bushy, orange tail bounced through metal beams and brackets. Sparkie circled the tower, catching wind under his wings and spinning with a flourish.

"He's here," Thorn said. She slammed to a stop at a chain-link fence. Rolling coils of barbed wire lined the top, and though Thorn had no problem plowing over it, she knew Samira couldn't. Sparkie arched overhead, diving gracefully onto her shoulder as Samira reached her side.

"How do you know?" she asked through heavy breath. Thorn turned toward her, confused, but her chest twinged as it suddenly occurred to her…

Samira had never met Leroy's Familiar.

Sparkie chirped as a tiny, furry thing wedged beneath the fence, fighting through a knotted mess of weeds growing into the links. Samira stared, her lips parted in awe, as the red squirrel detangled itself.

Then it jumped onto her, squealing wildly. It climbed the folds of loose fabric until it reached her shoulder. Samira shrieked and took a few steps back, but when the squirrel pressed its little face to the underside of her chin, she froze. Her eyes went wide and filled with tears as she raised a hand to the animal. A fuzzy head rubbed against her shaking fingers.

"This is…" Samira began, staring up at Thorn, but her voice was too tight to finish the sentence.

Thorn smiled and nodded. "Leroy's," she said. "They've missed you."

A blustering, desperate laugh erupted from Samira's mouth, and that laugh turned to sobs as she clutched the creature nuzzled up against her throat. For a moment, Thorn was swept up in it, her chest stinging as Sparkie flattened his cold body against her. She shook her head, grabbed Samira by the elbows, and steadied her on her feet. The Virtue looked up, tears dripping down her cheeks, and Leroy's squirrel peeked through her fingers.

"He'll know where we are," Thorn said. "Let's go get him."

Samira nodded, and she let go of her husband's Familiar. The animal ruffled its bright, orange fur, ran its back and tail across Samira's jawline, and leapt to the ground. Then it turned and took off back the way they'd come. Thorn followed it into the middle of the road.

A man was sprinting toward them. A towering man with umber skin, broad shoulders, and no soul.

"Samira!" he screamed.

Samira began to sob again. She covered her mouth with her hands, her whole body shaking, as she cried Leroy's name and ran to him. Thorn kept her distance. Gave them space. When the two finally met, Leroy wrapped his arms around Samira's middle. He eclipsed her, his massive frame overshadowing hers by miles. Thorn expected him to lift her up from the ground, but instead, he fell to his knees. He collapsed, embracing her with all of who he was, his face burrowed beneath her chin as she cradled his head in her arms. The squirrel joined them, burying itself in Samira's silky, black hair until it all but disappeared.

Thorn stood back and watched. She could do almost nothing else.

Except take out her phone, open a line to Chris, and send a quick message.

"We've got him."

"God, Samira," Leroy said, his husky voice grinding with emotion, muffled against her collar. "Thank God."

He was filthy, his whole body coated in a fine layer of white dust that made his washed-out jeans and black shirt look nearly the same color. It embedded into his textured hair, beneath his nails, even in the creases lining his face. Samira didn't seem to mind. He tilted his head up to her, and she grabbed the sides of his face fervently, pressing her lips hard against his. Thorn averted her gaze, looked down at her device, and read Chris's response.

"Good. No sign of the Sins."

That should have been a relief. Thorn frowned.

Why wasn't it a relief?

"Hey," she said, clearing her throat. Samira and Leroy pulled apart just far enough to turn their faces toward her. "We've got to go."

Samira nodded and dabbed at her eyes with the backs of her hands, but no matter how many times she swiped them away, the tears kept falling. Thorn walked toward them as they got to their feet, and Leroy stepped in front of his wife. Thorn bristled, but he extended a hand. She paused, then took it. His grip was firm.

"Thank you," he said. His dull, brown eyes glistened, and his voice cracked. "I owe you everything."

Thorn didn't know what to say to that, so she just nodded.

The walk back to the vehicle felt longer. With Leroy at her side, his hand in hers, Samira seemed less hurried. Thorn strode a few paces ahead of them, listening to the small talk, the catching up without actually discussing things they'd rather say in private, but her mind was elsewhere. Worrying. Wondering.

When Alan called, Thorn's stomach was already tied up in knots.

"We found him," Thorn said upon answering as she unlocked her SUV, hoping that's all this was—hoping Alan just wanted an update.

"We have a situation," he said instead. Thorn froze with her fingers on the handle. Samira and Leroy stopped on the far side of the vehicle. Thorn felt their attention on her.

"What happened?"

"I'm sending you a message," Alan stated. Thorn threw her door open and stepped inside. Samira and Leroy climbed into the back, closing themselves in as Thorn started the engine. The screen on the dash glowed up at her, and Alan's text displayed upon it. "I got this five minutes ago from an encrypted source. Miss Andrews can't trace it."

It was a set of coordinates followed by a note.

"I have Darius. Meet me at 8:30. Come alone, or he dies."

A dull, rushing panic ripped through Thorn, pulling the air from her lungs and the thoughts from her head. She stared at the screen, vaguely aware of Samira and Leroy doing the same behind her. Sparkie let out a harsh cry from her shoulder.

"We have checked the whole Underground, and Darius is not here," Alan continued. Fury rumbled under the surface, rolling in Thorn's chest, filling the cavity with heat. "We did, however, discover his phone and watch, as well as Mr. Wolfe tied, sedated, and bleeding behind a vehicle in the corner of the garage."

The fury faltered as Thorn's eyes shot wide open. "You found *Nicholas?*"

"Unconscious," Alan said, as though to clarify. Thorn shook her head as he went on. "Elijah is—"

"Fuck," Thorn cut in, throwing the car into drive and peeling away from the side of the road. "It's Jacob."

"Pardon?"

"Jacob is working with the Sins," Thorn said, her heart pounding. They flew down the country road toward the highway. "It's not DuPont. It's Jacob. Fuck!"

There was a pause on the other end of the line. "If he is working with the Sins, this must be a trap."

"Call Chris," Thorn said. "Send her the coordinates. Get her teams there as soon as possible, but have them keep their distance, a block perimeter, then send the rest of TAC in—everyone who's cleared for duty. I'm going to drop Samira and Leroy off at the Underground. Then I'm headed in, too."

"Be quick," Alan said. The grim tone of his voice made Thorn want to scream.

"I will."

She disconnected the call and roared, slamming her palms on the wheel. As she made to turn right and get onto the I-9 Westbound, a warm hand landed on her shoulder. She whipped around.

Samira had wedged between the chairs behind her, and she watched Thorn with a steady, resolute expression.

"Let's go get Darius," she said.

Thorn put the car in park so quickly that it jolted forward, and she turned around in her seat. Leroy sat behind his wife, his jaw dropped, eyes wide, displaying every ounce of surprise twisting inside Thorn's gut. His familiar chittered, agitated, on Samira's shoulder.

"There are going to be Sins there," Thorn said. "It's dangerous."

"I know," Samira said. "But Darius needs us. He needs *you*. You got us out of Georgia. Without you, we'd be dead. We can't let them get to him. We just... we can't."

Thorn's lips parted, and she glanced over Samira's shoulder. "You good with that?" she asked Leroy. Samira turned to him, too, and he looked between the two women for a moment before he nodded.

"Where Samira leads," he said, placing a palm on her thigh and squeezing tight, "I'll follow."

Thorn nodded, grateful, relieved, and furious, as she turned back to the road, threw the car into drive again, and took a hard left. They surged onto the freeway toward New York City as the sun dropped lower in the sky.

———————————

Darius sucked in a gasp, his heart pounding so fervently that his whole chest cavity felt like a drum. The beat intensified, making his breathing faster, harder, and his shoulders shook in chills that left him incapacitated for a moment. His face was pressed up against musty, gray upholstery. Rough fibers scratched against his cheek and caught to the stubble on his chin as he turned his head to look around, but he couldn't make sense of where he was. The world seemed to move. The light changed—brighter, darker, and bright again—and a familiar rushing sound filled his ears. Warm, human energy was all around him, flowing nearer and further. He didn't recognize any of it. Without warning, Darius was thrown to the side, his hip slamming into a wall, and he winced through his teeth.

A car. He was in the cargo area of an SUV.

For a few helpless seconds, Darius tried to reposition himself, but his arms were trapped behind his back. He yanked at them only to feel plastic bonds digging painfully into his wrists. His ankles were tied, too. The pit of his stomach sank. Darius rolled onto his back, a shot of pain moved through his shoulders, and he groaned.

The vehicle jolted before straightening out again.

"Jacob?" Darius called. No response. Darius wormed his way back to his belly, anchoring his shoulder into the upholstery to get the leverage he needed to pull his knees up beneath him. They turned left, and Darius lost his balance, slamming down again. "Damn it!" He turned back over, this time successfully propping himself up, and he leaned his weight into the corner between the back window and rear seat. All he could see of Jacob was a blurry outline. Darius closed his eyes and shook his head.

"Jacob!"

Again, Jacob didn't respond. Didn't even move. Darius tried to look out the tinted window and get a sense of where they were, but his eyes still wouldn't focus. Had he been drugged?

"Where are you taking me?" he asked.

Still nothing.

Darius sighed and tilted his face against the leather headrest. It was cool, and the clammy sweat on his forehead slid against it. He could practically hear Thorn when they found out what had happened to him. Here Darius goes again, doing something *stupid* because he wasn't *thinking straight*.

He had to think straight now.

For a few moments, Darius considered his situation. Jacob was clearly having an episode, and somehow, his Programming had been affected. Darius had no idea if anyone knew he was missing. Otherwise, he was fine. Aside from the tingling in his hands and feet, he didn't seem hurt. His pockets were empty, and the watch had been torn from his wrist, which meant he had no tracking device on him. Panic tightened between his lungs.

"You don't have to do this, man," Darius shouted to the front of the car, hoping to reason with Jacob enough to get the man talking. Maybe if he could convince him to remove these bindings, Darius would have the chance to use his Influence. It wouldn't be a long-term solution, but it could get him out of the back of this damn car.

Jacob, however, continued to ignore him. He turned toward the left. The sun changed again, glaring off a flat surface in the distance. A body of water?

Darius shook his head. His vision was improving, and he could make out the things closest to him. Piles of folded clothes. Water bottles and a garbage bag filled with food wrappers. A handgun—Darius's heart skipped a beat—sitting next to a black gas mask on the ground.

Jesus, that was right. The thing Nicholas had confronted Jacob about. It had been the gas mask.

He lowered himself to the floor in the back of the SUV,

his heart lodged in his throat. A tight pain bolted through his shoulders as he rested against his arms. The binding around his wrists pulled so tightly he thought it might cut into him, but he pushed through it as he angled his feet toward the rear window. Darius gritted his teeth, drew his knees into his chest, and thrust his legs out with as much force as he could.

His heels slammed into the window. It groaned but didn't break. Darius kicked again. And again. That got Jacob's attention. He screamed something Darius couldn't make out, and suddenly they jerked to the left. Darius lost his momentum. As he went to kick again, the movement yanked him around, and he slammed his feet into the siding instead. The SUV hurled to a stop. Before Darius had a chance to right himself, Jacob threw the hatchback open.

"Stop!" he roared, climbing into the vehicle while other cars on the highway sped past them. Darius cried out as Jacob pinned him down and got up in his face. His fingers were tight around Darius's collar. He wore a pair of driving gloves, guaranteeing Darius made no skin-to-skin contact. So much for Influencing his way out of this. "STOP. TALKING. I have a plan, and you're going to *ruin it*."

"Damn right I am," Darius said, trying to twist out of Jacob's grip, but the other man shoved a knee into Darius's chest to keep him from moving. He leaned over the back seat and shuffled around. When he returned, he had a roll of duct tape and a bundle of socks. As he pulled the socks apart, Darius shook his head. "You're trying to kill me!"

"No!" Jacob's eyes went wide. Manic. He pulled at his lower lip with his teeth, peeling the chapped skin back until he exposed the pink beneath. "This is *not. About. YOU.*" Jacob grabbed Darius by the face, digging his fingers into his cheeks until his jaw was forced open, and he shoved a sock inside. Then he ripped a length of duct tape free and slammed it over Darius's mouth. "Now *shut up*. Sit still. If you keep kicking, I'll knock you out."

Jacob pushed Darius back down and jumped out of the

SUV. Darius tried to get to his knees again, but as they peeled away from the edge of the highway, he rolled to the side. This time, he stayed there. His hands and feet were so numb he could hardly move them. Out the window, all he could see were clouds. He watched them turn from white to blood orange, wondering what Jacob was planning and how long it would take for the Martyrs to realize he was gone.

Minutes later, the clouds disappeared, swallowed up by concrete and shadow. Darius lifted his head, but he couldn't see more than a dark gray ceiling. The sensations were familiar, though: squealing tires, the vehicle turning in one direction, going up, up, up…

They were in a parking garage.

Suddenly, the sky came back. Rich sunset light blasted the tinted windows as Jacob stopped the SUV, grabbed the gun from the middle seat, and got out. Darius felt him walk away, and as the pattering of human life moved several stories below them, Jacob stood completely still. Darius didn't know for how long. The sun faded further. Orange shifted to navy, and just when Darius felt like his fingers were going to fall off, something tapped on the door by his feet. He looked down, and he gasped.

Sparkie peered at him through the glass.

A surge of desperate, grateful air pushed through Darius's nose as he nodded at the lizard. He watched Darius for a moment longer before vaulting upward and disappearing. An urgent, pleading hope made Darius's heart start racing again. How close was Thorn now?

He got his answer moments later—by the feeling of a Virtue nearing from somewhere below. His stomach twisted.

She'd brought Samira.

The pull stopped at the bottom level. As soon as it did, Jacob came sprinting back and threw open the SUV. He was hard to see in the growing darkness as he tossed a pair of binoculars onto the ground and grabbed Darius by the shoulders.

"Coward," he hissed, dragging Darius out. "He's a fucking *coward!*"

"Who?" Darius tried to ask, but the word came out muffled against the sock inside his mouth. The muscles in his jaw hurt from being forced open for so long. Jacob didn't acknowledge him as he tugged Darius out of the vehicle. They were at the top level of a parking garage. It was dim, lit only by six lights along the two outermost edges. He couldn't see much more than that. Jacob grabbed Darius by the elbows, wrenched him around, and pressed the barrel of the pistol against his temple. Darius's heart stopped.

Across the top floor of the parking garage, he saw Thorn.

CHAPTER TWENTY-NINE

Seventy feet and a dozen cars separated them, a gulf of concrete and steel. The sun was setting behind Thorn's back, outlining the silhouette of her body in an eerie, dusky glow. Her features were swallowed up in the dark, but she marched across the rooftop with a violent purpose, like a tsunami barreling to the shore. Jacob moved back, dragging Darius with him, as Thorn's arms raised and pointed in their direction. Darius didn't need to see the gun to know it was there.

Three more steps, and she came into the light. Her fierce, black eyes locked onto Jacob's, and her mouth hardened into an unforgiving line. Sparkie sat on her shoulder. Darius felt like the animal was looking right at him.

For a moment, they stood in silence.

"How long have you been working for the Sins, Locke?" Thorn asked at last.

Jacob's grip around Darius's arms tightened. Cool metal quivered against his head. "You think you know everything," Jacob snarled. "You think you're *so smart!* But you have *no idea* what you're talking about."

"You're right. I don't," Thorn said. Her dark voice was steady, but under the surface, under the calm, Darius heard the fire. It made her words sharper. Quicker. "So, why don't you tell me?"

Jacob didn't speak. Darius heard the wet sound of him licking his lips by his ear and swallowing hard. Thorn's eyes locked onto him, her form steady and perfect, ready to pull the trigger the second she saw an opening.

"Why did you send the Sins to the garden?" she pressed. Still nothing. Nothing but harsh breathing and gloved fingertips digging into Darius's flesh. "Lina died—"

"She wasn't supposed to *be there!*" Jacob roared, his voice so sudden and so loud that Darius stumbled to the side. Sparkie perked up on Thorn's shoulder as Jacob pulled him back to shield himself more fully, and he kept screaming. "She wasn't the one who was supposed to get hurt!"

"Who was?" Thorn asked.

"*You!*"

Thorn's brows shot high on her head, and her eyes went wide—two black circles surrounded by pools of hard, stark white. The line of her mouth parted just enough to take in a low, quiet gasp.

And the admission poured off Jacob's tongue in a flood of stinking, rotting hatred.

"I knew *you* would go!" he screamed. "I sent them there—sent you after them—but they fucked up! Again!"

Thorn's jaw dropped further. *"Again?"*

"I could never be strong enough to get rid of you," Jacob went on, throwing words like daggers across the lot, trying to land one in Thorn's chest. "But the Sins—the *Sins!* They are! I sent them after you here, but you had too much help. These people you've brainwashed—they'll protect you! They'll fucking *die for you.* So I thought, maybe Washington. Maybe Georgia. When you're alone. But no! The Sins were too scared! *Even the Sins are fucking scared of you!*"

Finally, Jacob stopped. His breath was hot against the back of Darius's neck, sending a sickening, moist discomfort down his spine. Thorn stared at him, and Sparkie, still, watched Darius. At last, she shook her head.

"Why do you want to kill me?"

"Because you *destroyed* the Martyrs!" Jacob's whole body shook now, and the gun pointed at Darius's head shook with him. He nearly lost his balance, and Jacob heaved him upward again. Sparkie bristled as Jacob kept ranting. "You and all the corrupted like you! Blaine! DuPont! That guy from the cemetery! You think you're doing the right thing, but you *can't* because you're *fucking broken*. You throw us into your battles. You lie to us. You get into our brains and change our memories to keep us complacent."

Thorn's eyes opened even wider. "Jacob—"

"*I killed my little girls,*" he roared, nearly sobbing. Darius flinched as the gun pressed harder to his temple. "I killed my wife! You knew, and you hid it from me, and you let me come here and hurt more people! You're getting people killed, and it needs to stop!"

Then Jacob shook his head. "No. We need to start over. No corruption. No *poison*. The new Martyrs without the Sins' evil growing inside!"

Thorn was losing him—Darius could tell she knew it. She took a half-step backward, and Jacob came toward her, forcing Darius ahead of him. He was shaking harder now, his grip on Darius less controlled, but the pistol still pointed at his head. It was only a matter of time before he pulled the trigger, and Darius had no intention of dying here tonight. He threw a look to Sparkie then gestured his chin toward the ground. The reptile's head tilted.

"And you think you're the person to put this together?" Thorn asked. "This new order of Martyrs?"

"No!" Jacob yelled. "*He* is." His fingers tightened on Darius's arm as he jostled him front to back. "When I get you and Blaine and the others out of the way, *I'm* doing the right thing. Ending my life, like you should have let me do twenty fucking years ago."

He took another step toward Thorn. Darius hopped forward on his bound feet one last time, looking at Sparkie, then at the ground, hoping to god the animal understood.

Jacob's voice practically whispered by his ear as he glared at Thorn.

"Put that gun in your mouth," he told her, "and pull the fucking trigger, or Darius dies, and the Martyrs die with him."

Sparkie nodded at Darius, and Darius went limp. His full, dead weight pulled toward the ground, and Jacob scrambled to hold him. A gunshot went off over his head, then another, deafening him as he slammed to his knees and then to his face on the concrete floor. The warmth of Jacob's aura snapped as he collapsed behind Darius. A loud, sharp ringing clouded his senses, and he couldn't focus.

Then someone took him by the shoulders and pulled him up. Thorn filled his view. She grabbed his face, her hands cool against his skin as she tore the tape off his mouth. He cried out, or he tried to, but the sock was in the way, so he forced it out with his tongue and inhaled a deep, freeing breath. Thorn was still holding his head, and she said something to him, but he couldn't hear it over the tone in his ears. Sparkie's smooth body pressed against his numb fingers as he chewed through the plastic zip-tie clasping Darius's wrists together, and Thorn grabbed a knife from her pocket and cut the binding at his feet. Darius glanced back at Jacob Locke lying dead on the ground behind him. His brown eyes were open, just as intense in death as they had been in life, staring at the night sky. A single, clean hole cut into his head above his brow.

Thorn's voice finally started to come through. It was muffled like he was hearing it through cotton.

"—okay?"

"What?" he asked, shouting over the roaring in his brain.

"Are you okay?" she repeated. Her hand came toward his face again, a frown on her lips, and she gently touched his jawline by his right ear. When she came back, her fingertips were dabbed in blood. "Fuck. Your eardrum ruptured."

He thought that's what she said, at least, but she was only at half-volume. Darius reached up to his ear, but he couldn't feel anything. His fingers and toes burned as sensation rushed back into them. He looked to Thorn. She was getting back up, and she held her hand out to help him do the same.

But as soon as he put weight on his feet, he crumbled and hit the ground again. He swore, and Thorn moved to his left.

"We've got to go," she said as she pulled his arm over her shoulder and wrapped hers around his waist. Her voice was louder on this side, and he glanced at her. She started toward the stairwell at the far end of the lot while Sparkie took to the sky and disappeared in the night. "The Sins are coming. We're barricading the garage."

They tore across the rooftop. Thorn supported Darius's weight effortlessly, like he was just an extension of herself. By the time they reached the stairs, Darius's feet had begun to gain feeling again. First, it was painful—the hot, sharp sting of knives being driven into his heels. By the time they reached the third level, the pain had faded to rolling static, like having bare soles swarming with ants, but the hairs along the back of Darius's neck stood up on end.

Samira's Virtue was moving upward, circling in their direction while the bottom floor flooded with hot, human energy. Indistinct sounds—Darius couldn't make them out—bombarded his injured ears in a swirling mess that could have been anything. An explosion rocked through his feet, and he stumbled backward.

Suddenly, Thorn pulled him away from the stairwell, tucked behind a nearby truck, and forced him to his knees. Samira's Virtuous pull roared up in a maroon SUV. The vehicle veered to the side, parking longways across the driving lane, and the doors flew open. Samira and Leroy leapt down. Another TAC car followed and mimicked their maneuver. Thorn waved them over.

When Samira whipped around the corner, she gawked at Darius. He was vaguely aware of his name coming out of her mouth, but it sounded clouded and distant. A little red squirrel sat on Samira's shoulder, watching as she grabbed

Darius's face in her hands. Hot, healing energy poured through his head and deep into his ear canals. It was like coming up for air. In a rush, his hearing cleared, and the world around him was howling.

Sirens. Gunshots. Eight TAC members screaming to each other as they crouched at the top of the stairwell or behind the wall of cars. Another two black-clad Martyrs ran across the third floor, away from the opposite set of stairs, which was filling with smoke. Below them, around them, people pushed in. Blue and red emergency lights glowed through the open walls, adding to the warm color of the yellow bulbs above. Darius turned back to Thorn, aghast, as she shoved a kevlar vest into his hands. She wasn't wearing one anymore. The blood drained from his face.

How many times was she going to give up her protection for him? Because *he* did something stupid and got them into a situation like this?

"You wanted field duty," Thorn said, pushing the armor further against him. "Welcome to field duty."

Darius's mouth went dry as a wall of heat drew nearer, riding a wave of siren calls. "What's the plan?" he asked as he threw the vest around his shoulders, but he struggled with the straps. Thorn forced his hands away and began to tighten them for him.

"Moore's on scene," she said. Leroy hovered over her shoulder, a tower of dust and anger as he looked out at the garage. Thorn went on. "Wrath, Greed, and Lust are closing in, but so is our backup. We're going to hold out here until they arrive."

"What was that explosion?" Darius asked.

"We destroyed the other stairs from level two, so they can't climb up," Thorn said. "Makes it easier to defend. There." She cinched the last strap on his vest and pressed her hand against it, lingering for a moment, fingers splayed right over Darius's heart. She looked up to meet his eyes. There was a terror behind them he didn't often see.

"Stay with me," she said.

He nodded.

"Thorn!" Chris shouted. Like the rest of TAC on-site, she wore basic gear over her standard uniform, and she hoisted a rifle into her hands, the barrel pointed at the ceiling. Behind her, a solitary shot vibrated up the stairwell. "We've got vehicles blocking both entrances, but Moore's police are moving in on foot."

"Khoury!" Thorn shouted, turning to Leroy as she got to her feet and tightened the ponytail at the base of her skull. "Are they Puppets?"

"The ones inside are," Leroy said with a nod.

"Then cut them off," Thorn commanded.

For the next few minutes, the garage filled with hot energy and hotter bullets. Chris bellowed orders into her headset, and the Tactical team expertly defended both the stairs and the blockade of cars cutting level three off from everything below them. Underfoot, a group of Puppetted officers moved forward, shooting around the corner whenever an opportunity presented itself. Leroy stood by Seth Graves, who was kneeling behind the Martyrs' bulletproof cars on the front line. His eyes narrowed as he fell into the void between worlds. Every so often, one of the cops closing in collapsed, but another would immediately take their place, running in from the ground floor.

The whole time, Thorn moved, and Darius tracked her. Somehow, she seemed to stand taller than the rest—armorless, wielding nothing more than a handgun that she hadn't had to use yet—as she assisted TAC and dragged wounded off the line for healing.

A gunshot went off, someone screamed, and Thorn and Darius ran in. Seth fell backward, blood pouring from a wound by his shoulder. Darius rushed to his left, Thorn to his right, and together they pulled him back toward the stairwell. Samira was tucked behind a concrete wall there, where she couldn't be spotted by the Puppets coming in. As soon as they were out of the line of fire, she came forward.

"Take it easy!" Thorn shouted over a new round of

gunfire. The Martyrs at the line ducked down, shot back, and Darius felt a point of warm energy beyond the barricade disappear. He pushed his palm under Seth's helmet and touched his skin. Healing power poured into him, and Thorn pointed a finger at Darius's face. "Pace yourselves!"

"Here." Samira placed her hand beside Darius's and took over. Her fingers shook, her dark skin dusky, but she kept calm. Darius had to give her credit. She was handling this better than he would have this early in his life with the Martyrs.

"How you holding up?" he asked her.

She glanced over her shoulder, where another warm energy collapsed. Leroy's Familiar stuck with her, clinging to her vest with tiny claws.

"Praying for a rescue," Samira said. "But I won't be waiting for one."

The auras beneath them shifted. A new surge neared the building, and Thorn's voice called across the concrete cavern.

"Get ready," she said. "Lust and Greed just joined the party."

"Preserve your ammunition," Chris screamed from the front line. She knelt by the hood of the maroon SUV. The metal was dented and warped from bullet fire. "We've got to make it last!"

Thorn swore and turned around, reaching out to grab Seth, now fully healed. She hauled him to his feet, and as he rushed back into the fight, Darius looked up at her. "How close is backup?"

"Ten, maybe fifteen minutes," Thorn said, touching her earpiece, eyes darting across the garage.

More people came at them now. Two forces so large Darius assumed each held at least twenty Puppets pushed around the cars blocking the entrance and exit. He shook his head.

"And Wrath?" he asked. Thorn looked down at him, meeting his eye. "How close is she?"

The expression on Thorn's face told him he didn't want to know the answer.

A greater surge of people flooded up the garage. The Martyrs were outnumbered six to one. Gunshots went from intermittent to never-ending, and swaths of civilians sprinted up the driving lane toward the Martyrs' blockade. Thorn moved more than ever, informing TAC of Puppet locations and working with Darius to drag the wounded away for healing and put them right back in the line of fire. Leroy's Influence was hardly enough now—every time he cut a soul off from Gluttony, it felt like more came in to take its place. A bullet slammed into the concrete ceiling, tearing pieces off and showering them with gray powder.

Another hit a Martyr in the throat.

"Fuck!"

Thorn rushed forward, Darius on her heels. They turned him over, but his energy had already disappeared. Darius shook his head, his lungs tight, but Thorn immediately tore the dead man's helmet off and shoved it into Darius's hands. "Take it," she said as she started removing his vest, too.

While she strapped the armor around her chest, Darius slipped back to where Samira was still tucked behind the wall, keeping low, ducking below the new rainfall of cement dust pouring over their shoulders. She grabbed him as soon as he came up.

"Are you okay?"

Darius nodded and handed the helmet to her. "Here. Put this on. This is gonna get worse before it gets better."

The color left Samira's cheeks, but she pulled the helmet over her head all the same. It wasn't the right size for her—too big, the way the vest was too big—but better than nothing. Darius turned back toward the firefight just in time to see Thorn dragging the dead Martyr away from the endless spray of bullets. When she noticed Samira wearing the helmet, her eyes darkened, and she looked at him.

But she didn't say anything about it. Instead, she tapped

her headset and said, "Wrath's here."

A hot, angry mob of energy pushed in below them, easily doubling the number of Puppets already in the building. The blood drained from Darius's face as he looked at Thorn.

"How many people can she control?" he called over the screaming and shooting.

"Too fucking many," Thorn snarled.

They plowed into the garage. A horde of mindless, helpless victims at the end of Autumn Hunt's fingertips, running mechanically through the other Puppets, between battered and beaten cars, and right toward the Martyrs with no regard to the lives Wrath was willing to sacrifice for them. Chris screamed something else to her people that Darius couldn't understand. More gunshots went off, but he couldn't tell if they hit their marks—couldn't tell if people were getting killed because now all the hot energy was so crammed in together there was no way to tell it apart anymore.

Smoke started filling the third floor, and Samira grabbed his hand.

"They're telling us to go up!" she shouted as Chris began to direct people into the stairwell. Thorn and Seth moved down the steps to maintain control over the Puppets trying to get in there, taking shots at people as they came in from the second story. The rest of TAC backed through, lobbing black devices over the masses. They exploded in light and sound and smoke, creating more confusion in the chaos. Leroy all but lifted Samira off the ground as they headed to the fourth level. A cut on his forehead had already healed, but a streak of blood dripped down the side of his face. Darius followed on their heels.

As soon as their last man came through the ingress, Thorn and Seth moved up—Seth shooting, Thorn reaching out with her Influence and snapping people off from Wrath without lifting a finger—leaving a barricade of unconscious bodies behind them. Darius felt Puppets roll forward. A wave of warmth washed over the cars, around the corner, and headed toward them from the other side.

They were going to be surrounded.

Thorn seemed to sense it. She pulled back, and Chris stepped in to take her place, securing the stairs as Thorn sprinted up them two at a time and joined the rest at the top. She did a quick headcount—and Darius did the same. Seven. Including Chris and Seth, they only had seven TAC officers left. Thorn swore and looked out the open wall to the ground below, where blue and white police lights blared up at them.

She snapped back to face Darius, Samira, and Leroy.

"You," she said, pointing at Leroy. "Cut off any cops. The fewer guns we've got to worry about, the better. You two—" she indicated Darius and Samira this time "—take cover."

Then she started to head away, but Darius followed her.

"I can fight," he said. While the rest of TAC rushed past her, Thorn spun around to argue, but Darius kept talking. "You *know* I can. We need all the help we can get!"

For a moment, as the warm energy below drew nearer, the pounding of several dozen feet echoing up and around them, Thorn stared at him. Her jaw slammed shut, and her black eyes filled with fury and fear. At last, she nodded, took a step toward him, and pushed her pistol into his hands. She held it against his palms for a breath, her fingers tight around his.

"Keep close," she said. "Don't get yourself fucking killed."

They ran around the driving lane and tucked in behind a van. The other five TAC officers were already in position while Leroy stayed with Samira. He barricaded her behind a concrete wall near the stairwell and stood in front of it like he was made of steel instead of flesh and bone. Darius swallowed hard as Sparkie swooped in through the walls and perched upon his shoulder.

Puppets started coming.

At first, it was slow. A man or woman sprinting around

the corner. TAC would shoot them in the leg, knocking the Influence right out of them with a little bit of pain, or Thorn tapped into her link to Wrath and cut them off. But then, the swell came. More than two dozen people rushed up to the fourth floor, a disorienting mix of armed and armored cops with civilians. Darius took a shot here or there, aiming low, hitting people in the thighs or abdomen, but it wasn't slowing the drove. They moved with an inhuman urgency—single-focused and hive-minded. There were too many of them. The Martyrs couldn't stop them all.

They slammed into the front line. Hand-to-hand combat replaced firearms. Thorn flew through them like a machine, ducking, dodging, and deflecting. She knocked a hole in the wall of human energy. People fell around her with the violence of a hailstorm. Bodies cracked to the concrete and didn't move again.

But Puppets still got around her.

A man rushed toward Darius, and he ducked, driving an elbow into his thigh. The Puppet crashed to his knees, and Darius swung his pistol like a club, clocking the poor guy right in the temple. He went down at Darius's feet just as another warm burst of energy came up behind him. He threw his arms out as a shield as a woman grabbed for his throat. Darius knocked her to the side, and her empty, emotionless eyes locked onto his as he forced the heel of his palm into her nose. The link to whichever Sin controlled her shattered, and she collapsed, too.

When Darius turned again, though, his eyes widened. The swell pushed past Thorn. Around her. Surrounding her and the TAC team on all sides, piling onto people like fire ants on a fresh kill. Two. Three. Four people ran at him. Darius stepped back, avoiding one punch as Sparkie screamed and jumped from his shoulder to attack a different Puppet's face. Then another tackled Darius from the side. He landed hard on the concrete, slamming his chin into it. A sharp sting of pain moved up his jaw and into his teeth. Samira screamed from the other end of the room—

A deep, haunting howl poured through the garage.

Darius flipped around as a massive, black wolf dove onto the Puppet pinning him to the ground. Rae drove her fangs into the woman's shoulder and tore at her like a wounded animal. When she lost consciousness, Rae rose, and her maw split open. The building rang with an echoing, gravelly bark that made Darius's lungs contract and his blood run cold. More power moved in now—more human warmth pushing at the perimeter of the garage.

The force of Puppets inside split into two parts. More than half started retreating toward the main level. Rae stalked after them as someone grabbed Darius from behind and helped him to his feet. He turned around to see Chris, her cheeks red, sweat dripping down the sides of her face.

"Backup just got here," she told him as Seth rushed past her to help the other Martyrs on the fourth floor. Her eyes moved to Darius's chin, and he felt hot liquid dribbling down his neck. "I have orders to get you and Samira the hell out of here."

Darius glanced over his shoulder, where he felt the force of Martyrs starting to push forward, driving the remaining Puppets back down the garage. Thorn screamed commands and flew into the mindless civilians with a fury, holding them back. Sparkie suddenly appeared on Darius's shoulder again, clinging to the kevlar vest.

He turned to Chris and nodded.

She led him the opposite way, back toward where Samira and Leroy were waiting behind the stairwell wall, but before they reached it, the hairs along Darius's neck stood up. Samira's face paled, and she caught his eye, shaking her head. Leroy stepped in front of her. The muscles along his broad shoulders were tight and ready to snap.

Someone was moving up the steps—three auras Darius didn't recognize—and he gasped.

Terrance Moore filled the doorway, a semi-automatic rifle in his hands and armor stretching across his chest. He raised the weapon, and Darius grabbed Chris by the shoulders. They both hit the ground as a spray of bullets clattered against a concrete pillar. Moore's voice boomed around them in a laugh.

"If it isn't my old friend," the Sin taunted. "Not so brave now, are you, Kindness?"

He lowered the rifle, pointing it right at Darius's face. Chris scrambled in front of him, shielding his body with her own. Moore sneered and stepped forward, into the garage.

The second his boots hit the ground, Leroy tackled him.

"Leroy!" Samira cried.

Chris leapt up and shoved Darius away from where Gluttony and his Forgotten Sin grappled by the stairs, fighting for control of the rifle. Two armed, Puppetted police officers came up, pistols in their fists, as Chris sprinted back and grabbed Samira by the hand. One of the men pointed a gun at Chris's head, but the squirrel on Samira's shoulder let out a horrible, screeching cry as it vaulted onto his visor. The shot struck uselessly to the ceiling as Chris dragged Samira away from the fight.

Tight fingers wrapped around Darius's wrist, and Thorn shouted beside him.

"Let's go!"

She pulled Darius back down the ramp. Chris wrapped her arm around Samira as she continued screaming her husband's name, but they kept running. They rushed past Puppets and Martyrs, ignoring the fight as they tried to reach the ground floor. Sparkie swooped overhead, guiding them through the mayhem. Samira dragged behind, constantly looking over her shoulder until they rounded the edge and hit the next floor down. Thorn never left Darius's side, a constant, reliable figure.

Until a rush of hot energy barreled into her.

Thorn was thrown sideways and pinned against a car. Darius's gut seized as Autumn Hunt grabbed Thorn by the ponytail and threw her face into the back windshield. The glass broke against her forehead, spiderweb cracks flowing with crimson. Darius tried to turn, but Chris forced him forward.

"*Run!*" she screamed.

His heart torn in his chest, Darius glanced back at Thorn one last time as she roared and twisted around, but she disappeared as they moved onto the second floor. Smoke and dust filled this level. Dead and unconscious Puppets lay around their feet as the living and breathing stomped over them. Darius coughed and covered his mouth with his hand as Chris darted between cars, dragging him and Samira with her.

Someone took a shot at them. The bullet crashed into the armor on Chris's chest, knocking the wind from her lungs, and she fell back. Darius looked up to see Carlos Ruiz. Like Moore, Lust wore a ballistics vest over his clothes. Somehow, his sleek, styled hair seemed untouched, the black strands perfectly put together despite the concrete dust sprinkling down on him from above. His handsome expression warped with a sinister smile as he raised his gun again. Just before he pulled the trigger, he glanced to his left, and another body tackled him. Darius gaped.

Gabe DuPont.

Decked out in full TAC riot gear, Gabe used the butt of his rifle as a bludgeon, swinging it in an arch with all his weight and smashing it into Lust's face. The Sin's head snapped sideways, a cut slicing open across his cheekbone. When he turned back, all semblance of that cocky smile disappeared.

"Darius!" Samira yelled, and he turned to her. Chris was fighting for air on the ground. While Lust roared and came after Gabe, Darius knelt down. Samira tilted Chris's head back, and he shoved his fingertips under the top of her black turtleneck to find skin. He felt a cracked collarbone and two broken ribs pull themselves back into position. In the process, Darius's stomach gave an uncomfortable flip.

Chris suddenly took a deep, gasping breath, her green eyes wide, and she stood back up. Darius came with her and turned around. Gabe knelt on the ground at Lust's feet, three Puppets holding him back. When one ripped his helmet off his head, Lust pointed a pistol right between his eyes. The Sin grinned through the blood pouring from the healing cut across his face.

A shot went off from across the garage, and Lust flew backward. More than twenty energies crumbled at once, falling silent and still on top of other bodies and bloodshed. Darius's jaw dropped as the smallest TAC member he'd ever seen rushed up the drive. Mackenzie. He recognized her immediately by her fuzzy aura and the bright orange hair sticking out at the base of her helmet. She dashed to Gabe as he got to his feet and pointed her gun at the Sin. Carlos Ruiz convulsed on the ground, clutching his neck as he let out a harsh, inhuman scream…

And his aura disappeared as a massive, blue parrot materialized beside him.

The bird writhed on the concrete. It squawked madly, its shining, turquoise feathers picking up bits of stone and streaks of blood while it flapped around. Darius rushed over and grabbed Lust's face in his hands.

But it wasn't Lust. Not anymore. A man stared back, his half-empty eyes full of terror and confusion as he looked at Darius. He reached up, desperately trying to grab Darius's shirt. The flesh around the gaping wound in his throat began to mend.

Then Carlos Ruiz took a shuddering breath, his body seized one last time, and the bird disintegrated by Darius's knee. His heart pounded painfully in his throat as he looked back at Mackenzie and Gabe. Her eyes were wide behind the tinted visor, and her mouth parted in awe.

But it didn't last long. Someone roared furiously a floor above them, and when Darius got back to his feet, he turned to see Thorn sprinting through the mob. A shock of relief made his legs feel weak momentarily as she shoved her way through Puppets. Blood covered half of her face, and her fingers were coated in a gritty mix of red and black, but her eyes cut through the smoke and landed on Darius.

"Go!" she screamed. "Greed is pulling out! We've got to go!"

The remaining Martyrs turned and ran. They moved across the second floor toward the stairwell they'd been defending earlier. Bodies lay around it—unconscious and dead—and as they approached, Darius felt energy coming down from above. Samira felt it, too, and they glanced at one another.

As soon as they got past it, Leroy was thrown from the doorway. Samira screamed as her husband landed on the ground in a bloody heap. His nose was broken, one eye black and blue, and a healing bullet hole ripped through his shoulder, but he got to his feet. The red squirrel climbed up his arm, its tail twitching, as Gluttony stomped through the egress. He'd lost his weapon, and his dark face was a canvas of deep bruises and cuts. His broad mouth opened up in a snarl as he screamed, "You *son of a bitch!*" Then he snatched a pistol off the ground.

Thorn grabbed the gun out of Chris's hand and rapid-fired three shots into Terrance Moore's thigh, vest, and shoulder. The Sin howled in pain as he fell to one knee. Thorn went to pull the trigger again, but Samira jumped in front of her and forced her hands upward. The bullet clattered uselessly into the ceiling.

"Don't kill him!" she cried.

Thorn gawked, her black eyes glittering furiously. *"What?"*

But Samira didn't answer. Leroy limped forward on a damaged left leg and grabbed Moore from behind. He hooked his arms at the Sin's elbows and laced his fingers behind his neck, forcing the man to his knees with his hands above his head. Samira hurried up to him, and the Martyrs stopped retreating. Thorn and Darius exchanged a look, all too aware of Wrath and her Puppets turning the corner, sprinting down the lane toward them like a stampede.

Moore looked up, met Samira's eyes, and his mouth went slack. "You're—"

"Yes," Samira said. "I am."

She reached for his wrist. Moore was so much taller than her that she had to stretch. He thrashed, trying to escape Leroy's deadlock, but the Forgotten Sin braced himself and kept them still. Samira's hands wrapped around Moore's *Peccostium*, and the whole room slowed. Leroy's Familiar scampered to her, nuzzling up against her throat. She smiled. Her eyes filled with tears as she murmured something under her breath that Darius couldn't make out over Gluttony's furious roaring.

Then the garage erupted with light and sound. Samira's palms glowed with the white, hot intensity of a star, casting ghostly shadows across the concrete pillars and body-strewn floor. Air whipped around them, tearing through the garage, pulling into the open walls, and funneling down the drive with the force of a typhoon. The wind was so strong, so overwhelming, it stole the breath from Darius's lungs and sucked him forward. He fell to his knees, and Thorn landed beside him. Her hand found his on the concrete and gripped it tightly as she held the other up against the gale.

Moore was screaming. His voice contorted, the deep baritone rising and rising until it didn't sound human anymore. In the darkness, Gluttony's flesh glowed. He lit up like he was made of molten metal, the shadows of bone and sinew outlined against his skin. A plume of smoke burst from his lips and dilated nostrils, pouring from his eyes like hot, ashy tears. He choked out a deep, primal sob as his body shook in Leroy's arms.

And Leroy began to scream, too, through gritted teeth. A perfect circle of bright light glared from his right wrist. Samira's eyes went wide and fearful, but she didn't let go as she reached over Gluttony's head and pressed a palm against her husband's cheek.

Then a sharp, infernal cry exploded from Gluttony's throat, so loud, so high-pitched, that Darius thought his eardrum would rupture again. It pierced into his head, his body, his spirit, and Darius closed his eyes and hunched over, his jaw gnashed together.

When the screaming stopped, the wind died with it.

And Samira's Virtue disappeared.

Darius's head snapped up. Samira and Leroy stood together, the crumbling form of Terrance Moore falling to ash between them. The squirrel Familiar clinging to Samira's shoulder burst into a cloud of light and dust. Leroy's eyes went wide—dark circles on his gaunt face—and he sucked in lungfuls of desperate air. A warm, human aura suddenly materialized around him. Darius's mouth dropped open. He looked to Thorn to find her staring, too.

Then Samira stumbled into Leroy's arms. She gasped, her breathing fast-paced and panicked as she drew her hands toward her chest and clasped them together. He grabbed her by the shoulders and held her steady, speaking to her in quiet, loving tones.

Thorn let go of Darius's hand. She got to her feet slowly, Sparkie pressed up against her throat as she took a step forward. Darius moved to stand, too.

Wrath screamed. "NO!"

The word cracked like thunder, echoing through the concrete building in a violent rage. Darius jumped back as he looked to where Wrath was crouching twenty yards up the lane. Puppets lay in an unconscious mess around her feet, leaving her alone and unguarded. She grabbed a pistol off the ground. Thorn reached for one, too.

She didn't make it before the Sin fired six rounds into Samira.

They hit the armor on her shoulders and across her back, thudding into kevlar until the last two moved lower. Samira let out a strangled, guttural sound as the bullets landed in the small of her back, one after the other.

"Samira!" Leroy cried.

He fell to his knees, cradling Samira with one hand while the other pressed to her wounds. Blood surged through his fingers. The Martyrs ran past him, sprinting with Thorn as Wrath made for the open wall. Leroy kept screaming. "Help me! Someone, help!"

Darius pushed past Mackenzie, past Gabe, past Conrad and Chris and every other Martyr until he made it to Leroy's side and landed hard on the ground beside him. Samira's lips were already turning a dusky shade of blue. Darius's heart lodged in his throat as he lifted the back of her shirt and pressed his palms flat against the bullet wounds. The blood squirted out so hard it tried to force his fingers away, but Darius held tight.

Energy flooded out of him. It followed the path from Darius's soul, down his arms, and into his fingertips, where it joined with Samira and sank deep into her body. He felt the wounds—the fractured spine, the severed artery, the damaged nerves—and he directed his healing toward them. Bone began to click together, and tissue recovered, but Samira's body still convulsed in his hands. Her skin felt cold and clammy, and Darius's stomach buckled at the sickening warmth of blood soaking his jeans. A dangerous tickle ran up the base of his neck.

He ignored it.

The world around him started to fade away. He was vaguely aware of Wrath's energy tumbling down two stories to the ground floor below them, getting back up, and sprinting away. He hardly noticed as Martyrs ran to the stairs to try to head her off. The sounds of the garage swam in his ears, occluded and distant. All he felt was Samira, the bullets in her body trying to pinch their way out, and that little tickle growing to a roar. Goosebumps sprung up across his back and shoulders, down his arms, and his stomach filled with dread.

He should stop. He knew he had to stop.

But Samira shook again. She felt colder—too cold now that she didn't have an aura attached to her—and Darius was overwhelmed by the smell of iron and Leroy sobbing her name.

He couldn't lose another one.

So Darius pushed more energy into her. He pushed until

his vision went gray, his hearing dissolved, and the loudest sense he had was that of touch—the feeling of Samira in his hands, of a metal slug landing in his palm, of *something* fluttering onto his shoulders.

Then those shoulders shook, and he was aware of that, too...

"*DARIUS!*"

CHAPTER THIRTY

The first thing Darius noticed was the beeping.

A high-pitched, rhythmic tone. Every few seconds, it repeated itself, tapping on his awareness like a fingernail against glass. Hardly noticeable at first, but the more it tapped, the more annoying it became until it was all he could focus on.

Beep… Beep… Beep…

Next, he noticed his body. It seemed to be tapping him, too. On a tempo almost identical to the beeping but just off enough to be jarring, all his muscles tensed, held, and relaxed. For a few seconds, his world was an obnoxious cacophony of stimulation he had no control over. Beeping. Buzzing. Flexing. Relaxing.

Darius opened his eyes.

He was lying at an angle, slightly propped up, and the white expanse of a drop-panel ceiling spread out above him. The lights were blinding, and he tried to shield his eyes, but something pulled against his arm. His muscles were so weak that his hand felt like it was tied to a twenty-pound weight. With a frown, he looked down.

The hospital ward. Darius was in one of the private rooms in the hospital ward. Electrode patches dotted his arms and threaded up his gown, pulsing currents into his body that forced his muscles to move. The wiring tethered him to a machine by his side. It wasn't the only thing. An IV was also attached to the veins on the back of his hand, and he saw, no, *felt* a catheter at his groin.

With a groan, Darius moved to sit up.

Something cried from the corner of the room, and before Darius knew it, a red and blue blur thudded against his chest. He jumped, the heart monitor on the left beeping more urgently now as Sparkie ran in circles around his throat. Cold, smooth scales and leathery wings brushed against his bare skin, sending a chill down Darius's spine, and the tiny, sharp points of Sparkie's claws bordered on painful without ever crossing the line. Darius breathed a sigh and raised a hand, gently brushing it along Sparkie's back. The Familiar trembled beneath his touch.

Then a warm energy rushed to the door. It flew open, and Raquel stormed through. Her eyes filled with tears.

"Oh, my god," she said, barely holding onto the sob stuck in her throat. "You're awake!"

Raquel ran into the room. Sparkie did a final lap around Darius's shoulders, pressing his body close to the nape of his neck before he spread his wings and took off through the open door. Raquel nearly fell onto Darius in a hug, her tears wetting his cheeks and falling into his beard—

Darius raised a hand to his face and felt a thick layer of facial hair across his chin. His heart did an uncomfortable flip. As Raquel pulled back, he looked at her.

"What happened?"

The froggy, unpracticed voice that came from his mouth didn't sound like his. Darius swallowed hard. His throat scratched together like gravel.

"You've been in a coma," someone said from the door.

Alan walked into the room. He strode to Darius's bedside in four long, smooth steps, his black slacks and crimson button-up a sharp contrast to Raquel's sea foam scrubs. Darius's eyes went wide.

"A *coma?*" he asked. "For how long?"

"Thirty-five days," Alan said as he pulled up a chair.

Darius touched his chin again and looked around, seeing the situation in a new light. The table by the foot of his bed was covered in cards and dried flowers. A menagerie of foil balloons in various stages of deflation hovered above them. Get well soon. Fourth of July. Happy Twenty-Fifth Birthday, the five scratched out and replaced with a nine in Mackenzie's handwriting.

His stomach twisted up in knots, but before he had the chance to speak, Alan said, "Miss Hernandez, please shut this machine off, and let Elijah know Darius has woken up. He can run his tests shortly."

Raquel nodded and did as she was asked. The moment the door clicked shut behind her, Darius blurted out, "Samira—is she...?"

"Alive," Alan said with a nod. "Without your quick action, she would not be."

A rush of relief made Darius lay back on his bed again, and he closed his eyes. "Oh, thank god."

"Yes," Alan said, but there was a strange tone in his voice, and Darius looked back up. Alan held his gaze for a moment, his lips tight behind his goatee. "Though there were complications. When you lost consciousness, one of the bullets was still lodged in Samira's spine. She is paralyzed from the waist down."

The relief drained from Darius's chest in a cold stream. "Maybe I can fix it."

"Virtues cannot heal old wounds," Alan said, repeating a lesson Teresa Solomon had taught Darius years ago. "It has been over a month. The bulk of the damage is irreparable."

"I'd like to try."

"Perhaps," Alan said. "But not today. Elijah believes you healed past your limit, triggering your seizure and subsequent coma, so you will understand that we want to take this very slowly."

Darius's mouth dropped open again. "I had a seizure, too?"

"For almost two minutes," Alan confirmed. "You stopped breathing, and Christine had to administer CPR before you could be safely moved to the Underground. Once here, we managed to stabilize you, but to be frank, Darius… we weren't sure you would ever wake up."

Darius didn't know what to say, so he cleared his throat and looked down at his hands.

"I'm sorry," he began, but Alan held up a palm to stop him.

"You saved a life," Alan said. "Many lives. I have read dozens of accounts on the incident, and no fewer than nine people credit you for getting them through that evening. Next time, I hope you see the value in *your* life. We certainly do."

Alan smiled, and he got to his feet. Before he turned around, though, Darius said, "I have one more question."

"Of course."

"Jacob," Darius started, and Alan's face went cold. The muscles along his jaw tightened dangerously.

"We can discuss this later," he said. "You have been through—"

"No," Darius cut in. He sat up, frustrated that his arms felt so stiff under his weight. His elbows ground together like they'd started to tarnish. "I don't want to discuss this later. Maybe it's been a month for you, but for me, it happened less than an hour ago."

For a moment, Alan watched him, but then he sighed and took his chair again. He leaned forward, lacing his fingers between his knees. "What do you know about Jacob?"

"I know Pride used him as a hitman," Darius said. "That he killed his family and you removed the Programming when he came here. I also know he wanted to keep the Martyrs safe… so, how could this happen?"

Alan provided a somber nod. "Jacob did want to keep the Martyrs safe, more than anything, and that is exactly the problem."

Darius frowned. "I don't understand."

"Once we knew Jacob was involved, we traced his steps," Alan said. "It was… a challenge, and it took our teams nearly two weeks to find what we were looking for. Eventually, we discovered a storage facility in Long Island, and it was full of boxes with information… Manifestos, journals, photographs, maps, plans, all with one focus: how to save the Martyrs."

The warmth drained from Darius's face, and he swallowed hard. His throat was so dry it stuck together. "From Thorn?"

"Thorn," Alan confirmed. "Myself, and anyone who was 'corrupted' by the Sins. Thorn was his primary target, if only because she was the *easier* target. Making her death look like an accident in New York City would have been simple enough."

"What about his do-no-harm Programming?" Darius asked. "I thought it was supposed to stop him from hurting Martyrs?"

"As far as he was concerned, Thorn and I were *not* Martyrs," Alan said, shaking his head. "Yet another way Programming the human mind can be so complicated. That Programming did, however, make it almost impossible for him to be directly involved. That was why he decided to use the Sins. He was very careful. His communications were all encrypted and untraceable. For years, he sent them information, coordinates, any detail that he thought could result in Thorn's death, and they never even knew his name."

Darius sighed and pressed his fingertips against his eyes. "He mentioned something about sending them after her in Georgia and Washington."

"We did connect him to both of those incidents, as well as dozens more throughout the years," Alan said. Then he paused, and when Darius glanced up, he found Alan watching him with a dark expression.

"What?" Darius asked.

Alan drew in a measured breath. "He was also responsible for the altercation that claimed Eva's life last year," he said, the timbre to his voice low. "And for Cyrus Murphy's death."

A sudden, numb wave poured over Darius's body, and he felt distant from himself. "Cyrus?" he asked. Alan nodded. "That means…"

"Jacob, intentionally or not, led the Sins to you and your family."

A sterile silence surrounded them. With the machines attached to Darius turned off, it was deafeningly quiet. All he could make out was the irregular pattern of his breathing and his heart pounding in his ears. When he closed his eyes, three-year-old memories of dead children came back as bright and vibrant as though he'd lived them just yesterday. He tapped his thumb against his fingertips, focusing on the bright lights, the weight of his limbs, and the smell of antiseptic to ground himself here and avoid falling too deep into that grief again.

"How the hell did we miss this?" he asked, his voice tight.

"Because I was foolish," Alan said, and the pure candidness of the statement caught Darius off guard. "Isla Diamandis's Programming was intense, more so than anything else I had ever dealt with before, but despite that, and despite the damage to Jacob's mind, I was confident that I had removed or covered anything dangerous. When issues arose, I simply addressed them with more Programming. He seemed fine, if not a little anxious, and for ten years, he was.

"Then, Diamandis was killed, and her Programming, wiped out." Alan let out a soft, slow sigh. "*My* Programming, apparently, was not enough. He wrote detailed accounts of the resurfacing memories, including the incident where he murdered his family, and he felt betrayed that we had hidden it from him. I… can't say I blame him."

The room went quiet again, and Darius slowly shook his head. "I can't believe he kept that secret for so long."

"The signs were there," Alan said. "His disdain for us grew, and he became more convinced of our negative impact on the Martyrs. The increased bloodshed of the last few years was a trigger for him, and he started getting desperate. He was willing to sacrifice himself, to reveal your Virtue, to drug the entire Underground, just for a shot to destroy us. If I'm completely honest, Darius, I am terrified by how close he came."

A cold rush constricted Darius's chest. "You'd think his aura would have reflected this."

Alan's mouth played with the idea of a dark, humorless smirk. "The soul is a tricky thing," he said. "Jacob Locke believed, with all of who he was, that he was *saving lives*, not ending them. Nothing blurs the line between good and evil, between right and wrong, more than intention. He was not an evil man, nor truly a corrupted one. He was unwell, he was alone, and we relied so heavily on Programming to keep him held together that we missed the signs he was hurting. We failed him, and we all have paid for it."

With that, Alan got back to his feet and headed toward the exit. He paused at the doorway.

"Dr. Harris will be in to see you shortly, and assuming your tests are fine, you will be free to go," he said. "But the Underground has changed a lot in thirty-five days. Please, take it slow, and get some rest."

Then he opened the door and swept through it like a shadow.

***

After giving the standard spiel ("No healing, no exercise, no training of any kind, and if you don't show up for physical therapy every day for the next two weeks, I will hunt you down and lock you in this room"), Dr. Harris signed Darius off with a clean bill of health. Raquel returned his belongings to him—a phone, a watch, and a set of fresh clothes—and sent him on his way. After checking for new messages, which there were none, Darius hopped into the hospital shower.

When he got out, he wrapped the towel around his waist. God, no wonder his body felt worn so thin. *He* was thin. Months of training had melted off of him. He frowned as he looked into the mirror.

That wasn't all that was new. At least a week's worth of coarse hair covered his chin and cheeks. Darius rubbed his fingers over it and shook his head with a grimace.

Yeah, that had to go.

Half an hour later, he walked out of the hospital ward cleansed, clothed, and clean-shaven. He paused in the waiting room, closed his eyes, and took a deep breath.

Alan said this place was different, and it *felt* different. The energy moving in the courtyard underfoot wasn't the same energy he was used to. It was more active and *bigger* somehow. Shifting his focus to this floor, he glanced down the hallway toward the Martyr directors' offices. Part of him wondered if Thorn was there and, if so, why she hadn't come to see him yet...

But Thorn had no aura, so Darius couldn't sense her. What he *could* sense, though, was Chris. She paced her office while Gabe stood still in the middle of it. Darius headed that way. He didn't bother knocking. Instead, he strode right up to her door and pulled it open.

Chris spun around like she was ready to scold whoever walked in, but she froze when she saw Darius. The shock on her face disintegrated, and she smiled so widely that it crinkled the bridge of her nose and the corners of her eyes. Those eyes glistened with tears as she slammed a tablet onto her desk and threw her arms around Darius's shoulders. He was so unprepared that his legs trembled beneath him as he caught her.

"Darius!" Chris breathed before she pulled back and lightly shoved him. "Jesus, you scared me!"

He laughed as Gabe stepped up and shook his hand.

"Glad to have you back," Gabe said. "How you feeling?"

"Fine," Darius said, unsure if it was true. He crossed his arms. "It doesn't feel I've been out for a month."

Chris's smile fractured. "Funny," she said. "Feels like longer to me."

Darius's empty stomach flipped, and Gabe gently touched Chris on the back of her elbow. She glanced at him and cleared her throat. "Anyway, we were just heading downstairs. Join us! We have a *lot* to tell you about."

When they stepped into the hallway, Darius drew his phone from his pocket, saw no new notifications, and glanced at the door that led to the lobby outside Thorn's office. He was tempted to pop in and check if she was there, but Chris called his name, and he followed her to the elevator. The dining area below them was full of warm, human energy. *Too* full. While Gabe hit the button, Darius asked, "Is TAC grounded?"

"No," Chris said. "We're busier than ever, actually. Why?"

"It just seems like there are a lot of people here," Darius said.

"There *are*," she said with a smile. "We've recruited over forty new Martyrs since you've been out."

Darius's jaw dropped as the sliding doors opened. "You're *kidding?*"

Chris shook her head, they got onto the elevator, and Gabe said, "All cops. When Moore was destroyed, his Programming wore off. As you can imagine, a lot of us are starting to remember the awful shit he made us do."

Gabe's voice drifted off, and he hit the button for the lower floor. Chris gave him a sympathetic look before she turned to Darius. "Cassius LaFleur, Moore's right-hand man, has taken the commissioner position, and he's trying to keep it quiet. Anyone who has spoken openly about these resurfacing memories has been removed from duty and locked away."

"Locked away?" Darius asked.

"In psych wards," Gabe said, "but there have been a few

arrests. They tried to challenge the system, and the system hit them hard. These people lost everything."

"So," Darius said slowly, "you went and grabbed them?"

"Essentially, yeah," Chris said. "When we track someone down, Holly makes sure they're a good fit, then Gabe and Thorn go talk to them. If they want to join, we break them out. If not, Thorn Programs them to block those memories again."

Jacob Locke's face filled Darius's head, and his gut clenched uncomfortably. "Isn't Programming them risky?"

"It's not foolproof," Chris agreed, "but leaving them trapped in some institution isn't better, is it?"

Darius took a deep breath. He supposed not. Maybe this was one of those things Alan was talking about. The line between right and wrong felt really blurry now.

"How does the rest of the team feel about having a bunch of cops in the Underground?" he asked.

Chris shrugged and glanced up to Gabe as the elevator slowed to a stop. "Better than you'd think," she said. "We all want the same thing: the Sins gone."

"And we're a hell of a lot closer now," Gabe said.

The doors pulled open.

As soon as Darius stepped into the courtyard, the room paused for air. A sudden, chilling quiet swept through the Martyrs gathered outside the kitchen. Then the quiet exploded. People shrieked, called his name, and jumped to their feet as they barreled toward him in a wave of hot energy. For a moment, Darius was stunned—shockingly reminded of that night in the parking garage that felt like just yesterday to him—and his heart pounded hard.

But then the warmth pushed in on all sides, wrapping him safely inside it. The Martyrs reached to touch him, grabbing his shoulder or shaking his hand ardently, almost urgently. John pulled him into a hug while Parker and a few other researchers held back tears. But not everyone rushed forward, and Darius searched the room. A couple of tables were full of men and women he didn't know. They watched the spectacle with raised eyebrows and whispered over their food. Others, like Conrad and Skylar, smiled from a distance.

He didn't see Thorn.

"All right, ya animals!" a sharp voice rang out. "Everyone, give the man some space!"

Mackenzie forced her way through the mob. She stepped up in front of Darius, waving wildly and forcing people back. In the last month, her roots had grown out, dark against dye that had faded to a toasted yellow color. She propped her hands on her hips, and she smiled, a glint in her bright, blue eyes. "Everyone but *me!*"

Then she slammed into Darius and wrapped her arms so tight around his middle that she squeezed the air from his lungs. He forced out a laugh and glanced at Chris, who smiled with a shrug. Gabe ushered the crowd back to their business as Mackenzie pulled away and looked Darius over from head to toe.

"I hope you enjoyed your vacation and all that beauty sleep," she said with a wink. Chris quietly, gratefully, grabbed Darius's shoulder before she moved off with Gabe. Mackenzie crossed her arms and grinned. "Now that you're back, I'm gonna put you hard to work. We're swamped."

"What's going on?" Darius asked. He started to walk toward the dining area, scanning tables. "Aren't we down to just two Sins right now? I thought that would make things a little slower."

Mackenzie barked a laugh as she kept pace at Darius's side. "You'd think, wouldn't you? But no. Shit's messed up in a *big way* with both Lust and Gluttony gone. Lots of systems are totally fucked."

"Yeah, I heard about the issues with the NYPD."

"Right." Mackenzie glanced around at the new members. "Still weird to have so many of them down here, but I gotta admit, it's a good plan. I've never seen newbies this motivated to punch the Sins in the teeth."

Darius's eyebrows arched high, and Mackenzie caught

the look. She wrinkled her nose up and shook her head, waving him away with the flick of a wrist. "I know, I know. I was wrong. Shocked me, too."

A smile cut across her face, and Darius laughed. He looked around the room one last time, drew a short breath, and said, "Thorn must be busy, too."

"Insanely," Mackenzie said. "Wrath is gunning for control over the media, the cops, first responders… all the stuff Gluttony and Lust were in charge of. Thorn's trying to pin her down. I haven't seen her in the Underground in, god, five days now."

Darius nodded, considering the Martyrs again. With a sigh, he wrapped his arms around his chest. Then someone waved at him, and he glanced to the edge of the courtyard.

Samira and Nicholas. Somehow, Darius hadn't seen them sitting there—two Former Virtues, talking quietly over their meals. Leroy was with them, the only person at the table with an aura. They watched Darius, and though Samira looked more tired than usual, she wore a soft smile as she waved again.

Darius's eyes moved down. She was sitting in a wheelchair.

His chest constricted, and he quietly excused himself from Mackenzie. As he approached the table, Leroy got to his feet.

"Glad to see you up," Leroy said as he shook Darius's hand. His deep voice rumbled like an old engine.

"Me, too," Darius said. He sat across from Samira. Dark shadows sprung up beneath her dull, brown eyes. "I'm so sorry. I wish I could've—"

"Stop," she cut in. "You saved my life."

"But not my head," Nicholas grumbled, reaching back and feeling his scalp through his hair. "I'll have these scars forever."

"You can't even see them," Leroy growled, unamused. Samira raised her eyebrows and patted her husband's hand. Nicholas's lips curled into a smirk.

"That's right," he said. "You can't. I guess you're off the hook, then." He glanced at Darius, his smile widening. "How are you?"

"Fine," Darius said, no more confident in that answer than he had been when Gabe asked the question. He focused on Samira again and tilted his head in her direction. "How are *you* feeling?"

"I'm okay," she said. "Every day is a challenge and a gift."

Leroy's brows drew together, his fingers tightening around his wife's on the tabletop. Darius looked down at their hands and saw that Leroy's *Peccostium* looked different. The black had burned away, leaving a pale scar behind in its place.

"What are you going to do now?" Darius asked.

Samira took a deep breath. "I want to continue helping people like we did at the farm," she said after a moment. "Mr. Blaine found a place for us in Missouri. It's beautiful. Perfect for healing."

Darius's brows drew together. "Healing?" he asked. "How?"

Samira's smile widened. "I don't need to be a Virtue to help people heal," she said. "Our lives are so… hectic. We try to make sense of it all by getting swept up in who we think we are, what we think we're supposed to be. Carrying those burdens is devastating, and releasing them is… absolutely liberating."

Samira closed her eyes and pressed her palm over her heart. Darius's chest filled with tender warmth. "Sounds like a good mission," he said sincerely. "Is that God's next plan for you?"

"I've come to realize," Samira said, opening her eyes to consider him, "that plans are human—just another attempt to understand the unimaginable. Cain was right. The world is chaos. *God* is chaos. The beautiful, awe-inspiring chaos inside us and around us."

A brief silence fell, and Nicholas broke it with a scoff.

"Can you believe this?" he said, gesturing a palm toward Samira. "She's making me look bad." He smirked, and Samira's cheeks flushed at the compliment. Leroy glowered at him.

"I told you, you're welcome to come with us," Samira said. Leroy's face soured further, and Nicholas looked between them before he shook his head.

"I appreciate it," he said, "but where you want to heal, I want to get rid of these bastards. The best place for me to do that is here." His smile glistened in his half-empty eyes. Then the smile faded as he gave a soft sigh. "Though I still think you should try to convince Abraham to join you. Having a shrink on site would be helpful, and it's gotta be better than wherever he's planning on going."

The warmth broke, and Darius shook his head. "Wait. Abraham is *leaving?*"

Abraham's warm energy walked around his room with a slow, somber rhythm. When Darius knocked, that energy froze. Abraham stood still for a moment—just long enough that Darius considered the possibility he might ignore him entirely. At last, Abraham shuffled toward the door. It unlocked with a click, and a sliver of light appeared through a crack. Abraham's face pressed against it.

"Ah, Darius," he said. He opened his room and welcomed Darius inside. "I heard you woke up. I'm glad. I was starting to worry I wouldn't get to say goodbye."

Abraham's quarters were nearly empty. Any personal items or effects had been packed, leaving dusty rectangles on the walls and streaks across the dresser. The bed was covered by a mess of folded laundry, wrapped packages, and stacked photographs. Darius looked down at them, and a grim history of familiar faces stared back. Stella. Lina. Jacob. He swallowed hard and turned around to find Abraham watching him, twisting a pair of socks between his palms.

"I'm sure everyone here has already tried to talk you out of this," Darius said. He shoved his hands deep into the front pockets of his jeans, shrugging his shoulders up. "But I couldn't let you go without trying myself."

Abraham let out a bittersweet chuckle. "I appreciate it, really," he said as he walked to Darius's side and tossed the socks on top of a dozen other pairs inside his suitcase. "But I can't stay here." With a shaky breath, Abraham lifted one of the photographs. His wedding. He and Stella stood arm in arm, Lina and Jacob beside them. "My family is gone."

"We're your family, too," Darius said. "We can get through this together."

Abraham glanced up, his brown eyes full of unshed tears. "With all due respect, Darius, I am *tired* of losing family. I'm tired of waking up every morning to just 'get through' this. I can't do it anymore."

A bleak silence surrounded them. Darius nodded into it. "Where are you going to go?"

"I don't know," Abraham admitted quietly. "It's impossible *to* know. I asked Alan to cover all my memories of this place."

"*What?*" Darius's mouth fell open, and Abraham swallowed hard. "That's got to be two decades! Your mind—"

"Will be fine," Abraham interrupted, turning back to his suitcase and zipping it shut. "The Program is simple. No long-term damage. It will be more like having amnesia. I won't be a security threat to the Martyrs, and I won't have to remember the hell I've been through here."

A swell of emotion gripped the words, and Abraham cleared his throat, blinking tears away. Darius's gut twisted.

"You also won't know what happened to your wife," he said. "Or Lina and Jacob."

"No, and that will be hard," Abraham said, "but I'll be in good company. There are still people out there who knew me, people who have spent the last twenty years searching for answers about what happened to all of us. Like my dad." Abraham's long face filled with sorrow. "He's almost eighty now. It will be nice to give him some closure and spend time together before he's gone, too."

The air in the room felt dense, and Darius's lungs ached. He couldn't wrap his mind around the idea of an Underground without Abraham. He'd been one of the first people Darius had talked to when he and Eva had come in, bloodied and terrified. The first one to hold out a hand, even if Darius hadn't wanted anything to do with it at the time.

Abraham had seen the skinny, sick, and scared person Darius had been, and he'd never stopped trying to make him feel welcome here. Never stopped trying to make the Underground feel like home and the Martyrs like family.

Darius's eyes stung. "I'm really gonna miss you, man," he said at last.

The muscles along Abraham's neck tightened, and he gave a stiff nod.

"God, I wish I could say the same," he murmured, "but I won't remember you at all."

When Darius walked across the courtyard a few minutes later, from the western wing of rooms to the eastern, the dining area was still full. People wandered through and sat down. Talked and laughed. Their voices and their warmth hovered in the air, comfortable like a sunny window on a spring morning. Darius paused as he reached the hallway and looked over them. Their energy was welcoming and inviting.

But Darius didn't want to join in it. Not right now. He felt like being alone.

The Underground was different. Alan had said it: a lot *had* changed. Darius sensed it in the people. In himself. Even the walk to his quarters wasn't the same. New plaques had been affixed to several doors, showing names Darius didn't recognize belonging to people he'd never met. He could almost hear Jacob's voice in his head.

The new Martyrs. No corruption. No poison.

His room was just as he'd left it, and for a moment, he was struck by how much it looked like Abraham's now. Empty. Boring. Nothing on the walls or the surfaces to show that this space belonged to anyone at all, let alone Darius. If his name weren't nailed to the door, it wouldn't stand out from the hundreds of others left unoccupied. He left as much of an imprint as a ghost.

Darius walked to his bed, sat down, and opened the side table drawer. Inside, the Bhagavad Gita lay waiting for him like an old friend. As Darius pulled it out, he wiped away a fine layer of dust, and the red, leather cover shined like new. He flipped through the pages, revisiting them, and his heart plunged at the notes he found inside. Teresa's, written in the margins, and Lina's, on scraps of paper trapped between the pages.

Tears filled his eyes, and after he closed the cover, he brushed them away with the back of his hand. Darius took a deep breath as he put the Bhagavad Gita down again, this time lying face-up on the table. That was a little better.

Darius didn't want to die like a ghost here.

For the next few minutes, he went through the motions of normalcy. He plugged in his phone and set it next to the book on his nightstand, headed to his dresser, and pulled out a pair of lounge pants. After changing, he turned off the light and flung himself onto his mattress. Then he stared at the ceiling in the dark, and he thought about Abraham. He thought about twenty years of pain, of trauma, of heartbreak being washed away, and what a relief that could be. His stomach fluttered at the idea of it—of starting over. A fresh slate.

But it was so much more complicated than that. It was also twenty years of passion and triumph and love. Twenty years of *life*. Twenty years that had turned him into the person he was today. He couldn't trade any of them. He wouldn't.

Samira was right: every day was a challenge and a gift.

Darius closed his eyes and took a long, slow breath. For the first time in months, he thought about Eva on purpose. He thought about Lina and Teresa and all the people he had ever loved and lost and let the grief wash over him. It poured through his chest and sat like cement in his lungs. He breathed into it, through it, until he didn't feel like he was drowning anymore. Soon, Darius was drifting off to sleep.

Who knew being in a coma for thirty-five days could be so exhausting?

He woke up to beeping again.

A tone trilled next to his bed, and when Darius's eyes opened, it was to a dim light shining up from his nightstand. He turned to look at it when another notification pushed through to his phone, beeping again. He sat up and checked his watch.

Who would text him at a quarter to midnight?

Darius knew the answer before he touched the device. He swiped it up and saw Thorn's name sitting above a chain of two messages, sent seconds apart:

"Hey."

"You hungry?"

Darius typed back immediately.

"Starving."

The screen showed Thorn responding, and moments later, he read, *"I'm in the kitchen."*

Darius jumped to his feet, grabbed a shirt, and threw on his shoes. The walk from his room felt warmer than usual—more people, more bodies, pressed in around him. Lights over the courtyard looked down with a dim, lunar glow, making it easy for Darius to walk through the tables in the dining area without running into any of them. As he neared the kitchen, he didn't see Thorn immediately, but the rich, nutty aroma of freshly ground coffee hit his senses.

Past the walk-in refrigerator, the stovetops, and the ovens, he found her. She stood over the machine, her back to him, as she watched the last drips of brew hit the pot. Pale fingers pulled her dark, silky hair around one shoulder while Sparkie sat on the other. The animal's head lifted, and Thorn turned. For a long moment, they just watched one another.

Then Thorn's thin lips pressed into a smirk, and she tossed him a fork. Darius barely managed to catch it. When he looked at her again, she had started pulling clamshell boxes out of a paper bag on the counter. Chinese lettering scrawled across the side in flaky, red ink.

"I don't want you to embarrass yourself," she said, tearing the paper open on a pair of chopsticks and snapping them apart. She put them between her fingers and clicked them together.

Darius laughed. "Wow," he said, raising his brows as he walked toward her. He rested his hip against the counter and crossed his arms. The smell of Kung Pao chicken, fried rice, and chow mien made Darius's stomach rumble. "I've been in a coma for over a month, and this is how you say hello?"

"I've been in a coma," Thorn said. "It's nothing special."

She picked up a slice of water chestnut straight from the container, popped it into her mouth, and watched him. Her eyes moved between his, from the right to the left and back again. Now that he was closer, the dark, sleepless circles beneath them stood out, making her slender face seem hollow. After a few moments, when Darius still didn't speak, Thorn pulled her lower lip between her teeth and frowned. "What's wrong?"

"Nothing," Darius said, shaking his head, and he leaned over the takeout, too. He took a bite of chicken. "I heard Wrath's been keeping you busy."

Thorn nodded through a breath. "She's trying to stabilize the police," she said as she reached for the coffee pot and poured herself a cup. "This kind of thing happens every time a Sin's host is destroyed, but it's always bigger with Gluttony. The NYPD is one of the most militarized organizations in the country, and losing control of it is a huge blow, so the other Sins scramble to keep it under their thumb until Gluttony can step in again. This time, it's different."

She lifted her mug to her face. The steam wafted around her, and she closed her eyes, breathing it in, as her shoulders rose and fell in a graceful but weary sigh. Darius's brows drew together.

"Because Gluttony won't come back," he said.

"And only two of the Sins have hosts right now," Thorn said. "Greed is a coward, so Wrath has to do all the heavy lifting. I need to take advantage of it."

"What do you mean?" Darius asked.

"Hunt is almost impossible to track," Thorn said, and she threw out a bitter scoff. "I should know. That's my job. She's constantly on the move. It's how she's managed to keep her host for so long. After ninety years, she's sunk her teeth into so many different areas of New York's infrastructure… Local gangs. Wall Street. Even the United Nations."

Thorn took a sip before putting her mug down and reaching for her chopsticks again. Darius had almost forgotten there was food in front of him, so he shoved another bite in his mouth as she went on. "Wrath has hundreds of holes to crawl into, and she's never in the same place long enough for us to get a solid read on where she's going to be. This last month, though, she's been easier to find."

"What does that mean for us?" Darius asked.

Thorn cast him a dark look through her lashes. "It means she's distracted. Vulnerable. I want to take her down before Lust and Envy repossess."

A jolt of surprise made Darius's eyes widen. As Thorn took a bite, he leaned toward her. "You really think you can?" he asked. When Thorn shrugged in response, he shook his head. "How much time do you have?"

"We rarely see a repossession happen before two years," Thorn said.

"It's two years for Envy this January," Darius argued.

"Then I guess I'd better be quick."

Thorn turned back to the food, and Darius did the same.

For a few minutes, they ate in silence. Every so often, Darius glanced at her. The next time Thorn reached for her coffee, she said, "Why do you keep doing that?"

"Doing what?"

"Giving me that look."

Darius's mouth parted, and Thorn's eyes glittered as she tilted her chin to the Familiar still sitting on her shoulder. Sparkie's attention was glued to the side of Darius's face. He laughed and shook his head.

"You just seem tired, that's all."

Thorn drew in a slow breath as she reached for the pot again. "I *am* tired," she said, topping off her coffee. "But I've been tired before. More tired than this. I'll be fine."

"You've got to take care of yourself," Darius said. Thorn paused, the rim of her mug pressed to her lips, and one slender brow arched high on her forehead. Darius laughed. "Trust me. I should know. I'm a great example of how to do it wrong."

This time, Thorn didn't even respond to him. Her mouth pulled into a smirk as she took a sip. No matter how much coffee she drank, it didn't seem to work. Thorn still looked exhausted. A thought suddenly occurred to him.

Caffeine wouldn't work. It couldn't. Not when she was still a Forgotten Sin.

"So," he started, crossing his arms as he leaned back against the counter, "how does it feel, seeing Leroy human again?"

Every muscle in Thorn's body froze, and her eyes gleamed in the darkness. At first, she just watched Darius, her brows slowly drawing in, before she took a breath. "I don't know," she admitted. Her tone fell deeper, darker, and she shook her head. "We've always thought this was possible, but I never really believed it would happen. Not for me. It seemed so far away."

"Seems a lot closer now," he said, and he smiled. Thorn didn't.

"Closer." Her jaw clenched. "Maybe. But I hate that

someone else has to suffer so I don't have to."

Darius frowned. "Samira doesn't seem like she's suffering."

"She feels that pain," Thorn started, but Darius interrupted her.

"Why does pain have to mean suffering?" he asked. "Even with her spine broken, with her soul cut in half, Samira is *excited*. She's happy." Darius scoffed, surprised at the surge of emotion in his chest, and he glanced at the ground. Thorn shifted. He heard the soft *clunk!* of her mug landing back on the counter. "It's not right to decide she's suffering for her, and I don't want you deciding for me, either."

He looked up to Thorn again, finding her eyes wide and lips parted. Her tongue darted across the bottom of her teeth, and Sparkie disappeared down her back. At last, she nodded, never moving that intense gaze away from Darius's face. The shadows under her cheekbones seemed darker, highlighting her weariness.

They stood in an awkward quiet for a moment, Darius's chest feeling a little heavier, Thorn's eyes looking a little more somber, until she cleared her throat. Whatever comfort they'd shared began to fade. "I should get to bed," she said, and she started packing things away.

"Don't worry about this, okay?" Darius said, gesturing to the food but hoping she understood that he meant more than that. "I've got it."

"It's fine—"

"Thorn," Darius cut in. He laid a hand on her shoulder; her skin felt cool under his touch. "For god's sake, it's just a couple of take-out boxes. Go the hell to bed. You're exhausted."

The muscles along Thorn's jaw relaxed. "Thank you."

Darius nodded. "Any time."

As he stepped away, clearing a path for Thorn to walk past him, she paused. Through the tiredness in her eyes and the worn shadows beneath them, Darius recognized a flicker of gratitude. Finally, she took a step forward...

And Thorn wrapped her arms around him.

He stood there, stunned, as Thorn held him tight. A long, deep breath stretched down her spine, drawing him closer, and her fingers dug into his shoulders like she was terrified he might slip away. A smile warmed upon Darius's face. He sank into her embrace, relishing the pull of her hands on his back, her silky hair against his cheek, and the smell of sandalwood and vanilla.

"Take it easy," Thorn murmured. The words vibrated from her chest into his. "I've been waiting a month to put you on the field. Don't keep me waiting."

Then she let go. Without another word, Thorn slipped through the dark kitchen, merged with the shadows, and disappeared entirely. Darius stared after her long after she was gone before he turned back to the counter. He lifted Thorn's chopsticks and played with them until he held them between his fingers. He reached into the chicken and, after a couple of minutes, lifted a piece. His smile stretched into a grin.

Suddenly, he found his appetite roaring back.

CHAPTER THIRTY-ONE

Hunt's Point was an absolute shit-hole neighborhood that Mayor Richmond Bently avoided as much as he could. He hated the gross, industrial stink polluting the air and coming through the ultra-filtered air conditioning in his 2093 Mercedes-Benz Lux. He hated the roads, which were constantly under construction, and what did they have to show for it except for more goddamned potholes? But mostly, Bently hated the people.

Polls always showed one thing: if you lived in Hunt's Point, you didn't vote. The lowlifes. As far as Bently was concerned, if they weren't going to show their support for him, fuck 'em.

The coupe slowly rolled down Oak Point Avenue, squeezing its way through blocks of ugly brick warehouses, boarded-up windows, and parking lots of shitty cars trapped behind barbed-wire fences. Bently wrinkled his nose and leaned forward, his face hovering inches above the leather wheel as he read street signs. Barretto. Casanova. Tiffany. Jesus, even the intersections here sounded like a bunch of cracked-out prostitutes. He grimaced.

Soon, he found what he was looking for. Another brick warehouse, jutting up from the ground. The upper half of the building was covered with foggy, glass windows, most of which had been broken, while the lower part flaunted a handful of garage doors painted with all kinds of crudely drawn genitalia. When Bently parked in front of it, staring right into the single eye of a particularly pornographic piece of graffiti, his stomach twisted.

God, he hated this fucking place.

But he had business to attend to, so he got out of his car, shut the door, and walked around to the trunk. From it, he pulled out a tattered old vehicle cover he used strictly for moments like this. The last thing he needed was to come out of this meeting to find his beautiful car vandalized or stolen. As he started unfolding the canvas, he looked himself over in his reflection on the Benz's glossy, violet paint. He pulled back his shoulders, turned to the left, and straightened his suit jacket. Then he leaned forward and considered his face, running his fingers over his smooth jaw.

Not bad. Those diet pills had done the job, and the plastic surgery healed well enough. He didn't look like a man nearing sixty, which was exactly what he'd been going for. Immortality would be a hell of a lot more fun when he looked this good.

His lip curled into a sneer. Immortality. He bitterly threw the cover over his car, tucking it around the wheels as he shook his head. He'd been promised immortality.

And someone had broken that promise.

With the car covered, Bently straightened his jacket again with a sniff and made his way up to the warehouse. All but one of the doors were locked and chained shut, so he went in the side entrance, careful to touch as little as possible. It was a massive, open space, filled with crates upon crates of imported shit Bently didn't care to know more about. A handful of dividers had been lazily put together at the back wall, building "offices" for the people who "worked" here. A rickety, metal staircase led to the second story. He'd never been up there before, but he could imagine it was more of the same shit. As he shut the door behind him, voices carried across the room.

"They're not holding up their part of the deal," Cassius LaFleur was bitching.

Bently frowned and walked across the concrete floor, his size-ten Louboutins clopping as he went. One of the "office" doors was cracked open, and Bently heard even more bitching float through it.

"How long did Dane say it would take?" another man asked.

"A year max, and he's been gone for almost twice that long!" LaFleur exclaimed.

"Calm down, Cash," a woman said.

"Don't tell me to calm down," the interim commissioner snapped.

Bently pushed the door open, and four pairs of eyes flipped up to him. Four pairs of angry, bitter eyes. He stood in the doorway, his jaw gnashed together, and he shook his head. "You started without me?"

Connor Amoretto, the man seated across from LaFleur, glanced down at an expensive gold watch. "You're twenty minutes late," he said, his manicured brows pinching together.

Bently's teeth clenched even tighter as he glared at Amoretto. The man worked for one of the top advertising agencies in the city, famous for helping Bently's campaign create catchy slogans about cleaning up New York. Reading between the lines, that really meant getting rid of undesirables in tax brackets so low that they didn't even *pay* taxes. The man was also damn near super-model perfect, with his blonde hair, dimpled cheeks, and blue eyes. No amount of surgery could make Bently look thirty-four again.

"I had work to do, unlike the rest of you," Bently growled.

"Fuck you," LaFleur spat as he threw Bently the same venomous look Commissioner Moore always had. "You have no idea how much work I've had to do in the last month!"

"Easy, boys," Neema Davis said as she crossed her arms. Her dark, full lips pouted into a frown while those brown eyes shot daggers at him. "No need to get so salty."

Bently scoffed while LaFleur flipped Davis the bird. She just giggled. Davis was from one of those old "New York" families and was so loaded with money hidden in various accounts and assets that it was almost disgusting. She dug her talon-like, manicured nails into everything—including politics—and she'd made a big show of supporting Bently's competition in the last election just to piss him off.

"Rich, take a seat," she said with cocky nonchalance.

"Don't call me that," Bently snapped. "We're not friends, *Davis.*"

Davis's lips pulled into a haughty smile as she gestured to a seat across the table from her, beside the only person in the room whose name Bently never remembered. Mar-something? Unlike Amoretto, LaFleur, and Davis, she didn't do anything important at all. Supposedly, she was an assistant for the Gibson Artist Agency, some little nobody pushing papers and making phone calls. The girl looked like an immigrant—not that there was anything wrong with that, he liked to remind his voters, so long as they did it legally— and she never talked, so Bently was half convinced she didn't speak English. Even now, she kept her mouth shut as she glared at Bently like he was a sinner pissing on the Vatican's front steps.

He never understood why Cassandra Smith chose her as her successor, but then again… He never quite saw the value in Smith anyway. Besides, of course, her power. God, his life would be so much easier with that power.

"It has been a while since we've all gotten together," Davis said, her voice carrying a slight accent that Bently was pretty sure she faked to sound more sophisticated than she was. "None of you have changed, then?"

She glanced around, pointedly considering them with a knowing glint. Bently shook his head.

"No," he said, pulling out a folding chair. Before he sat

down, he grabbed a violet handkerchief from his breast pocket and wiped the dust off the seat, his nose curling up. As he lowered himself into it, he threw the handkerchief onto the table. Around the room, Amoretto and the other woman shook their heads.

"This is *bullshit*," LaFleur snarled furiously as he slammed his fist on the plastic table. "I was promised more than just the commissioner job—I was promised Moore's fucking magic. All my officers are losing their goddamned minds. Do you know how hard it's been keeping them quiet?"

"The last time I talked to Anton Claytor, he told me this process can take time," Davis said with a quaint shrug.

Bently's brows drew together, and a nervous bubble twisted in his recently-tucked gut. "You didn't tell him we were meeting tonight, did you?"

Davis scoffed and waved her hand. "Of course not. Don't be stupid." Heat raised to the apples of Bently's cheeks, and Davis watched him through those heavily made-up eyes of hers, the bright yellow powder striking against her brown skin. "Why do you think we're meeting *here?*" She gestured around the warehouse. Her family owned a lot of property all around the city, and their assets in this area were used as a holding ground for contraband they smuggled in. "If we went to one of my nicer buildings, he would find out. He has people at almost all of my properties."

"That's bullshit, too," LaFleur said. "He doesn't fucking trust you."

"Or he's keeping tabs on the assets that he'll have control over when he shares Neema's body," Amoretto reasoned.

"*If* he ever shares it," LaFleur challenged. He turned to Bently, his lip curled indignantly. "We were *promised* this power. If their current bodies died, they'd need new ones, and in return, we'd get the perks. That's what they told us. Well, Derek Dane and Cassandra Smith have been gone for over eighteen months, and there's no sign that they're coming back for us. So what d'ya say, *Rich*? You helped Dane set up this little 'fan club.' Why aren't you and Marlena living the high life as gods yet?"

Marlena! That was her name. Bently glanced to the Latina on his right, and her dark eyes looked him up and down while her nose scrunched up.

"I have no idea," Bently said, turning back to the table. LaFleur, Davis, and the Marlena woman watched him, but Amoretto's brows suddenly drew together. He frowned and glanced down at his lap, where his hands were tucked away. Quietly, he adjusted the sleeves of his button-up shirt and removed his watch. Bently sighed and pinched the bridge of his nose. He could still feel where the doctor had scraped the bone away, making it look more elegantly *Roman*. "I thought it was just taking longer than anticipated, but now there are *four* of them missing… I am starting to wonder…"

"I'm telling you, they fucking lied to us," LaFleur said. Amoretto looked up, the muscles in his jaw rigid as his focus landed on LaFleur. The commissioner kept ranting. "They never had any intention to let us share their power. We've been fucking had, and I say we fight back."

"You're *crazy*," Marlena said, and Bently was so shocked by the sound of her voice that he nearly jumped. The tone was deep and dangerous. Her eyes flashed around the table. "You *all* are! You've been chosen by *gods*, and you think you can challenge them? They'd kill you, and you'd deserve to die."

Amoretto glanced at her, his lips pulled into an appreciative smirk, as LaFleur threw his hands up with a scoff.

"Gods!" he hissed. "For all we know, that's a lie, too!"

"You've seen what they can do," Marlena argued.

"So what?" LaFleur snapped back. "There are only a few of them left now. They can't take us all out."

"What exactly do you propose to do, Cash?" Davis challenged, the sarcasm thick in her voice. "Throw your army of *mentally unstable* officers after them? And who would we even fight? Like you said, Dane, Smith, Ruiz, and Moore are *gone.*"

"Then we go for Claytor," LaFleur said, crossing his arms, and Davis's eyes went wide with shock. If this situation weren't so serious, Bently would have reveled in that look on her stupid face. LaFleur leaned forward. "And that one bitch who keeps coming by my precincts and trying to do *my damned job.* Fuck 'em. Fuck the lot of 'em. I won't be used anymore."

A single eyebrow raised in a dramatic arch on Amoretto's flawless forehead. He dropped his watch into his front pocket, leaned forward on the table, and clasped his fingers on top of it. "You *really* think that's a good idea?" he asked. The way he said it felt off. The tempo was a little slower, a little more sultry than Bently was used to. "You *really* think you can take down Anton Claytor *and* Autumn Hunt?"

Bently frowned. Autumn Hunt? Was that the name of the woman LaFleur was complaining about? He glanced to Davis, who seemed just as confused as he was, and then to Marlena. His stomach buckled. She was watching the side of Amoretto's face with wide eyes, and her painted lips parted just enough to see a line of pink behind her red lipstick.

But LaFleur scoffed and said, "Just watch me."

The corner of Amoretto's lip drew up into a smile, and he got to his feet. "You're making a big mistake," he said slowly as he unbuttoned the cuffs on his sleeves and started rolling them up. When he got to the left, Bently caught a glimpse of a black tattoo sitting just below his wrist. He didn't remember the man having a tattoo.

LaFleur's jaw slammed together, and he jumped up, too. He was a broad guy, thick with muscle Amoretto didn't have. With a posturing grunt, he puffed his chest out. "You wanna find out, pretty boy?"

Amoretto's eyes darted up, the deep, dark blue glistening hungrily. He shook his head. "No."

His right arm flew out, his fist wrapping around LaFleur's throat and squeezing until it crunched like a raw egg. Davis screamed as Amoretto opened his palm. Cassius LaFleur crumbled to the concrete floor, gagging and gasping for breath as blood bubbled between his lips. Bently shoved himself so far away from the table that his chair toppled backward, and he landed hard on the concrete. Marlena leapt up without a sound, her eyes glassy and awestruck as Amoretto grabbed Bently's used handkerchief from the table and wiped crimson droplets from his fingers.

"You're—" she began, but when Amoretto looked at her, her voice stuck in her throat.

"Oh *yes*," he purred. "And I must say… I'm *disappointed*."

He pulled his chair back out and sat upon it. Beneath the table, Bently could see Davis's legs shaking, her hands clasped tightly in her lap. LaFleur writhed on the ground beside her, a trail of red dripping from the corner of his purple lips as he choked. The sight of him made Bently's stomach twist, and he scrambled to his feet but didn't sit back down.

"I'm sorry," Davis stammered, shaking her head so urgently that the braided bun she wore threatened to come tumbling down. "We meant no disrespect. It's just—"

"We have provided you with *so* much," Amoretto the God went on. He leaned back in his chair and propped his heels on the table with a haughty elegance that sent a chill down Bently's spine. "Notoriety, wealth, information, resources…" He slowly looked from Bently to Davis, Marlena to LaFleur, before his eyes landed on Bently again. "And you pay us back with *treachery?*"

Bently's face went cold, and he stammered, "N-no, of course not."

"Then what do you call *this?*" Amoretto gestured widely around the room.

Davis's lip quivered. "We were just—"

"Do not *lie!*" Amoretto howled, his voice disjointed with his calm, collected posture. The laced fingers on his lap tightened, and he shook his head. "I should kill you. All of you."

A cold current shattered the summer heat leaking through the broken, upper-story windows, and Bently glanced at the door. He might be able to make it, but LaFleur's body was twitching, gurgling, dying on the ground right in front of it. Bently brought a hand to cover his own throat as Amoretto went on.

"But I won't," he said with a sigh. Amoretto opened his hands, palms up, and held them out to the room. Bently recognized the tattoo now. It was the mark they got when the power transfer was finally complete—the mark of the gods. "Because I *am* merciful, and I understand the concerns you have. After all, Derek and Cassandra have been gone for quite some time. I'm sure it's *very* frustrating."

For a few seconds, no one moved. A whimper from across the table drew Bently's eyes to Davis. She stared, open-mouthed and dumb looking, as Amoretto let that sink in. Then she closed her lips, swallowed hard, and said, with a voice so small Bently hardly heard it, "Why is it taking so long?"

Amoretto's eyes devoured her head to toe with an animalistic appreciation before he shrugged. "Maybe these two haven't done their jobs well," he said, gesturing his head in Bently and Marlena's direction. He placed a hand flat against his chest. "Clearly, *this* one did all Ruiz instructed. He was... very primed for me. We get along quite well."

"That's insane," Bently blustered. His face filled with heat as he stepped forward. "I have done everything Dane asked me to do—*everything!*"

"Yes," Amoretto said, a coy smile turning his mouth up. "Plastic surgery *was* high on his list."

Bently's indignation flopped in his chest as he blubbered.

"But," Amoretto said as he turned away and flipped his wrist lazily, "I don't think that's the real issue. We've been having some... problems... with an insurgent group.

They've been throwing kinks into our plans, which surely slowed Derek and Cassandra in moving into you." He glanced at Bently and Marlena again. The two of them shared a quick look.

"Insurgent group?" Marlena asked.

"They're like a nest of rats," Amoretto said bitterly, and he paused before gazing around the room with a slow, sensational flair. He looked each of them in the eye with intention, and when he landed on Bently last, it felt like those eyes were seeing him as the man he was before the dieting, the surgery, and the implants.

Bently swallowed hard. "What do you want from us?"

Amoretto's charming smile opened up, showing off a pair of dimples and perfectly straight, white teeth. He got to his feet. "I could be persuaded to forget what I saw here tonight," he said, walking around the table and behind Davis's back. One of his hands touched her right arm and trailed a path from it all the way across her shoulders as he moved past her. Her body shuddered. When he got to the other side, he looked down at the ground where LaFleur's body had finally stopped thrashing. Amoretto dug his heel into the commissioner's shoulder and flipped him to his back. Dead, bulging eyes stared at the ceiling. "All I ask is your help with one little thing."

"What?" Davis asked at the exact same moment Marlena said, "Anything!"

"There's a woman," Amoretto said, putting his hands in his front pockets. "We want her."

"Of course," Bently said. "Who is she?"

Amoretto's eyes moved onto his face. When his smile widened, it sent a nauseous chill into Bently's gut.

"She's the key," Amoretto purred, "and if we have her... we *win*."

ABOUT THE AUTHOR

MC Hunton is a bright personality with a shockingly dark taste in the stories she writes. She graduated with her bachelor's degree in Creative Writing in 2010 and has been working on her debut series, The Martyr Series, since 2005. The first book, Resurrection, won first place in the fantasy category of Writer's Digest's Best Self-Published E-Book Awards in 2022 and took home the win in the paranormal category in the Indie Reader Discovery Awards in 2023. She has a penchant for fast-paced action, deeply-rooted sociopolitical and spiritual themes, and emotionally driven plot and character development.

Check out what she's up to by visiting her website:
www.MCHunton.com